Dress Rehearsal

Jennifer O'Connell

A SIGNET ECLIPSE BOOK

SIGNET ECLIPSE
Published by New American Library, a division of
Penguin Group (USA) Inc., 375 Hudson Street,
New York, New York 10014, USA
Penguin Group (Canada), 90 Eglinton Avenue East, Suite 700, Toronto,
Ontario M4P 2Y3, Canada (a division of Pearson Penguin Canada Inc.)
Penguin Books Ltd., 80 Strand, London WC2R 0RL, England
Penguin Ireland, 25 St. Stephen's Green, Dublin 2,
Ireland (a division of Penguin Books Ltd.)
Penguin Group (Australia), 250 Camberwell Road, Camberwell, Victoria 3124,
Australia (a division of Pearson Australia Group Pty. Ltd.)
Penguin Books India Pvt. Ltd., 11 Community Centre, Panchsheel Park,
New Delhi - 110 017, India
Penguin Group (NZ), 67 Apollo Drive, Rosedale, North Shore,
Auckland 1311, New Zealand (a division of Pearson New Zealand Ltd.)
Penguin Books (South Africa) (Pty.) Ltd., 24 Sturdee Avenue,
Rosebank, Johannesburg 2196, South Africa

Penguin Books Ltd., Registered Offices:
80 Strand, London WC2R 0RL, England

Published by Signet Eclipse, an imprint of New American Library, a division of
Penguin Group (USA) Inc. Previously published in a New American Library edition.

First Signet Eclipse Printing, June 2007
10 9 8 7 6 5 4 3 2 1

PUBLISHER'S NOTE
This is a work of fiction. Names, characters, places, and incidents either are the product of the author's imagination or are used fictitiously, and any resemblance to actual
persons, living or dead, business establishments, events, or locales is entirely coincidental.
    The publisher does not have any control over and does not assume any responsi-
bility for author or third-party Web sites or their content.

In memory of my mother-in-law,
Janice O'Connell,
whose joy for life we continue to miss every day,
and who could always be counted on
for a plate of chocolate chip cookies

Acknowledgments

There were so many women without whom *Dress Rehearsal* would be just another idea cluttering up my head. My agent, Kristin Nelson, and my editor, Kara Cesare, were instrumental in bringing Lauren's Luscious Licks to life and encouraging me to stick it out. Laura Caldwell was always there to listen to me bitch and complain and share her own experiences. Debby Rivera of Ambrosia Patisserie was kind enough to invite me into her kitchen and share her wedding cake stories. My daughter, Carleigh, was an invaluable companion whose curiosity made our "field research" in Boston so much fun.

And of course the two men in my life, John and Tanner, are always there to make me smile.

Life is uncertain. Eat dessert first.
—Ernestine Ulmer

1

"*L*auren!"

I glanced over my shoulder in search of the shrill voice calling my name like a dog whistle. Past the snaking line of coffee-starved patrons jonesing for their morning fix with all the jittery expectation of patients in a methadone clinic, I spotted her. Gwen Stern was standing on her tiptoes in the doorway, frantically waving her French manicure at me even as a Starbucks barista was yelling for her to move out of the way and let the other customers in.

"Lauren! I can't believe it!" Gwen gushed, pushing her way through the line, completely oblivious to the fact that there were ten people ahead of her on the verge of tackling her Jazzercised body to the floor and beating her silly with cinnamon scones. Gwen reached out and pulled me into a bear hug, squeezing me so tight I could feel the firm resistance of silicone spheres before she twisted to her left and grabbed the elbow of a reluctant Brooks Brothers suit trailing behind her. "Charlie, this is Lauren Gallagher—of Lauren's Luscious Licks."

Charlie took a quick look around to gauge the crowd's hostility before holding out his hand. "Nice to meet you, Lauren. I've seen your cakes in *Boston* magazine."

"Lauren, this is Charlie Banks, my divorce attorney. He's with Goodman & Moore—a *partner*," Gwen announced proudly, as if her status as a client of the blue-chip firm was the result of a stringent selection process rather than her ability to pay blue-chip rates.

"Hi, Charlie." I attempted a genuine smile, but considering I was still two people away from my morning caffe latte, I wasn't sure I was all that convincing. "So I guess David is . . ." I let my voice trail off, waiting for Gwen to fill in the blank.

"About to have his clock cleaned by Charlie and his firm," Gwen answered for me, almost gleefully.

"I'm sorry." I shook my head sincerely, even as I was going through my mental database trying to recall their cake.

"I was, too, but Charlie's making it easier."

Not to mention more lucrative.

"I guess I expected things to change once we were married, but I was never a priority in David's life—in fact, I was running a distant third behind the Dow Jones and his company's balance sheet." Gwen sighed before abruptly grabbing my shoulder with one hand and covering her mouth with the other. "I hope you don't think I blame you! The cake was lovely, absolutely perfect. I promise I'll be back for the next one."

The girl in line ahead of me moved toward the register, and I gratefully stepped up to the counter to place my order.

"Thanks, Gwen. I'm sure you will."

Less than five minutes later, I was standing in front of Lauren's Luscious Licks inhaling the sweetly bitter aroma of Belgian chocolate being pumped through the vent over the doorway. As I unlocked the door and made my way through the starkly decorated cake gallery, I could already hear Maria barking orders in the kitchen.

I'd stopped baking the cakes when Lauren's Luscious Licks moved from my studio kitchenette to our Newbury Street storefront, and now I spent my time promoting the business and making sure we stayed one step ahead of the competition. Whereas I had been declared "the new face of wedding cakes" by *Boston* magazine, Maria Contadino was strictly old-school. In fact, the bakery she used to work for in the North End still used plastic bride-and-groom toppers complete with a miniature veil poking out of the bride's head and a top-hatted groom. But Maria knew her stuff. When she responded to my ad for the position of pastry chef/kitchen manager, I got the impression that she believed she was interviewing me more than the other way around. When our conversation was over and I offered Maria the job, she told me that she'd have to think about it—as if I'd be lucky to get her. And I was. Now, while I took care of the cake boutique out front, scheduling client tastings and ensuring that the business ran smoothly, Maria ruled the kitchen with the knowledge and pride of someone who'd been baking for more than forty years, and with all the charm and tact of Mussolini.

"Hello, all." I pushed through the swinging door to the kitchen and greeted my staff, for which I received three *holas*, a *bonjour*, and a *'bout time* from Maria.

I headed straight to my desk next to the walk-in refrigerator and pulled a five-by-seven filing box out of the top drawer. Sure, I had a computerized accounting system and inventory program, but when it came to keeping track of client preferences, I still relied on good old-fashioned handwritten notes and index cards.

I found the card titled STERN, DAVID AND GWEN, and reviewed my comments.

Gwen and David Stern—August 15, 1998. She'd wanted a heart-shaped white cake iced with a high-gloss fondant and trimmed with a chain of fresh gardenias. They'd settled on stacked square tiers of citron vodka cake with lemon-scented buttercream icing. No filling, no florals, no extraneous adornments. The cake was nothing more than a confectionary cocktail symbolizing the closing of yet another business deal. No wonder Gwen required the services of Charlie Banks and his firm. I could have told her she was destined for divorce court before she even set one foot down the aisle.

"How many anniversary cakes do we have next week?" Maria asked me as she effortlessly worked the double-scalloped crimper.

"So far we're four for six. The Novaks' number was disconnected, and there was nothing listed with information. I still have to get in touch with Judy Dennison."

One of Lauren's Luscious Licks' most popular offerings—something that we originated years ago and which our competitors have since copied—is our Year to Remember package. When clients order their wedding cake, they can include a five-inch replica to be delivered on the anniversary of their big day. Aside from the Novaks, the Dennisons were the only couple I hadn't been able to reach regarding next week's deliveries.

I picked up the phone and dialed Judy Dennison's home number for the third time since Monday. She finally answered on the fourth ring.

"Hi, Judy. This is Lauren Gallagher from Lauren's Luscious Licks. I'm just calling to confirm delivery of your anniversary cake next week."

"Anniversary cake?" Judy repeated. "What anniversary cake?"

I glanced at the index card in my hand and read from my notes. "The hazelnut genoise washed with cognac, layered with dark chocolate ganache and iced with espresso buttercream—the anniversary version of your wedding cake."

"Don't bother."

"But it was part of your Year to Remember package," I reminded her. "It's already been paid for."

"Jim moved out last month," Judy said flatly. Then she seemed to warm up to the idea. "But I guess you can go ahead and send over the cake, as long as I paid for it. I did love the hazelnut genoise."

Judy confirmed her address and I put the cake on Maria's schedule for next Tuesday. Before I placed Judy Dennison's card back in the file box, I reviewed my comments. Jim Dennison was allergic to hazelnuts. *Large red welts and severe itching*, I'd written along the side margin. And right below it, a note scribbled in two days later—*Judy okay'd hazelnut, said Jim didn't need to have a piece.*

And another couple bit the dust. Judy and Jim had planned a cathedral ceremony with more flowers than the Rose Parade and were even featured in a *Town & Country* spread. But it didn't matter. I'd seen enough designer gowns glide down the aisle to know that neither the wedding, nor its price tag, had any bearing on the happiness of the couple or the longevity of the marriage. The cake, on the other hand, was beginning to tell a different story.

"Maybe it's really that simple." I placed the last of the powder pink receipts on the desk next to the adding machine. The stack of slips, elegantly engraved with the Lauren's Luscious Licks logo, stood three inches high.

"Nothing's that simple," Maria disagreed, not even bothering to look up at me as she wiped down the stainless steel workbench.

"Look." I sifted through the pile of index cards I'd removed from the filing box on my desk and held out a card for Maria to see. "It's all right here."

"I'm not listening to you," Maria practically sang, like a child who holds her fingers in her ears and hums "It's a Grand Old Flag" so she can tune out the noise around her.

"Look at this," I said even louder and pointed to the card. I felt kind of like Glenn Close in *Fatal Attraction*: *You didn't think I'd let you ignore me, did you, Maria?*

Maria didn't flinch, and as she reached to wipe off the electric pasta machine we used to create icing gathers, pleats, ruches and swags, I grabbed for the shiny metal tool. It wasn't exactly a boiling bunny, but it got Maria's attention.

"It's undisputable," I said.

"It's crap," Maria replied and swatted me away like I was nothing more than a pesky mosquito.

"Remember the couple who chose the Wedgwood blue fondant-iced dome with the white chocolate swags?" I read from the card in my hand.

"August eighteenth, two thousand and one."

"Lasted less than a year." I pulled out another card. "That woman who insisted on the coffee sponge cake with rum-laced custard, mocha mousse and rolled chocolate icing?"

"July twenty-fourth, nineteen ninety-nine."

"He left her for his therapist—his sex therapist. Named Harvey. I'm telling you, I know which couples will make it and which won't just by watching them select a cake." I looked up at Maria, who was bending over to lift the black rubber fatigue mats off the tiled floor, her thick, compact body packed into a white chef's coat and checkerboard trousers. "I'm a marital Magic 8 Ball."

"More like screwball, if you ask me." Maria folded the mats and laid them by the back door. She liked to shake her head at me and frown a lot, furrowing her brow until her thick, bushy black eyebrows practically formed a single sleeping caterpillar across her forehead, but after working with her for almost seven years, I knew she got a kick out of me—even if she enjoyed acting like I was an annoyance rather than her boss.

"Come on, you've seen it—how some women won't hear of anything but pure piped white buttercream while their fiancés only want a dark chocolate layer cake with chocolate mousse filling. Or how it becomes a debate of fresh versus pastillage flowers? I mean, I can see it as they're flipping through the pages of the portfolio—the way a man rolls his eyes when his fiancée points out a cascade of sugar blossoms and butterflies. And don't even get me started on the dreaded groom's cake." I pushed back my chair and stood up. "That's the kiss of death, a sure sign that a man isn't ready to trade in his single status for a wife."

"Ask not for whom the bell tolls; it tolls for couples with groom's cakes?" Maria shook her bandanna-cloaked head, which kept her short, cropped black hair from peeking out and letting anyone know there was a real woman inside. "Lady, just sell the cakes and keep the fortune-telling to yourself."

So what if Maria didn't believe me? After years of observing couples, I'd become adept at predicting everyone's future but my own. Like people, cakes had distinct personalities, and from my stool at the tasting table I could tell which personalities would clash and which marriages would crumble. My clients could save themselves, not to mention their families and friends, the hassle and expense of a wedding if they'd just ask me up front whether I thought the marriage would work. But then I'd also eliminate the four-figure price tags that accompanied five-tier wedding cakes with white chocolate draping and basket-weaved buttercream, not to mention the subsequent baby showers and birthday parties where our individually sized crimped fondant-iced cakes had become a must-have for my clientele.

"Fine; suit yourself. Deny it all you want, but it doesn't change the fact that I'm onto something here."

Maria responded with a few carefully chosen words in Italian, a practice she knew annoyed me to no end. The only Italian words I could decipher were along the lines of *rigatoni alla Bolognese* and could be found on the menu at Lucia Ristorante. And Maria knew it.

"What was that?" I asked, expecting a translation of some obscene gesture I was supposed to perform on myself.

"I said I'll have a large cheese pie with pepperoni," Maria repeated and then laughed, amused at herself.

I sat down at my desk and turned my back on Maria. My fingers flipped quickly through the filing box until I found the index card labeled MANNING, MARK AND ROBIN. I held the card in my hand and revisited the tasting that had repercussions I still felt on a daily basis, like the aftershocks following an earthquake.

I'd known Robin and Mark weren't going to make it long before I received what I'd thought was an obscene phone call but ended up being the sobbing-induced hiccups of a just-dumped Robin. Once the heavy breathing subsided, Robin was able to tell me about her newly imposed single status. And, even as I told her that it would be okay, that she'd survive just fine without Mark, the only words going through my mind were *I told you so*. Only I hadn't told her. There was no way you could tell one of your best friends that she was making a mistake when her newly minted emerald-cut diamond was twinkling at you. But I'd known, simply by observing the way Mark turned away from Robin instead of leaning in to her as they sat at the tasting table. The way he shrugged dismissively and said *I don't care; whatever you want* when Robin picked the lemon cake with lemon mousse filling, fresh raspberries and lemon-scented buttercream. Besides, he kept stealing glances at his watch, which is never a good sign in any situation, but definitely an indicator of trouble for two people about to say *I do*. Yes, I'd known that very afternoon, six months after their engagement and four months before they took that fateful pledge. And I hadn't said anything—to anybody, not even Paige. And so Robin had to find out the hard way, when she discovered Mark's duffel bag packed and ready to go in the hall closet, like a getaway car.

"Hey, Gypsy Rosalie, what time is Paige's appointment tomorrow?" Maria called out from the broom closet.

"Five o'clock."

"Anything special, or just the usual?"

"The usual, but she was also interested in trying the white cake with blackberry filling and white chocolate mousseline, so include that, too."

Maria muttered something in Italian and closed the closet door with the force of a man twice her size. I wasn't surprised that Maria had never married. She was like a human cannoli—it would take a man with extraordinary patience to discover the sweet filling that I was sure was tucked deep inside her hardened exterior.

"I'm telling you, Maria. I'm onto something here. I'm a baked goods bridal barometer. I have the predictive power of pastry." I was cracking myself up, but no giggles emerged from the broom closet, just a scowling Maria, who carried the clean mats back into the kitchen and laid them in place at the foot of the convection oven and the three-hole sink.

"How about using those powers for something good, witchy woman—like telling me if the bus will be on time for once."

I ignored Maria's request for transit telepathy and continued. "Maybe there is something we could do when I can tell it's a mismatch—like suggest a Thinking It Over party instead."

"Don't we get paid for baking wedding cakes, not Thinking It Over cakes? Besides, who'd take relationship advice from someone who hasn't been on a date since her membership in the Milli Vanilli fan club was revoked?"

The same people willing to buy a cake from someone who hasn't had her hands on a wire whip mixer or worn a cotton apron since Lauren's Luscious Licks opened its doors. "But it'd be a win-win for everyone: the woman can wear her princess gown, the guy can invite all his buddies to a party with an open bar and we can create a new category of cakes that eliminate the middle men—divorce attorneys." I was going to let Maria's dating remark slide—she retained embarrassing facts the way other women retained water— but I couldn't resist adding, "And just because I'm not willing to settle for just any guy doesn't mean I can't get a date; besides, that membership was a present from Paige, and it wasn't revoked. The club disbanded."

What Maria also failed to acknowledge was that I'd willingly decided to sit on the dating sidelines for a while. I mean, after spending my days with couples in the throes of love, couples on the verge of committing to a lifetime together, a dinner at Legal Sea Foods didn't exactly measure up. And even though fifty percent of the couples who sat before me, and an even higher percentage of those ordering groom's cakes, would end up dividing their assets in court, I couldn't help but think that if someone couldn't hold my attention for a two-hour date, there was no way he'd keep my interest for more than two decades.

I once told Paige that dating in my thirties had begun to feel like standing in line at a cafeteria. I was waiting my turn, eyeing my options and trying to see past the strawberry Jell-O, chick peas and pickled beets, even as other women were growing impatient, worried that the longer it took to get to the front of the line, the less there'd be to pick from. Nobody wanted to settle for the dish of syrupy fruit salad when the person before her carried away a piece of chocolate layer cake with a brilliant red cherry on top.

Maria shook her head at me before unhooking her coat from the wall and stuffing her pillowy arms into the sleeves.

"You can wait for your magic carpet, but us regular folk still have to rely on public transportation." She wrapped a natty wool scarf around her neck and pulled on a pair of Isotoner gloves with suede patches sewed into the palms. "See ya."

I watched Maria check the oven one more time to make sure it was off, and then, out of habit, flip off the light switch before exiting through the swinging door and leaving me in the dark.

"Good night, Maria."

2

What are you doing tomorrow night?" Robin demanded, not even acknowledging my pleasant greeting.

"Hello to you, too." I balanced the cordless phone against my shoulder and continued folding laundry. "Steve and Paige are coming for their tasting at five, and we were thinking of going out for a drink afterward."

"Shit, I forgot." Robin heaved an aggravated sigh, as she did every time someone mentioned anything to do with marriage, men or monogamy—which meant there was always a gust of air blowing from Robin's direction. "How's she doing?"

"Paige is hanging in there. She still hasn't convinced Steve that it's absolutely necessary to be transported from the church to the reception in a horse-drawn carriage, but she's working on it."

"Well, come over afterward; I want to talk to you about something."

"Not another seminar." Robin was constantly testing out new seminar ideas on me and Paige, but since Paige was in the middle of planning her wedding and couldn't be relied upon to provide objective feedback on programs designed for disgruntled women, I'd become Robin's sole sounding board. Apparently I more closely resembled Robin's target audience.

"Let's just say it involves getting screwed," she said, purposely leaving me hanging.

"Sounds intriguing; any hints?"

"As a professional speaker and seminar aficionado, I know better than to give away the punch line." Robin paused for effect, which, despite the fact that I knew it was coming, worked. "You'll find out when you get here."

I placed folded stacks of T-shirts and underwear and jeans into the laundry basket and hoped that Robin's need to talk had nothing to do with Mark. After two years of post-divorce retaliation, there wasn't much left she could do to make Mark rue the day he met Robin Cross. Then again, she was very creative.

"So, what's for dinner tonight, chef girl? Perhaps a little herb-crusted leg of lamb? A simple salmon and asparagus *en croute*?" Robin struggled to affect a convincing French accent.

"Let's see." I made my way past a sad excuse for a dining room table and into the kitchen, where the remains of my dinner still sat on the Formica counter. "I prepared a mélange of flaky albacore in white sauce, sprinkled with freshly grated aged cheddar and nestled on a bed of toasted organic nine-grain loaf."

"A tuna melt on whole wheat?"

"Bingo."

"Just because you're cooking for one doesn't mean you have to eat like a ten-year-old," Robin scolded. "You know, for someone who makes a living because she supposedly knows her way around the kitchen, you're certainly a big disappointment to those of us who know you."

I removed the cooled griddle from the burner and set it in the sink with this morning's cereal bowl. "You know what they say—the cobbler's kids and all. Besides, my living is made outside the kitchen, where it's all about presentation."

"Speaking of which, I've gotta run. I'm writing a new workbook for the SCALPEL program, and there's a publisher interested in taking a look at it. An editor's taking me to dinner."

"Brave soul."

"Smart soul. SCALPEL's booked through June. Tell Paige and Steve I said hi. And don't let them pick anything with nuts. You know how I feel about nuts."

Mostly that she liked to bust them.

Robin's company, Women in Action, was originally a small organization that coordinated classes for bored housewives and single women—pottery classes and candle making, macramé and flower arranging. When Robin joined the company right out of college as an event coordinator, she immediately saw the possibilities. Instead of offering night classes on how to create memory quilts, Robin had bigger plans. She bought the company from the owner and set about re-creating the firm, and today Women in Action developed seminars and workshops based on the phases in a woman's life—from adolescent angst to incontinence, Robin liked to say.

The themes of Robin's seminars seemed to follow along with the events going on in her life. When she first purchased the company, she created programs for working women—seminars with the names Sleeping Your Way to the Top: Using Your Dreams to Achieve Professional Success and Is That Spinach in Your Teeth?: What *Not* to Say During the Interview Process. After she married Mark, she started focusing on couples' issues, with The More the Merrier: Group Sex for Married Couples and I'm Not Your Mom, So Pick Up Your Own Dirty Underwear: Setting Boundaries That Make Marriage Work. Unfortunately, Robin's been more successful telling other people how to live their lives than figuring out her own. Since the divorce, she's struck it big teaching women how to get over lost love, even as she struggles to take her own advice. Love Stinks: Getting Over It and Moving On was so successful that it led to the entire Relationship Circumcision series, which included Men: Can't Live with Them—And Why Would You Want To?, Sexual Healing: Nothing a Little K-Y Jelly and Batteries Can't Cure, and finally, the complete SCALPEL method of relationship recovery. In her program SCALPEL: Cutting Out the Man Who Ripped Out Your Heart, Robin takes women through the seven steps necessary to move on after splitting up: *S*creaming, *C*rying, *A*nger, *L*oneliness, *P*ayback, *E*levation and *L*etting Go. Robin's still kind of stuck in the payback phase herself, but she claims to be working on it.

The seven-week series begins with Robin standing on a

darkened stage wielding a scalpel, the instrument's slender blade illuminated by a spotlight, reflecting shards of light into the audience. Once the drama of the scene sinks in, the audience quiets down and turns its full attention to the stage. In a voice that is at once thunderous and controlled, Robin announces that men are as useless as foreskin. Those are her exact words: *Men are as useless as foreskin.* The women go crazy, clapping and whooping, pumping their fists in the air. That line alone convinces her audience that the seminar was worth the seven-hundred-and-fifty-dollar admission fee. Clever gal, that Robin.

In a way, we're kind of at opposite ends of the spectrum. I was there to see women get caught up in the fairy tale, and Robin was there to help pick up the pieces when Prince Charming rode off into the sunset with the chambermaid.

Robin thought I was in danger of becoming a wedding junkie, which was akin to becoming a serial killer, in her opinion. But after watching the transformative power a compressed piece of carbon can wield on otherwise sane women, I was the opposite of a wedding junkie. I'd seen successful, competent professional women get blinded by yards of raw silk and glittery tiaras, and I'd witnessed rational women come unglued at the thought of sacrificing just one creamy white Pascali rose even as their wedding budget was nearing that of a third world country's gross national product. It turned out that even Paige wasn't immune to the hysteria, which is why every conversation we'd had lately seemed to revolve around such thought-provoking topics as big band versus swing and Calphalon versus All-Clad.

In fact, if Dante was around today, he'd add a tenth circle of hell: other people's wedding plans. But in my line of work, I didn't just have to grin and bear it—I grinned and baked it.

Even though Robin insisted that I was destined for disappointment, that being around giddy brides every day would leave me hopelessly buying into the myth of marital bliss, I knew she was wrong. If anything, watching couples go through the process of planning a wedding has made me even more convinced that I shouldn't settle for anything less than Mr. Absolutely Right. And I definitely wasn't desperate to get married like other women who hit the big three-oh and felt their biological clocks turn into time bombs—even if I did have my wedding cake picked out (raspberry-filled almond cake with chocolate ganache), I knew where I wanted to live with my husband (the Back Bay with a view of the Charles River), and I habitually ripped pages out of the Pottery Barn catalog and saved them in a folder marked SOMEDAY, which drove Maria crazy. And Maria wasn't the only one.

Robin and Paige couldn't understand why my apartment was still decorated in early-career Ikea, even though Lauren's Luscious Licks was booming. They couldn't believe I hadn't traded up, that I still relied on my old standbys—the particle-board dressers, queen-sized futon and rice paper lamps. But there was no denying that my apartment was homey, and I always had fresh or still-not-dead flowers on the dining room table that doubled as a TV tray when you folded down the two leaves. So what if my kitchen coordination consisted of matching the white laminate cabinets with the six ribbed glasses I got for free when I purchased one hundred dollars' worth of groceries at Star Market.

No matter what Paige and Robin said about my apartment, its three rooms still reminded me of the day I swallowed hard and signed the lease on the Newbury Street store. I took a huge financial risk by signing that lease and then compounded my leap of faith by moving into a one-bedroom on Comm Ave a week later. But because I was either terribly naive or just desperately hopeful, I believed in the boutique. I knew I could make it a success, and signing the lease meant that failing wasn't an option.

My kitchen was a drastic contrast to Paige's, with its granite countertops, and Robin's, with its Sub-Zero fridge. My refrigerator wasn't even full-sized, much less a five-foot-wide behemoth with enough freezer space to keep Walt Disney cryogenically suspended until science developed a cure for cancer. I didn't have a dishwasher, either, which is why the dishes tended to pile up in my sink until I was forced to either wash them or drink straight from the milk carton. Paige and Robin were fully aware of my dirty little secret, which is why they always declined my offer of any beverage in an opened container.

But if I didn't care, why should they?

Well, actually, I did know why Paige was so concerned. She was hell-bent on finding me that Back Bay condo and cashing a very hefty commission check when I signed on the dotted line. But I'd always thought that when it came time to buy real estate and invest in adult furniture, *adult* meaning pieces that came preassembled and didn't require hex nuts and wood glue, I would share the decision with someone else. Why invest in French country if my future significant other preferred mission style? It never occurred to me that I wouldn't be making the decision with someone else whose tastes I'd have to take into consideration, someone whose color preferences I'd have to reconcile with my own. Buying a place was a huge decision, a commitment that I just wasn't ready to make, when the man of my dreams might want to live in Cambridge.

Even if my decision to wait patiently caused me to be on the receiving end of Robin's feminist manifestos and Paige's daily e-mails about declining mortgage interest rates, I was fine with it. Besides, I'd had my chance to marry Neil. If I was really a wedding junkie, I would have accepted his offer, and right now, instead of running Lauren's Luscious Licks, I'd be in Washington, D.C., popping out little Neil juniors and enjoying all the perfectly pleasant perks that surely accompanied the title of Mrs. Neil Morrow.

Instead, two weeks after Neil moved, I found myself without a boyfriend, without a job and without any money to buy a gift for Paige's birthday. I could barely afford a cab ride to the party, much less a present, so I picked up a Martha Stewart cookbook for two bucks at a used bookstore in Cambridge and went to work. Before that afternoon, the closest I'd ever come to baking was the time Paige, Robin and I attempted to make hash cookies—hash brownies requiring too much effort, as the Duncan Hines mix actually necessitated the measuring of water and cracking of an egg. But cookies—that we could handle. All they required was slicing open a roll of Toll House cookie dough and placing the dollops of dough on the toaster oven's miniature cookie sheet. Even without the hallucinogenic effects of hash, the chocolate almond torte I'd made for Paige was a hit, and soon I had people asking me to make desserts for parties and, eventually, after I'd taken classes to learn the proper technique, weddings.

Eight years later, Lauren's Luscious Licks was the toast of the town, Neil was long gone, and I was getting ready to make Paige another cake.

I ran some water over the dishes and griddle and headed back into the living room where my clothesline-fresh laundry, and hopefully a juicy Lifetime movie, awaited me.

Lifetime TV—what an ingenious idea. How could a woman possibly feel bad about her own life after watching two hours of women who are cheated on, betrayed, struck with amnesia, jailed, mutilated or held captive by stalkers? Besides, it's given life back to a whole generation of sitcom actresses who were spiraling into entertainment oblivion. I've gotten sucked into so many movies starring Meredith Baxter Birney as a psycho husband killer or adulterous sex addict, I had a hard time picturing her as sweet Mrs. Keaton anymore.

As I folded my bath towels, I thought about Robin out at some expensive restaurant getting wined and dined by an editor while I devoted an evening to ensuring that my socks were matched and my underwear was folded into quarters. Funny thing is, I knew that Robin would give it up in a heartbeat—the articles that quoted her as an "expert," the requests to appear on TV, and the all-expenses-paid dinners with publishers who were trying to woo her—and all it would take was one phone call from Mark saying he wanted her back.

If I'd offered Robin the option of a Thinking It Over party five years ago, there was no way she would have taken it. Even though they'd lived together for four years, no one, not even me or Paige, assumed that marriage was on the horizon for Mark and Robin. As a couple, Robin and Mark prided themselves on their respective independence; they were the consummate contemporary couple comprised of two separate but equal participants. Their relationship was an exercise in self-preservation, with two tubes of the same toothpaste and a conscientious decision to avoid having a designated side of the bed—too conventional and routine, even though Robin preferred sleeping next to the alarm clock and Mark liked having easy access to the phone. No, we never asked Robin and Mark when they'd get married, but we did ask *if*. And when we asked, Robin held her breath.

Despite herself, Robin had become one of those women she hated: a woman who needed more, a woman whose neediness was breeding discontent and something completely foreign to Robin—insecurity. The longer Robin and Mark lived together without the mention of a ring, not mentioned because Robin believed that no self-respecting woman should have to bring it up, the more she needed it. When they walked to the grocery store together on Saturday mornings she found herself stealing glances in the jewelry store windows, the expansive plate glass mercilessly reflecting what she herself had started to see—fear. When Mark finally proposed, five years from the day they met and one week short of the date Robin gave in her ultimatum, she was finally convinced that she'd gotten what she wanted.

Of course, the best-laid plans are usually the ones that come back to bite you in the ass. When Mark left Robin, he proclaimed that he didn't want to be married anymore, implying that it was the institution that he found distasteful, not the person he'd chosen to enter into the institution with. But Robin knew what he meant. He meant he didn't want to be married to her.

Unlike Mark, I didn't have a problem with the institution of marriage; I had a problem planning a life with Neil.

"I have an offer you can't refuse," Neil had told me over a candlelit dinner at L'Espalier. "Move to DC with me."

"He said what?" Paige had cried when I told her about the après-ski dinner. "An offer you can't refuse?"

"What is he, a used car salesman?" Robin started waving her hands in the air like the guy from the Fast Freddy's commercial. "Come on in today, folks; we're wheeling and dealing; we've got a man with an offer you just can't refuse!"

"That is the lamest proposal I've ever heard," Paige chimed in.

"It wasn't exactly a proposal," I'd told them. "It was more like—"

Robin cut me off before I could answer. "A sign you should seriously wonder why you're dating this man?"

No, it wasn't a proposal, but I realized, just by looking at the expectation in his eyes, that Neil's offer was a prelude to marriage and a lifetime together. And after three years of dating, three relatively pleasant, stress-free years during which we bumped along without any significant disagreements but without any electrifying fireworks either, it seemed like the obvious thing to do.

"I'll think about it," I answered, but even then I knew that the only thinking I was going to be doing was the kind that resulted in an ironclad excuse that wouldn't make me look like the bad guy.

But would things have turned out differently if Neil had given *me* the opportunity to say yes to a Thinking It Over party? Maybe with more time I could have learned to live with the little things that started to make me question whether we belonged together. It was as if the more real the prospect of our spending our lives together became, the higher I turned up the microscope on his habits and ways of doing things and revealed imperfections that, once uncovered, I couldn't overlook. Like how he'd laugh a little too hard at his own jokes, as if hoping his listeners would follow along. Or when he'd tell me he could care less and I wanted to scream at him, "You *couldn't* care less; the expression is you *couldn't* care less."

Okay, minor things, I know. In retrospect, maybe I was blowing things out of proportion in the end. It was an expression lots of people got wrong. But it became like a humming noise in the background of our relationship, and the harder I tried to ignore it, the louder it grew. It wasn't that Neil was Mr. Wrong. He just wasn't Mr. Right.

You get what you settle for, Maria once told me. I think at the time she was referring to the low cocoa-butter content in a shipment of chocolate we received, but it applied just as well to relationships. We didn't hesitate to send the shipment back and order from another supplier. And if I wasn't willing to settle for anything less than perfect when it came to ingredients for our cakes, I sure as hell wasn't going to settle for anything less when it came to my personal life. After all, everyone knew that the best things come to those who wait.

3

Thursdays were always crazy in the kitchen. We had the Friday-night ceremonies for the late planners and the couples looking to save money on room rentals, not to mention preparations for Saturday's onslaught of nuptial madness. Luckily, at this point I rarely had to make a personal appearance at the receptions anymore and instead relied on our drivers, who were also trained to assemble the cakes on-site when necessary. After all, as the proprietor of Lauren's Luscious Licks, I was much too busy to be navigating the streets of Boston in a refrigerated truck—or at least that's what I led my clients to believe. The truth was, if I had to sit through one more round of outdated, humiliating wedding traditions, I'd hurl myself onto the cake knife and beg the caterer to put me out of my misery. Whether it was watching adult women lift their thousand-dollar dresses to expose a four-dollar garter belt like some tart at the Mustang Ranch, or the bride and groom kissing like a couple of Pavlov's dogs every time some relative from Topeka clinked a glass with a fork, I'd had my fill. I mean, toss a handful of hundred-dollar bills into a crowd of single women instead of a secondhand wilting bouquet—they could use the cash a hell of a lot more than twenty-hour-old roses and the promise that they were next down the aisle. Even I'd join in on that little ritual.

Typically I didn't even offer tastings past noon on Thursdays, but when it was one of your best friends getting married, you made an exception.

The boutique's cake gallery didn't have a clock, but I could tell by the noises coming from the kitchen that it was just past four o'clock. All today's orders were filled by now, and it was cleanup time. I headed into the kitchen to check on Paige's tasting selections and found the staff preparing tomorrow's cake boards with a thin layer of rolled sugar paste while Maria stooped over one of the butcher-block benches.

"We all set?" I asked Maria as I took the serving tray down from a speed rack.

"Almost." She squeezed the pastry bag gently, piping just the right amount of raspberry puree into an elegant spiral on the last plate. "Now we're ready. Paige will be happy."

Maria loved Paige. Whenever Paige stopped by the boutique on her way to a client's house or between appointments, Maria turned from a grand monster into the consummate Italian grandmother. She let Paige taste icings and fillings and always put together a little something for Paige to take home with her. Even though I thought Maria did it as much to annoy me as anything else, you'd be hard-pressed to find someone who didn't love Paige.

When I walked into my room on the second floor of Pomeroy my freshman year at Wellesley, I was curious to meet the owner of the three matching Samsonite suitcases on the otherwise empty floor. My roommate for the next nine months had wasted no time during our brief phone conversation filling me in on what she thought I should know. In less than four minutes I learned that Paige Carmichael was valedictorian of her graduating class (but it wasn't such a big deal, Paige had assured me; there were only a hundred kids in the entire class, and most of them were morons), that Paige was going to major in economics and go into real estate (Boston's answer to Donald Trump, only without the gilt-covered tributes to her ego or entourage of starlets), and that Paige Carmichael absolutely, completely, to the core of her being, detested applesauce (*but if you like it, then I'm sure we can come to some sort of compromise,* Paige had offered, as if I might be planning to hoard jars of Mott's under my bed).

I had pictured a very tall, very attractive, self-assured blonde (we'd never gotten around to asking each other what we looked like; even though we were curious, we felt it belied our intellect and burgeoning feminism to care about such things), so when a petite brunette in a pink corded headband showed up with the last of her belongings, I was surprised; all that confidence was packed into someone so tiny, so completely the antithesis of what I had pictured, that I was immediately at ease. How could you not like someone who looked like the leader of a pep squad, sported a T-shirt that read VISUALIZE WHIRLED PEAS, and feared the concept of pureed apples? We wouldn't be sharing clothes, which was a bummer because I figured one of the benefits of having a roommate was the doubling effect it would have on my wardrobe, but I hoped we'd become good friends.

Even after we'd met Robin, smoking a cigarette on the steps of the bookstore, Paige and I shared a level of familiarity and candor that could come only from surviving close living quarters, monthly mood swings, and all the firsts that went along with our newfound independence. Even now, I found it hard to believe that the Paige who was getting married, the overachieving real estate agent who wouldn't consider going outside without sunscreen much less without undergarments, was the same girl who had Robin and me on the floor of Donovan's poolroom searching for her lost underwear. And how did we get Paige Carmichael, birthday girl, Phi Beta Kappa member and anal-retentive president of the class of 1993, to remove her underwear in a bar? We didn't, but the Harvard senior feeding her celebratory shots of Jägermeister did.

"Could I have lost any more dignity in that room just now?" Paige asked when Robin and I caught up to her in the hallway outside the poolroom and learned that she'd had to sacrifice her underwear in a mad dash to get dressed. Apparently a group of rugby players was about to turn on the overhead lights and discover her splayed out on the pool table in her birthday suit with a guy named Digger. As she was leaving, one of the rugby players uncovered her pair of lacy bikini bottoms and decided that instead of returning them to Paige, as she'd asked him to do, he'd use her underwear for a game of hot potato.

"That would mean we thought you had dignity to begin with." Robin cracked a smile, but by now Paige's Jägermeister buzz had given way to a throbbing headache, and her sense of humor was left in that room along with her underwear.

"Look at it this way; you have a hell of a story to tell your tenants when they refuse to leave the premises: the case of the vacated panties—why possession is still nine-tenths of the law," I managed to say before we all burst out laughing.

"You ever repeat this to anyone and I'll sue your asses for defamation."

I threw an arm over Paige's shoulder and led her back toward the bar. "At least our asses will have underwear on them."

That was probably the last time I saw Paige do anything irrational. Since then she's managed to keep her head, and her underwear, screwed on tight—unless you counted sleeping with a science teacher from Roxbury on a scuba diving trip she won for having the highest quarterly sales in her office. I guess oxygen deprivation and a wet suit with fins can do as much to impair one's judgment as a few shots of Jägermeister. In Paige's case, she literally opted for a shot of sex on the beach instead.

I was arranging the gallery's tasting table for Paige and Steve, placing two Reed & Barton dessert forks every eight inches until there were six matching sets, when simultaneously the phone rang and the front door opened, letting in a burst of winter air.

I took the call and held up a finger to indicate to the visitor that I'd be a minute.

"I'll be right with you," I mouthed, pointing to the cordless phone I had pressed up to my ear.

The man smiled and turned his back to me as he looked up at the oversized cake portraits hanging on the gallery walls. It was actually a very nice smile, an easy smile. Usually the men who came in alone were uptight, as if just by walking into a cake boutique they were at risk of losing their manhood. If they thought Lauren's Luscious Licks was intimidating, they wouldn't last five minutes in the lobby of Women in Action.

I sat down at the tasting table and opened the scheduling diary to next week. But even as I went through the available openings, I had trouble diverting my eyes from the black overcoat making its way across the floor. A few snowflakes dotted the shoulders and arms of the coat, and I watched as they melted away, replaced by shiny droplets of water.

After we finally settled on Wednesday afternoon, I penciled in the caller's name and turned my attention to the dark-haired man slowly moving from one photo to the next.

"Can I help you?" I offered and waited for my unexpected visitor to turn around so I could get a better look at who those broad shoulders belonged to. The wait was worth it.

"Lauren? I'm Charlie Banks." He started toward the tasting table, where I was still seated on my stool. "We met the other day in Starbucks."

"Oh, sure; I didn't recognize you." I stood up and went to shake Charlie's hand, which was warm from being nestled in his coat pocket.

Is this what I was missing every morning by walking around half-comatose before my daily dose of Starbucks? How could I have not noticed what a great smile Charlie Banks had? I glanced at his left hand for evidence of a precious metal, a skill most women have mastered by the time that little detail starts to matter, and noticed it was bare.

One benefit of working in a cake boutique was being able to immediately find out if a man was already taken. Of course, one of the disadvantages was that ninety-nine percent of the men who entered the boutique were accompanied by their fiancées.

"Are you interested in a cake?" I asked, screening him for a future Mrs. Banks.

"Actually, I'm here because Gwen Stern was afraid that if she came here herself, you'd hold it against her, and she's still got her heart set on one of your cakes for her next wedding." Charlie stuffed his hands back into his overcoat and shrugged, as if he was embarrassed to even be having this conversation. "Anyway, she'd like her photo removed from your portfolio. She says the emotional strain of knowing other couples will see it is too great."

"Sure. No problem." I started back toward the tasting table to retrieve the portfolio.

"I feel ridiculous even doing this." Charlie apologized and followed me, each step of his polished wing-tipped shoes echoing throughout the sparse gallery.

"Don't. It's not the first time," I assured him, even though it was the first time a client sent a six-foot-tall attorney with caramel brown eyes.

"It's a first for me. But, you know, we do share a lot of the same clients."

"Do we?" I gestured for him to take a seat and started slowly going through the portfolio page by page even though I knew exactly where to find the Sterns' cake.

"Oh, sure. I've seen a lot of your cakes immortalized in photo albums that are touted around as proof. My male clients don't usually bother trotting out the wedding photos, but for some reason the women like to take me through every page in painstaking detail, pointing out how happy they were and how their soon-to-be-ex-husbands should have to pay for making it all go awry. I swear, sometimes I think I can tell they were going to end up in my office just by looking at the pictures of the bride and groom feeding each other cake—some couples just look so gleeful at the opportunity to take a four-pronged utensil and drive it at their spouse's face, like they wish it was a pitchfork."

Charlie's admission was an instant aphrodisiac. It seemed the Goodman & Moore partner and I shared more than a roster of clients. We shared insight that was as valuable as insider information. But while his instinct may be right on when his client is signing the retainer check for his services, I could tell which couples were destined for a seat in his downtown office before they even tied the knot. Still, it wasn't often that I met someone who shared my propensity to predict coupling catastrophe.

"That's funny. Sometimes I think I can tell just by watching them pick out a cake, like it's my sixth sense—I see divorced people."

Charlie let out a laugh and grinned at me. "Maybe there's an opportunity for us there—a joint venture of sorts, or at the very least I could offer you a referral bonus or something."

"Sounds lucrative, but that would eliminate all the romance, wouldn't it?"

"I don't get to see much of the romance, as you can probably imagine. In my line of work, marriage is more a form of job security than anything else."

I stopped turning the album's pages and looked up at Charlie. He held my glance for a moment before looking away, and it wasn't until an embarrassingly long breath escaped from my mouth that I realized I'd stopped breathing.

"Is that it?" he asked, pointing to the citron vodka cake displayed behind a sheet of nonglare plastic.

"That's it." I slid my hand behind the stiff covering and removed the photo. Reluctantly, I handed it over. "Here you go."

Charlie took the photo and carefully slipped it into the chest pocket of his overcoat. "Thanks. I better get going; I'm not quite sure how I'll explain this on my time sheet—there's not exactly a column for billable hours spent retrieving cake portraits."

I followed Charlie to the front door, inhaling the deliciously foreign and unsweet scent of him as I lingered in the wake of his cologne. I tried to think of a way to get him to stay a little while longer, but my arsenal of witty banter and feminine wiles ran out years ago.

The best idea I could come up with on such short notice was to ask Charlie if he'd like any other clients' photos, or even just a cup of coffee before venturing outside again. Not exactly original, but also not something he'd be likely to turn down in twenty-degree weather, either. Just as I was about to say something, Charlie stopped in the open doorway and peeked his head back into the gallery, his cheeks already turning pink from the wind. "Thanks again, Lauren."

I smiled mutely, choking under the pressure. I, a woman who once addressed an entire auditorium filled with wedding planners, couldn't get out the words necessary to offer a man a cup of coffee. Quite pitiful, even for someone out of practice. Obviously, getting a date wasn't like riding a bike. Or if it was, I was a candidate for training wheels.

When the door closed behind him, I wrapped my arms across my chest and let out a little shiver. Charlie Banks was more than just a divorce attorney who managed to be charming even as he was revoking a client's cake portrait. He had something most men lacked—intuition. A man with intuition who didn't wear skintight silk T-shirts, perch his hands on his hips and call everyone sweetie. I didn't know they existed.

As far as I was concerned, there were two kinds of guys—the aforementioned hip-swaying variety was automatically excluded, of course. In my experience, which I wish I could say was vast but was more like selectively sporadic, there were the guys you met and enjoyed talking to for a while before it dawned on you that maybe this was someone worth getting to know. It had been like that with Neil. Then there were the guys you met and even though your lips were moving and the conversation was bumping along nicely, the only thing going through your head was *What's this guy like in bed?* And which group did Charlie fall into? Come on; it wasn't even a toss-up.

Maybe I could call Judy Dennison and recommend that I introduce her to a divorce attorney at Goodman & Moore. Or maybe a joint venture wasn't such a bad idea after all.

After my seven years of self-imposed dating exile, Charlie was like a mirage in my dating desert. I wasn't going to let him slip away that easily. While the thought of recommending Charlie to Judy Dennison was tempting, she was probably on the market again and already looking for husband number two. I didn't need the competition. So how could I get Charlie back into the boutique?

I straightened up the cake gallery and mulled over my options. Thankfully, straightening up consisted mostly of arranging the client chairs and my chrome stool. Everyone always thought that *cake boutique* was just a fancy term for bakery, but in fact the room was modeled after the upscale art galleries that my clients loved to ooh and aah over even as they passed over the works of art for the art of networking.

The seventeen-by-twenty-five-foot room had the requisite polished blond hardwood floors and recessed lighting, but large blowups of black-and-white cake photographs were mounted on the ivory walls where canvases would usually hang. Readying the gallery for tasting appointments simply required realigning the two Mies van der Rohe Barcelona chairs that faced the client side of the glass-topped tasting table. The chairs, with their white quilted leather seats and chrome-plated metal frames, may have seemed a little sterile for an environment that should conjure up childhood memories of licking batter-covered spoons and stealing fingertip-covered swipes of sugary icing, but the crowd that flocked to Lauren's Luscious Licks wasn't exactly traditional. My brides wore chic sheaths and strapless gowns that showed off sculpted bodies and cleavage sprinkled with bronzing powder. There was nothing frilly about my clientele—they approached wedding planning with the managerial savvy of a CEO and the acute knowledge that a wedding was only as good as it looked. Right down to the cake.

At Lauren's Luscious Licks, we didn't adorn the gallery with all the homey touches normally associated with weddings—there were no elaborately carved and uphol-stered Victorian side chairs, no salmon and pink chintz cur-tains ballooning over the large picture windows running along the sidewalk, no Oriental rugs lining the floors or grand chandelier hanging from the ceiling. In fact, if it wasn't for the fresh tulips tucked into a solitary Lalique vase standing on the glass-slab tasting table, passersby probably would have thought the storefront was deserted. But, even as clients sank into the plush leather seating and swayed gently to the music of George Winston softly wafting from the built-in speakers, I knew that the Zen-like quality of the gallery was all an illusion, because beyond the cream-colored swinging door in the center of the back wall, the real work was getting done.

Maria kept an immaculate kitchen, all shiny stainless steel, with a place for everything and everything in its place, as she liked to remind me. Maria's only personal touch was a handwritten piece of paper taped up on the wall above one of the butcher-block benches. In her tight, sharp script she'd scrawled, *The only way for a woman, as for a man, to know herself as a person is by creative work of her own*. It wasn't as if Maria went around quoting feminist writers, so I figured she must have seen the Betty Friedan line on a calendar or something. When I asked her if she'd ever actually read *The Feminine Mystique*, Maria didn't miss an opportunity to put me in my place.

"Of course I've read it. And I didn't have to take out eighty thousand dollars in student loans to have some professor put it on a required reading list."

And my snappy comeback? "It's called a syllabus."

"Everything's ready for Paige," I now told Maria, who was rinsing a spatula in the sink.

"Why'd you let him go?" she asked.

"Who?" I feigned indifference, as if I had better things to remember than the handsome lawyer who'd just disappeared into a gray March afternoon and left me stirred up south of the border.

Maria frowned at me, a frown that said she knew I was full of shit.

"Were you spying on me?" I teased. "I didn't know you cared."

"I don't."

"Then why all the concern? Why are you watching me with those beady Sicilian eyes?"

"That's what the little glass window in the kitchen door is for, isn't it?"

"The window is there so I can spy on you."

"You're right; I'm usually more interesting." Maria held up the wet spatula and pointed toward the front of the boutique. "He's back."

"What?" I turned around and saw that Maria was right. Through the kitchen door's window I could see Charlie standing on the black floor mat I kept in the entryway to keep customers from tracking sand and salt throughout the gallery.

"I know you haven't done this in a while, but maybe you should go see what he wants." Maria smacked the spatula against the side of the sink and I jumped. "Go!"

* * *

"Don't tell me you have another client who can't bear the thought of some other bride viewing her cake." I tried not to seem too anxious as I approached him, but after spending my days in the realm of premarital planning, I'd all but forgotten what went on between men and women before the reception hall was booked.

"You wouldn't like to go to dinner sometime, would you?" Charlie asked, forgoing any small talk that would have given me a chance to collect myself before practically croaking, "Sure I would" like a death-row prisoner who'd been asked if she'd like to take a call from the governor.

Charlie tipped his head to the side and smiled, once again regaling me with what I was sure was the result of teenage years filled with orthodontist bills. "Great. I'll call you tomorrow."

"I have a date," I sang to Maria, who was sterilizing the long, sharp dowel rods we used to keep the tiered cakes from shifting.

"Will wonders never cease?"

Talk about taking all the guesswork and risk out of relationships—with our joint abilities, Charlie and I would know right away if we were a sure thing. And, if we were, who knew where it could lead?

"A date," I repeated. "Do you believe it?" Had it really been so long since I'd met a guy who was even vaguely interesting that the mere idea of a date could obliterate seven years of hard-earned cynicism and get me wondering whether the diaphragm buried under my bathroom sink with a crusty bottle of Nair and a curling iron was more than a shriveled up disc of cracked latex that had seen better days?

"Stranger things have happened. Maybe he'll even find you mildly attractive." Maria turned to me. "But I wouldn't count on it."

"I have a date and I didn't even have to leave the comforts of my own boutique," I announced proudly, and dipped my finger in a bowl of buttercream. "Maybe he has a friend for you, a nice elderly lawyer who's looking for a little Italian lovin'."

"Get out of here; you're making a mess." Maria smacked my hand with a dowel. "See what you make me do? Now I have to sterilize again. Out!"

I danced through the swinging door to wait for Paige and Steve, regaling Maria with my best Ginger Rogers impersonation even as the door smacked me on the side of my head.

"That ought to knock some sense into you," I heard Maria grumble in the kitchen.

But neither the lump growing above my ear nor Maria's grumblings could wipe the smile from my face—because, even though I hated myself for becoming the very cliché I despised, I was already wondering how Charlie felt about raspberry-filled almond cake with chocolate ganache and a view of the Charles River.

4

$\mathcal{W}$hen Paige and Steve rang the buzzer at five o'clock, I could already tell that we were in for a long night. As I went to unlock the door, they stood outside solemnly, without sending a wave or a smile in my direction. And this from a couple who mailed out Groundhog Day cards and actually celebrated Sweetest Day and other specious Hallmark holidays.

"Let me take your coats." I held out my arms and waited as Paige slipped off her leather trench and Steve peeled off his L.L.Bean layers. "Can I offer you a cappuccino, herbal tea or sparkling water with lemon?" I asked instinctively, clicking into hostess mode.

"Hot tea sounds great," Paige answered, rubbing her bare hands together. "It's freezing out there."

"I told you to wear gloves," Steve reminded Paige and then turned to me. "It's March and she refuses to wear gloves."

"I wear gloves, but I just had a manicure and I didn't want to ruin the polish." Paige held up her hands for my approval.

"Very nice." Paige seemed vindicated by my show of support and smirked at Steve, whose own hands had been covered in the kind of rugged fleece-lined gloves favored by men who shopped for clothes in catalogs that also offered hip waders and kerosene lanterns.

"Water's fine for me, thanks." Steve attempted to fold his

body into one of the pristine leather chairs. "Do all your clients get such special treatment?"

"They do if their check clears," I called back over my shoulder before disappearing behind the ivory door. When I returned, they were both seated at the tasting table, where Paige was anxiously tapping her glossy nails on the glass and Steve looked like he was preparing to choose his last meal.

"We're still eligible for the family discount, right?" Paige took the fragile china cup from me and held the steaming tea up to her lips.

"Even better. My wedding gift to you is the cake of your choice."

"That's really generous," Steve acknowledged and smiled for the first time since they'd arrived. I also thought I noticed his shoulders relax a little once he realized he wouldn't be footing the bill.

"Yeah, that's me, Miss Generosity." I winked at Paige and sat down on my chrome stool across the table from them.

"Well, you're not the only generous one. I have a great place coming on the market and it has your name all over it."

"Does she ever stop?" I asked Steve, who just shrugged at me before taking a sip of his Perrier and frowning at the bubbles.

"Let me finish before you say no. It's a two-bedroom brownstone on Comm Ave; it's got hardwood floors, crown molding, built-in bookshelves in the living room, and—get this—a rooftop deck. The kitchen should really be gutted, but you have a kitchen here, so you'd survive while it was under construction."

"Comm Ave's so far in—" I started to object, but Paige cut me off.

"It's four blocks from the river," she corrected me.

"But I want something overlooking the river."

"You and everyone else. Look, Lauren, you're going to have to compromise—with your expectations, you'll never find the perfect apartment, but this place is so right for you."

"You're right; it sounds great," I agreed.

"So why don't you save me the trouble of listing it?"

"Because I'm not looking to buy a place right now," I told

her for the hundredth time. "Now, let me go get the tray and we can start."

"Don't do anything special for us," Paige called after me. "Just act like we're any other couple that comes in here expecting you to create miracles with sugar and flour."

I returned from the kitchen carrying a sterling silver Tiffany tray with the practiced efficiency of someone who'd done this a million times and the care of someone who understood that in Paige's mind, today was unlike any other.

I carefully removed the six pieces of cake from the tray and placed the Waterford dessert dishes between the forks I'd already laid out. This was all about showmanship, and the performance was about to begin.

"We're going to start from the inside out. Here we have five samples of our most popular cakes, and the blackberry filling with white chocolate mousseline that you requested. As you taste each one, note what you like and don't like—the texture of the filling, the consistency of the icing, the bounce of the cake. I'll make notes and then we'll move on to the client portfolio, where we'll go over the design, coloring and shape of the cakes."

"We can mix and match what we like, right?" Steve asked, eyeing the plates suspiciously.

"Absolutely," I assured him. " 'Your cake is a reflection of you,' I like to say."

I took my place back on my four-legged chrome perch, ready to silently observe their reactions to each impeccably sliced and plated piece of confectionary perfection. As Steve slowly and methodically savored each bite, Paige moved swiftly from one plate to the next, as if she knew exactly what she was looking for. They were a study in contrasts, those two.

I'd always thought they made a nice couple, if not exactly a predictable one. While people always commented that Neil and I looked like we belonged together, meaning that we were both well educated, equally attractive and took a good picture, Paige and Steve were more like the people you saw walking down the street and thought *What could they possibly have in common?* Or, my first thought, after noticing the obvious difference in size, *How the hell do they have sex?*

Not only was Paige a successful real estate agent with lines on the hottest properties in the city and a cell phone glued to her diamond-studded ear—she also happened to be all of five foot two with a perky brunette bob that bounced behind her like it was trying to keep up. Steve, on the other hand, stood a foot taller, could palm Paige's head like a basketball, moved with all the grace of a man on stilts and taught earth science in Roxbury—and he even looked the part, with Coke-bottle glasses, shaggy blond hair that was perfect for windswept beaches but not for huddling over Bunsen burners, and khaki pants that always needed pressing.

Paige was the most organized person I knew (she still cursed Bloomingdale's for discontinuing those undies with the days of the week printed on the front; they had saved her a lot of time), while Steve could walk around for hours looking for the glasses that were inevitably resting on top of his head.

When Robin and I first met Steve, we thought maybe Paige was just clinging to the dwindling remains of a waning tropical romance. There was no way Paige would have given Steve a second look if they'd met on the murky shores of Boston Harbor instead of on the turquoise blue waters of the Florida Keys. Then Robin and I figured it was just a stage Paige was going through, getting back in touch with her rural Vermont roots or something. But even after their tans faded, Paige and Steve still looked at each other like they were more than just a vacation hookup. Almost six months later, they were still going strong and we'd grown used to Steve turning bike rides along the Charles into good-natured lectures on aquatic ecosystems.

Finally, Steve placed the last fork on its plate, and Paige sat forward in her chair, anxious to hear his verdict. "You first."

"No, you," he acquiesced, like most men did in this situation—after all, most of them had more experience comparing the synthetic filling in Twinkies to that in SnoBalls, not royal icing to buttercream.

"You." She lobbed the ball into Steve's court again.

Steve forced a smile and pointed back at Paige.

I was about to put an end to this nauseatingly cute banter,

which seemed more than a little strained, when they both said their choices aloud at the same time. It sounded something like *carrot cupcakes with spiced marzipan*.

"What was that?" I asked, thinking surely I'd heard wrong.

"The carrot cake with orange-scented cream cheese filling and vanilla-spiced buttercream icing," Paige told me, as sure of herself as any thirty-two-year-old bride who'd waited long enough and done all the things a modern woman was supposed to do before succumbing to marriage— college, a career, the requisite girls' weekends where she'd leave Steve behind to assert her independence. This was where it ended, where she gave in to the impractical impulses left over from a childhood spent marrying off Ken and Barbie. She knew exactly what she wanted to be feeding her guests on her wedding day. And it was carrot cake with orange-scented cream cheese filling and vanilla-spiced buttercream icing. Period.

"I'd like cupcakes with marzipan fish," Steve weighed in.

"What?" Paige and I cried in unison.

"Fish cupcakes." Steve couldn't miss the look of horror registering on Paige's face, and he attempted to clarify his selection. "Lauren could stack them on different tiers so it looks like varying ocean depths."

"Varying ocean depths?" I've pretty much done it all at Lauren's Luscious Licks, including a collection of jagged coconut-crusted cakes protruding from a bearskin rug for a couple who met in Aspen, but I've never created varying ocean depths with cupcakes.

"You know; because we met scuba diving off the Keys," Steve explained. "I meant tropical fish, not bass or trout or anything."

To recap what had just happened, I repeated it aloud slowly so we were all on the same page. "So, Paige would like a carrot cake and Steve would like cupcakes with fish on top."

"Marzipan fish," he corrected me. "My mom used to get us these marzipan snowmen every Christmas, and my brother and I would devour them. And this way, every guest gets their own fish. Cool, huh?"

Steve watched me and waited for the lightbulb over my head to go on. It didn't. "Right. Marzipan fish."

I looked over at Paige, whose mouth was firmly set in a straight line. She was less than thrilled with Steve's selection. In fact, she looked like she was ready to throttle him.

"I thought you were both interested in the blackberry filling with white chocolate mousseline," I reminded them, but the frost had already set in. Neither Paige nor Steve was interested in blackberry filling or my attempt to avoid what I could tell was coming.

"I thought we decided to nix the cupcakes." Paige kept her voice even and avoided looking directly at Steve.

"No, you'd decided to nix the cupcakes. I told you I liked the idea of everyone having their own personal cake. It's fun."

"Fun?" Paige's voice was rising and she turned to face Steve. "This is a wedding; it's not supposed to be fun."

Steve let out a breathy laugh, and Paige realized how she sounded.

"What I meant was that cupcakes are for children's birthday parties, not two hundred of our closest friends."

"Let's not go there again, Paige." Steve turned to me. "Can I use your men's room, Lauren?"

"Sure." I pointed toward the ivory door. "Through there and to the right."

Once Steve was out of earshot, Paige shook her head. "Sorry about that. We seem to have different ideas of what it means to plan a wedding. It was all figured out and now he wants a small, intimate gathering—not a 'lavish affair,' as he likes to call it."

"And he's telling you this now, after you've already booked the hotel? Why didn't he say something earlier?"

Paige hesitated. "He kinda did."

"Paige, you know better." And she did. Paige had heard my horror stories about wedding-obsessed women who would give away their firstborn for a Badgley Mischka gown and the ballroom at the Ritz.

"Lauren, it's my wedding! He just doesn't understand how important this is to me. You only get married once, right?"

Not if your husband wants aquatic cupcakes and you want carrot cake, I wanted to say. Instead, I kept my mouth shut. Paige was practically pleading with me to understand, and I did. I couldn't fault her for wanting a day as perfect as the magazines promised, any more than I could blame Steve for wanting a day that was simple and personal.

"I know it's about the money, but he won't admit it," Paige continued in a thinly veiled attempt to convince me that Steve was the one who was all wrong here. "I can afford it, but whenever I say anything he acts like I'm rubbing it in his face. Can't I just have this one thing? I mean, it's not like I'm naive; I'm a realist. I know all the things that can go wrong, but I have a career in case he leaves me; I have my own savings and investments. Can't I be indulged this one little girlhood dream?"

"We'll see what we can do," I promised Paige, and she reached over and gave my hand a thankful squeeze.

When Steve returned, I suggested we move on. "Let's take a look at the portfolio and see if that helps us narrow down the choices."

Although I always presented it as something akin to the holy grail of wedding cakes, the portfolio was really nothing more than a black leather-bound photo album containing snapshots of the cakes we've created for clients. Sometimes the pictures included the happy couple slicing the cake or performing the ritual fork-feeding that was supposed to symbolize something, although I never understood how feeding your new spouse like an infant demonstrated anything other than that it was time to reevaluate wedding traditions. But mostly the photos were of the cakes situated atop linen-draped tables, looking untouched, unreal and too perfect to eat.

"So, what do you think?" I asked, after closing the book.

"I think cream cheese is for bagels, not a wedding cake. Besides, a carrot cake has no meaning," Steve insisted.

"As opposed to fish? Do fish symbolize the carbon dioxide headache I had for days after diving, or the black eyes and temporary hearing loss?" Paige crossed her arms over her chest, not waiting for an answer from Steve.

He stared down into his lap and looked so hurt that I

wanted to stand up and remind them that it was just a wedding—but I didn't know which side they'd think I was on. For Paige, *just a wedding* meant that she wasn't asking for any more than every other woman who used to fasten bath towels to her head as a girl and pretend she was marching down the aisle to the familiar chords of "Here Comes the Bride." For Steve, *just a wedding* meant the day he married the woman he loved, not the day he played host to a bunch of strangers he was paying more than one hundred dollars a plate to feed. And me? For me, it was just another wedding, another glimpse into the future of the couple before me—and I didn't like what I was seeing.

Paige wanted a cake made from carrots, one of the few cakes that actually used an ingredient that grew in soil. Steve wanted to pay homage to the sea. And everyone knew that when mixed together, soil and water just made mud. As if that wasn't enough, the fact that Steve couldn't even share a cake with his guests certainly called into question whether he was ready to share his life with Paige.

I had to forget the fact that Paige and Steve were my friends and play the peacekeeping role I'd slipped into so often that I was the veritable Kofi Annan of wedding cakes.

I took a deep breath. "Let's start over."

After negotiating for an hour to come to a compromise, Paige and Steve finally settled on a sea-inspired theme rather than the cupcake fish tank Steve had us envisioning. There would be no fish, just sugar-paste shells nestled against seagrass and coral constructed of rolled fondant. The cupcakes were replaced with multiple undulating carrot cakes covered in vanilla-spiced buttercream and intended to resemble dunes. There would be no cream cheese filling and no marzipan, although Steve lobbied hard.

Once I'd written up the order, an order that should have had a big red stop sign on it, I carried the plates back into the kitchen and tried to think of a way to gracefully bow out of our plans for cocktails. I couldn't go out with Paige and Steve after what I'd just witnessed, besides the fact that they were barely speaking even as I wrote up the final specifications for the cake.

I grabbed a stack of invoices off my desk and returned to

the gallery, where Paige and Steve were already bundled in their coats waiting for me.

"You know, I don't think I'm going to be able to do drinks." I held up the invoice slips to show them there was no way I could possibly take off. "We have all these to fill tomorrow, and I should really get some of the paperwork completed."

"Maybe meet us when you're done?" Paige suggested halfheartedly, probably thankful I didn't want to prolong the agony of the evening. "And don't forget; we're meeting at six o'clock in front of Filene's next Thursday morning. If we're any later we'll never have a chance at the best dresses."

"I'll be there."

I let them out the front door and waved at the departing couple through the plate-glass window. Even as they neared Dartmouth Street, I continued watching until they crossed the street to hail a cab, their bodies huddled against the March wind blowing Steve's wool scarf around like a kite tail.

Maybe I was wrong. Maybe Paige and Steve wouldn't end up like all the other couples I'd had a hunch about. Sure, they were an odd couple, but that didn't mean they wouldn't work out. Look at me and Neil. Everyone thought we were a great couple. And where were we today? He was in DC and I was still here in Boston, making sure I didn't settle. Then again, look at Robin and Mark. If I'd said something, maybe Robin wouldn't be plotting how to best leverage her knowledge that Mark was deathly afraid of Siamese cats.

Even as I replayed the last two hours in my mind, the strained voices and cutting remarks, I knew I was kidding myself. Paige and Steve were a mismatch, and Robin and I had known it from the beginning. Anyone could tell just by looking at them.

As soon as their cab pulled away, I ran into the kitchen and grabbed my jacket. Two minutes later, the lights were off, the alarm was set and I was on my way to Robin's to break the news about our best friend's doomed marriage.

5

*Y*ou're not going to believe this—Steve wanted fish on the cake, only he didn't even want a cake; he wanted cupcakes." I took the glass of wine from Robin's hand and downed a generous gulp even before I removed my coat.

"Like sushi cupcakes?" she asked, pouring herself another glass of merlot and leading me into the living room. "A wee bit odd, even for Steve."

"No, he didn't want the fish *in* the cake; he wanted them *on* the cake—swimming on the cake, as he put it," I explained, taking a seat in an overstuffed shabby chic armchair.

"And Paige?"

"Carrot cake."

Robin wrinkled her nose. "That's weird."

"They don't agree on anything. Paige has her heart set on a big formal wedding and Steve wants nothing to do with it. That's not just weird, Robin. That's all wrong." I tossed my legs over the arm of the chair, held out my glass for another helping and started to tell Robin about my theory.

Robin let me finish but didn't waste any time letting me know what she thought. "Okay, now you're weird."

"It's true; I swear. Every time I hear that one of my clients split up, I go back to my notes, and most of the time it's right there in black and white—totally incompatible."

"All that from a lousy cake?"

It wasn't as ridiculous as Robin was making it out to be. Watching people interact at a pivotal moment is telling. And if people are willing to buy into horoscopes, why shouldn't your tastes and preferences also reveal something? At least with a cake, unlike astrology, you were making a conscious decision. I was a fairly intelligent, rational person, and I believed it. It just made sense.

"First of all, my cakes aren't lousy. And second of all, it's not just the cake. It's their body language and the way they interact."

"You didn't know with Mark and me," she pointed out, tucking her bare feet under her and reaching for a magazine on the coffee table.

I didn't answer and instead took a sip of wine and busied myself with a loose thread clinging precariously to the chair's slipcover.

Robin stopped flipping through the magazine and looked up at me.

"Did you?" she asked, sensing that I was holding out on her.

"Well, maybe I had an idea," I started, but it wasn't even worth the effort. There was no such thing as hedging your bet when you were dealing with Robin.

"Don't give me that crap. Did you know?" she demanded, narrowing her eyes in a bad imitation of interrogation tactics she'd probably seen Sipowicz use on *NYPD Blue*.

"I thought maybe you'd have issues," I ventured, trying to tread lightly into dangerous territory.

Robin tossed the magazine back onto the table with such force it skated effortlessly across the glass and off the other side onto the floor.

"Issues? Like him leaving me on our second wedding anniversary type of issues? Like him making a toast to 'future possibilities' and then telling me that his future didn't include me type of issues?"

I nodded and Robin jumped off the sofa so fast her merlot splashed right out of the glass and onto her sweater.

"Did Paige know? Did you tell her what you thought?" Right around the time Mark was divorcing Robin, Paige read an article about the growing popularity of starter marriages—first marriages that last less than five years and don't result in any kids. But Robin didn't find any solace in

Paige's declaration that Robin wasn't a failure—she was trendy.

"I never told anyone. I've never told any of the couples, even when it was so obvious to me." I almost held up my two fingers and swore on my Brownie badges, but I figured Robin had to believe me. After all, I'd never told her about any of this before now.

"I can understand not telling your clients, but me? I'm your best friend. You would have saved me two miserable fucking years being married to a guy who couldn't even commit to getting monogrammed towels."

"I'm sorry. Maybe I should have said something—as if you would have even listened to me."

"If I'd known your track record maybe I would have listened."

"So, now you know. What are we going to do about it?"

"Well, we sure as hell can't let Paige marry Steve."

I laughed and then realized Robin was serious. "Um, yeah, we can."

"Do you know how much money I've spent subscribing to gay porn and having it sent to Mark's office? How much time I've spent making sure he's on the mailing list of every transsexual support group in New England? Do you have any idea how humiliating it is to sit down with a man who promised to spend his life with you, only to find out that after six years of being together there isn't one goddamn thing you bought together that he wants to keep?"

Mark wasn't gay or a transsexual; in fact, he even started dating again shortly after he left Robin, which only fueled her efforts to make him regret he ever proposed to her.

"I'm not letting Paige go through that, and neither are you," Robin informed me, her woman-wronged speech concluded.

"So, what are we going to do about it?" I asked slowly, the wine starting to erode my better judgment. I was actually beginning to buy into Robin's little lecture. I was ready to take action—Robin was the Norma Rae of bad relationships, and I was willing to follow her into battle.

Robin came over to my chair and knelt on the floor next to me. *"Operation Save Paige."*

"Operation Save Paige?"

"We're going to figure out a way to help her see the light before it's too late."

I knew it wouldn't be that simple. "But Paige thinks Steve's the one."

Robin patted my knee and then rested her elbows on her thigh, like a teacher addressing her student. "Baby doll, if you've learned nothing else from me, you've learned two things. Number one, spit don't swallow. And number two, there's no such thing as *the one*."

"She's in love with Steve, and he's a good guy." I could still picture him staring into his lap as Paige maligned his memories of their scuba diving trip.

"Sure, Steve's a nice guy, but he's not the right guy for her." Robin could tell she was getting to me, and so she went in for the closer. "Look," she began, her voice getting lower and more serious. "They've been together less than a year, and he proposed after three months. You can't tell me you think that's long enough to know you're ready to spend the rest of your life with someone. Love does not conquer all—I should know."

I wanted to disagree with Robin, to tell her that I was confident Paige and Steve wouldn't end up like her and Mark. But I couldn't, because deep down I wasn't sure.

"So how do we convince her? We're supposed to help her pick out a wedding dress in all of"—I turned to face the clock on the wall—"seven days and ten hours."

Robin moved back to the couch and curled up against a pillow while she considered my question. We'd promised to help Paige navigate the legendary one-day bridal sale at Filene's Basement just like Paige and I had helped Robin. With a fairy-tale white gown hanging in her closet, there was no way Paige would listen to us. "Shit. I'll have to think about that. But as soon as I come up with an answer, I'll let you know."

"Well, we better move fast; if she finds a dress, it will be that much harder to get her to change her mind. I don't know if I can take the crying and handholding and histrionics of another friend's divorce."

"Gee, I'm sorry it was so hard on you," Robin cracked

dryly before reaching for the wine bottle and draining it into her glass. "Hey, if anyone can come up with a plan, I'm the one. Do you doubt me?"

How could I doubt a woman who slipped into Mark's parking garage unnoticed and replaced the staff's Armor All leather conditioner with rubber cement—a swap that went unnoticed until the valet had completed conditioning the driver's seat of Mark's BMW?

I shook my head and changed the subject. "So what's going on? You obviously didn't ask me over here to talk about Paige and Steve."

"You've got that right." Robin got up and brushed past the end table on her way into the kitchen to retrieve another bottle of wine. The table shook, and a picture frame holding a vividly colored photograph of a little girl grasping a beach ball fell over. The little girl in that frame appeared shortly after Mark walked out, just like the black-and-white picture of the Tom Cruise look-alike nuzzling a golden retriever, and the elderly couple holding hands on the beach as they looked off into the sunset—both held in frames reclining on Robin's fireplace mantel.

After Mark left, Robin purged her apartment of all things ex-husband-related, which included removing, and burning, any pictures she had once proudly displayed as a testament to their happiness. More than two years later, she still hadn't replaced the snapshots of bitter memories with new ones, and so every time Paige and I sat in Robin's living room we were forced to look at pictures of strangers from stock photo archives.

Robin returned from the kitchen with an open wine bottle and took her place back on the couch. "I'm being sued."

"By whom?"

"So far all I know him as is Plaintiff. His girlfriend tried to cut his nuts off. I guess she took SCALPEL a little too literally, and now he's taking me to court."

"Is it serious?" The last time Robin was in court, when the divorce was finalized, I thought they'd have to put her in shackles to keep her from lunging at her soon-to-be-ex-husband. Plaintiff had no idea what he was dealing with.

"Hell, yeah, it's serious. He says I was negligent, that I

demonstrated a lack of concern for whether an injury would occur as a result of my seminars. The bastard's looking for monetary damages—even though she didn't even succeed. Just one more guy trying to screw me."

"You were bound to piss off someone sooner or later." Actually, I thought Robin was lucky it took this long to catch up with her. I was sure Mark would have taken out a restraining order against her by now.

Robin stood up and took my empty glass. "It's called free speech, Lauren, and someone's got to teach these women how to stand up for themselves. Besides, why would I tell someone to do that? I'm not stupid."

"You're not exactly careful, either."

"Women need to know they can live without men."

"Like you?" I asked, knowing that almost one-third of all Robin's waking hours were consumed with thoughts of Mark.

"Exactly." Robin nodded. "More wine?"

I nodded. "Fill 'er up."

"So my attorney suggested that I rally the troops. I may need you and Paige and some of my better-adjusted clients to vouch for me."

"Vouch for you how?"

"By confirming that I'm a legitimate businesswoman and not some psycho instructing seminar attendees to seek revenge on men's genitalia."

"So you want me to lie?"

Robin didn't crack a smile. "Seriously, Lauren. This is important."

"Okay, if I'm needed I'll swear on a stack of Bibles that you're the picture of mental health and not a militant manhater masquerading as a self-help guru."

"Thanks." A weak smile replaced the genuine look of concern that had clouded Robin's face.

"So, that's it? Anything else to tell me?" I asked, realizing that I'd been around the caustic Robin so long I'd almost forgotten that before Mark left she actually had moments of vulnerability.

"Isn't that enough?" she groused, already firmly back on the path to acrimony.

I briefly considered telling Robin about my date with Charlie, but since Paige's engagement implied that she'd defected to the other side, I'd become Robin's de facto coconspirator. And with her self-help empire on the verge of being tried in court, the last thing she needed was to find out that I was reentering the world of male-female relations.

Instead we flipped on the TV to catch the last few minutes of *The Stag* while we drained yet another bottle of wine. I must have dozed off from the constant stream of merlot, because when I glanced over at the green numbers illuminated on the VCR it was almost eleven o'clock and I could hear soft snores coming from Robin's direction.

I stood up and shook my leg, trying to get the blood flowing through the pins and needles that made my foot feel like I'd stepped on a porcupine. The inside of the living room window was steamed over, creating a cloudy coating that distorted the lights on the downtown high-rises and made them look strobelike. Without even rubbing the window clean I knew what waited outside, and I was already wishing I was at home in my own bed and not about to venture into the frigid night.

"I better be going if I'm expected to be bright-eyed and bushy-tailed tomorrow morning."

Robin stirred and then stood up slowly, stretching her arms out over her head.

"You'll be okay catching a cab?" she asked, walking me to the front door.

"I'll be fine."

"Hey." Robin grabbed my shoulder and stopped me from leaving. "Don't forget about Operation Save Paige. She needs us."

I hugged Robin and stepped through the door into the hallway. "I know she does."

I realized that Paige needed our help to save her from making a big mistake. I just wasn't sure that a woman with a grudge against the male of the species and a cake clairvoyant were the ones who should be doing the saving.

6

$\mathcal{G}$et the telephone," Maria ordered, pointing to my desk.

My arms were stacked full of powder pink cardboard cake boxes, but since I thought it might be Charlie calling to confirm our date tonight, I laid the boxes on the floor, cleared my throat and reached for the phone.

"Lauren's Luscious Licks," I purred into the mouthpiece and watched Maria roll her eyes toward the ceiling.

"You selling cakes or porn?" Robin asked.

"I was expecting a call from someone else," I told her, recovering from my attempt at a sultry greeting. I swallowed hard and then admitted, "I have a date tonight."

I'd braced myself for Robin's wrath, and true to form, she didn't miss a beat. "Well, while you've been out meeting men, I've been thinking about how we can help Paige."

"I haven't been out meeting men; he walked into the boutique," I argued, managing to feel a twinge of guilt even though I hadn't done anything wrong. Since Neil left I'd been on a few first dates and even fewer second dates, and none had managed to arouse my interest as much as the ten minutes I'd spent with Charlie. He'd stuck with me like a song you heard once and couldn't get out of your head.

Robin cleared her throat a little too pointedly. "In any case, can we get down to the matter at hand?"

I'd managed to put Operation Save Paige out of my head since our last conversation, hoping that Paige would call and tell me that it had all been a misunderstanding and that she and Steve had decided on the white cake with blackberry filling and white chocolate mousseline after all. But no call arrived, which I interpreted as a sign that the weekend hadn't done much to thaw the situation. Obviously, Robin held out little hope for a happy ending, and I just hoped that her brilliant scheme didn't involve breaking the law or damaging property—two things she seemed to excel at when it came time to get even with Mark.

"I don't have to purchase a black turtleneck and ski mask, do I?"

"Nothing that elaborate, although if my first idea doesn't pan out, we may have to consider more drastic measures. In the meantime, you just follow my lead."

"Don't I get any details?"

"All in good time. I don't want Paige to guess we're up to something. Just show up at Filene's Thursday morning ready to go."

I held the phone away from my ear and gave Robin a silent salute.

"So where's this date taking you?" she asked.

"Sonsie."

"That's mighty trendy of you." Robin sounded impressed.

"You know me, a real trendsetter."

"If this cake theory of yours holds true, you might be more of a trendsetter than you ever imagined."

Maria was glaring at me and tapping her watch, a not-so subtle reminder that the UPS guy was waiting for us to make space in the supply room for our deliveries. I said a quick good-bye to Robin and followed Maria to the back room.

Trendsetter. I kind of liked the sound of that. The last time I was trendy, acid-washed jeans were in style and I used a hair scrunchie to keep my ponytail in place on the top of my head. Unless you counted the cake boutique, of course, which was the first one of its kind in Boston. Ah, to be at a vanguard for the masses, or at least those about to wed.

"And what trend are you setting?" Maria inquired, once again prying into a conversation she wasn't invited to enter.

"Oh, nothing. It was just something silly Robin said."

"That makes more sense," Maria reasoned. "Leading-edge isn't exactly the phrase I'd use to describe you."

"I used to be pretty leading-edge; remember when we experimented with the layers of Black Beauty roses between the tiers of cake to make it look like the whipped cream layers were floating on the flowers? And we were the first ones to offer a Year to Remember package."

"And how long ago was that?"

I knew I should have just quit when I was ahead. "I don't remember."

"Well, I do, and I think you were wearing acid-washed jeans and a hair scrunchie at that time."

"I was not." Maria was off by at least a year on that one.

So I hadn't introduced any earth-shattering innovations lately, but if Robin was right, that could be changing. Maria thought I wasn't leading-edge, but we'd see about that.

I was quietly logging in a new shipment of meringue powder and almond extract when a little girl called, looking for Maria. I knew something was wrong as soon as I passed the handset to her. Maria never got personal calls at the boutique.

"I've got to go," she told me, undoing her apron strings before she even hung up.

"Is everything okay?"

"Does it look like everything is okay? Do I usually rush off in the middle of the day after receiving a phone call?" Maria was especially testy. "I'm going home to watch my niece's children."

Maria was out the door before I could even offer to pay her cab fare. Or find out when she'd be back.

"We need to decorate tomorrow's anniversary cakes," Dominique reminded me.

"What are we going to do about the three cakes we need to bake for Wednesday's Year to Remember deliveries?" Georgina asked, looking to me for direction.

They were my troops now that Maria was AWOL, and I had to step up to the role of fearless leader, even if I was feeling anything but fearless at the thought of making the cakes.

I took a deep breath to get my bearings straight. How long could Maria be gone? She'd definitely be back in time to take care of this weekend's orders, so I just had to take care of the anniversary cakes. That couldn't be too hard.

I stood tall and made my first executive decision. "I'll get the anniversary cake orders and we'll go over what we need to do today." So it wasn't really a decision, but it was a step in the right direction.

The order forms showed that we had to decorate a pale buttercup yellow *broderie anglaise* anniversary cake with hand-painted eyelet for tomorrow. That meant hours of meticulous cutting and forming the lace detail. I'd be taking a pass on that one. What was the point of being the boss if you couldn't delegate the more daunting tasks?

We also needed to bake a mocha cake, a strawberry-rum cake and an amaretto cake for Wednesday's customers. A few cups of flour, some sugar and a paddle mixer. That was definitely more my speed.

"You two take care of decorating tomorrow's order, and I'll handle the baking."

While Dominique and Georgina got started on the *broderie anglaise,* I buttered the bottom of the anniversary-cake pans and lined them with parchment paper. After brushing the paper with more butter and dusting the pans with flour, I was ready to make the batter. And that's when it occurred to me. I had no idea how to start.

"Where's Maria keep the recipes?" I asked Dominique, swallowing my pride and hoping she wouldn't tell Maria how clueless I was in her absence.

She looked at Georgina and shrugged. "The recipes? I don't know. We don't use them unless it's something out of the ordinary."

Not a stellar beginning. I scoured the shelves and drawers and finally found a folder labeled RECIPES in the filing cabinet. I removed the folder and its yellowed pieces of paper stained with oil drippings and splotches of batter.

I managed to locate the lesser-used ingredients, the espresso powder and coconut extract, and then followed the recipes' directions exactly as described. The cups of flour were filled and then the tops leveled with a knife before being poured into the stainless steel mixing bowl. The sugar was sifted to remove any lumps and the softened butter added when my finger left a dent in the glistening exterior and told me it was at room temperature. All was going according to plan.

I took an egg in each hand and tapped them against the rim of the mixing bowl, but my touch was too light. I tried again, tapping harder this time; the shell cracked into fragments instead of the single controlled fissure I'd learned to make years ago. As the yolk and the whites spilled into the bowl, I gripped the eggs too firmly and splinters of shell shot into the batter.

"Shit," I muttered under my breath, but not softly enough to escape notice.

"Everything okay over there?" Dominique asked.

"Everything's under control," I lied.

Normally, sticking one's fingers into the batter is a no-no. I knew lots of baking scenarios that required the poking and prodding of fingers, but mixing cake batter wasn't one of them.

I grabbed a wooden spoon from the utensil tray and turned my back to block Dominique and Georgina's view. With the spoon in hand I tried unsuccessfully to scoop out the shells. Next I attempted to scrape out the shells with a spatula, which only ended up burying the shells deeper in the batter so I couldn't even tell where they were.

At that point I had two options. I could leave the shells in the batter—they were small pieces, after all—or I could use my fingers and go fishing. As much as using my fingers was a last resort, I knew I didn't have a choice. Amaretto sponge cake wasn't supposed to be crunchy. I washed my hands and dug in.

When I finally slipped the pans into the preheated oven, I felt a sense of triumph. I may have been a little shaky at first, but I'd managed to survive just fine. Not bad for someone who hadn't baked a cake in years.

"You could have just run the batter through a strainer to get out the shell," Georgina told me as I was stacking the mixing bowls in the sink.

Then Dominique decided to pipe in. "Of course, Maria never has to do that, but it does work."

I nodded knowingly, hoping they'd think I was aware of the strainer option all along but was using some ancient technique that I learned from a wise baking sage. "Sometimes it's better to do things by hand."

"And sometimes it's better to use generally accepted kitchen practices," Georgina concluded. "More sanitary that way. Not to mention faster."

They'd been hanging around with Maria too long.

I washed my hands and avoided their stares as I went out into the gallery to wait for my first appointment of the day.

Gloria Caldwell was one of the most revered wedding planners in the city, and her list of clients read like a who's who of Boston society. With her fluff of short white hair and an air that was at once society matron and showgirl, Gloria always reminded me of Carol Channing. The only thing missing was a silvery boa tossed over the shoulder of her tight-fitting Chanel suits.

As expected, Gloria's entrance could not go unnoticed.

"Lauren," Gloria cried, throwing her arms out dramatically, as if expecting me to run into them like a child. "Come here, you beautiful girl! Let me see you."

Because she's Gloria Caldwell, I did as she instructed.

"How are you, dear?" she asked, pulling me into her bosom and then holding me at arm's length so she could examine me from all angles. "Oh, you are a breath of fresh air. I love the blond highlights; now you don't look so mousy. I hope you went to Giorgio, as I advised. He's the only one doing good highlights these days."

"He spoke very highly of you," I told her.

"Of course he did, dear. I gave that man his start. Without me he'd be at Supercuts in Revere still giving women the Rachel. So what do you have for me?" Gloria made her way over to the tasting table.

I followed her and we sat side by side in the Barcelona chairs usually reserved for clients. Gloria's visit wasn't just social, and after our initial niceties she was ready to get down to business. The portfolio was already opened to the most recent cakes, giving Gloria some ideas that she could take back to her clients.

"Love the imperial dome crown with checked satin pleats." Gloria tapped a long red nail on the plastic page. "And the ribbon tapes are a nice touch."

"She wanted sprays of white ginger and orchids, but I told her it would be too busy."

Gloria squeezed my arm. "Good advice. Sometimes they can go overboard with the flowers. What's inside?"

"That was a chocolate fudge cake with white chocolate mousse and white chocolate buttercream icing. We served fresh raspberries on the side."

Gloria let out a little gasp. "Perfect. So tasteful. Now, I'm seeing more brides going against the traditional white cake, which I have to admit is a nice change from the white on white on white we saw a few years ago. They're asking for some pastel colors or chocolate. What do you have?"

We flipped through the portfolio and found cakes that fit Gloria's description.

"This has been popular; it's a yellow sponge cake with amaretto-laced custard, dark chocolate mousse and rolled chocolate icing."

Gloria wrinkled her nose and made a face.

"Not what you had in mind?" I asked.

"No, it sounds divine. But do you smell that? Is something burning?"

There was only one thing in the oven. The cakes.

"Excuse me, Gloria. I'll be right back." I darted toward the kitchen and burst through the door. Georgina and Dominique were hunched over the rotating cake stand, diligently working on the eyelet detail.

"Don't you smell that? The cakes are burning!"

Dominique looked up. "We didn't hear the timer go off so we just thought you dripped some batter in the oven when you slid in the pans."

I pulled open the oven door and inhaled a billow of dark smoke. "Shit! Grab me something!"

Georgina brought me a dish towel and stood by as I removed three pans from the top oven, and then three pans from the bottom, dropping them all onto the butcher-block workstation with thuds. Over an hour of work, almost a dozen eggs, several pounds of butter and flour—all of it shot to hell. Every cake's golden crust was charred.

"Why didn't you set the timer?" she asked, pointing out the obvious.

"I forgot," I blurted out and then realized I may as well have just said, *Lauren Gallagher is a complete baking farce.*

Georgina looked over at Dominique, whose head popped up when she heard the boss admit such an amateur mistake. Needless to say, the *broderie anglaise* on their cake was flawless. If I didn't know better, I'd swear the icing was mocking me.

"I've got Gloria Caldwell out there and then three more appointments after her. Can one of you throw these out when they cool and then start over?" I asked, the heat from the oven warming the kitchen and allowing the stench of burned cake to spread.

Georgina nodded.

"Great." I peeked out the kitchen door's window and caught Gloria restlessly shifting in her chair. "And let's not tell Marla about this, okay? I don't want her to worry that we can't handle things when she's gone."

On my way into the gallery I thought I heard Georgina ask when Maria would be back.

Dominique quickly answered her. "Not soon enough."

"Is everything okay?" Gloria asked, angling for a better look inside the kitchen as the door swung closed behind me.

"Sure, it's fine."

"Were cakes on fire in there?" She pointed to the kitchen like it was the scene of a crime. "My clients wouldn't look favorably upon Lauren's Luscious Licks burning their wedding cakes."

"I assure you, everything is under control."

Gloria let the subject drop, but as we went through the pages of the portfolio I couldn't help but get the feeling that she was thinking the same thing I was: *Has Lauren Gallagher lost her touch?*

It was such a careless mistake; I'd barely burned a cake when I was just starting out. Now here I was in front of the most influential wedding planner in the city, and instead of acting like a seasoned pastry chef I was trying to cover up my oversight like a guilty kid. Even if the only thing I was guilty of was being out of practice; well, that and leading everyone to believe that I actually had a hand in every cake that was made. If I couldn't bake a two-layer anniversary cake without setting the kitchen on fire, what was I doing?

Thankfully, the rest of the afternoon was relatively uneventful. Georgina and Dominique managed to finish decorating the *broderie anglaise* cake and bake the three anniversary cakes for Wednesday.

My appointments went well, a nice contrast to Thursday's fiasco with Paige and Steve, and as I sat across from the couples I put Gloria's insinuation out of my mind and let my thoughts wander to Charlie and our impending date. I was still Lauren Gallagher, über pastry chef, as far as my clients were concerned.

I couldn't help but let the anticipation of seeing Charlie grow, like when you order a soufflé at the beginning of a dinner and then spend the entire meal building it up in your mind—the way the batter slowly rises in the oven, vulnerable to loud noises or unexpected interruptions that could undo hours of work. I imagined the two of us sharing stories about our clients like modern-day anthropologists, delving into the ingredients for a successful relationship and recipes for disaster. We'd be like Louis and Mary Leakey, only instead of exploring human evolution, we'd explore something just as complex and intriguing—the evolution of male and female relationships. And we wouldn't have to travel to the far reaches of Africa. Or live with native tribes or learn a foreign language—unless you counted deciphering what men really meant when they told a woman they'd call.

Maria returned around three o'clock, grabbing her apron and heading straight for the delivery boxes without offering an explanation for her absence or an excuse for leaving us to fend for ourselves.

"Everything okay?" I finally asked, peeking my head into the storage room.

Maria kept her head down, checking off supplies on the list in her hand. Her answer was short and not too sweet: "Yes."

"Everything went smoothly here," I assured her, even though she didn't seem too worried. "No problems at all."

Maria stopped logging the supplies and looked up at me, stifling a knowing smile that I could tell was growing at my expense. "That's good to hear. Remind me to show you how to work the timer when I'm done with the supplies. I know it can be tricky with all those minutes on the dial, but maybe if you practiced you'd get the hang of it."

Damn Georgina and Dominique. They probably couldn't wait to tell Maria about the burned cakes. My troops had defected. I was the emperor, and Maria was holding my clothes. "What did they tell you?"

"*They* didn't tell me anything, but from the way the kitchen smells, it's obvious you handled the baking." Her point made, Maria flipped over the list and continued writing. "Just in case you've forgotten how to tell time, too, your date is at seven o'clock. That's when the big hand is on the twelve and the little hand is on the seven."

I left Maria alone in the storage room to enjoy her little joke. I may have forgotten to set the timer, but I could still tell time. In just a few hours I'd be meeting Charlie for dinner, and no matter how much Maria made fun of me, it didn't change the fact that I was about to go on a date.

7

I jogged the five blocks to the restaurant, not because I was running late but because the skies opened up and unleashed a freezing downpour as soon as I'd stepped out of the boutique. Of course, there wasn't a cab in sight, so with my chin tucked under my collar I dashed down Newbury Street, trying to avoid the growing puddles and dollops of rain that poured off the roofs of neighboring buildings.

I noticed Charlie first and ducked behind a couple waiting at the hostess stand for a table. The cuffs of my wool pants were dotted with splatters of white from the salt on the sidewalk, and my formerly stylish high-heeled boots were probably dyeing my toes black as I stood there. There wasn't much I could do to turn my blond matted helmet into the carefully coiffed 'do I'd had going on in the boutique, but I shook my damp hair anyway and hoped Charlie liked the wet look.

Charlie was meeting me straight from work, and he was already standing at the bar holding a half-empty martini glass. His suit jacket hung casually over the back of his bar stool, and although he still wore his red-striped necktie, it hung loosely around his neck. The bartender, a tall, thin guy with a shaved head, was doubled over laughing as Charlie animatedly waved his arms in the air, amusing him with a story. Even in his power-lawyer uniform, Charlie looked as comfortable as most men did in a baseball cap and a worn pair of jeans.

"Hello, counselor," I greeted him, sidling up to the mahogany bar and taking Charlie by surprise.

"Hey, Lauren." Charlie set his cocktail on the bar and turned to face me. Although his navy chalk-striped pants were still crisp, Charlie's brown hair was tousled from his storytelling.

"Got caught in the rain, huh?" he asked, helping me off with my soggy coat and shaking it so the last clinging droplets fell to the floor. "Master of the obvious—one of my more lawyerly skills."

He turned back toward the bartender. "Mel, this is Lauren, the pastry chef I was telling you about."

"Hi, Lauren." Mel smirked and gave Charlie an approving thumbs-up, a gesture he didn't even attempt to hide from my view. "Charlie was just telling me about some of the clients you've shared. Sounds like you two have lots of war stories."

Charlie ordered me a drink and then excused himself to go check on our table.

"He's a good guy, Charlie," Mel told me, placing a cocktail napkin on the bar before setting my merlot on top.

I nodded. "So far, I can't argue with you."

Mel set his elbow against the lip on the bar and leaned in toward me. "So, you're Lauren Gallagher," he repeated, sounding curious.

"That's me."

"A lot of your clients come in here after their appointments at your place. You know, people in your line of work are a guy's worst nightmare," Mel stated matter-of-factly.

He thought people in *my* line of work were nightmares? Apparently he'd never heard about lecherous bartenders attempting to masquerade receding hairlines with trendy Kojak sleekness.

"And what line of work is that?"

"Table's ready," Charlie interrupted, pointing to the hostess waiting for us at the front of the restaurant.

Before he could clarify his statement for me, Mel moved over to the cash register to close out our tab.

After paying Mel and grabbing his suit coat, Charlie placed his hand on my back and guided me to our table. His touch was firm and familiar, and he navigated us through the restaurant as if he owned the place. Sonsie was buzzing with after-work activity, professionals who flocked to the European bistro for its renowned martinis and angled for premium seats at the bar. In the summer, the high French doors lining the front of the restaurant were pushed back, transforming the cozy dining room into a sidewalk café, where the classic tunes of Louis Armstrong and Billie Holiday floated outside.

Sitting across from Charlie, I had a hard time picturing him as a divorce attorney. He didn't seem threatening enough, and he was way too happy. I always thought men who specialized in broken marriages were slick lotharios who consoled their distraught female clients all the while scheming how to get them into bed.

But with a small scab on the underside of his chin where he'd probably nicked himself while shaving, and his shirt-sleeves rolled up exposing a digital Boston Red Sox watch, he didn't exactly come across as all that menacing a guy.

"What are you thinking?" I asked, scanning the specials listed on the menu.

"The cream of winey mushroom soup looks good, but after the day I had, the last thing I need is to listen to my food complain." Charlie drummed his hands on the table like a vaudeville comedian cuing his audience for a laugh. "Ba-da-bum."

Despite myself, I followed his prompt.

"Do you use that line on all your dates?"

"So far, you're the first one; what do you think?"

"I think there's a reason lawyers aren't known for their sense of humor."

Charlie dropped his chin into his chest as if he'd been stabbed, and pretended to pull a sword out of his gut. "Ouch; you're a tough crowd."

"Were you expecting a standing ovation?"

"Nah, maybe just a little audience appreciation."

I reached for the small candle in the center of the table and held it in the air like a lighter at a rock concert. Charlie seemed pleased.

"I've got to be honest with you. I'm not even that hungry. I had dinner meetings all last week, and after my carnivorous display at 75 Chestnut last night, I don't know if I can handle another big meal."

I loved 75 Chestnut. Okay, so I'd never actually been to 75 Chestnut, but I knew I'd love it. A converted townhouse tucked away among the brownstones of Beacon Hill, 75 Chestnut was the perfect romantic restaurant, the kind of intimate setting where a man got on bended knee and a woman said yes. I'd peeked in the large-paned front window, my nose close enough to glimpse the small marigold-and-jasmine-colored dining room but not so close that they'd chase me away with a bottle of Windex.

"That's a pretty nice place to go for a business dinner," I commented, wondering whether the dinner had in fact been business or pleasure.

"A lot of our clients like to go there—of course, as long as the firm is paying, any four-star restaurant will do. Ever been there?"

"No, not yet."

"You should go; it's great."

"It just doesn't seem like the kind of place you'd go for an ordinary dinner."

"It's just a meal, Lauren, not a state dinner. Take my advice; don't wait too long to try it."

"I'll keep that in mind."

"I'm going with the pineapples Foster," Charlie declared, replacing the menu in his hand with a full wineglass.

"Pineapples Foster isn't a meal."

"Says who?"

"Says the people who put it on the dessert section of the menu."

Charlie leaned in over the table and checked over his shoulders to make sure no one was listening. "If you won't tell, I won't tell," he whispered.

During my dinner, and Charlie's dessert, the conversation was easy and rambling. One topic blended into another effortlessly and seamlessly, as if we knew we'd have plenty of time to go back and cover what we'd missed. The first sixty minutes with Charlie were already worlds apart from my last date, seven months ago, when a management consultant named Matt spent our entire meal trying to convince me that six sigma quality processes would revolutionize the manufacturing of electrical components. I didn't bother telling him that the only sigma I was familiar with was a fraternity guy from Dartmouth.

"So, any premarital premonitions today? Clients whose choice of whipped cream ensures an early demise and the filing of joint petitions for dissolution?"

"No, it was pretty run-of-the-mill. A few brides, a wedding planner who came by to scout some cakes for her clients, that sort of thing. The beginning of the week is usually kind of slow."

"Wedding planners—the five-star generals in the war between the sexes."

"Hey, don't knock it till you've tried it. Lots of couples use wedding planners these days, and it makes my life a hell of a lot easier dealing with pros who know the inside scoop on how to get things done."

"You're all like a little secret society, aren't you?"

"Being a secret wouldn't be so good for business, now would it?"

"Right you are, Ms. Gallagher. And exhibit A would have to be that article in *Boston* magazine. Very impressive."

"Why, thank you, Mr. Banks, but most of the credit goes to my friend Paige; she knows the publisher."

"I never would have thought a bakery was newsworthy. Not that I haven't been known to have a deep appreciation for a really good Boston cream pie."

"It's a boutique," I corrected him.

"Po-tay-to, po-tah-to—either way, they're still spuds."

For a minute Charlie sounded like Maria, and come to think of it they almost shared the same amount of facial hair, even if he was much easier on the eyes. Although I always defended our "boutique" status to Maria, the way Charlie put it, I almost agreed with him. I didn't bother trying to explain the difference. What started out as a marketing concept had mushroomed into a new vocabulary that was quickly picked up by our trendy clients and abhorred by Maria.

As I sat across from Charlie spooning pineapples Foster from a deep-dish bowl, I was reminded of my dinners with

Neil. The dates in between Neil and Charlie had felt more like a meeting between prisoners of war, where we shared name, rank and serial number, but not much else during two hours punctuated by uncomfortable pauses and polite murmurs of agreement—conversations that moved along barely creating a ripple, like the stones kids skip across the surface of a calm lake.

Charlie didn't seem to notice whether or not the waiter approved of his main course of pineapples flambéed with brown sugar and rum, and when he ordered our wine he simply pointed to the wine list and said, "We'll have a bottle of this" instead of making a big deal out of perfectly enunciating every syllable with the appropriate accent. And as much as I was enjoying our evening, Charlie's warm smile and quick laughter made me think I wasn't the only one.

"How are things going for Gwen?" I asked.

"She's working through her grief—mostly by working her way through David's bank account." Charlie gave me a conspiring wink. "I think she'll pull through."

"So what makes someone become a divorce attorney?"

"Mostly the glamour, the public adoration and the look of respect on people's faces when they hear what I do for a living—not to mention the prestige of being on everyone's most-hated list."

I laughed. "Divorce attorneys are right up there with foreign dictators, aren't they?"

"On good days," he pointed out, smiling. "Seriously, my grandfather left my grandmother with four kids to raise, a house that was about to be foreclosed on and forty dollars in the bank. He left a note that said he was going to Texas to seek his fame and fortune as a rodeo star and my grandmother couldn't do a damn thing about it."

Charlie Banks—nemesis of assholes and savior to divorced grandmothers everywhere. I loved it.

"Have I ever heard of him?"

"Not unless you stopped at his trailer park on your way through Abilene. What about you? Were you one of those little girls who spent hours with her Easy-Bake oven?"

"I was more into my Snoopy Sno-Cone machine."

"So you didn't dream of being a pastry chef?"

I had to think about that one for a minute. The last time I remembered *dreaming* about being a pastry chef I was signing the lease for the boutique, when I thought my dream was coming true. Funny how a dream can become reality and go from being something you aspired to to something that was more like a restless night's sleep.

"When I was a kid, I wanted to be a ballerina. You don't want to be with me at Christmastime when Tchaikovsky's *Nutcracker* comes over the sound system at Star Market. It's not pretty."

Charlie threw his head back and squinted at me. "Ah, some dreams die hard."

When the waiter cleared our plates, Charlie and I ordered some coffee.

"Dessert?" he offered.

The lemon crème brûlée sounded tempting, but I decided to pass. "I'm stuffed."

I almost wished Charlie would order a piece of cake. I wanted to see what he'd choose so I could put my frosting forecasting talent to the ultimate test—my own.

"Maybe next time," Charlie suggested.

"Maybe," I agreed, not missing the subtle suggestion that there'd be a next time. I couldn't help smiling as a warm flush spread through my body—or maybe it was the bottle of red we'd finished off.

"I think it's only fair to be up-front with you," Charlie said, taking a sip of his espresso.

All I could think was *Oh, no, here it comes*. I knew it was too good to be true. This was where he told me that he had a girlfriend or some incurable disease that renders him impotent, or maybe he still lived with his parents and collected Beanie Babies. I knew there had to be a reason Charlie was still single.

"I know a lot of women see every man as potential marriage material, and I just want you to know that I'm not."

"Not what?"

"Marriage material, at least not any time soon. It's not that I'm afraid of commitment or anything, but I've just seen it go wrong so many times. So if that's what you're looking for, I'm not your man." Charlie watched me, waiting for a reaction. "Does that bother you?"

Was he kidding me? I was a college-educated woman, a successful entrepreneur, someone who'd lived on her own for ten years—quite well, I might add. Did it bother me? Of course it did!

I may not buy into the myth of the wedding, but I wasn't ready to write off men and marriage like Robin. I'd had a Barbie doll, too. And if Barbie didn't have Ken, she was simply a camper-driving, ballroom dress–wearing stewardess who came home to an empty townhouse, even though it was a really cool townhouse. And when Barbie wasn't tooling around town in her convertible Corvette, she could have Skipper over for an afternoon of hanging out by the pool. When I thought about it in those terms, Barbie actually had it pretty good without Ken, if you didn't count the small issue of her breasts outsizing her waist two to one, making it nearly impossible for her to stand up in real life without keeling over.

I hesitated before answering, taking a sip of my coffee to buy time. If I told Charlie it bothered me, then I'd be as bad as all those women I made fun of, the ones who were taping Tiffany ads to their boyfriends' bathroom mirrors after the first date. But if I said it didn't bother me, would I really be telling the truth?

Years of experience had taught me how to read someone's choice of cake, but how did I interpret the choice to not have a cake, period? If I had any question about what Charlie saw when he gazed into his own Magic 8 Ball, I'd just received my answer. He saw a lifetime of dating.

"You're assuming a lot on a first date. One, that I just want to get married, and two, that I'd even consider you for the position."

"That's not what I meant." Charlie seemed surprised that I'd turned the tables on him, but I also got the feeling that he was glad I didn't fold easily. "It's just that I've been out with women I really enjoyed, and when I wasn't talking about our joint retirement account on the third date, they acted like I'd led them on or something. I don't want to chase you away, but I want to be fair with you." Charlie set his espresso cup on the table and waited for my answer.

He wanted to be fair with me? His *fair* was like the warning on a cigarette pack—CAUTION: THIS RELATIONSHIP MAY BE DANGEROUS TO YOUR MENTAL HEALTH. And like all those people walking around coughing up their lungs, I was about to throw caution to the wind.

"I stand forewarned." I sipped my coffee and let the warm, bitter liquid slide down my throat. "So can you elaborate for me? If it's not commitment you're afraid of, then why write off every relationship?"

"It's just the opposite. I'm not writing off a relationship; I'd love to meet the right person. I just want the relationship to be based on more than an arbitrary timeline we have to meet because the Caribbean is offering great deals on honeymoon packages."

I must not have looked convinced.

Charlie sat back in his chair, clasped his hands together on the table and tried to put it in terms I could understand.

"You and I meet two entirely different couples in the course of our day. You see couples on their way into the tunnel; I see them on their way out."

"You make it sound like an amusement park ride."

"It is in a way, isn't it? You wait in line together for a roller-coaster ride with twists and turns you can only imagine and long straightaways that can drop off into oblivion before you realize it."

"This is quite an elaborate metaphor you've got working here."

"But it applies, doesn't it? My clients are screaming for the ride to be over."

"And mine are trying to push their way to the head of the line, right?"

"Yep. It's not for the weak of heart."

"Or the queasy," I added.

Charlie laughed, and I couldn't help but join him, picturing Gwen Stern buckled into the roller coaster's lead car, her arms waving in the air and a wedding veil flying out behind her as she and David prepared for the drop.

"Okay, I think we've exhausted that metaphor," I told him.

"So, what do you think? Would you like to see me again?"

Even as I was answering, I hoped I was making the right choice. "Yeah, I would."

Charlie grinned. "Great."

8

*W*hen Lauren's Luscious Licks first opened, I was fascinated every time a couple came into the boutique. I couldn't wait to hear about their wedding plans, the bridesmaids' dresses, the song they'd dance to as their guests looked on clinking champagne glasses with spoons, demanding one more kiss. I'd get so genuinely excited, so wrapped up in the anticipation, that the brides could have been my sisters or my best friends. I listened raptly as they took me through the moments of their event, hanging on every detail. I let their intoxicating engagement stories fill me like helium.

As they described their gowns in vivid detail, I could hear the rustle of the crinoline, feel the grainy texture of the raw silk against my fingertips. When they recalled the flowers, I could smell their sweet fragrance and see the prisms of light reflected from tall, slim crystal vases overflowing with sprays of lilacs, and freesia and dusty blue hydrangea. Even without the brochures, I basked in the sun of their Caribbean honeymoons, imagining the powdery sand between my toes. But that was years ago, and my attitude had changed since then. Now attending anyone's wedding felt like my very own version of a busman's holiday.

I couldn't put my finger on exactly when that genuine curiosity had changed to benign observation. I did know that it happened around the time Robin started planning her own wedding. Or, more accurately, the morning we participated in our first "running of the brides" at Filene's Basement.

Like most people around Boston, we'd heard tales about the department store's deeply discounted bridal blowout. There's no slow marching up those department store aisles, just mad dashes to grab armfuls of dresses, regardless of the size or style, in hopes of finding the perfect gown, or at least some good leverage for trading.

Arriving a mere fifteen minutes before the doors were set to open, we thought we'd be fine. Even though we should have known better—after all, most of the dresses were slashed to only a few hundred dollars—we were ill-prepared for the legions of women lined up outside the store's entrance. When we found our place at the end of the line, there were about three hundred women ahead of us, and by the time we made it into the store, the racks were barren, and barely dressed women were negotiating with one another using their stashes of dresses as the currency of choice.

Paige and Robin set off in search of other people's unwanted leftovers, while I looked around the fluorescent-lit room in awe. I watched future brides and their sisters and mothers and friends on a modern-day treasure hunt, and that's when it hit me. All the time and effort and money devoted to an ephemeral event as if it was the pinnacle of achievement—the Big Day. The Big Day commemorated the peak of a couple's relationship. It implied that they'd reached the summit of the mountain, the highest point, whereupon they could look down one side and see how far they'd come.

But what bothered me was the other side, the side that wasn't fraught with the obstacles a couple faced in the beginning, but instead represented the difficulty of staying on that peak, the inevitability of things going downhill from there.

From that day on, I wasn't in a rush to plan a big white wedding. I wanted to stay on the top of the mountain for more than just one day, to set up camp and stake out a safe, level spot for the entire duration of a relationship. I guess from that standpoint, I was in safe hands with Charlie. I couldn't help but remember one of my mom's more sage pieces of advice: be careful what you wish for; you might just get it.

Robin, Paige and I ended up leaving Filene's empty-handed that day, but the sale wasn't a complete waste. Robin decided to introduce her own seminar on how to navigate the treacherous waters of the Filene's sale—Bargain Basement or Bridal Hell: Bribing and Bartering Strategies for Filene's Running of the Brides.

Paige learned from Robin's mistake, and she was ready to give the running of the brides another shot. Eager brides were already lined up outside the doors facing Washington Street when we arrived at the ungodly hour of 6 A.M. After careful consideration, she'd determined our optimal strategy and come up with our plan—a three-woman tag team. Paige insisted that we be able to find one another in the sea of frantic brides-to-be, so we paid homage to our hometown team and wore Red Sox baseball caps and red T-shirts. Paige also said we needed to keep our energy up, so she wore a fully stocked fanny pack with bottled water, bagels and granola bars. Yes, a fanny pack. Paige is lucky we even acknowledged we knew her.

Once we'd staked out our place among the seventy or so women who must have slept on the sidewalk the night before, Paige walked to the head of the line to feel out the competition.

It was right then and there, on the sidewalk preparing to scurry around Filene's Basement like the crowd at Pamplona, that Robin decided to put Operation Save Paige into action.

"She can't come away from here with a dress," Robin instructed me, keeping an eye on Paige's intelligence mission. "No matter how great she looks, we have to tell her to keep looking. Got it?"

I nodded but didn't have time to ask any questions before Paige made her way back to us.

"The women up front got here at one-thirty this morning," she told us. "And they brought walkie-talkies. Damn." She shook her head, disappointed she hadn't thought of that too.

For the next two hours we chatted with the women around us, sharing information about their upcoming weddings. I heard about ceremonies on the beaches of Cape Cod, a destination wedding in Aruba and a good old-fashioned wedding on a small vineyard just west of the city. The brides-to-be shared every detail of their wedding planning, from the centerpieces to the first song they'd dance to with their new husbands.

When one of the women asked Paige where she was getting her cake, she told them Lauren's Luscious Licks. The woman grabbed the arm of her sister and bit her bottom lip before letting out a single "Wow."

Paige looked like she was waiting for me to jump in and introduce myself, but I was there to help her pick out a dress, not drum up business for the boutique. Besides, this crowd took no prisoners when it came to wedding planning. I was afraid if I said anything I'd get mobbed.

"Are the cakes as incredible as they say?" the woman asked, a group of other brides beginning to huddle around us.

Paige laughed and leaned in toward the women like she was about to share a coveted secret. "Even better."

"You are so lucky," the woman breathed. "I heard that Lauren has to approve you as a client before she'll even book an appointment."

I caught Robin stifling a chuckle.

"I read that Lauren can refuse to make a cake if she doesn't like what you've picked," another woman added.

One of the brides announced, "My friend told me that Lauren uses an astrologer to help you select the right cake."

"Okay, enough," I finally cut in. "First of all, all you have to do is call for an appointment. It's easy. Second of all, you can have any cake you want. And that stuff about the astrologer, that's just plain old ridiculous."

The women turned on me as if I'd just told them there's no such thing as Santa Claus.

"Oh, yeah? How do you know?" the first woman challenged.

"Because I'm Lauren."

She snickered at me and the other women followed. "Yeah, sure you are. And I'm Vera Wang."

I was branded a poser by the crowd, and they quickly moved away from me.

"Imagine pretending to be Lauren Gallagher," one of the women whispered as she walked away. "How pathetic."

Sure, I could have protested or pulled out my license and proved I really was Lauren Gallagher. But what was the point? These women wanted the proprietor of Lauren's Luscious Licks to be a fairy godmother, sprinkling her pixie dust over buttercream icing like some magical spell. They thought it was like their wedding day every day at Lauren's Luscious Licks, but what they didn't realize was that I did four or five times a day what other women waited a lifetime for. You can't exactly tell people that without sounding jaded and slightly annoying. So why burst their bubble? I kind of liked their version of my job better.

As it got closer to eight o'clock, all friendly banter ended, and I swore I caught a few women stretching their hamstrings, as if they were preparing to run the Boston Marathon. The line bent around the corner so that I couldn't even tell where it ended.

When the security guards unlocked the front door, it was as if a starter's gun had been fired. Women took off, and the three of us were carried along in the current of eager brides. We were in the store sixty seconds before the racks were picked clean by women with crazed looks in their eyes, like piranhas in a feeding frenzy.

I'd managed to stuff three gowns in my arms before my rack was reduced to a mere skeleton of its former self. I clutched the dresses greedily to my chest and looked around the frenzied room for Paige and Robin. I spotted two Red Sox hats in the corner and ran over, stepping over naked women in the throes of trying on dresses as I walked.

Did I mention there were no dressing rooms?

"Here." I let the gowns fall to the floor in front of Paige. "Try these."

Paige had already stripped down to her bike shorts and sports bra, an ensemble she'd determined ideal for optimal efficiency and minimal flesh exposure. A devious mother of the bride crept toward us on her hands and knees and slyly reached out to grab one of the gowns I'd dropped. Paige firmly planted a foot on the pile to keep it from going anywhere, and the woman slithered off to prey on other unsuspecting shoppers.

Robin helped Paige shimmy into a gown with a skirt so

full it looked like she could house a family of four under its box pleats. We watched as she struggled to twirl around, the heavy skirt and trailing train just ending up twisted around her legs like a wrung mop.

"Not very dance-friendly, is it?" she asked, frowning.

"Once the bustle's up it won't be so bad," I observed, bending down to gather the train.

Robin rushed in to help and "accidentally" knocked me over onto the floor. "Sorry," she apologized, giving me the evil eye before turning to Paige. "Don't listen to Lauren. A bustle that big will just make your ass look fat."

"Maybe you're right." Paige let Robin undo the row of pebble-sized buttons running down her back and stepped out of the dress.

Now that I'd seen Operation Save Paige in action, it was my turn to pitch in. I picked up the next selection, an ivory A-line gown with cap sleeves, and slipped it over Paige's head.

"That's way too big," Robin complained as I grabbed the excess material at the back of the dress and pulled it taught so it hugged Paige's boobs.

"But it's gorgeous. Besides, what do you expect for two hundred and forty-nine dollars? Even after alterations it'll still cost less than it should." Paige held up the price tag and showed Robin. "It was nineteen hundred dollars—it's a steal."

"Can you say *flat chested*?" I asked, maneuvering Paige sideways so Robin could see her profile.

"Lauren's right; you look like a fourth grader," Robin confirmed.

"A fourth grade *boy*," I added, getting into the swing of our mission.

Paige looked down at her boobs, which were, in fact, nicely nestled underneath the bodice's seed pearls and lace. "Really?" she asked, squeezing her elbows together until a deep hollow of cleavage formed between her boobs. "Maybe I could have pads put in."

I let go of the excess material and the dress dropped to the ground without my even unbuttoning the back. "Moving on."

"It's bartering time," Paige told us, collecting the two discarded dresses and handing them to Robin. "Go see what you can get for these."

I helped Paige in and out of the gowns she and Robin had picked out and managed to dismiss all of them in a matter of minutes.

"Too uptight," I weighed in on an empire-waisted satin gown.

"Too Pamela Lee," I judged the silk crepe sheath with boned bustier.

A ballroom-skirted dress with puffy sleeves and bows was "Too Princess Diana."

I rejected a filmy organza gown for being "Too Stevie Nicks."

I discarded a full tulle ballerina dress as "Too Lara Flynn Boyle at the Golden Globes."

"Too Jenny Craig," I commented on the last dress in our pile.

"What's that mean?" Paige asked, getting a little frustrated with me at that point.

I puffed my cheeks and held my arms out in a circle. "Fat."

I waited for Paige to say she could see right through me and our attempts to sabotage her wedding plans. There was no way a woman who was barely over a hundred pounds and just cleared five feet could look fat in anything, and especially not in a silk chiffon slip dress.

Luckily, just then Robin returned carrying the same dresses she'd left with. "Sorry, Paige. I couldn't trade them for anything."

"Oh, this is crazy." Paige stood there in her bike shorts and sports bra watching women trade dresses left and right.

"Let me try," I offered, taking the dresses from Robin. "I'll go see what I can find."

I walked around the large room, navigating past giddy women in strapless dresses and their adoring families of fans.

There were still some pretty dresses being traded, but I bypassed those for a few that caught my eye. I spied the first dress being used as a rug by a group of young women with South Boston accents.

"Can I have that?" I asked, pointing to the dress crumpled under their feet.

"Take it," one of the girls answered and tossed it to me. I lobbed one of mine back.

She seemed surprised. "Wow, thanks. I would have given that nasty thing to you for nothing."

I managed to collect two more dresses before heading back to Paige and Robin.

"Put this on," I ordered and handed over the first dress I'd bartered for.

Paige made a face but obeyed.

"That is totally you," I told her once Robin had zipped it up.

"Lauren, it's gray," Paige protested.

"Chic, don't you think?"

"No, I don't. I think it's *gray*. I don't want a gray wedding dress."

"It goes great with your eyes," Robin added, seeing where I was going. "They say gray is the new black."

"I don't want a black wedding dress!"

I held up another one of my picks, a gothic black number best suited for women named Morticia. "Then I guess you won't like this one, will you?"

Paige shook her head.

"Okay, you win," I conceded. "Try this instead."

Paige couldn't get out of the gray dress fast enough.

"That's it. That's the one." I nodded at Robin, who joined in my love fest for dress number three.

"That is stunning," she gasped, clutching her chest.

"What are these, wings?" Paige asked, holding up two panels of fabric that hung off the entire length of the sleeves—from her armpit to her wrist.

"Very ethereal, don't you think?" I asked, and Robin quickly agreed.

"Angelic in a way."

"Are you guys kidding me?" Paige flapped her arms, and we watched as her wings took flight behind her.

Robin acted surprised. "Not at all. Lauren and I love it."

Every dress we discarded, we traded for another equally atrocious one until we'd worn Paige down and possibly convinced her we had the worst taste of any women she'd ever known.

"I can't believe this." Paige finally sat down on the floor, deflated. "There have to be over two hundred dresses here, and we can't find one that looks halfway decent on me? Not a single one?"

I didn't answer. Paige had looked more than halfway decent in most of the dresses she tried on—she looked beautiful. She looked exactly like a bride was supposed to look.

"Maybe it's just not meant to be," Robin consoled, taking a seat on the floor next to Paige. I was hoping she would get the true meaning hidden in Robin's comment, that maybe Paige and Steve weren't meant to be.

But instead she just shook her head and smiled. "I think I know what's going on here."

"You do?" Robin and I answered in unison, our eyes meeting as we tried to prepare a plausible defense.

"Sure. But I understand." Paige reached out and patted Robin's knee. "It must be hard coming back here and dredging up all those memories of when you were looking for a dress."

Paige stood up and put an arm around my shoulders. "And I know you're afraid that once I'm married we won't spend as much time together, but I promise that won't happen. We'll still have our girls' nights."

I shrugged and looked down at the fraying carpet, as if embarrassed Paige had found us out instead of relieved she didn't figure out our true motivations for selecting such horrible dresses.

Paige reached out a hand to pull Robin off the floor. "Let's get out of this place. I've had enough."

"We're going to hell for that," I told Robin on our way out of the store.

Robin shrugged. "It ain't pretty, but somebody's got to do it."

Phase One of Operation Save Paige was completed.

9

"My fiancé will be here any minute," Julie apologized for the fifth time. "He's just taking a cab from downtown."

"That's fine. I'll be in the kitchen checking on things." I had turned my back to go when I heard the front door open and Julie call out to her fiancé.

He started toward us with a harried look on his face. "Sorry I'm late; the meeting went longer than expected."

When he reached us, he gave Julie a quick hug before putting his briefcase on the floor and holding out his hand to introduce himself to me, a gesture that was halted in midair when he finally took a minute to look at the woman whose hand he was reaching for. "Lauren?"

My breathing grew shallow and I could hear my heart pumping, its rapid pulsing reverberating in my ears like tribal drumbeats.

He said my name as if it was a question, like he wasn't even sure I was the same woman he'd asked to move to DC with him. While Neil and I silently took each other in, Julie's face registered that there was more going on here than her fiancé meeting a pastry chef.

"Hi, Neil." I recovered, wiping my moist hand discreetly on my pants before holding it out in the most professional manner. Neil looked at me with the same blue-gray eyes I'd woken up next to for so many mornings, the same eyes that used to remind me of the color of the ocean on an overcast day.

"You're the Lauren behind Lauren's Luscious Licks?" he asked, even though at that point it was pretty obvious.

"The one and only." I exhaled slowly, taking deep cleansing breaths like I'd seen once in a yoga infomercial.

"Neil?" Now it was Julie's turn to be confused.

I couldn't wait to see how Neil explained this. Would he tell Julie we were old friends or would he venture even further and tell her the truth—that before Julie there'd been another woman Neil had wanted to marry, and she was standing right in front of them.

"Lauren and I used to date a long time ago," Neil explained, as if we'd gone out to Chili's a few times for dinner instead of sleeping together for three years. And how come Julie didn't already know about me? You'd think Neil would tell his future wife about the woman who broke his heart.

"That's so funny; what a small world." Neil's explanation seemed to satisfy Julie, and she turned her attention to the matter at hand. "So are we ready to start? I can't wait to see what you have for us."

I held up a finger, acutely aware that it was trembling even as I was managing to keep my voice steady. "I'll be right back."

I walked straight through the kitchen and into the bathroom, locking the door behind me.

"Neil," I said into the mirror and watched my lips form his name. "Fucking Neil."

I ran the taps and let the water get so cold it numbed my fingers. I tore three paper towels from the roll and held them under the faucet before dabbing my forehead with the damp wad. In the mirror I watched my chest rise and fall with each breath.

Neil was in the gallery. *My* gallery. And he was about to marry someone who wasn't me.

Maria pounded twice on the door. "What's taking so long? You got the runs?"

I ran the water over the towels and placed them on my neck before answering. "I'm fine."

"Then get out here," she barked. "We've got clients waiting."

I had to compose myself. In the medicine cabinet I found

my lipstick and carefully filled in my lips before blotting them on a tissue and dabbing on some gloss. I ran a brush through my hair and bent over, hoping the blood that had run out of my face the moment I realized Neil was my four o'clock appointment would find its way back into my cheeks. One more glance in the mirror, and I walked out ready to face Neil and his fiancée.

Maria was waiting for me with the sample tray. "I hope you washed your hands."

I thought I had. I'd thought I'd washed that man right out of my hair long ago, too, but now here he was—the ghost of relationships past.

I kicked the kitchen door open, carried the sample tray into the gallery and laid the plates on the table. After going through my spiel, I sat back and watched them each try a slice of cake. I suppose I should have gone into more detail about the fillings and icings as they worked their way through each piece, but watching Neil, *my* Neil, sit on the other side of the table like all the other grooms before him, had rendered me speechless.

While they worked their way from plate to plate, I studied Neil, as if for the first time. How come Julie wanted to marry Neil when I didn't? Why was she sitting there with Neil instead of me? Did I miss something that had been right in front of me all along?

"So what brings you back to Boston?" I finally managed to ask, breaking the silence.

"Julie's from Newton, so she wanted to get married back in Boston."

So Neil was getting married on my home turf—and I was supposed to bake for the occasion.

"All my family's here, and we're moving back next month," Julie added between mouthfuls. "We'd like our kids to be around their grandparents and cousins and all."

Kids? Well, that explained it. Poor Neil was just doing his duty.

"So, you're pregnant?" I pointed to Julie's stomach.

Julie gasped. "Oh, God, no. That's not what I meant. I was talking about sometime in the near future."

They were sitting here eating my cake, sharing their joyous news, and now I had to hear about their mating plans? What was next, the play-by-play of last night's positions?

"This must be so much fun, making wedding cakes," Julie continued, oblivious to the fact that I was still trying to digest the idea that Neil and this strange woman were planning a family together. "When my mom and I used to bake cakes, I loved making all sorts of funky colored icing and eating the batter. By the time we were done, my fingers were stained some atrocious purply color and I had a stomachache from licking the bowl clean."

"All class, my future wife," Neil teased.

"Ignore him." Julie swiped a glob of icing from the sour cream fudge cake and playfully dabbed Neil on the nose. "You know, I always pictured pastry chefs as fat men in tall paper hats with flour on their cheeks, but you don't fit that stereotype at all—you're like a celebrity chef!"

Okay, could this woman be any nicer? I mean, what was she trying to pull, acting all sweet and unassuming? Maybe if she knew that her fiancé used to turn my stuffed bear around so he couldn't watch us having sex, she wouldn't feel so friendly. What would she do if I inquired about the status of the eraser-shaped birthmark on Neil's right ass cheek?

"I can't believe Neil knows you," Julie marveled. "Your cakes are legendary."

Now this was getting intolerable. "I don't know about that," I answered with false modesty, fully aware of the fact that my cakes were legendary, that Lauren's Luscious Licks made the best damn cakes in all of Boston!

"Oh, they are. All of my friends want your cakes."

"How'd you end up doing this?" Neil asked.

At first I thought Neil was asking how I made the apricot sponge cake with meringue buttercream he was eating, and I froze. I had no idea how the hell the cake was made. That was Maria's department. But when Neil gestured around the gallery, I realized he wanted to know how I started Lauren's Luscious Licks. Now that was a question I could answer, and you could bet they'd get the Merchant Ivory version of my story.

I told them about making a cake for Paige's birthday and how it mushroomed from there. I conveniently left out the part about losing my job and taking up residence in my bed for three straight days, wrapped up in my own version of Egyptian cotton sheets—six hundred thread counts of self-pity.

"That's amazing." Neil was impressed.

It was hard to tell whether he meant amazing that Lauren's Luscious Licks had become so successful, or amazing that a woman whose culinary skills were once limited to tuna melts and scrambled eggs could actually bake elaborate wedding cakes.

"What do you think of this one?" Julie asked Neil, tapping her fork on the edge of the third plate.

"I'm not a big fan of lemon. Maybe we could have something more subtle. Any suggestions, Lauren?" Neil asked, looking up at me.

"Well, we could do another citrus, like orange, or a banana." Neil and Julie didn't look thrilled. "We could do a strawberry rum or almond cake."

"Almond sounds good." Neil turned to Julie. "What do you think?"

"Sounds great," she agreed.

"So if we're going with the almond cake, can we still have the raspberry filling, like the lemon sample here?"

"Sure you can."

"What about the icing? I don't want something too sweet. How about chocolate? But not just a typical chocolate icing, something with a little more pizzazz."

I knew what I had to suggest. It was the obvious choice. But even after I'd opened my mouth and the words were out, a voice in my head was screaming *don't say it*!

"Like a chocolate ganache?" I asked slowly, not liking where this was going.

"That's the stuff they make truffles out of, right?" Neil asked, and Julie nodded her head. "Perfect."

Julie beamed. "Lauren, that sounds amazing."

An almond cake with raspberry filling and chocolate ganache—sound familiar? Neil just described my perfect cake! He picked the cake I wanted for my wedding! The boyfriend I dumped, the man I thought was the wrong guy for me, had just described exactly the same cake I wanted when I found the person I would spend the rest of my life with.

The next twenty minutes went by in a haze as I went through the motions of showing the portfolio and suggesting designs but couldn't stop thinking about what I'd just witnessed or the revelation that maybe I'd been wrong all along—maybe I'd made a huge mistake when I let Neil go.

"Thanks for being so helpful, Lauren. There's so much to do for the wedding, it's getting to be a little overwhelming. Next week I have a meeting with the florist, and then I have to go look at invitations, and on Wednesday afternoon I'm going to check out Gamble Mansion for the reception."

"Nice." Definitely not a place that catered to the pigs-in-a-blanket crowd.

"So, we're all set, then?" Julie asked, signing the order form that confirmed their selection.

"Just a sec." I wrote Neil's check number on the form, and then handed over the pale blue copy.

They stood to leave.

"Thanks so much, Lauren." Julie leaned over and gave me a squeeze. "I can't wait to tell my friends that Neil knows you."

He did more than know me, I thought. He wanted me to be where you are right now.

After they left I was filled with nervous energy. I paced around the room trying to figure out my next move. Did I call Paige and Robin and tell them that of all the cake joints in all the city, Neil had just walked into mine? Should I clean up the tasting table or just sit down and try to convince myself that Neil's cake preference was merely a coincidence? A total fluke? A slap in the face? A kick in the ass?

Oh, this was ridiculous. It was Neil! How could he be *the one*? Sure, I used to love him, but that was years ago. This had to be a mistake.

I was about to carry the loaded tray into the kitchen when the front door opened and Neil reappeared.

"Forgot my briefcase," he explained, pointing to the black leather attaché case against the wall.

Neil picked up his briefcase and came over to me. "You know, it's really great to see you."

"You, too." Had Neil grown taller? And what was that fantastic cologne he was wearing?

"I'd love to talk more, but with Julie here and all . . ." Neil paused. "Well, you understand."

"Sure." It was completely reasonable that he wouldn't want to drop to the ground and declare his undying love for me in front of his fiancée.

"Maybe we could get together sometime? Like for a drink or something? I've got business in our Boston office that I'm working on, so I'll be traveling back and forth."

Was Neil asking me on a date?

"Well, you've got my number." I pointed to the business card he had tucked in his jacket pocket. The jacket that was covering the chest I used to rest my head on before falling asleep.

"Right. And you've got mine, too." He held up the blue order form. "I better go."

Neil was halfway to the door when he stopped and turned back toward me. "You know, I never would have thought it eight years ago, but this place is perfect for you."

You are, too, I almost replied, thinking that there was more truth to my answer than I used to believe.

I had to tell someone about Neil. I couldn't just let him come into the boutique and order my cake, and chalk it up to a twist of fate. But Paige was out on appointments, and Robin was teaching a seminar at the Park Plaza. I'd never thought of Maria as a surrogate friend before, but she had proximity in her favor.

"Did you see that couple?" I asked Maria, placing the tray on the butcher-block bench.

"Yep."

"That was Neil. *My* Neil."

"So?" Maria dipped a delicate paintbrush into the shallow reservoirs of color on the palette in her hand and painstakingly brushed flecks of mauve on the ivory tea roses of a cake topper. Her hand was steady and sure even as I hovered impatiently, waiting for Maria to grasp the magnitude of what I just said.

"So?" Maria's lack of recognition was staggering. "So, I could have married him!"

"And I could have married Mario Spinelli. Big deal."

Someone wanted to marry Maria? What kind of masochist was this Mario?

I threw up my hands in defeat. Leave it to Maria to upstage my reunion with Neil. "Wait a minute. Who's Mario Spinelli?"

"None of your business."

"Okay, fair enough. But why didn't you want to marry him?"

"He didn't pick the right cake," Maria drawled sarcastically and then laughed at me.

"How long did you go out with this Mario?"

Maria ignored my question and continued dipping the paintbrush into the small pools of food coloring.

"What kind of wedding cake did Mario want?"

"I'm sorry; did you miss the part where I said we didn't get married?"

"Well, Neil picked the same almond cake with raspberry filling and chocolate ganache that I've been saving for myself."

"So, what are you going to do about it?"

I hadn't gotten that far. I was still digesting the fact that five minutes ago Neil was practically asking me to run away with him.

"Are you saying you think I should do something about it?" I asked. Maybe Maria was right; maybe I shouldn't just let Neil walk off with Julie to start a new life. Maybe there was a reason he showed up on my doorstep after eight years—or at least the doorstep of my boutique.

Maria shook her head and let out a frustrated sigh. "Go home, Lauren," she instructed. "I think you're getting delusional."

I wasn't delusional. In fact, I may have been thinking clearly for the first time in a long while.

10

"Tonight's the night." Robin sounded almost giddy on the other end of the phone.

"For what?"

"Phase Two of Operation Save Paige—the intervention. Paige is frustrated she didn't find a dress at Filene's, and we've got to strike when she's most vulnerable."

Robin was sounding more and more like she was orchestrating a coup.

"But I've got another date with Charlie tonight." Yes, my life was feast or famine. For eight years Neil could have showed up and picked my cake, but instead he decided to reveal himself when a noncommittal divorce attorney wanted to start dating me. Even though Neil's taste in cakes was frighteningly similar to mine, there was no way I was cutting Charlie loose. Especially now that I'd told him I was above worrying about the marriage thing. The timing would look too coincidental. Besides, I hadn't figured out what I was going to do about Neil. There had to be a logical explanation for the cake—maybe Maria put him up to it.

"Oh, well, in that case, forget it." Robin's abrupt tone was dripping in sarcasm. "When Paige is headed to divorce court with two children on her hip and years of her life down the tubes, I'll just tell her that we could have prevented all her pain, but *Lauren had a date*."

"Fine; you're right. So, what are we doing for this intervention?" I asked, trying to keep my voice low so Maria couldn't hear what I was saying. Maria looked like she was concentrating on creating the six satin sugar roses needed for the Murphys' cake topper, but I noticed she had an ear cocked in my direction.

"I've got it all planned out," Robin assured me. "We'll tell Paige about your theory and what you noticed when they were picking out a cake. Then we'll tell her that you knew about Mark and me, blah, blah, and then we let her know that we don't want her making the same mistake."

"She's going to hate us."

"Look, we like Steve, but this isn't about him. It's about Paige."

I agreed to meet Robin at Paige's apartment by six o'clock. The plan was to ambush her when she got home from work. Operation Save Paige was starting to look like a full-on military maneuver.

"What are you planning with that lunatic Robin?" Maria asked me after I placed the phone back on its cradle.

"Nothing."

Maria narrowed her eyes at me. "Did you find a dress for Paige?"

"No."

"What do you mean, no?"

I looked away, just in case Maria planned to use her Jedi mind trick to pull the truth out of me. "Nothing looked right on her."

Maria shook her stubby finger at me and warned, "You better not be doing anything to my Paige."

Her Paige. Who was Maria kidding? She probably didn't even know Paige's last name. When I first introduced my best friend to my new pastry chef there was instant rapport between them the moment Paige declared that she'd take a misshapen homemade chocolate chip cookie over a ninety-nine-cent Mrs. Fields cookie any day. Maria told me later that Paige reminded her of herself when she was younger, although I couldn't imagine the two of them having anything in common.

I piled the cake boxes on a shelf in the storage room before taking Charlie's phone number with me into the gallery.

The kitchen phone was too close to Maria's curious ears, and I didn't want her to hear me canceling my date.

I dialed Charlie's office and left a message on his voice mail explaining that we'd need to reschedule our dinner. I found myself rambling on until a beep interrupted me and indicated that my time was up. Reluctantly, I hung up and started back toward the storage room.

"No date tonight?" Maria asked, reading my mind—or more likely eavesdropping on my conversation.

I shook my head no.

"Now was that a date with Charlie or Neil that you were canceling? I can't keep all your men straight these days."

"Charlie, of course. Neil's getting married," I reminded her.

Maria raised her eyebrows at my declaration of innocence. "Let's keep it that way."

"Hey, what are you guys doing here?"

"Freezing," Robin mumbled, jumping up and down on the sidewalk to keep warm while I sat on the front steps watching my breath escape in cloudy puffs into the night air.

Paige sorted through the keys on her key chain until she found the right one and slipped it into the lock. "This isn't some sort of surprise bridal shower, is it?" she asked, almost sounding hopeful.

"We just wanted to see you. Our morning at Filene's wasn't much fun." Robin nudged me and I realized that was my cue.

"We thought it would be nice to order a pizza and hang out."

Paige shrugged and opened the door. "Sure. Come on in."

Robin and I followed as Paige climbed the stairway to the second floor of her two-story brownstone. This was the first building Paige had bought after saving for years to begin her quest for real estate domination. And even though she'd added four other properties since then, I knew that no matter how many buildings she had in her portfolio, Paige would always have a special place in her heart for the two-unit investment property in Brookline that she'd ultimately turned into her home.

When Paige first took me to see the run-down building that was just off Beacon Street, I thought she was crazy. It took more than a can of paint and some Spackle to be able to see beyond the purple marbled wallpaper in the bathroom and the bronze dining room chandelier with the squirrels and acorns—it took fearless vision. But Paige persevered, and today she rented out the first-floor unit for a pretty hefty sum while her own apartment's foyer opened up to a living room with a creamy granite fireplace and floor-to-ceiling windows that gave Paige an amazing view onto the tree-lined street.

While Robin passed out bottles of Corona from the twelve-pack we'd brought with us, Paige ordered a pizza from Pino's.

"It'll be about thirty minutes," she told us. "Take a seat and put on a CD; I'm going to change my clothes."

Since Robin was already kneeling next to the fireplace trying to get the flames going, I headed over to the stereo. I flipped through the CDs, which were all neatly lined up and arranged alphabetically inside the built-in bookshelves. I selected five discs and slipped them onto the CD player's tray.

"Hey, Lauren. I heard you had a date," Paige yelled from her bedroom as the sounds of Natalie Merchant filled the room and a mellow orange glow swelled from inside the fireplace.

I glanced over at Robin, who shrugged. "I didn't tell her."

"Who told you that?" I called back.

"Maria, when I called yesterday." Paige reappeared wearing a pair of gray sweatpants and a flannel shirt. "So, who is he?"

"His name's Charlie Banks. He's an attorney."

"Is he a litigator?" Robin interrupted. "He better not be representing that dickless prick who's suing me. Maybe he's a plant from the opposition; maybe they're trying to get to me through you."

"Right, because God knows the only way I could get a date is if he's being paid by Plaintiff's crack legal team. No, he's not a litigator," I assured Robin.

"And?" Paige waited for me to spill some salacious tidbits. But what could I say? *Charlie's great; too bad the idea of marriage repulses him.*

"And what? He's cute and he seems to have a good sense of humor."

"So, is he a candidate for Mr. Absolutely Right?"

"So far he's just a candidate for dinner." Not that I was complaining. Dinner at trendy restaurants sure beat a peanut butter and jelly sandwich at home.

"Well it's about time someone filled Neil's shoes." Paige grabbed a pillow from the couch and sat on the floor. "Let's just hope this one doesn't need lifts."

Without realizing it, Paige had just handed me the opener for the can of worms I was dying to set free. Ever since Neil showed up at the boutique I couldn't stop wondering what he meant by *go out for drinks*. Was that code for *take you to bed and show you what you've been missing*? I wanted to tell Paige and Robin about Neil's little visit, but the night we were going to put the final stages of Operation Save Paige into action didn't exactly seem like the right time.

"You know, the lifts never bothered me so much," I told her, defending Neil's orthopedic shoe implants. But then I couldn't resist adding, "In fact, *I could care less*."

Paige let out a gurgled laugh and had to cover her mouth to keep from spraying beer on her parquet floors. "To Neil," she toasted, holding up her bottle. "He's got three hot chicks in Boston toasting his fallen arches, and I'm sure he could care less."

"I don't know," Robin broke in, ignoring the toast as she continued to formulate conspiracy theories in her head. "It's a little curious, this guy showing up at exactly the same time I'm served papers."

"He's not a litigator, Robin. He's a divorce attorney."

"Oh, Jesus." Robin flopped down on the floor next to Paige and laid her head in Paige's lap. "And here I thought he was a sleazeball lawyer. Silly me."

After the pizza arrived and we'd managed to polish off eight slices of a large cheese pie in six minutes flat, we stretched out on the area rug in front of the fireplace and listened to the crackling flames.

"It's so cozy in here," I mumbled to no one in particular as I watched the fire create flickering shadows on the walls of the living room.

"We could rent a movie or go out for a drink if you want," Paige offered, even though her eyes were closed and she didn't look like she'd budge to go to the bathroom, much less outside where it was about thirty degrees and sleeting.

"We actually wanted to talk with you about something important." Robin sat up and smacked my arm.

I didn't feel like moving, but I knew Robin wanted to present a united front so I pulled myself up and sat Indian style next to Robin.

Paige opened her eyes. "Is this about the bridesmaids' dresses? Because I promised you could help pick them out. And I saw a dress on the Vera Wang Web site that was so beautiful; it's the kind of dress—"

"We can both wear again," Robin and I chimed in unison before Paige could finish.

"Why does every bride say that? All these women come into the boutique and tell me how their bridesmaids will be able to reuse the Bubble Yum pink floor-length gown with matching shawl, and I'm always sitting there wondering if they really believe that or they're just trying to justify asking their best friends to spend four hundred dollars on something completely useless. I mean, even the nice ones aren't exactly recyclable—I've never worn the navy strapless number from Robin's trip down the aisle." I turned toward Robin. "No offense."

"None taken." Robin paused briefly before forging ahead. "Look, it sounds great, but before we start picking out bridesmaids' dresses, Lauren and I wanted to talk to you about the wedding."

"What about it?"

Robin took a deep breath and exhaled before laying it on the line. "We think you should call it off."

"Or at the very least postpone it," I added, trying to soften the blow.

Paige looked at us with a crooked smile on her lips, as if she was waiting for the punch line to the joke she'd obviously just missed.

"You can't be serious." Paige turned to me. "Lauren?"

"We're serious."

"What are you talking about? We put deposits down on the church and the hotel and now we have the cake."

I shifted onto my knees to keep my legs from falling asleep. "Yeah, about the cake—"

"What about the cake?"

"The other night, watching you and Steve pick out the cake reminded me of some other couples I've worked with—like Robin and Mark, and Gwen and David Stern and a bunch more."

"So?"

"So they all ended up getting divorced."

Paige waved away the implication with a flick of her wrist. "That's crazy."

"No, it's not."

"Yes, it is," Paige insisted.

"It's just that maybe if Lauren had said something to me, I would have thought twice about marrying Mark," Robin explained. "I don't want you to make the same mistake I did. You know, every time I had to call a customer service representative to change a credit card or household bill back to my maiden name, they'd always ask if I was changing my name because I was getting married. And like an idiot, I always said yes, because the thought of telling anyone that Mark left me, even a total stranger who didn't care, was just too"—Robin shook her head and paused, looking off into the darkened bedroom before finally finding the right word—"mortifying. I don't want you to go through that."

"Steve isn't Mark, Robin." Paige stood up and moved to the couch, where she pulled a pillow onto her lap and stared into the fire.

I waited for Robin to become defensive, but instead her voice softened and she got up from the floor and took a seat on the couch next to Paige. "I know that, Paige. I'm not saying this to you because I never want you to get married or meet a guy or because I don't like Steve. We just think that maybe you're rushing into this, and you have to admit, Lauren's been pretty accurate in her assessment of couples so far." Robin gestured in my direction as if she expected me to start spouting statistics of my successful pastry prophecies.

"So you could really tell with Robin and Mark?" Paige asked.

I nodded. "And others, too."

"But Steve's about the most genuine person I've ever known." Paige hugged the pillow closer. "And I love him."

Robin let a hand fall lightly on Paige's shoulder before continuing. "We know that. But we also know that you're two totally different types of people. He isn't anything like the other guys you've wanted to date, and we're just worried that you're rushing into this. You've only known Steve for six months—and you've been engaged for three of those. Can you honestly say that before you met Steve you would have even considered marrying a guy you knew for only a few months?"

Paige was silent.

"Or that if you took out that checklist you made senior year, Steve would be able to check off all the boxes that you listed as criteria for a husband?"

Paige cringed. We'd all made those damn checklists our senior year, and at the time it seemed like a good idea. I made a mental note to see if I still had mine packed away in a box with my yearbooks.

"What did I know back then? I was twenty-one. Besides, what makes you two experts at this?" Paige sat up a little straighter, as if ready to challenge us. She stabbed a finger in Robin's direction and then turned it on me. "You're divorced and you won't even go out on a date because every guy you meet is flawed in some minuscule way."

Paige managed to get in a few zingers with her keen observations, but neither Robin nor I rose to the bait. It's not like I expected Paige to toss her engagement ring into Boston Harbor like Robin had. I couldn't argue with Paige's logic; our own track records didn't exactly inspire confidence. If she knew that I was planning dates with Charlie even as I was figuring out how to bump into Neil again, Paige would probably kick us to the curb on the spot.

"Why should I listen to either of you?" Paige asked defiantly.

"Because you know we love you and we only want you to be happy—long after the wedding is over," I answered and then decided to be honest, even at the risk of sounding like I was pointing a finger at Robin. "I've seen it, Paige. All the excitement surrounding a wedding day and the idea of happily ever after. And I've seen what happens when happily ever after ends. I'm just scared for you."

"It's just that you and Steve are such an unlikely couple," Robin forged on, building our case. "You've always had a grand plan, while Steve's content to live each day as it comes. If I asked you where you'd be in ten or twenty years, you'd be able to give me an answer right away, down to the day and maybe the hour, but Steve doesn't even think about what he's going to have for lunch tomorrow, much less what he'll be doing years down the line."

Paige's chin dropped into her chest and she stared sadly at the solitaire poised on her left hand. She didn't argue.

"And it's all happened so fast. You haven't even known each other for that long, and here you are planning the rest of your lives."

"You know we're not saying this to hurt you, right?"

Paige tipped her head back onto the couch and stared at the ceiling as if looking for an answer amid the stippled plaster. "Man, this sucks."

Robin and I nodded. "We know."

While Paige let the night's turn of events sink in, I got up from the floor and reached over into the cardboard case, taking out three Coronas. After removing the caps, I handed one to Robin, who seemed grateful for the offer of alcoholic refuge.

"At least promise us you'll think about it," I said, holding out a Corona for Paige.

She hesitated, looking briefly at Robin and then at me, before she reached out and reluctantly took the bottle. "I promise."

11

*Y*ou know what today is?"

I glanced at my alarm clock and tried not to drop the phone as I snuggled back into the warm cocoon of my down comforter.

"Saturday?" I ventured, my voice muffled under a tangle of flannel sheets.

"The day I was supposed to go pick out my wedding ring," Paige reminded me.

"Are you okay?" I asked, the reality of last night's intervention truly sinking in for the first time.

Operation Save Paige was a success, if you could consider breaking up your best friend and her fiancé an achievement. I tried not to think about how heartless that sounded, and instead focused on the positive: Paige wasn't going to make the same mistake Robin made when she married the wrong guy.

"Am I okay? What do you think?" Paige's tone was verging on sarcastic, and for a minute I thought she was getting ready to rip into me. Instead, she let out a frustrated sigh. "You know, I'm not saying I think you and Robin are one hundred percent correct, but I just got off the phone with my mom, and apparently you weren't the only ones with concerns."

"So what are you going to tell Steve?"

"I already called him."

"And what happened?"

"Well, he was asleep when he picked up the phone, but once he realized what I was saying, he wasn't exactly understanding."

"You can't blame him for not understanding, Paige. Just a few days ago you were picking out your wedding cake." As soon as the words escaped, I closed my eyes and waited for Paige to echo what I was already thinking myself—that while Paige couldn't blame Steve for not understanding, she could blame Robin and me for stirring up this mess.

"Anyway, by the time we hung up we'd agreed to take some time apart to think things over." I could hear the crunchy stream of Special K in the background as Paige poured herself a bowl of cereal. Paige is religious about her morning routine, which consists of a bowl of Special K with bananas and skim milk, her One-A-Day vitamin and tomato juice. She spent the night at my apartment once after a Red Sox night game, and all I could offer her as a substitute was Frosted Flakes and Bloody Mary mix. Paige didn't stay for breakfast.

"So, now what?" I curled up on my side, bringing my knees into my chest to try and shake the morning chill.

"You want to go skiing?" she suggested, her voice hopeful. Paige's parents owned a motel near Okemo, and whenever she needed to clear her head, Paige's first instinct was to hit the mountain. It wasn't a big deal to take off for a ski weekend when we were in college and the only thing we were skipping was an afternoon drinking milkshakes in Schneider Center, but if Paige was willing to cancel her Saturday showings, she really needed to get away.

"Today?"

"Now. I'll swing by and pick you up. I already told my parents we were coming, I gave my appointments to Sheila, and I'm picking up Robin in half an hour."

"I don't know." I peeked my head out from under the covers and watched the stiff, frozen branches swaying in the wind outside my window. Last night's unexpected snowfall was still piled up on the windowsill a good three inches.

"Do you have to go to the boutique? I thought this was an off Saturday."

The boutique was open only two Saturdays a month,

mostly to encourage couples to schedule tastings during the week, but also because the kitchen was crazy on Saturdays and the last thing I needed was for clients to hear Maria screaming obscenities at an uncooperative meringue or unruly floral tape. Even if our clients weren't fluent in Italian, it was obvious that Maria wasn't exactly reciting the Hail Mary. Although I usually went in every Saturday anyway, even when I didn't actually have anything to do in the kitchen besides get in the way, the truth is, once the cakes were selected, my role in the process was over.

But it wasn't work I was thinking about at that moment—it was my toasty bed and the fact that it was barely seven-thirty in the morning and the last thing I wanted to do was get up and drive to Vermont in the backseat of Paige's car. I tried to remember the last time I saw my ski pants and thought I recalled seeing them somewhere in a Rubbermaid tub in my closet along with my gloves and thermal long johns. As long as I didn't have to go searching around in my basement storage locker for all my ski gear, I could probably be ready by eight-thirty.

"Okay, I'm in. Come by in an hour; I'll be out front." It was the least I could do, given the circumstances.

Whether out of guilt on our part, or denial on Paige's, or the fact that we were given explicit instructions upon entering her car not to mention Steve, no one brought up what transpired the night before in Paige's living room, or why we were currently passing through Contoocook, New Hampshire.

"Hey, I forgot to tell you that my editor may be calling." Robin handed me a blueberry muffin from the Dunkin' Donuts bag in her lap.

"What's she want with me?"

"Apparently she's heard of you, or at least she's heard of your cakes. She wants to talk with you about an idea for a book."

I caught Paige eyeing me in the rearview mirror as I broke off a piece of the muffin, and I quickly scanned the backseat for errant crumbs and my apple juice bottle. Paige always reminded us that in her business, a car was akin to a mobile office and should not be mistaken for a traveling receptacle.

"What kind of book?" I asked, making sure the apple juice cap was screwed on tightly.

"She said a sort of coffee-table book, lots of big glossy photos of your cakes organized by season or something like that."

"And this is something she thinks people would buy? A book of cake photographs?"

"Are you kidding me? People would eat it up."

"No pun intended, of course." Paige rolled her eyes at me in the mirror, and when I glanced down at her hands on the steering wheel I noticed a bare finger where her engagement ring once took up residence.

Robin didn't seem to notice. "Of course. We all know that Lauren's cakes are made more for viewing than eating; otherwise, people would be ordering their cakes from the Stop & Shop bakery section instead of shelling out big bucks for something that sits on a table and gets stale while guests do the electric slide and the chicken dance."

"It's nice to know you hold my profession in such high regard. And there may be a hustle or two, but I can assure you, there's never an electric slide or a chicken dance." I balled up my napkin and tossed it at Robin.

"Hey, no throwing your garbage around my car," Paige scolded. "And I have Wet Ones in the glove compartment so you can wipe your hands off; I don't want your greasy fingerprints on my leather seats."

If I felt bad earlier about Steve and Paige, the car ride to Vermont was reminding me why Operation Save Paige took place. I knew for a fact that Steve's Subaru Outback had a collection of old Burger King wrappers and a few French fries under the backseat, not to mention half a dozen saliva-covered tennis balls from his dog, Clyde.

"I'm a respected pastry chef," I reminded Robin.

"Come on, Lauren. You haven't been a pastry chef since Maria took over. You're like a florist, and Maria's like a gardener—she makes things, and you make things look beautiful." Robin turned around to face me. "And I have nothing against florists; in fact, I wish I was on their receiving end more often, so don't get all sensitive on us."

Robin turned back and started flipping through the CDs

Paige kept in a holder Velcro'd to the visor. While she told us about her lawyer's latest attempts to get the lawsuit dismissed, I couldn't stop thinking about what Robin had said. Maria was a gardener, and I was a florist—what the hell did that mean? It didn't sound like an insult, but then why did Robin's comment make me feel uncomfortable, like there was something in the comparison that didn't exactly put me in a favorable light? It was almost as if she knew about the burned cakes and the eggshells in the batter.

"So did he, Lauren?" Paige asked, stopping at a red light.

"Did he what?"

"Did the divorce lawyer call you back to reschedule your date?"

There was a message on my machine from Charlie when I got home from Paige's last night, but I didn't think he'd appreciate a call from a drunken woman at two o'clock in the morning. Besides, even though I wanted to call him back, I was afraid if he made any sort of offer for a late-night booty call, I'd take him up on it.

"He left a message about getting together tonight, but since I'll be in a different state, I don't think that's going to happen."

"I love it—an independent woman blowing off a guy for a weekend with her girlfriends." Robin slid a Melissa Etheridge CD into the player. "We've come a long way, baby."

I wasn't sure we'd come a long way, but I knew that we were driving three hours to get away from guys we'd be pretending not to think about all weekend. Only it wasn't just an ex-husband, an ex-fiancé, and a lawyer with ambiguous intent that we'd left behind; it was also an ex-boyfriend who'd picked out the same wedding cake as me.

"Neil came by the boutique the other day," I said quietly, testing out the words to see how ridiculous I sounded.

Paige's boot immediately fell onto the brake pedal and my forehead slammed into the driver's seat headrest. "Are you kidding us? What'd he want?"

"To pick out a cake with his fiancée."

Paige promptly stepped on the accelerator, and I was thrown back against my seat. "Thank God. I thought you were going to say he came back to reclaim you or something dumb like that."

"Why would that be such a bad thing?" I asked, pretending to be fascinated by the tractor trailer out my window. It was an eighteen-wheeler, after all.

Robin twisted around to face me. "Are you kidding me?"

"Besides, Maria told me that Charlie seemed like a great guy." Paige nodded at me in the rearview mirror.

"She did?" I wasn't sure I liked the idea of Maria discussing my love life with Paige behind my back. But I had to admit, I also found it quite disturbing that Maria seemed to like a guy she glimpsed through the kitchen door better than she liked me.

"Yeah. She said you were all swooning and stuff after he asked you out. Now, I don't even know the guy, but the fact that Charlie got you all worked up over just one date tells me that he's your man."

I stared raptly at the writing on the side of the trailer: BUTCH'S MOVING & STORAGE. "But what if Neil did come back to reclaim me? What if I wanted to be reclaimed?"

Robin smirked at me. "What are you, a mitten in the lost and found?"

"I just meant that maybe Neil and I were meant to be but I was too young to know it before."

"I'm sorry; I have to put a stop to this right now." Paige flipped on the blinker and pulled over onto the shoulder of the road. She unclasped her seat belt and turned to face me and Robin; the expression on her face was nothing short of exasperated. "Is it possible for us to go even one day without creating upheaval or disarray in our lives? Can we please just go skiing and try to have some semblance of normalcy and order for two lousy days?"

Robin and I remained quiet and appropriately chastised.

"Well?" Paige asked again. "Is it?"

"Just two days, right?" Robin quipped. "Because any more than that and I'll have to think about it."

Paige stuck her tongue out at Robin and fastened her seat belt. The rest of the ride was as normal and orderly as we could manage on six hours of sleep.

By the time we parked the car and made it to the lodge, it

was almost one o'clock. Paige was anxious to get started, so she gave us our marching orders and told us to meet her by the South Ridge Quad in fifteen minutes. Robin and I went to rent skis, and Paige set off to buy the lift tickets.

When Robin and I met up with Paige again, we were awkwardly balancing poles and skis in our arms while we struggled to walk in so many layers we looked like Michelin men with goggles. Paige, on the other hand, was all business. In her black stretch bibbed ski pants, mirrored wraparound sunglasses, and a red and white microfiber ski jacket that had more strategically placed meshed vents than the space shuttle, Paige was ready to ski the mountain into submission. But with the tempting smell of hamburgers cooking on the lodge's outdoor grill, the only thing I wanted to submit to was lunch.

"Ready to go?" Paige asked, stabbing her poles in the snow while Robin and I snapped our boots into our bindings.

"Just a sec." I reached for the hat I'd stuffed in my coat's inside pocket and pulled it on, making sure my ears were completely covered.

"What the hell is that?" Robin asked, reaching over and flinging a pom-pom hanging from one of the floppy points on my fleece hat.

"It was a gift from Maria a few years ago."

"You know she was just playing a joke on you. She never expected you to really go out in public looking like a court jester."

"Or a motley fool," Paige threw in.

"Well, I looked in all my closet bins and couldn't find any other hat. I wasn't about to go downstairs into the storage room at eight o'clock in the morning and start rummaging through boxes looking for something worthy of the Kate Spade ski team."

Paige shook her head at me. "If you moved into a bigger apartment that actually had closet space, you wouldn't have to keep half your stuff in a musty old basement along with your neighbor's taxidermy collection and sixteen pairs of mildewed army boots."

I ignored them both, straightening my hat and pulling my

goggles down over my eyes so that everything around me took on a muted gold tinge. "Are we going skiing, or are we just going to play pick on Lauren all afternoon?"

Paige worked us hard, dragging our butts all over the mountain and down trails that Robin and I had no business navigating without the assistance of either a burly ski patrol or a beefy Saint Bernard with a keg of brandy tied around its neck. After two hours of playing catch-up with Paige, my shins were aching and my thighs were burning. I figured this was Paige's way of putting us through some perverse form of penance.

"Doesn't it make you feel alive?" Paige asked, as the triple chairlift slammed into the backs of my knees and forced my ass onto the icy seat.

As our chair drifted quietly above Timberline Trail, Robin reached over the safety bar and struggled to unbuckle her right ski boot. When the clip finally released with a loud pop, she let out a sigh of relief and looked over Paige's head at me. "Are you thinking what I'm thinking?"

I nodded. "Beer."

"Oh, come on; don't quit on me yet," Paige protested.

As our chair approached the drop-off area, I placed my gloved hands inside the pole straps and prepared to unload. "Sorry, Susie Chapstick. You can keep going, but our day on the slopes has come to an end."

We watched Paige ski off on her own in the direction of Jackson Gore Peak, and then Robin and I raced down Upper Tomahawk toward the Base Lodge with more energy and enthusiasm than we'd managed to muster all day.

After parking our skis and poles on the racks outside, Robin and I found a table upstairs in the loft area of Sitting Bull and ordered a pitcher of beer and a plate of Macho Nachos. A grungy-looking guy in a poncho was tuning his guitar on the stage below us.

"How do you think she's holding up?" Robin asked me before devouring a handful of cheesy chips.

"She's acting fine; a little too fine, if you ask me. I don't think it's really sunk in yet. Maybe she's in denial."

"The ring's gone."

"I know. So is the heart bracelet he got her for Valentine's Day."

Robin shrugged. "I think coming here was a good idea. She needed to get away from the city."

In college, we were used to Paige dragging us up to Vermont, and we'd usually get in a good six weekends of skiing before the snow gave way to dirty brown patches and hanging out on a campus that was coming back to life was more tempting than a three-hour car ride. Back then, ski weekends seemed like more fun, or maybe our expectations were just so low that we didn't realize guys who took pride in the homemade craftsmanship of their beer bongs and dotted their sentences with *dude* like grammatical confetti weren't exactly the cream of the crop. Still, we had a hell of a time lowering our standards. Now the lodge seemed filled with families, with parents trying to wrangle their kids or wiggle them out of ski clothes, or young professionals like us who saw skiing as a two-day respite before returning to reality.

It seemed as if every year since graduation we ventured to Okemo less and less. Whether it was a growing lack of tolerance for subzero temperatures and the skyrocketing price of lift tickets or just the reality that Paige and I had fewer weekends away from work, our ski weekends had become fewer and farther between. In fact, this was our first trip all season.

Eight years ago Neil asked me to move to DC right after we'd spent a weekend at Okemo with Paige, Robin and Mark. From the drive up that Friday night, to the Sunday we got home and Neil told me we had reservations at L'Espalier, I'd sensed that he was up to something. I never suspected anything bad—he wasn't the kind of guy to sneak around behind my back—but I never thought he was planning a romantic proposal of sorts, either. It wasn't that Neil didn't make romantic overtures, but more that his romantic overtures were pretty standard—red roses on Valentine's Day, a special dinner on my birthday, that sort of thing. Asking me to move away with him on a Sunday night after a ski weekend—that wasn't something I'd thought he had in his repertoire.

After four hours of skiing and a three-hour ride back to Boston, all I wanted was a hot shower, my fuzzy slippers and a made-for-TV movie. Instead, I changed into a pair of black wool pants, threw on a black turtleneck sweater and caught a cab to the restaurant to meet Neil looking like I was embarking for a funeral instead of a romantic French restaurant.

Now, you don't just decide to take someone to L'Espalier on a Sunday night without a degree of forethought and a plan. So when the maître d' showed us to our table I was thinking Neil had planned one of two things. Either he was going to ask me to marry him, which after three years was perfectly logical, or he was going to make some sort of monumental announcement, like that he'd decided to go ahead and apply to business school (the measurement of *monumental* obviously being in the eye of the beholder).

During dinner Neil kept the conversation going while I attempted to discern if the odd creases around his blazer pocket were in fact the outline of a small velvet box or just a sign of a poor dry cleaner. When dessert arrived and he still hadn't told me anything, I almost suspected I'd dip my spoon into my soufflé and emerge with a few Grand Marnier–covered carats. But when neither the diamond emerged nor did Neil drop to his knees, I was relieved and started to enjoy the end of our meal. And then he told me about his job offer in DC.

It's not like we never talked about going to DC together, so Neil's announcement didn't come as a total surprise. I didn't run from the table screaming in fear at the thought of losing my boyfriend, or stand up and do the happy dance that finally our long-laid plans were coming to fruition. Our conversations about DC had been more of the *Gee, Georgetown has amazing bars* variety than in the league of *We need a two-bedroom apartment with air-conditioning in a decent school district.*

After Neil moved, I felt a kind of survivor's guilt. After all, when you boiled it down, I hadn't simply told Neil I didn't want to move to DC. I'd in essence told him that I didn't want to be with him anymore, that while he was good enough to date and sleep with when he was a short T ride away, once our relationship required any sort of sacrifice or effort, I was going to take a pass and send him on his way alone. Did I cry in the weeks after he moved? You bet I did.

Were they tears of loss and a profound realization that my soul mate was hundreds of miles away? Not exactly. They were tears that sprang from the well of failure, or more accurately, my fear of failure. In a perverse form of universal retribution, I was laid off from my job at a small ad agency the week after Neil left. Sure, I'd been feeling restless with Neil and my *Groundhog Day* existence, but I never in a million years would have chosen getting laid off as a way to shake things up. A new haircut probably would have done the trick. Instead, I was living proof that what goes around comes around, but at least I wasn't heartbroken and alone in a strange city. I knew I'd gotten the better end of the deal—I still had my friends and all the familiar surroundings of Bean Town.

I pictured Neil pining away for me in DC, wandering aimlessly around national monuments and through museums celebrating our country's history while he reran our own history through his mind like a grainy black-and-white movie: the weekend we escaped to a little bed-and-breakfast in Cape Cod when the idea of spending another sticky summer weekend in the city was just too unbearable, or how we'd sit on the banks of the Charles River and watch the crew races during the Head of the Charles, sharing thermoses of vodka and tonic on our blanket. I mean, those sound like intimate, meaningful moments shared between two people who loved each other. How could he not be thinking about them without longing for what we'd shared?

I soon learned how: by not calling me or even sending a single postcard from our nation's capital. It seemed that the moment Neil's U-Haul pulled away from his building, he'd left more than his dead ficus plant behind. I figured he was just too hurt to keep in touch, that any contact with me was probably like rubbing salt in his wound. At least, I'd hoped there was a wound, even if it was an itsy bitsy one that would eventually heal once his new life got rolling and I became nothing more than a story he'd tell in a bar like the one I was seated in at this moment.

But now Neil was back in Boston and I was the one feeling like a Band-Aid had been ripped from my skin, taking my scab with it.

By the time Paige met up with us in the lodge, Robin and I had finished the nachos, and the guitar player was seated on the shallow stage strumming the beginnings of a Dave Matthews song.

"Man, I needed that," Paige declared and fell into a chair, her pink cheeks shiny from carving some serious turns down black diamonds. "Did you guys order anything to eat? I'm starving."

We flagged our server and waited as she made her way through the growing après-ski crowd.

"Are you saving these seats for anyone?" A guy in a navy blue turtleneck sweater pointed to the four empty chairs surrounding our table.

I shook my head. "Nope, go ahead and take them."

The guy waved to three friends waiting over by the stairs, and I scooted my chair in so he could get by.

As the three others headed toward us, Mr. Turtleneck Sweater squeezed between the table and the loft railing and started removing his layers of wool and Thinsulate, revealing a buff physique and a bad case of hat head.

"I'm Jeremy, and this is—"

Robin cut Jeremy off before he could finish the introductions. "Mo, Larry and Curly?"

Instead of being put off, Jeremy grinned and ran a hand through his matted blond hair. "You're close. It's Mitch, Denny and Bill."

"Well, take a seat and join us." I moved my jester hat off the table and cleared a spot for our visitors. "We were just about to order another pitcher."

After ordering two more pitchers and another round of appetizers, we all exchanged small talk about the trails we'd skied and the fresh powder that this week's end-of-season snowstorm had dumped on the mountain. Needless to say, Paige held up our part of the conversation, recalling every run, mogul and ice patch to the complete amazement of our four tablemates. But even though Paige and her extensive knowledge of the mountain and skiing in general kept Mitch, Denny and Bill enthralled, Jeremy kept trying to start a conversation with Robin.

"So, are you up here with your boyfriends?" Jeremy asked, refilling Robin's cup with fresh beer.

She shook her head before providing clarification of her single status. "Divorced."

Four pairs of male eyes homed in on Robin, curious specimen that she was—the seemingly normal woman afflicted with an old person's disease for which there was no cure: acute divorce.

Robin seemed pleased with her ability to shock the unsuspecting group of men.

"Do you come up here every weekend?" Jeremy charged on, recognizing Robin's answer as the land mine it was and choosing to steer clear.

"No, just whenever we need to get away. Paige's parents own the Chalet Motel in town."

"Are you all from Ludlow?"

"Nope, we live in Boston."

"No way. Us, too." Jeremy smiled at Robin and waited for a flicker of acknowledgment, but she wasn't giving him a break.

"So then guessing what you all do for a living shouldn't be too hard. Usually all we meet are investment bankers or lawyers who are under the impression that a pair of Rossignols and a gold card make them the answer to every woman's dreams."

"What gave us away? Was it the paisley neck warmers, the pin-striped ski pants or the smug air of superiority?" Jeremy asked, feigning the affected speech of a Kennedy.

Denny laughed. With his own nasal South Boston accent he'd never be mistaken for New England royalty. "Actually, Bill and Mitch are in sales, Jeremy's with a tech firm and I'm what they call *in transition*."

"Luckily his transition just happened to occur when our lease on the ski house kicked in," Bill pointed out. "And luckily he's playing babysitter for my uncle's rottweiler in Wellesley while he and my aunt are in Florida for the winter."

Denny's fair cheeks were blushing. "I'm a lucky guy; what can I say?"

"We went to college in Wellesley," Paige told Denny.

"You went to a girls' school?" Jeremy asked Robin.

Paige and I waited for the fireworks. Poor Jeremy. He had no idea who he was dealing with.

"Wellesley is a women's college," Robin calmly corrected him, "not a girls' school."

"Oh, of course. So then you must think it's okay to have country clubs that only permit male members, right?" Jeremy asked, baiting Robin into a conversation. "After all, what's good for the goose is good for the gander."

Before we could stop them, Robin and Jeremy were off and running, debating the merits of a single-sex education and the differences between a social club and a place of higher learning.

While they battled wits, the rest of us tried to carry on a conversation over the escalating dispute. Our efforts were thwarted, however, when Robin punctuated one of her points by telling Jeremy that he was full of shit.

"Come on, you guys, keep it down or they're going to throw us out of here," Bill warned.

Even the guitar player on the ground floor was looking up at our table, and from what I could tell, he was more than a little annoyed that Robin and Jeremy were stealing the crowd's attention away from his acoustic version of "Brown Eyed Girl."

For every point Robin made, Jeremy seemed to enjoy playing devil's advocate. Robin was used to putting men off balance, but Jeremy refused to get rattled. I guess even he had his limits, because after fifteen minutes he held up a paper napkin and waved the white flag.

"Okay, you're right."

"That's it? I'm right? You can't just give up like that." Robin seemed more flustered by Jeremy's ability to surrender than by his contrary points of view.

"I'm not giving up; you've convinced me." Jeremy reached for Robin's cup and poured her another beer. "You had some interesting arguments."

Robin didn't know how to reply, so she just took the cup and drank, all the while watching Jeremy with piqued interest.

By the time the guitar player finished the last chorus of an Eric Clapton song, the crowd had thinned, and we were one of just a few tables still loitering. When the waitresses started stacking the chairs on the tables, we took the hint that we'd outworn our welcome.

Jeremy was the first to stand. "We're going to head over to Luigi's for some home-cooked Italian food; do you want to come along?"

I looked at Paige, who looked at Robin, who looked back at me. In the ensuing silence I realized that I was going to have to be the one to make the decision. Paige probably didn't care one way or the other, and there was no way Robin would admit that she actually wanted to go. But lasagna sounded good, and at least it would provide a distraction from the reason we were up there in the first place. Who needed to sit around pretending that we didn't just ruin Paige's life? In the short term, anyway.

"Sure, just let us go back to the motel and we'll meet you there in an hour."

Robin shrugged casually, but from the way she watched Jeremy's reaction, I knew I'd made the right choice.

"I drank way too much beer." Denny patted his stomach and let out a groan as we walked through the lodge's parking lot. "Where's the car?"

"This way." Jeremy pulled on his gloves and bent down to scoop up a handful of snow. "You better not blow off dinner," he warned us, forming a snowball and tossing it at Denny.

Denny dodged out of the way of Jeremy's toss, and instead ended up getting sprayed with slush as a car passed by.

Paige shook her head and yawned. "We've had two early mornings, so it's not going to be a late night."

"Oh, come on," Jeremy protested, patting another snowball between his gloves. "Robin?"

Robin almost looked torn, but she agreed. "This is Paige's weekend."

Jeremy lobbed his handiwork at Robin in dissent, hitting her squarely in the stomach. Not to be outdone, she quickly retaliated with two snowballs from a three-foot bank that also included enough sand, salt and dirt to leave a brown stain on the arm of Jeremy's coat.

Without delay, another perfectly round ball soared out of Jeremy's hand toward Robin, and then snow started flying in both directions.

I grabbed Paige and retreated behind a car to avoid the line of fire. On the snow-covered ground, Jeremy's and Robin's battling shadows were illuminated by the headlights of the oncoming cars. For someone as competitive as Robin, her throws seemed more playful than strategic, landing softly against Jeremy's parka and disintegrating upon impact.

"What's up with those two?" Paige asked me.

"I don't know. Maybe he likes a challenge."

"Then he must be in his glory."

If Jeremy's glory included a tongue as sharp as a Ginsu knife and the attitude of a samurai warrior, then he'd found what he was looking for. Robin's tolerance for flirting went MIA when Mark left, as if every man who expressed an interest in Robin was a stand-in for her ex-husband and therefore deserved the same treatment as someone who'd walked out on her anniversary. But all evening Robin had been feeling Jeremy out—not flirting exactly, and I don't even know if I'd call it being friendly, because telling someone his head was up his ass wasn't usually how you made friends. It was more like Robin was testing Jeremy. And he seemed to be passing with flying colors.

Although it was nice to see Robin's edges dulled a little, I couldn't help but think that Paige was watching the scene from an entirely different point of view—the point of view of somebody who saw two people tentatively coming together even as she and Steve had just come apart. No wonder Paige had pulled over this morning asking for some normalcy and order—I'd been blathering on about Neil after Maria had told her what a decent guy Charlie seemed to be. I was double-dipping in the well of dating while Paige had just pulled the plug on her fiancé and watched her relationship go down the drain.

"Come on, Robin, we're going," Paige called out in the direction of Robin's laughter.

"I'm coming," she screamed and then slid into place next to us before a snowball landed on the car's hood with a dull thud.

"I told Jeremy we'd meet them at Luigi's in forty-five minutes," she told us, breathing hard. "Now, come on; if we hurry we can make a run for it."

"Robin! Over here!" Jeremy waved us over to a corner table with a red and white checked tablecloth and the requisite Chianti-bottle candleholder. There was barely any wick left in the well-worn candle, and the little wax that remained on the stub slowly slipped down the side of the bottle until it froze in place on top of the petrified drippings.

The guys were already downing garlic bread and calamari, and before we even sat down the waiter arrived with another basket of fried mozzarella sticks.

"Put it in front of her," Denny instructed the waiter, pointing to Robin's seat. "We took the liberty of ordering an appetizer for you."

A waitress wasn't too far behind with another bottle of wine.

"We thought we'd be needing another bottle of wine, too," Mitch explained, draining the bottle that was on the table. "How about a toast? To new friends."

I picked up one of the short, stout jelly jar–like glasses filled with wine and joined in the toast.

Jeremy grabbed for one of the mozzarella sticks, and although Robin didn't offer to share with him, she didn't slap his hand away either. "Denny said you wouldn't show, but after this afternoon's show of hospitality in Sitting Bull, I knew you had a heart."

Robin wasn't taking any credit for having a heart. "Thank Lauren. I was ready to turn you guys away."

"I could tell. Come on; you thought we were lawyers? Are we really that bad?" Jeremy winked at Robin, and despite herself, she cracked a smile.

Capitalizing on Robin's obvious disdain for the legal profession, Jeremy reached for another stick and regaled the table with a lawyer joke, which went over big, and soon everyone was joining in. Everyone except me, of course. I felt a little loyalty toward Charlie. Not enough to stop the fun, mind you, but enough to sit quietly without fueling the legal fire.

"Nope, can't trust 'em. Lawyers suck," Denny concluded, although with his South Boston accent and dropped *r*'s it sounded more like *loyas suck*.

Robin joined in on the lawyer bashing. "You know, that's what I told Lauren. She blew one off this weekend to go skiing with the girls."

Mitch gave me a thumbs-up. "Nice move."

"I'm involved in this lawsuit right now and I swear my lawyer is ticking off the dollar signs on his desk while we talk," Jeremy told us. "Every time I call him I can practically hear the flag pull of his meter—like he's a taxi driver, and I'm the one being taken for a ride."

"And his lawyer's his brother-in-law!" Mitch pointed out, and we all burst out laughing.

"What's the lawsuit?" Paige asked.

Jeremy looked away from us and picked at the garlic bread on his plate. "Let's just say my ex-girlfriend went a little off the deep end when we broke up."

Mitch slapped Jeremy's arm and let out a chuckle. "Yeah, you could say that—she tried to make him a soprano with a carving knife."

Robin slammed her drink down on the table, shattering the glass and sending a splatter of wine flying through the air. Her mouth dropped open as she processed what Jeremy had told us. "You're Plaintiff?" she finally spat. "You're the prick who's suing me?"

The table fell silent and we all watched Jeremy's face twist in utter confusion as he tried to understand Robin's transformation from enjoyable drinking buddy to ranting lunatic.

"What are you talking about?" Jeremy looked from Robin to me, and then back again. "I'm suing some psycho seminar chick."

Robin stood up and deliberately pushed her chair back abruptly before walking around to Jeremy's side of the table and holding out her hand. "Let me introduce myself, *Jeremy*," she said evenly, pronouncing his name as if it left a bad taste in her mouth. "I'm Robin Cross, president of Women in Action—and resident psycho seminar chick."

Although he seemed to be devising exit strategies, Robin had Jeremy cornered between her and the table, and she wasn't budging. "You're the woman I'm suing?"

"You've got that right. And you're the guy who's blaming me for your ex-girlfriend's actions, when what you should be doing is wondering what you did to make her want to castrate you in the first place."

Jeremy held his hands up to defend himself, and possibly to create a protective barrier between himself and Robin. "Hey, I didn't do anything wrong. I just told her things weren't working out; I was just being honest with her—what'd you want me to do? String her along so she doesn't attempt to maim me?"

"How about taking her feelings into consideration? How about not making promises you can't keep?"

"Hey, how about keeping it down, you two," Bill cut in. "People are starting to stare."

Bill was right. All the tables around were watching quietly, waiting to see what happened next.

"Robin, why don't we just go?" Paige suggested and started to gather up our coats.

"No fucking way. I'm not the one taking him to court." Robin crossed her arms over her chest and moved aside to let Jeremy get up.

"Come on; all the tables are full." Bill tried to appeal to Robin's sense of fairness, which probably had something to do with the fact that there was a line of people waiting to be seated, and leaving our cozy corner pretty much meant an end to dinner. "Can't we just eat our meal and then all go our separate ways?"

"He's suing me!" Robin practically shrieked, and Bill sunk lower into his chair to avoid the stares from the surrounding tables.

"Look, it's nothing personal," Jeremy explained. "My brother-in-law says I have a case. You just can't go around telling women to get even with every man who's broken their heart."

"I can't? Well, let me tell you something, *Jeremy*." Robin bent down so that her eyes were level with Jeremy's and her nose was about two inches away from his face. "When I get your ass in court, you'll see what I can do, and if you think getting your balls cut off is bad, then you have no idea what you're up against." Robin stood up and pulled her jacket off the back of her chair. "Let's go."

Robin was halfway across the restaurant before I even made a move to stand up.

"Well, gentlemen, enjoy your evening." Paige gave the group a weak smile.

I almost felt sorry for Jeremy. He hadn't said a word since Robin stormed off, but I noticed that he watched her move through the crowd until she disappeared.

Finally he turned to me. "You've got to understand. My ex came at me with a knife. Does Robin know that?"

"She's just trying to protect her business," I answered, reaching for my jester hat.

"I don't want to take her business." Jeremy shook his head and stared out the window at the fluorescent LUIGI's sign casting a red tint on the snow outside.

He obviously wasn't out to screw Robin, like she'd thought. I doubt he'd even be suing her if it wasn't for his brother-in-law.

Jeremy looked back at me. "Doesn't she get that sometimes it just doesn't work out and there's not any one reason? I just wanted her to realize that shit happens, and that doesn't mean that you have to blame someone for it or devote hours of seminar time to prolonging the agony."

Paige was anxious to get going, but I couldn't just walk away from Jeremy without some sort of response.

"I know. You and everyone else."

Normalcy and order, Paige had requested. Next time we really had to try harder.

12

$\mathcal{W}$e packed it in early on Sunday, leaving before the lifts even closed. There wasn't the usual girl talk on the ride home, and as I sat in the front seat watching the street signs pass by, I kept thinking I should tell Robin what Jeremy had said. But when I looked in my visor mirror, Robin was curled up on the backseat, her sleepy breathing interrupted by the rough grinding of teeth, and I figured that saving one friend a weekend was more than enough action for me.

"She sleeping?" Paige asked quietly.

"Yep."

"Good. She needs it. I thought she'd never go to bed last night." Paige lowered her voice. "What are we going to do about her?"

I shrugged. "Just let it run its course?"

"It's been almost two years, Lauren, and it doesn't seem to be getting any better."

Paige and I rarely talked about Robin's post-divorce trials and tribulations, even though at times it felt like she was auditioning for a guest spot on the panel of a *Jerry Springer* show. Like last night's blowout with Jeremy. Between scheming new ways to embarrass and humiliate Mark, and carrying around a chip on her shoulder the size of the rock of Gibraltar, Robin appeared to be getting it out of her system, and Paige and I had tacitly agreed to let her do it her way. We figured it was how she was working through the divorce process. Of course, we never thought she'd still be go-

ing at it two years later like the Energizer bunny with a
nuclear-powered grudge.

"What are our choices?"

Paige couldn't come up with an answer, and we drove on
in silence past the WELCOME TO MASSACHUSETTS sign.

We'd all obeyed Paige's instructions to avoid talking
about Steve all weekend. Even Paige's parents didn't mention the broken engagement and instead acted like we'd just
decided we needed to drive three and a half hours to freeze
our asses off. But with reality about to set in when we
reached the city, I wanted Paige to know that I was willing to
listen if she needed to talk.

"Do you want to talk about Steve?" I asked.

"What's there to talk about?" Paige kept her eyes on the
road.

"The fact that you've gone from talking about having
children with Steve to acting like he never existed."

"Why? Because I'm not crying? Or second-guessing my
decision? Do you really think talking about it will help the
situation?" She continued staring straight ahead, her mouth
set in a line as flat as the highway that lay out before us. "No,
I don't want to talk about it."

If she didn't want to talk, I couldn't force her.

After a few minutes, Paige's grip on the steering wheel
loosened and she turned to me. "So, Maria said that this
Charlie guy seems nice."

I found it odd that Maria was suddenly taking an interest
in my love life, and I couldn't help but wonder if she was
hoping I'd get dumped on my ass.

"He is," I told her, but my voice wasn't exactly filled with
enthusiasm.

Paige wrinkled her nose and frowned at me. "What's the
problem?"

"Nothing."

"You like this Charlie, right?"

"As much as you can like someone who tells you that he
doesn't want to marry you." Did that sentence sound as pitiful as it felt?

"What? He said that?"

"He didn't mean he didn't want to marry me, exactly. Just

that he didn't want to marry anyone, at least not in the near future."

"Do you think he's afraid of commitment?" she asked.

"He said he's not; he said he wants a relationship."

Paige seemed confused. "So, he likes you, he wants to keep seeing you, but he doesn't want to marry you?"

I nodded.

"Okay, then what's the problem here? If you asked Robin, she'd probably say he was doing you a favor. Besides, you like him and he likes you. That's half the battle right there."

"I know."

"Look, maybe you can't have your cake and eat it, too. That doesn't mean you shouldn't enjoy yourself."

Robin shifted in the backseat and I waited for her to chime in with her two cents. Instead she rolled onto her other side and fell back asleep.

Paige looked over at me, scrutinizing the expression on my face under the glow of the passing highway lights. "So, why the long face?"

I shifted in my seat, wishing I could explain it, even to myself. "I don't know."

"Sure you do. You know exactly what the problem is; you just don't want to admit it."

"Admit what?"

"That even though you'd like to believe you're above buying into all the fairy-tale crap, you're just like all those clients you love to make fun of."

"I am not," I objected too quickly.

Paige smiled knowingly at me. "What do you do for a living?"

"I bake cakes."

"No, you don't. You focus on conclusions."

"But I hate all that wedding bullshit, all that time and energy on something that only lasts a few hours." Paige's face tightened up and I felt like a callous idiot in light of the fact that Robin and I put the kibosh on her few hours just two days ago.

"Sure you do," she agreed quietly. "Because all that stuff gets in the way of what you really want, the culmination of it all, the big finale—the cake. It's your version of the happily ever after."

"So?"

"So, Charlie telling you that there is no conclusion, no final destination—it bothers you, because you've been waiting for the big finale, and if it's not coming, then what's the point?"

"That's not it at all."

"Sure, it is."

"No. It's that we're two people who watch clients make relationship choices for a living, and we know. We've seen firsthand when it works and when it doesn't. We can tell when it's a mismatch, and yet we still want to see each other. And if we can tell that there's something there worth pursuing, it's almost like a guarantee."

"There are no guarantees, Lauren. Take it from Robin; her guarantee expired when Mark left."

"But I could have had that with Neil," I mumbled, a little too loudly.

"Ah, yes, Neil." The lightbulb went on in Paige's head. "Now I understand. Charlie tells you he isn't interested in getting married and then Neil walks into the boutique ready to say *I do.*"

I felt so transparent that Paige could have just called me Casper.

"You let Neil leave without you for a reason, Lauren," Paige reminded me.

I was sure I had, but at the moment I was having a hard time remembering what that reason was.

When Paige dropped me off in front of my building, it was almost seven o'clock. As I let myself into my apartment, I could see the blinking red light from my answering machine casting an intermittent light into the air every few seconds. It was probably asking too much to expect a message from Neil explaining that he understood the significance of his cake selection and realized we were meant to be together. On the other hand, a part of me, the part that was controlled by hormones run amuck and the irrational desire to see where the next date led, hoped it was Charlie. Although I'd wished Charlie had been frantically calling me all weekend, there was only one message. One message wasn't exactly frantic. It was pathetic.

I pushed the PLAY button and went into the kitchen to pour myself some juice while the tape rewound. I'd left in such a hurry yesterday morning that there were no clean glasses, and so as I hoisted the Tropicana carton to my mouth, I waited by the counter for Charlie's deep voice to welcome me home. Instead, a different, albeit familiar, man's voice made its way across the living room.

"Please call me when you get this message," Steve practically pleaded, each labored word a stab at my heart. "Paige called off the wedding and I just don't get it."

Steve's message ended with a beep, and the machine informed me that there were no other new messages. I pushed the ERASE button and wondered how many more times Steve had tried to reach me that weekend, only to hear my recorded greeting.

Poor Steve. He sounded so confused, so utterly at a loss from the sudden turn of events with Paige. I liked Steve. I really did. But Paige was my best friend. She was the one who held my hair off my face as I deposited an evening's worth of Cambridge's best tequila into the public toilet stall at the Hong Kong. She was the one who drove three hours to pick me up at a Yale formal when I discovered my date in the stairwell with a look of ecstasy on his face, and then looked down and saw his roommate's girlfriend on her knees and realized why he was smiling. Not to mention the fact that I probably wouldn't even have a business today if it wasn't for Paige's support in the beginning. The least I could do in return was try to save her from making a huge mistake.

Without mentioning Steve once all weekend, Paige had managed to convince me that she was taking the intervention seriously. Unlike the guy who'd left the desperate message on my machine, Paige didn't waste her time moping around. She'd summoned up the strength of a woman who didn't believe in dwelling on things once she'd made up her mind. Unlike Robin, who seemed to marinate in her feelings for ages, Paige seemed almost too resolute, too comfortable with her decision, like she'd decided to redecorate her living room instead of rearrange her life.

Of course, running into Plaintiff Jeremy kind of set the weekend off on a different trajectory altogether. There wasn't much time to mope, with Robin ranting and raving about Jeremy the rest of the weekend. But even if Paige didn't let on that anything in her carefully managed existence had changed, I was sure that it would take more than two days' skiing in Vermont to get Steve out of her system.

Tonight, after parking her car and unpacking, Paige would be alone. Not just alone in her apartment, but really alone for the first time since she met Steve. I imagined her going through her date book, crossing out all the appointments she'd made—the florist, the caterer, the band, the travel agent. The months she'd been counting down with anticipation instead seeming to lie before her one after the other until her calendar reminded her to purchase another year.

Was it sad? Yes.

Did I wish Paige and Steve had picked the same cake and lived happily ever after? Of course.

Was I proud of the fact that Steve and Paige were no longer together or that I was the reason they were probably trying to make sense of the last forty-eight hours?

Absolutely not.

But if I could save Paige from getting hurt or making a mistake that years from now she'd regret, didn't I have to tell her? If I found out that she was about to buy a house that was built on an unstable foundation, wouldn't I say something, even if it meant she lost her down payment? If she was about to invest in a company that I knew was cooking the books, I'd tell her in a heartbeat. And so that's exactly what Robin and I did, because Paige was about to invest in one of the riskiest ventures out there.

If only more people learned to recognize the signs of trouble *before* they got to the tasting table. If only I could point out the indicators that said it was time to call it quits. Now *that* would be a book worth buying.

Maybe Robin's editor would be interested in a book

about my cake theory instead of the cakes themselves. Plenty of investment advisers wrote books on how to mitigate risk; I could do the same thing—only my advice would taste better.

I could explain how I was able to identify the relationships that were junk bonds. Sure, the upside could be huge, but were you willing to risk everything you had on the slight chance it would pay off? Then there were relationships that promised a steady, if average, return that was guaranteed— like municipal bonds or certificates of deposit. They didn't have the excitement of junk bonds, but they also didn't have the uncertainty. At least when you went to bed every night, you knew that your nest egg would still be there in the morning. I guess using that logic, Neil was my treasury bond.

I knew it wasn't a coincidence that starter marriages flourished during the dot-com era. I saw so many weddings funded by dot-com dollars and IPO stock options, you'd have thought there'd be a ticker-tape parade following all the happy couples hopping in their rented Bentleys on their way to the airport and a honeymoon at Cap Juluca. Of course it was a time when everyone bought into the propaganda of IPOs without looking too closely at the details or examining whether all the hype was warranted. Inevitably, when the bubble burst, these couples were left completely ill-prepared to deal with the fallout of relationships built on flimsy future promises, and we ended up with an entire generation divorced before the age of thirty.

So, when it was all said and done, I was relieved that Paige had decided to take our advice and cash out. And, given her experience with Mark, I wasn't surprised that Robin had decided to stay out of the market altogether. And me, I was banking on an emotional savings account.

If I were writing the *Lauren's Luscious Licks Guide to Emotional Investment,* what would my own strategy be? I'd continue waiting for the highest guaranteed return with the least chance of a downside, even if economists would argue that no such thing existed. In a perfect world, I could hedge my bets and put the odds in my favor by exploring things with Charlie *and* trying to find out if I'd missed something about Neil, something that I'd been oblivious to eight years ago when I let him move away.

Neil *and* Charlie. Now that was a great idea. It didn't have to be an either/or proposition, at least not until I figured out who offered the better return. Talk about a sound investment strategy.

That's why, after I unpacked and gave him another twenty minutes in which to dial my number, I decided to phone Charlie and reschedule our date. This was no time to play coy games or follow arbitrary rules created by women who saw dating as a dance between cat and mouse. I'd been the one to cancel at the last minute, and so it was only fair that I be the one to call him.

"I was starting to think maybe you thought I'd be bad for business," Charlie joked after I explained the impromptu ski trip. "So you had a good time?"

"We prescribed a little downhill therapy for my friend. She just broke up with her fiancé."

"That's too bad. Did your therapeutic approach work, Dr. Freud?"

"Maybe. Anyway, I was wondering if we could reschedule our dinner."

"I've got a pretty busy week, but how about lunch?"

We worked out the details, and after we hung up I resolved to stop worrying about Steve and Paige and Neil and let myself enjoy the prospect of Charlie—the only man I'd met who shared my insight into the coupling process. Maybe his altar aversion was something that would change with time. After all, he'd never dated me before.

I filled the tub with my favorite French vanilla bubble bath and climbed in, surrounded by all the lotions and potions any self-respecting woman felt obliged to waste her hard-earned money on. The warm, fragrant water melted away the post-skiing soreness in my muscles, and as I lay there with my eyes closed, my thoughts grew lazier. I pictured summer weekends on Martha's Vineyard with Charlie, sharing lobsters on the beach in Menemsha—until a sailboat floated by with Neil on the deck watching us through a pair of binoculars. I imagined autumn car rides to Vermont to see the fall foliage—and Neil following us in a state trooper car with a megaphone, demanding that we pull over and show him our license and registration. As hard as I tried to make my bath-time musings a Neil-free zone, he kept elbowing his way in, like those storm warnings that flash across the bottom of the TV screen and interrupt regularly scheduled programming.

I quickly dipped my fingers in the tub and splashed water on my face, replacing the vivid images with the white tiled wall of my bathroom. I needed to get some sleep. If I was going to start juggling Charlie and Neil, I needed all the energy I could muster.

13

"Jome lady called for you on Saturday."

"Did you get a name?" I asked, going over the packing slip of a delivery we'd just received.

Maria put down the bag of gum paste she was squeezing and slowly repeated her conversation with the caller as if I had the reasoning capacity of a four-year-old. "I asked if she wanted to make an appointment for a tasting and she said no. I asked if she was calling about a cake; she said not exactly. She wasn't buying a cake, and I'm not an answering service. She said she'd stop by today to see you."

I probably should have pulled rank and told Maria that taking messages *was* her job when I wasn't around. But as I watched her gently cradle the pastry bag in her hand and form perfect clusters of cornflower blue hyacinth petals to complement a pink tulip and chartreuse viburnum bouquet cake topper, I stayed silent. It would be one thing if I thought Maria's ornery manner was actually directed at me personally, but I knew that her irascible temperament had nothing to do with me or the boutique. Her sudden interest in my love life even made me think that maybe she really did care about me as more than the signature on her paycheck. I swear, sometimes I didn't know whether Maria was an example to me, or a warning. Besides, after experiencing what it'd be like without Maria in the kitchen, I was suitably humbled. Of course, there was no reason Maria should know that.

"So then everything went smoothly in my absence?"

"We managed just fine without your superior supervisory skills. I put the mail on your desk."

The boutique was always quiet in the beginning of the week, when business slowly simmered, building up day by day until the full boil of activity bubbled over into the weekend. On Mondays and Tuesdays, we recuperated from the flurry of Saturday's activity. The kitchen staff alternated days off, and without Hector and Benita on Mondays and Georgina and Dominique on Tuesdays, the kitchen was almost serene. Maria usually took Tuesdays off, so Mondays were spent compiling our supply list and receiving deliveries for the week's orders. Cakes were baked on Wednesdays and Thursdays, after which we wrapped the spongy circles and squares in plastic and placed them into the refrigerator to firm up before beginning the icing and decoration. While Lauren's Luscious Licks wasn't a cake factory, after eight years in business we were a fine-tuned machine.

As Maria had promised, on my desk I found a stack of white windowed envelopes from our suppliers and several handwritten envelopes. I bypassed the invoices and the personal letters that undoubtedly contained deposits from clients, and pulled out the Pottery Barn catalog that waited for me at the bottom of the pile like a four-color, eight-by-ten invitation to dream. As the other mail sat unopened, I slowly turned pages and studied the catalog photos in detail. The Bordeaux table stood in a faux dining room, its top set with linen napkins, wide shallow plates and wineglasses as if just beyond the seam in the catalog a French country kitchen waited with coq au vin steaming on the stove.

"Look at you circling pictures like a kid with her nose in the Sears Christmas Wish Book," Maria scoffed.

"Nothing wrong with a little wish list," I told her and circled the Brittany chandelier hanging over the table.

"Sure, as long as you're willing to wait twelve months for Santa to slide down your chimney carrying your wishes in his sack."

For some reason the image of Maria and Santa in the sack popped into my mind, her dark hair tucked into Mrs. Claus's kerchief as they rolled around like two balls under the sheets, never quite able to wrap their arms around one another. It wasn't an image I wanted to hold in my head for very long, lest it become indelible.

"Are you telling me you never believed in Santa Claus?"

"Oh, I believed in Santa, all right. I was the one who insisted on making macaroons and Italian wedding cookies for him just like my nonni did; I even stuffed the pastry shells with preserves all by myself."

Of course, Maria was a regular pastry prodigy. I could picture her as a child, standing on a milk crate so she could reach the kitchen counter, a red bandanna already keeping her pigtails from falling into the mixing bowl. I once asked Maria why a bandanna and not a chef's hat or hair net. "Please," she'd answered, as if the reasons were self-evident. "I'm working, not walking a runway."

Even as a young child with cookie dough between her pudgy fingers, Maria knew she'd found a place where she belonged. The kitchen wasn't just the room where her mother served dinner and her brothers started food fights. It was where she could experiment with different ingredients and surprise her family with new creations. She knew she didn't want to do anything else.

When I prepared that first chocolate almond torte from the Martha Stewart cookbook, I never thought I'd end up doing this for a living. I didn't even know what almond paste was, but because I was out of a job, I had the time to figure it out. Now, not only did I know that almond paste is a mixture of ground almonds, sugar, and glucose, I used to have a favorite brand imported from Denmark.

Unlike Maria, who seemed to be born with a wooden spoon in her hand, I stumbled into the kitchen—or was given a very firm shove in the form of a pink slip that arrived two days after Neil left for DC. My ego wasn't merely bruised; it was checked into intensive care, placed on life support and given a fifty-fifty chance of survival. The uncertainty, the feeling that I was flailing about for any life raft willing to throw me a line and reel me in, drove me to consider a job in any field that I could remotely be qualified for as a recent college graduate with a major in history.

I had no illusions that my bank balance would be able to

sustain me, and so I registered with every temp agency that would let me fill out an application and prayed my phone would ring with daily assignments until I was able to find another job. In our little world of independent overachieving women, I'd been prepared for much, but not failure.

Robin and Paige made their daily rounds, showing up at my apartment to check on my progress. I even offered to provide them with a clipboard to hang from the foot of my bed so they didn't have to duplicate questions: *Have you looked in the want ads? Did you go through your Rolodex for possible networking contacts? Is there another temp agency you can call in the meantime?*

But not once did either of them suggest I pack it in and follow Neil to DC, and they never asked the one question that now seemed to be begging for an answer—did I make a mistake letting Neil go without me?

If I hadn't had Paige's party to take my mind off the fact that I was about one month's rent away from having to call my parents to ask for money, I would have been a goner. In the days after Paige's birthday party, my meager galley kitchen, with its two-foot-wide linoleum floor designed to distinguish it from the rest of my sprawling four-hundred-square-foot studio, provided me with welcome distractions. After the success of Paige's birthday torte, I was asked to make a going-away cake for a woman in her office, an anniversary cake for another agent's daughter and dessert for a brunch. Without hesitating, I happily, and gratefully, accepted the requests and set off for the bookstore in search of more instruction. When I wasn't poring over cookbooks, I conducted my own form of field research, visiting local bakeries and patisseries to check out what I was up against. And I was up against a lot.

There was no way I could compete with the elaborate sugar roses and chocolate drapings that were propped up and displayed behind glass like precious jewels. Instead I decided to attempt desserts that were long on elegance and short on artistry.

For the going-away party, I settled on an apricot-ginger pound cake with rum glaze. I was scrupulously following the directions, making sure that all the ingredients were at room temperature and that I gently folded the apricots and ginger into the batter, when Paige called to see how things were going. I checked to see if the preheat light on the oven was still lit before telling Paige about my going-away party selection.

"*Pound cake?*" Paige had repeated, as if I'd said I was making mud pies with sprinkles on top.

"Not normal pound cake," I started to explain, even as I was beginning to doubt my choice. "I splurged on a cake pan with a decorative fleur-de-lis relief so it'll look elegant."

"Why a pound cake?" she asked again, obviously beginning to have second thoughts herself.

"Because you're having the party at the office, so you don't want lots of crumbs, and pound cakes are moist."

"Okay," she agreed and continued to listen.

"I didn't want anything with too much icing; that can get messy, and it didn't seem very professional to have everyone licking whipped cream off their lips. Besides, everyone in your office is addicted to coffee, and what goes better with coffee than pound cake?"

Paige was silent for a minute. "You know, you're right. You really know what you're doing, don't you?"

"Absolutely," I assured her, eyeing the paintbrush I'd bought at the hardware store as a substitute for the pastry brush the recipe called for. "I know exactly what I'm doing."

I had a small problem with the vanilla-bean cheesecake I'd planned for the intimate anniversary gathering. I figured any old cake pan would work in place of a springform pan, but when I tried to remove the forty ounces of cream cheese held together precariously by five eggs, I learned my lesson and ran out for the pan the recipe specified. I also learned a second lesson during that fiasco—there's a reason chefs tend to be generously proportioned, and if I was going to bake I couldn't eat my mistakes without paying a hefty price for it later.

After I'd bought another five packages of cream cheese and made a second attempt, my cheesecake emerged from the pan looking just like the cookbook's glossy photo—its velvety golden top meeting the edges of a firm shortbread crumb crust. I brushed some fresh violets with egg whites, sprinkled them with a light coating of sugar and placed the candied flowers on the center of my cheesecake. It was gorgeous.

I stood back and marveled at my creation. It could easily have been placed in the glass case of one of the bakeries I'd visited—it was that lovely. But what I really looked forward to, even more than the anniversary couple's delight at the candied pansies, was when my cake would be served to six people and they'd discover that my cheesecake was more than just a pretty face.

After the vanilla-bean cheesecake, word spread quickly—the colonial army wouldn't have had to rely on Paul Revere if they'd had Realtors. The agents in Paige's office told nearly every client about my desserts, and they in turn told their friends. Within a few months I was up to my elbows in flour and sugar and vanilla, and I'd run out of room in my kitchen for all the new gadgets I was buying on a daily basis.

Although I made a lot of mistakes in the beginning—an especially gruesome bittersweet chocolate cake comes to mind—I learned and kept moving forward. I started depending on recipes less and less, and relying more on my own tastes. And coming from someone whose sweet tooth once tended to lean more toward Devil Dogs than strawberry mascarpone trifle, that was saying a lot.

The kitchen counter quickly became overrun with my supplies, and every day another rectangular cake pan or copper cooling bowl crept toward the living area of my studio. A secondhand bookshelf held Tupperware containers filled with cake flour and confectioners' sugar, and I hung a makeshift utensil rack for my measuring cups and spoons.

The day I realized that I was sharing my night table with a twelve-pound KitchenAid paddle mixer, I knew it was time to acknowledge that I wasn't just making some extra money until I got a real job—I'd found a career. I decided it was time to find some retail space. Looking back, I could see that that decision was the start of Lauren's Luscious Licks and, in a way, the beginning of the end for me.

Before I moved to the boutique on Newbury and hired Maria, I loved the feel of flour, so fine after sifting that it was almost slippery in my hands. Watching a solid mass of butter thaw until it gave up its glistening shape and succumbed to the paddle mixer was almost surreal. I'd kept my nails short,

clipped square, so ingredients didn't get packed under—
even though the flour that sometimes found its way under
my nails did result in a quick French manicure.

I used to love getting my hands dirty, watching cakes rise
and egg whites stiffen, the way somehow it all came together, all the ingredients mixing together to make something entirely different yet something that was completely
reliant upon every component (as I learned when I thought
that there couldn't be much difference between baking powder and baking soda, and soon discovered that no matter how
similar ingredients may seem, they each had their purpose).

When the OPEN sign was officially hung on the front door
of Lauren's Luscious Licks, I'd willingly handed the baking
over to Maria, maybe a little too easily, to focus on the big
picture until I knew how many tastings I could schedule each
day and where the delivery entrances to Boston's finest ho-
tels were located, but not how each perfectly formed sugar
rose was created, one petal at a time.

"Hello," Maria called out to me, taking my attention
away from the navy Manhattan leather armchair that would
look so good in a study. "Can I get a little help over here?"

I closed the catalog, placed it on top of the pile in my
desk drawer and went to help Maria with the deliveries.

That afternoon I had appointments with three brides—four
if you counted the two women getting married to each other.
The first bride, a woman who brought me a swatch of material from her wedding dress and wanted to replicate the
alençon lace on a six-tier red velvet cake, was a layup. She
seemed surprised that I wasn't even a little concerned about
the intricate pattern, but I told her that I'd seen worse. When
I pulled out the portfolio and showed her the different laces
we've managed to etch into the sides of cakes, she called her
mom on a credit card–sized cell phone and squealed with
delight.

My next appointment was with our best repeat customer,
a dubious distinction for most people, but one that Alexandra
Cassidy almost seemed to wear with pride.

"Last time we went dark and rich with the white chocolate mousse filling and chocolate fudge cake," she reminded

me. "And even though Howard was as rich as the cake, unfortunately he was also just as dense." Alexandra paused as if waiting for me to agree before she continued. "But Spencer is so amazing; I have a feeling that this is *it*."

"I hope you're right." I smiled and Alexandra beamed back.

"This time I was thinking something light, something a little fun. After all, Spencer is only thirty-seven."

Did I mention that Alexandra was about sixty, although her lids had been lifted so often she easily passed for forty, even if her eyebrows seemed to be stretched taut in the center of her forehead like blond McDonald's arches.

I suggested a yellow cake with passion fruit and orange cream filling, and cream cheese icing. Alexandra was a pro, and less than five minutes later we'd decided on the shape and decoration as well.

Alexandra clapped her hands together and held them that way, like a TV evangelist. "That's it! I knew you'd come up with exactly what I wanted. You are *so* good." Alexandra took out her checkbook and started to fill in the deposit amount. She tore the check out with a flourish but held on to it before placing it in my hand. "You know, if this does work out, I'm going to miss you. We had some good years together."

She wasn't kidding. Our relationship had lasted longer than her last two husbands combined.

Amanda and Allison were planning their August wedding and were my last appointment of the day.

The two women knew exactly what they were looking for. Even though they politely sampled each of the cake slices displayed on the table, when I asked which piece they preferred, neither wasted any time before pointing to the same plate and declaring, "This one."

I loved it when couples were so in tune. It renewed my faith in marriage, even if in this case the couple was destined for almost half a year's worth of PMS.

I laid the portfolio on the tasting table and we went through the pages slowly, allowing Amanda and Allison to point out what they liked and didn't like about each of the cakes.

"How about using fresh flowers instead?" Amanda suggested when Allison pointed out a few sugar flowers she liked.

"That'd be pretty," Allison agreed. "Maybe we could use the same flowers we're having in the bouquets?"

"Sure, I could have the florist make a smaller version for a topper." I flipped through the pages of the portfolio and showed them a similar design.

Allison reached for Amanda's hand and squeezed it. They looked at each other for a second before nodding in agreement.

Amanda leaned in closer to the picture and scrutinized the photo of the lavender phlox, cream-colored vendela and blue curiosa cake topper. "You know, my mom actually asked me if we were going to have two plastic brides on top of the cake."

Allison laughed. "And my dad asked which one of us would be addressed as *Mr.* after we're married."

"When she registered she put me down as the groom," Amanda pointed out.

"I didn't have a choice!"

"Then why weren't you the groom?" Amanda let go of Allison's hand with feigned irritation before winking at me and breaking out into a smile.

Allison laid her arm over Amanda's shoulder and pulled her closer before planting a kiss on Amanda's head and telling me, "I couldn't pull off a tux."

The boutique's front door opened and a cold whisper of air invaded the warm gallery, followed by a khaki-clad man. "Hello, ladies."

Amanda and Allison had been expecting him. "Lauren, this is my brother, Hugh," said Amanda.

"Hi, Hugh." I stood up and started to clear away the tasting plates.

Amanda gave her brother a hug. "Hugh is one of the few people who doesn't look at us like we're crazy for doing this."

Hugh shrugged. "Hey, as long as I'm not asked to be the maid of honor, I'm fine with it."

"We keep trying to set him up with women, but he's not exactly a willing participant."

"Must I remind you that the last time I went on a blind date with a woman, she ended up falling in love with my sister? My friends still won't let me live that down."

"Hugh wasn't my type, but I didn't know it at the time." Allison stood up and leaned in to give Hugh a kiss on his cheek, but he grabbed her from behind, spun her around, and bent her backward into a very Fred Astaire–like dip before kissing her on her nose.

"He thinks all these fancy moves will show me I've picked the wrong sibling," Allison told me, her head hanging upside down so that the tips of her blond curls swept along the floor.

"It's a good thing I don't have a fragile ego," Hugh conceded and helped Allison upright.

"Hey, Lauren, know any women looking for a handsome, eligible mortgage broker?" Amanda asked.

"Let's not worry about my eligible status right now. What'd you two go with?" Hugh stuck a finger into the half-eaten slice of sour cream fudge cake and swiped a glob of icing before Allison could slap his hand away. "Good stuff," he noted, licking his finger.

"We went with the orange blossom yellow cake as planned," Allison confirmed.

"With raspberry mousse and pink pistachio-scented buttercream," Amanda added, completing Allison's sentence.

Hugh shook his head, disappointed. "I see my advice meant nothing to you two."

"Please." Allison bumped her shoulder against Hugh, nudging him away from the table. "This guy wanted us to get a carrot cake!"

"What can I say? I'm a sucker for old-fashioned carrot cake—my tastes are perfectly pedestrian compared to my sister and her girlfriend here."

"Fiancée," Allison and Amanda reminded him.

While the two brides went on to describe for Hugh the fresh magenta and coral poppies and peonies they wanted cascading down the cake's tiers, I reassessed the carrot cake–loving mortgage broker in front of me. Hugh was the polar opposite of Steve—preppy, clean-cut and involved in a fast-moving industry. His hair was conservatively cut, cropped close to his neck with neatly manicured sideburns that were probably kept in check every morning courtesy of Gillette. But a wave of hair falling casually across his forehead belied Hugh's otherwise exceedingly ordinary haircut and made me think that perhaps this guy was someone Paige should meet. He was probably five foot nine or five foot ten, max, which meant he was perfectly proportional for Paige, and any man who could find humor in the fact that his sister's future bride was originally supposed to fall for him, well, he couldn't take himself too seriously.

Besides, I felt like I owed it to Paige.

"So, you're a mortgage broker?" I asked Hugh.

"Yep. Why, are you buying a place?"

I shook my head and gave Hugh a conspiring smile. "No, but I have a friend that I think you should meet."

14

$\mathscr{M}$aria was gone and I was about to lock up and call it a day when the front door swung open and a tall blond woman in a black cropped wool peacoat rushed in.

"Hi, Lauren. I'm Vivian Linden, Robin's editor," she gushed, approaching me in long strides. "Sorry I'm late. I am so excited to meet you—just thrilled!"

I reached for Vivian's hand, but she brushed it away and embraced me like we were long-lost sorority sisters; the only thing missing was the secret handshake. "I have so many friends who love your work, and after talking with Robin, I feel like I already know you."

Vivian was a lot younger than I'd anticipated, which meant she was probably around my age. Whenever I pictured publishers or editors, I envisioned either caftan-wearing women with hair graying at their temples and pulled back absentmindedly into updos kept in place by number two pencils, or Diane Keaton look-alikes in vintage suits and funky berets. Either way, I figured they lived alone with mountains of manuscripts piled up on their night tables. But Vivian was neither hiding underneath a caftan nor an Annie Hall clone. And, considering she was dressed in trendy low-rise black pants that made it clear not only that her stomach was flat but that her ass was perfectly toned, I doubt she spent her nights alone in bed reading.

Vivian walked around the gallery with her arms stretched

out like Julie Andrews atop an Austrian mountain before she burst into song.

"This place is perfect," Vivian cooed, although she didn't bother elaborating on what it was perfect for. "Did Robin tell you my idea?"

"Sort of. She said you were thinking about a book of my cakes."

"Oh, Lauren, not just *a* book. *The* book. The definitive book on wedding cakes by Lauren Gallagher, creator of Lauren's Luscious Licks." Vivian held her hands up, her thumbs and forefingers in right angles as if she was trying to visualize how the boutique would look in a frame. "I see pictures of your cakes, glossy, high-concept photos by a master photographer, maybe Pietro Visconte or Randy Bock," she mused, naming photographers I thought shot only fashion models.

"Aren't there already books like that?" I asked, thinking that if I could prove my theory with Paige and Hugh, Vivian would really have a story worth publishing.

"Lauren, of course there are wedding cake books, lots of boring books by authors people have never heard of. But there aren't any books by Lauren Gallagher." I must not have looked convinced because Vivian tipped her head to the side and reached for my hand, which she patted. "I don't think you realize what you have here. People come to you for an ideal—a vision of how their wedding day is meant to be, the conclusion of months, sometimes years, of planning. Lauren's Luscious Licks is a form of wish fulfillment. Nobody comes here because your cakes taste good."

It sounded like Vivian had been talking to Robin. I knew there was supposed to be a complement in there somewhere. I just had difficulty finding it. "They don't?"

"Don't get me wrong; your cakes are fantastic, absolutely divine. But they're more about a standard. You've set the standard for wedding cakes the way Vera Wang has set a standard for wedding dresses. There are tons of books about wedding dresses, but when a bride sees *Vera Wang on Weddings* on the shelf in a bookstore, she buys it. And why? Because it's by Vera Wang."

Vivian went on to describe her vision for the coffee-table book, complete with cover art and a huge launch party that would simulate—what else?—a wedding reception.

"So, what do you think?"

"It sounds beautiful, but do you really think you could sell a book filled with just photographs?"

"Oh, but it's not just pretty pictures of cakes. They'd be organized any way you see fit: by season or month, or even type of wedding—formal, garden, destination. You'd have total creative license."

"And people would buy that?"

"Lots of people. Women, mostly—women like you, who believe that the cake represents more than just dessert, that it represents the crowning moment. It's all about anticipation, really, isn't it? We want to heighten that anticipation, let it build page by page, photo by photo, creating a cake-induced climax that leaves women glowing and satisfied, like it was all worth the wait." Vivian basked in her own afterglow for a few seconds before coming back down to earth. "Don't forget; while brides may be willing to devote hours to selecting just the right cake, when the big day arrives, sitting down and eating cake when you have two hundred guests to entertain isn't exactly a priority."

Right. As Robin pointed out, they've all moved on to the chicken dance.

"Think what it would do for your business. And then there are all sorts of tie-in possibilities—you could become like the Emeril of wedding cakes."

Vivian bit her lip and squeezed her eyes shut, as if the mere thought of my wedding-cake empire was just too great. "Think big!"

The Emeril of wedding cakes—it didn't get much bigger than that.

I wanted to tell Vivian about my cake theory, but I was afraid she'd react like Maria did and call my idea half-baked. Then again, she was Robin's editor, and if Robin was willing to consider that there might be some truth to my predictions, then maybe Vivian would, too.

"What if I told you that I thought the cake a couple

chooses says a lot about their relationship?" I asked cautiously, ready to drop the topic if Vivian wasn't convinced.

"I'd say I was intrigued."

"Then what if I said I thought I had a talent for predicting whether a couple will break up or not by watching them pick out a cake?"

"I'd say we had a best seller in our future." Vivian rubbed her hands together, savoring my revelation. "Have you ever been able to put two people together because of the cake?"

"Not yet; why?"

"Well, it's just that brides are optimistic people by definition; predicting disaster is probably not something they want to read about. I had more of a feel-good book in mind."

I saw Vivian's point, but I couldn't help but feel a little let down. "Sure, that makes sense."

"Great. I'll work up an offer and get back to you. You may want to get a lawyer or agent involved. Robin's agent is fabulous."

Robin had an agent?

"Tootles!" Vivian tossed a wave over her shoulder and as quickly as she'd arrived, she was gone.

After the whirlwind that was Vivian, I needed her idea to settle in. I closed up the boutique and walked down Newbury Street toward Clarendon, where Pottery Barn shone like a beacon for young, attractive men and women methodically setting the stage for their lives with backdrops of earth-toned Charleston sofas and Sundari kilim rugs, accented with carefully placed props of stoneware, glass and antiqued pewter.

As I pulled the giant glass door open, I was bathed in the smell of newness. Buttery leather sofas and glossy wooden end tables, jewel-colored chenille throws tossed casually over the arm of a chair—they all tempted me to sit down, throw my feet up on an ottoman, and declare myself home. But of course, my home looked nothing like this, yet. Someday it would, when I finally settled into a place that I knew I'd be in for a while, or when I just settled down, period. But for now I had no problem using the Newbury Street store as a substitute.

Although Vivian went on and on about how much she loved the idea of a cake book, she didn't mention how much she was willing to pay for one. Even so, just the idea that she'd get back to me with an offer sounded good. I mean how hard could it be to make a few cakes and have some spectacular photographer snap some shots of them? But if I could get Paige and Hugh together in time, maybe I could give Vivian the feel-good book she was after. There was no reason why my cake theory couldn't work in reverse— getting people together before they were seated at the tasting table. Besides, I liked the idea of being the harbinger of good news. It sure beat a lifetime of interventions.

I shifted into browsing mode and started on the left side of the store. A few customers wandered through the aisles clutching reams of paper I recognized from the bridal registry printer, pages filled with margarita glasses, Audrey flatware, serving platters and table linens. They kept glancing at the sheets of paper, comparing the SKUs on the pages with the items they held in their hands.

I wended my way through the store, pausing briefly when I recognized items Robin had picked for her own bridal registry. In an ironic twist of fate, the store where Robin and Mark had picked the props for their life together was also the place that gave it a final nudge over the cliffs into oblivion. I'd heard the story so many times in excruciating detail that I no longer had to picture what it was like for Robin that afternoon. I felt like I'd been there.

On their second wedding anniversary, Robin had taken Mark shopping for her assistant's birthday gift, and Mark had trailed solemnly behind, something she attributed at the time to nothing more than male shopping aversion. Every once in a while they'd walk past a display, a wall-less room impeccably laid out to tempt shoppers into thinking it was actually possible to create a similar environment at home without the help of merchandisers and design professionals. And when they passed those displays, Robin caught glimpses of herself in the distressed-framed mirrors and liked what she saw.

They looked good together, Robin and Mark. With her chestnut highlights falling over the shoulder of her black leather coat, her sleek blowout creating a stark contrast to the wavy hair curling at the collar of Mark's brown bomber jacket, they looked like an advertisement she might see in one of her seminar brochures. An ad that showed women how it was supposed to be when you grew up and finally married the guy you were never sure you'd get.

Eventually, Robin selected the fishbowl vase for her assistant and, on her way to the register to pay, stopped in front of the Emma cake stand.

"What do you think? For an anniversary cake?" she'd asked Mark, running her finger along the stand's scalloped and beaded edges.

"Sure," he'd answered flatly and then added, "I guess we should stop on the way home and pick up a cake."

On the way back to their apartment, Robin and Mark bought a cake at the grocery store, a white one with dandelion yellow piping and three fluffy yellow rosettes (even as she was picking it out, Robin knew I'd disapprove, of both the cake and the fact that she hadn't ordered one in advance from Lauren's Luscious Licks). Once I'd told her my cake theory Robin undoubtedly saw this event as ominous foreshadowing of what was to come.

That night Mark brought the cake out on the new Emma cake stand, a single flickering candle in its center struggling to breathe as he awkwardly placed the cake on the table in front of Robin. Looking back, she often wondered if he was trying to give her a hint—that the solitary candle trying to survive on its own was in fact meant to prepare her for what would follow. Mark told Robin to blow out the candle, which she promptly did, forgetting to even make a wish. When the flame was out, Mark said more than he had since they returned home from the shopping trip.

"I'm not happy," he said, his eyes fixed on the thin line of smoke wafting up from the candle she'd just extinguished. "I don't want to be married anymore. I want a divorce." (At this point in the story I always let my jaw drop open, as it was my duty to act shocked even though I knew it was coming.)

Once Mark made his proclamation, Robin knew it was over. There would be no therapy, no hashing it out until late at night, trying to figure out how to fix things. Even as his words echoed through her body before finally settling somewhere in the pit of her stomach, she steeled herself against him; she'd be damned if she'd disagree with him, if she'd humiliate herself by asking him the question that swam through her head: Why now? Before they got engaged, she'd given him reasons to get out. He'd even found out about one. But once Mark slipped that ring on Robin's finger, she'd stopped questioning where they stood or seeking answers from other men.

Sitting there facing Mark, with his blank face containing no sign of remorse or doubt, Robin felt compelled to agree, to tacitly admit defeat and save face, as if she'd been thinking the very same thing but had been waiting until after the cake to break the news. (This was where I usually nodded my head, a sign that I understood exactly what Robin was thinking at this precise moment.)

Mark left the apartment a few minutes later. But before closing the door behind him, Mark left a list of the things he wanted. It was a short list that included the stereo, a rubber tree plant he'd had since college and his CDs—a list that included the belongings that mattered to Mark but didn't include one single thing from their own Pottery Barn registry. ("What, not one single thing?" I usually cried, appalled.)

Later, when Robin brought the still uncut and uneaten cake into the kitchen and placed it on the counter, she picked up the matches and relit the candle. She closed her eyes and blew, wishing with all her might that Mark would drop dead. (I always patted Robin on the shoulder when the story was over, as if to say *Good for you; that son of a bitch deserves to be dead.*)

I'd shopped in this very Pottery Barn for the items on Robin's registry. Although it was only four years ago, it seemed like a lifetime, like a different Robin. She'd always been so concerned about not letting a man define her, and here she ended up letting a man's exit become the defining event in her life. Funny how that worked out.

I continued wending my way through the store, following the smell of potpourri and room spray until I reached a display of large, square Pottery Barn coffee-table books propped up on stands. The cover of the book titled *Bed* showed overstuffed pillows snuggled against a cozy shearling bedcover casually turned down at one corner. Three old-fashioned suitcases were stacked bedside for night tables, which, after thinking about Robin's story, didn't seem like such a great idea. Why give someone the opportunity to think about leaving as he was lying in bed with you? I removed the book from the display and flipped through the pages.

Was this what Vivian had in mind? A book of eye-pleasing photos that reminded readers that nobody's bedroom really looked like those pictures. Even the casual touches intended to give the rooms a lived-in feel didn't reflect real life—in real life all those woven wicker baskets would be overflowing with magazines and books and other things tucked into the tasteful bins that provided convenient hiding spots when company visited. But as I continued to turn the pages, I saw that the book had more than just pictures of professionally designed rooms; it also had tips and how-tos that showed readers that, in fact, they too could re-create an atmosphere that resembled the picture on the page. Now that was a hell of a lot more interesting.

As I replaced *Bed* and reached for *Bath,* my cell phone's techno-ring cried for attention.

"Where are you?" Robin asked impatiently.

"Pottery Barn."

"Oh, Jesus. Back to the mother ship, huh? So, I got your message; what's up?"

I sat down on a cranberry twill Pearce sectional and settled in like the store was my own living room. "Do you think we should set Paige up with someone?"

"Don't you think Paige has enough going on in her life right now?"

I'd actually been thinking that Paige didn't have enough going on. Sure, she was keeping busy with work, but what about all the hours she was alone? Paige needed someone else to keep her occupied so she didn't dwell on everything she'd just given up. And Hugh was just what the doctor ordered.

But the other half of Operation Save Paige obviously didn't feel obligated to try to make up for Paige's broken engagement. "Besides, who the hell would we set Paige up with? It's not like either of us is exactly surrounded by single guys all day."

"I met this guy; he was in the boutique meeting up with his sister."

Robin sounded skeptical. "So you want to set her up with a guy who helps his sister pick out a wedding cake?"

"No, he was meeting her for dinner. Anyway, he was exactly what I'd picture Paige going for, and he just happens to be a mortgage broker."

"So they can make beautiful property transfers together?"

"I was just thinking that maybe we owed it to her, considering we're the reason she's not getting married anymore."

"She still has the ring, you know," Robin informed me, but I wasn't sure what I was supposed to make of that bit of information.

"She does?"

"Yep."

"Well, I know she hasn't spoken with Steve. He left a few messages on my machine, but eventually he stopped calling. She didn't want me to talk with him."

Robin seemed to be weighing the two contradictory signals Paige was sending: Was she holding on to the ring because it meant there was hope? Or did she tell me not to talk to Steve because she knew it was hopeless?

"So, let's set her up with this guy, if he's willing," Robin agreed. "How much more damage could we do?"

I was hoping we'd be able to undo the damage we'd done. "Vivian came to see me today."

Robin laughed, as if remembering something funny Vivian said. "She's a riot, isn't she?"

"I didn't know you had an agent."

"I needed someone to make sure my interests were represented. So are you going to do the book?"

"Vivian's going to get back to me with an offer."

"You don't sound that convinced."

"I don't know. I picture all these brides-to-be drooling

over cake pictures like they're confectionary porn instead of delicious desserts that are meant to be eaten."

"And how is that different from what you do now?"

Maybe that was what really bothered me. I wasn't so sure anymore.

15

I'm going out for a little bit," I announced, pushing my chair back. It was Wednesday afternoon and Julie had her appointment at Gamble Mansion. I hadn't figured out how to proceed with Neil, but I figured I could at least get some answers from Julie.

It seemed impossible that the Neil I watched drive away in a rented moving truck could be the same guy who showed up in the boutique. There'd been nothing overtly wrong with him; he didn't even let one little annoyingly incorrect declaration that he could care less slip from his lips. Lips that used to kiss me, I might point out.

If anyone could convince me that Neil and I were never meant to be, that he and Julie settled on the same cake and I just happened to share the happy couple's tastes, you'd think his fiancée would be the one.

"Where are you going?" Maria asked.

"To check out a reception site."

"For who?"

I hesitated before answering. "Neil."

"You mean Neil and his fiancée, don't you?"

I shrugged.

"Is this still about that nutty theory of yours?"

"Of course! What else would it be about?"

"Charlie."

"Charlie? This has nothing to do with Charlie. Besides, who have you been talking to about Charlie?"

"Paige."

"Well, whatever she said, she's wrong."

"Then what's this about?"

"The cake!" I repeated. Didn't Maria listen? "Did you not hear what I just told you?"

"I heard you. I just don't understand you."

It didn't matter if Maria understood me. She wasn't the one who had the answers I needed.

"Don't do it, Lauren," she warned, her face fixed and serious.

But I was already on my way out the door.

Walking into Gamble Mansion is like stepping back to a time when wealthy merchants built elegant homes in Back Bay and introduced their debutante daughters at coming-out parties that rivaled even the most extravagant wedding. In fact, that's exactly why the mansion's Louis XV ballroom was built. I'd provided cakes to more than one hundred ceremonies at the mansion and was intimately familiar with all of its historical nooks and crannies.

While I knew what to expect of the tasteful foyer, I didn't know that Julie would be standing in the center of the foyer's Oriental carpet when I arrived, almost as if she'd been waiting for me.

"Lauren! What are you doing here?" Julie rushed over to me and grabbed my hand, pulling me toward her mother. "Mom, this is Lauren Gallagher. How'd you know I'd be here?"

"You mentioned something the other day and I had a question to ask you," I stammered, hoping she'd buy the line I'd been rehearsing. With any luck I'd get an invitation to stay. "I'm working on a book of cakes and I was wondering if I could include the cake you and Neil selected."

"Of course you can," Julie answered quickly, making me feel like an idiot for making the trip to the mansion for something so stupid. "But you didn't have to come all the way here to ask me."

"I'm on deadline," I lied.

"Well, since you're here, I'd love it if you'd take the tour with us and give your opinion. I'm still a novice at this."

Before I had a chance to answer, the events manager came toward us, a clipboard in one hand. "Hello, Lauren."

"Hi, Susan."

Julie looked confused and then hit the side of her head with the heel of her hand. I almost expected her to tell us she should have had a V8. "Of course you two already know each other. I should have realized that."

Susan nodded graciously. "You're lucky to have Lauren making your cake."

Julie met her mother's eyes and they turned to me and practically genuflected. "We know."

Susan clapped her hands. "We'd better get started; we have a lot to go over."

Susan led the way and we all followed as she navigated through the wood-paneled library where Neil and Julie's guests would enjoy cocktails before heading into the ballroom for dinner and dancing under about ten thousand crystal droplets that would sprinkle light like falling stars.

Julie kept glancing over at me, as if asking for my approval.

"It's lovely," I told her, and scanned the library for a decanter of scotch.

"Were you interested in holding the ceremony indoors or outside?" Susan asked Julie, who in turn shrugged and asked, "Lauren, what do you think?"

I think you shouldn't be asking a woman who's gotten up close and personal with your fiancé's penis. "Let's take a look."

Susan took her cue and made a grand gesture of releasing the French doors leading to a private courtyard.

"Why don't you walk outside and look around," Susan suggested, nudging Julie out the door. "It really is beautiful."

Julie crooked a finger at me and I trailed behind. I just hoped her mom couldn't see the forked tail tucked between my legs.

Susan and Julie's mother stayed in the library discussing the hors d'oeuvres, leaving Julie and me alone in the courtyard, surrounded by nothing but frozen flower gardens and the ghosts of weddings past.

While Julie tried to calculate how many chairs the space could hold, I figured it was now or never.

"When did you know Neil was the one?" I practically whispered.

"Probably on our second date." Julie paused and looked at me. "I know that sounds crazy, but it's true."

"What was it about him that made you know?"

"It wasn't one big thing, more like lots of little things. It's not like I made a list, you know?" Julie laughed at the ridiculous notion that anybody would make a list.

I laughed along with her. A list. How crazy.

"When Neil picked me up for our second date he brought me laundry detergent."

"I hear that's usually a gift reserved for the third date."

Julie giggled. "That's funny. No, really, when we went out on our first date I kept telling him how good he smelled, and he told me it was this detergent he used. So he brought me a bottle. Neil's a sweet guy."

Needless to say.

"He'll make a great dad," she added.

No argument there.

"And he's obviously intelligent," Julie pointed out.

Obviously.

She smiled shyly, and I was ready to clamp my hands over my ears, afraid Julie would reveal his prowess between the sheets and blood would start spurting from my ears. "And good-looking."

No blood, just agreement. He really was.

"And there's just so much more, you know?"

I nodded. I couldn't disagree with a single thing Julie said.

"So, what do you think?" Susan stood in the doorway, waiting for an answer.

"We love it," Julie sang.

We?

Julie skipped up the steps to hug her mom and then went off arm in arm with Susan to tour the ballroom.

Julie's mom waited for me to walk with her. "So, Julie told me you used to date Neil."

"Years ago."

"He's wonderful, isn't he? I bet you're sorry he got away." She nudged me good-naturedly, like we were two girlfriends sharing an inside joke.

But the joke was on her, because I didn't *let* Neil get away. I'd given him away. And I was about to change that.

16

$\mathcal{I}$ flipped through the *Boston* magazine I found on the seating area's coffee table while I waited for Paige. She was in the midst of negotiating a deal for one of the Boston Celtics, and they were down to their final offer. Paige had the Celtic on her cell phone while she played hardball with the seller's agent on her desk line.

Paige had asked Robin and me to go check out a house she was seriously thinking of buying. Apparently the property had been on the market for a while, and although she thought it was a great investment, Paige wanted three sets of eyes there to see whether she was missing something glaringly wrong.

Although I couldn't hear what she was saying, I knew from the look of concentration on her face that the call was nearing an end.

I crossed and uncrossed my legs, trying to get comfortable on the black leather couch that was designed more for aesthetic impact than client relaxation. Robin was already ten minutes late, but I didn't mind because I needed some time away from the boutique to decide my course of action. I was meeting Charlie for lunch tomorrow, but I still wasn't sure how to proceed with Neil. I knew he was temporarily working at his company's downtown office, but how would I explain that I just happened to be waiting outside his building when he showed up?

When the front door opened and set off the soft chime

used to notify the agents of a new arrival, I looked up for Robin.

But it wasn't Robin. In fact, it was the anti-Robin. It was Robin's ex-husband. And he wasn't alone.

Mark walked straight up to the reception desk and didn't notice me until he'd given the receptionist his name and turned to take a seat on the couch.

"Hello, Mark."

Mark stopped in his tracks, causing the woman trailing behind him to walk right into his back. The startled expression on his face led me to believe that even though he'd decided to use an agent from Paige's office, he never thought he'd find one of us waiting for him to arrive.

"Lauren, hi."

I waited for Mark to introduce the woman, but instead he reached for her hand and pulled her in closer to him. No introduction was forthcoming, and Mark's message was received loud and clear—he'd decided that she should remain nameless, probably for her safety and the safety of all involved.

I wasn't sure of the protocol one was supposed to follow when encountering a friend's ex-husband, but after knowing the guy for so many years, I assumed some level of familiarity was expected. Being cordial didn't diminish my allegiance to Robin, did it?

I stood up and leaned in to graze his cheek with an innocuous kiss, but Mark obviously had a more formal greeting in mind and quickly backed away from my puckering lips, leaving me kissing the empty space between us. I resorted to an awkward embrace/handshake combo, our shoulders bumping together as we both counted the seconds before we could let go without seeming obviously relieved.

With our greeting out of the way, I sat back down and pasted a friendly smile on my face, a smile that said I was completely comfortable in this unexpected situation. A smile so casual it never let on that almost every day I felt his presence in everything Robin did and said.

Mark and the woman took the love seat against the wall, putting some intentional distance between us.

"Would you like some coffee?" the receptionist offered, and we all jumped at the distraction with a resounding *yes*!

In a city the size of Boston, it was bound to happen sooner or later, and it seemed to me that we'd been lucky to make it this far without coming face to face with the object of Robin's preoccupation. For better or worse, Mark and I were bound together by the same circumstances that once required that we befriend each other and now demanded that we circle each other cautiously. The very recognition of our acquaintance was an acknowledgment that what brought us together in the first place no longer existed. The only thing we had in common was the very reason we could never really be friends—Robin.

"Are you buying a new place?" I asked, hoping I didn't seem nosy, but dying to find out why Mark and the woman were there.

"Sheila's showing us a two-bedroom duplex over on Marlborough."

Showing us? Mark was moving in with the woman seated to his right?

"Sounds nice." Sounds like Robin was going to lose it when she found out, which, considering she was due to arrive any minute, I expected to happen shortly.

"We're all set," Paige called out, walking toward me with a huge grin on her face. "They took the deal."

Mark stood up and stepped forward, his hand extended in what I assumed was an attempt to avoid another embarrassing embrace. "Hello, Paige."

When Paige realized that the man waiting for her hand was Mark, she blinked a few times as if expecting the evil apparition to disappear.

"Mark, nice to see you," she responded tersely.

I caught Paige checking out the woman on the love seat, and then looking around for our missing friend. "Maybe we should go," she suggested, taking the magazine out of my hand. "Now."

I grabbed my purse and was ready to get the hell out of there, when Sheila came through the front door—followed by Robin.

"Sorry I'm late, Mark. I hope you haven't been waiting long." Sheila rushed up to Mark, but he moved back, stepping in front of his girlfriend as if to shield her from what was about to take place.

Robin never made it past the doorway, where she stood silently watching the unlikely crowd gathered in the waiting area. After the initial shock, during which she must have clenched and unclenched her fists at least four times, Robin seemed to be deciding how to play the situation, carefully assessing her alternatives. Lucky for all of us, she'd chosen to take the high road—usually the one less taken by Robin when it came to Mark.

"Hello, everyone," she said coolly and then nodded in Mark's direction, her expression pinched. "Hello, Mark."

Even though Robin had chosen to act calm and composed, Mark didn't look like he was buying it. After responding with a perfunctory smile, he sat down and placed a protective hand on his girlfriend's knee, causing the veins in Robin's forehead to throb uncontrollably. The girlfriend stared at the floor, attempting to make herself invisible.

"Ready to go?" Robin asked, still holding the door open.

Paige snatched her jacket from the coatrack and we were out the door before Sheila could ask why we were making a run for it.

"What the fuck was that?" Robin snapped once we were on the sidewalk and out of sight. "Who the hell was that woman he was pawing?"

"They're looking at a place," I told her.

"*They're* looking at a place? Together?" Robin practically spat out the word. "And there wasn't another agency in all of Boston they could go to? He knows you work there."

"We're one of the biggest in the city, Lauren. I doubt he did it on purpose."

"Right." Robin wasn't convinced. "Screw him, and screw his happy little house hunting. Look, I'm not in the mood to go check out your place right now. That's okay, right?"

Paige nodded. "Sure."

We watched Robin storm off, muttering "I'll show him" as she passed pedestrians who quickly stepped out of her way.

"That was a close call," I observed, as we started toward Paige's car.

"He's lucky she didn't go ballistic. Think she'll be okay?"

"She'll be fine," I told Paige. "What's the worst thing she could do?"

Paige unlocked the car and looked at me over the roof. "I don't even want to think about it."

"So where is this place?"

Paige glanced down at the listing in her hand while trying to keep her eyes on the road. "Around Cleveland Circle, off Strathmore."

We were driving along Beacon Street, just past Washington Square and the quaint neighborhoods of Brookline. As we got nearer our destination, the pedestrians passing us at stoplights seemed to get younger and scruffier.

"Isn't it mostly students around here? You're going to buy a place for some Boston College seniors to pillage and plunder?"

"No, it's an old house that was converted into three apartments, a great buy around here. I'm just considering it right now."

The house was a dingy beige with white trim that had started to yellow where it wasn't worn away completely. The paint on its weather-beaten shingles bubbled up and curled over itself, peeling away from the house like skin after a severe sunburn. A large covered porch spanned the front of the Dutch Colonial–style house, a wooden swing hanging limply from its ceiling. I followed Paige up the uneven front steps, stepping cautiously for fear of putting my foot right through the rotted planks.

If the outside was a before picture from *This Old House,* the inside was an after picture from a police crime scene. Okay, so there wasn't any blood, although there were rusty stains on the carpet as if someone had gone from room to room dripping spaghetti sauce, and instead of yellow tape warning DO NOT ENTER, some spiders had gone to town and spun an elaborate afghan connecting the ceiling lighting fixtures.

Someone had laid down carpet in the seventies, an oxidized orange with flecks of brown and gold in its shaggy pile. I could just imagine the decades of grime embedded in the synthetic fibers, where the flow of the rooms was clearly discernible by following the paths that had worn the carpet bare, like dirt trails.

"Do you think it's haunted?" Paige asked, stepping over a creaky floorboard.

"The only thing scary about this house is the prospect of living here. You'd have to completely gut this place," I observed, peeking inside the bathroom and quickly retreating.

"Would not. Look here." Paige was on her knees with a Swiss Army knife wedged under the carpet by the kitchen doorframe. "There are hardwood floors under the carpet."

"But you'd have to change everything about it."

Paige stood up and made notes on the small pad of paper she kept in her well-stocked purse. "I think you're being a little harsh. It's great."

If great meant in need of a bug bomb and a wrecking ball, then the house certainly fit the definition. "The ants in the kitchen seem to agree with you."

"Come on; you can get rid of ants, but you can't get crown molding like that anymore, or a built-in china cabinet with that workmanship without spending a fortune."

"You'd have to pay me a fortune to live here."

"It's just been empty for a while," Paige replied, poking her head inside the soot-covered brick fireplace and looking skyward. "Wow; this is a working fireplace."

"Probably the only thing in this place that's working. I don't know how you can see past all this," I told her, signing my name in the dust on the kitchen counter. "I'd rather have a place built for me, with everything exactly the way I like it."

"It's not about changing everything until it's exactly the way I want it. It's about appreciating the unique character of the home."

"You are a better woman than I am, Paige Carmichael." As I watched Paige scribbling with her Montblanc pen, I remembered what Robin had said about Paige keeping her engagement ring. "Have you talked to Steve?"

Paige shook her head and changed the subject. "Did you reschedule your date with Charlie?"

"Yes, but that doesn't matter right now. I don't want to talk about my date. I want to talk about your date."

Paige removed a tape measure from her purse and started assessing the width of the windows. "What date? I didn't have a date."

"I know, and Robin and I were thinking that maybe you should go out with someone."

Paige let go of the tape and it retreated noisily into its neat coil as if it knew better than to stick around for this conversation. "Haven't you two done enough for me recently?"

"But I met this guy, a brother of one of my clients, and I thought that maybe you two would hit it off."

"Hit it off? I just broke off my engagement, Lauren."

"I know, and I'm not saying that you have to go on a *date* date. Robin and I thought that we could all go out together, as a group. I'd invite Charlie, and Robin would bring whoever she wants to torture for the evening."

"I don't know if I'm ready for that." Paige avoided looking at me, and I wondered if her steadfast facade was finally cracking. She pulled the tape out from its hiding place and hooked one end against the windowsill.

"Look, no pressure. We just thought you should get out for a night."

Paige stopped measuring and sighed. "Fine," she agreed flatly. "Set it up."

"Great. I will." And I'd also tell Vivian that I might have the happy beginning she was looking for after all.

After our house-hunting excursion, Paige dropped me off in front of my building. Instead of heading straight upstairs to my third-floor apartment, I took a detour down the tiled hallway that led to the laundry-room entrance, and descended into the basement.

My building was like most of the older white brick residential structures built along Commonwealth Avenue where the T's green line divided the street down the middle like the trolley in Mister Rogers's neighborhood. Unlike the neighborhoods closer to downtown, in which luxury condos were springing up where smaller, tired buildings once stood, the area hadn't been targeted for gentrification, and cars still dodged across the signal-less T tracks like kids skirting capture in a game of tag.

My area of the city was the neighborhood equivalent of that spot on the tarmac where airplanes went when they could no longer sit at the terminal but weren't quite cleared for takeoff. Located between the family neighborhoods of Newton and the trendy streets of downtown, it wasn't populated with partying college kids, nor was it the quiet refuge of the elderly. Instead, most of the tenants were in-between, kind of like the neighborhood itself, a rest stop on the way into the city or out to the suburbs.

In the basement of my building, two washing machines and two dryers stood against a wall under the long, exposed tubes of fluorescent lights. The basement was clean and brightly lit, but it was still a basement, with a cold cement floor and cinderblock walls painted an industrial battleship gray that formed a thick smooth coating along the cinderblock's pebbled surface, almost like rubber. Paige wasn't kidding about the taxidermy collection or the assortment of army boots—for some reason, either because he thought it provided some measure of decoration or because his wife wouldn't let him keep them anywhere else, the building's owner mounted his hunting trophies from the exposed wooden support beams running along the ceiling. The mildewed army boots were tied together and strung along the underside of the beams like Christmas lights.

There were twelve storage rooms in the basement, one for each unit in the building. The storage rooms weren't meant for valuables, and I was reminded of that by the handwritten sign that told tenants that the building owner wasn't responsible for lost or stolen articles. The walls between the stalls stopped short of the ceiling, to let in the light, and the remaining two feet were strung with chicken wire. But even with their plywood walls and makeshift plank doors, the stalls were dry and relatively safe—perfect for storing my boxes of out-of-season clothing and otherwise useless memorabilia.

I worked the combination on the lock I kept on my stall,

and scanned the floor—a four-by-six space neatly stacked with large Rubbermaid tubs containing my summer clothes, which I would swap out in April and replace with my winter wardrobe, and brown cardboard boxes labeled in thick black Magic Marker. The contents of my stall fell into two categories: things I didn't have room for in my apartment, and things I'd never have a use for but couldn't bear to throw away. I was looking for the latter.

Next to my grass-stained field hockey stick, I found a box labeled SENIOR YEAR and untucked the stiff flaps that were folded over one another to create a makeshift seal. There were textbooks and spiral-bound notebooks, my yearbook, a yellowed campus newspaper, and even my date book where I kept all my assignments. I'd saved it all, although God knows why. I never expected to have a sudden need to review Kant's theory of transcendental idealism.

I picked up the metaphysics textbook, and an envelope tumbled out from between its pages. I recognized the handwriting and immediately knew what it contained.

Freshman year my parents sent me a teddy bear in a care package—a brown Gund bear with a tag that told me his name was Chocolate Truffle (I don't know why I assumed a bear named Chocolate Truffle would be a boy, but I did). I renamed the bear Oliver and kept him on my bed all throughout college. By senior year Oliver had seen better days; his fur was matted, I'd lost the burgundy velvet ribbon that came tied around his neck, and his suede nose was all but rubbed off. Still, I slept with Oliver on my bed every night, and so when Neil came back to my room after our second date, he met my bedmate.

A few days later a letter arrived addressed to Oliver in care of Lauren Gallagher. Paige thought it was sweet. Robin thought Neil was trying too hard. And me? I was amazed that someone wanted so much to be a part of my life that he'd actually try to win me over by buddying up to my stuffed animal. It was weird looking back on it. Like I said, Neil's romantic gestures were pretty standard. I'm sure if Neil remembered he'd be horrified, but at the time I thought it was endearing.

Neil's letter wasn't exactly a proclamation of love, but

he'd added a P.S. at the bottom saying that he hoped Oliver wouldn't mind sharing me in the future. If I didn't mind, I couldn't see any reason why Oliver would feel put out, considering he'd had a near monopoly on my sleeping arrangements for almost four years. I was more than ready to move Oliver over onto my bookshelf to make some room for Neil.

Neil was a catch. In my head I knew it. The women in my residence hall knew it. People who met him knew it. By the end of my senior year I saw Neil as someone who was reliable and familiar, which isn't a bad thing when you're about to graduate and embark on a life filled with unknowns. So why didn't I move with him? As Paige said, I'd had my reasons, and they were very logical at the time. I had a job at an ad agency that I liked. A lease on a studio apartment. My friends. I told Neil I couldn't leave and I told Paige and Robin I wouldn't leave. I couched my reasons in terms they could understand, but I never admitted the truth.

I wanted to stay in Boston and see what I could do without Neil. I was just getting started, and moving to DC with Neil seemed to be a premature ending of my first year on my own. I deliberately didn't move in with Paige and Robin when they got a two-bedroom apartment in Brighton. I didn't move in with Neil, even though he offered. Graduating from college was the beginning of life without training wheels, without the soft landing. I wasn't ready to give that up so soon and trade it in for a bicycle built for two.

I folded Neil's letter to Oliver and placed it back in the envelope. I'd kept it for eleven years—why not a few more? Besides, it might come in handy sometime in the near future if I needed to jog Neil's memory. I picked up the date book and thumbed through the pages, watching my senior year unfold week by week. Tucked between the pages of the week of November seventh, a piece of notebook paper with frayed edges was folded into thirds. The List.

Robin, Paige and I had decided to write out our lists after a night of drinking, which explained why my handwriting was lopsided, each letter a little lower than the one before until by the last word it seemed the sentence was sliding down a hill off the page. At the time it sounded like a good idea, an easy way to sift through the clutter, as Robin had put it. It was as if by merely identifying what we wanted in a man it would mean that he could be delivered to order, that he actually existed.

My list didn't have a title on top, just lines numbered one through ten beside a few phrases that at the time didn't seem like asking so much. After all, I was probably seeing double at the time, so asking for just one perfect guy didn't seem like such an outrageous request.

"That sounds like Neil," Robin had pointed out when I read my list aloud. "You can't do that. It's cheating."

"And why is number one blank?" Paige asked.

"I don't know what number one is yet," I'd answered, pretending to be stumped. But what I didn't tell them was that I'd left the line blank for another reason—mainly that I was afraid if I wrote something down on paper it would be obvious that Neil wasn't the one for me.

Now I scanned the page and quickly calculated that Neil easily met seven of my top ten must-haves. That wasn't bad.

I knelt on the floor of my storage locker and ticked off the criteria, wondering how Charlie stacked up against my list. Even though I'd only seen him in suits, Charlie seemed athletic. He found me funny, which meant he obviously had an excellent sense of humor. As far as I knew he didn't smoke, he was an attorney so he was well educated, and since he was at least four inches taller than me, I could definitely kiss him in heels without having to stoop down. So Charlie had five checks in the plus column. He was halfway there.

It was too soon to know about the other five requirements.

5. Nice to children
4. Isn't afraid to admit he liked *When Harry Met Sally*
3. Gets along with his family
2. Good in bed
1. (To be determined)

That was quite a list. The only thing missing was world peace and justice for all. I'd practically described Gandhi, although I wasn't so sure about the good-in-bed part. I don't know who I thought I was fooling. It wasn't like other women were looking for chain-smoking, uneducated couch potatoes who abandoned their families and cursed at little kids.

By the time I'd finished going through the list, my knees were numb from kneeling on the frigid cement floor and I just wanted to go upstairs and get warm. I stuffed the list in my jacket pocket, grabbed my yearbook and closed up the box. Maybe it was time to revisit my list. And maybe Charlie and Neil could help me figure out what that first requirement should have been.

17

$\mathcal{I}$ was now officially represented by Robin's literary agent and on the verge of publishing greatness, or at least that's what Vivian kept leading me to believe. She'd been eager to get a contract signed and pulled out all the stops with some very serious wooing—in the twelve hours after Vivian first walked into the boutique, I received two voice mails, a call from Vivian's assistant, a gourmet cheese basket and a bouquet of flowers, which I should have kept to myself but in a moment of poor judgment decided to share with Maria and my staff.

"What's that?" Maria asked, when I walked into the kitchen carrying a flower arrangement so large I could barely see over the tops of the purple, lavender and fuchsia anemones.

"Aren't they gorgeous?" I placed the fishbowl-sized glass vase on the butcher-block bench and stood back to admire my unexpected delivery. I didn't even bother hiding the grin that seemed plastered to my face. "I think I have an admirer."

Maria turned up her nose at me. "Oh, please. So, who're they from?"

"I don't know. It could be Charlie, you know. We did have a wonderful dinner." I leaned down over a perfectly formed blue curiosa rose, its petals just opening from a tightly wound bud, and inhaled. "Then again, who knows?" I didn't say his name, but Maria narrowed her eyes at me and I knew she got my hint. Maybe it was Neil who sent the special delivery.

"Considering this is the first time anyone has sent you flowers, I hardly think you should be parading around like you've been crowned Miss America. Why don't you just read the card so we can get this over with?"

"Is that jealousy I hear in your voice, Maria?" I teased, because I *was* feeling like Miss America. The only thing missing was Bert Parks serenading me as I took my victory lap around the kitchen. "This isn't some FTD teddy bear holding carnations. This bouquet cost a fortune."

I reached for the miniature envelope peeking out from behind a spray of green celosia and slipped out the handwritten card. I read the message silently to myself and wished I'd just placed the flowers on the tasting table and kept my mouth shut.

"So, which of the many men you think are pining away for you sent them?"

I considered lying to save face, but with the card in my hand Maria could always confirm my story.

"Well?" Maria asked again, losing patience.

I was about to be publicly dethroned.

"Your biggest fan, Vivian," I read and then held up the card to show her. "Wasn't that thoughtful?"

"Vivian? The publishing woman?" Maria laughed at me and then attempted to look serious. "You know, Lauren, you're right. I'm jealous."

So, the flowers hadn't been sent by Charlie or Neil, but I took them home anyway and kept them on my kitchen table. They were beautiful, and I didn't need to listen to Maria crack any more jokes about my *female* admirer.

Vivian's persistence, and impeccable taste in florists, paid off. I spoke with Robin's agent that same day, and Vivian had a copy of the contract messengered over within the hour. As far as everyone was concerned, the book was a done deal.

But now that Paige had agreed to go out with Hugh, I wanted to talk with Vivian about incorporating my cake theory. They'd decided to fast-track the project to get the book out in October, and I didn't have time to lose, so I stopped by her office on my way to meet Charlie for lunch.

Although Vivian wasn't expecting me, I was immediately showed into her office.

After Vivian spent the first fifteen minutes telling me how excited everyone at Pegasus Publishing was about the book, I finally had a chance to tell her why I'd stopped by.

"I think I can give you that feel-good story you're looking for," I explained.

"Really?" Vivian tapped her pencil on her desk as she thought about my news. "I tell you what; wait here a second. I'll be right back."

Vivian left me alone for a few minutes with the stacks of manuscripts piled high on her desk. When she returned she was followed by a silver-haired man in a three-piece suit who had a face furrowed from summers sailing off Martha's Vineyard.

"Lauren Gallagher, this is Bradley Potter, our publisher."

"Hello, Lauren." Bradley Potter reached for my hand and took it firmly in his own leathery palm. "Vivian told me your idea and we think it's something that should be capitalized on immediately."

"Now, look." Vivian sat down on the corner of her desk and crossed her legs. "What we'd like to do is hold a press conference at the boutique and allude to the fact that Lauren Gallagher is going to reveal her closely guarded secrets in the book—really build the excitement and get everyone talking."

"The idea is to whet their appetite, so to speak." Bradley rested his hands in his pants pockets and jingled a handful of change. "We want to get our publicity department on this right away, hold a press conference next week. So what do you say; are you up for it?"

It was a little premature, considering Paige and Hugh hadn't even met yet, but I just knew it was going to work out.

"Absolutely."

"Great." Vivian hopped down from the desk and walked around to the other side, where she ran a finger along the weeks on her desk calendar. "We're thinking next Friday."

The day after Paige and Hugh's date. No appointments. It was perfect.

* * *

"So this is what a divorce attorney's office looks like?"

"Surprised there's no guillotine?"

"Actually, I was expecting something along the lines of lethal injection. Less screaming." I stood beside Charlie's floor-to-ceiling window, taking in the views from his office on the thirtieth floor of Exchange Place. Below me on the narrow downtown street, little ant-like people scurried into cabs or waited on sidewalks for the streetlights to change. "Nice view."

"We're lucky the windows don't open; otherwise, I'd be talking some of our more unstable clients down from the ledge. I'm not exactly a fan of heights, but it's nice to look at the water."

Charlie's office faced east, and since it was in one of the tallest buildings in the financial district, it soared above the other skyscrapers to reveal an unobstructed view of Boston Harbor. I could easily see the planes taking off and landing at Logan Airport, the noise of their engines muted by the thick panes of glass preventing Charlie's clients from inflicting bodily harm.

We'd decided to have lunch in Faneuil Hall, an outdoor marketplace that was part historical meeting hall, part modern retail bonanza. Although Quincy Market is derided as the most visited tourist trap in Boston, I never tired of the place. Where else could you follow the Freedom Trail right to the front door of Crate and Barrel?

Even though it seemed as if winter had finally given up and admitted it was spring, none of the usual jugglers or musicians were around as we walked along the cobblestone promenade. The rows of pushcarts selling stuffed animals and beaded jewelry were still shielded by the thick plastic curtains that protected them from the elements until the weather warmed up for good.

We passed by the carts and entered Quincy Market's first-floor food court, a circus for the senses where old New England favorites—clam chowder and lobster rolls—battled for your taste buds against the staples of a modern meal—burgers, pizza and frozen yogurt. Once inside we followed the house rule—every man for himself—and while Charlie waited in line for a steak sandwich, I found my way to Pizzeria Regina for a fat wedge of cheese pizza. We met up again in the center atrium where the tables were filling up quickly with the lunchtime crowd.

"We could sit outside," Charlie suggested and led the way.

All the benches were empty, but Charlie stopped in front of one with a bronze statue of a cigar-smoking Red Auerbach, the legendary Celtics coach, reclining comfortably. "We could sit with Red, but the Celts sucked this year and I don't want to ruin my appetite." He moved one bench down and we took a seat.

Even though we were precariously balancing our lunches on our laps, Charlie wasn't distracted, and as we talked about our mornings and the parallels of our jobs he carefully watched me when I spoke, as if he didn't want to miss a word.

"Ever see *When Harry Met Sally*?" I asked between bites of my pizza.

"Ages ago."

"What'd you think of it?"

Charlie thought for a minute. "Are you testing me to see if I think men and women can be friends? Because I'm not exactly having lunch with you because I want to be your friend."

"So you don't think men and women can be friends?"

"I don't think you can be friends with someone you find attractive."

"That's not true," I disagreed. "I've been friends with guys." Although come to think of it, none of them were exactly candidates for a Calvin Klein underwear campaign.

Charlie finished his potato chips and continued. "Really? Okay, then let me put it this way. Say I met a woman who made me laugh. And then I found out that we had some things in common; we even shared some acquaintances. Then we hung out together and had a good time. Sounds like a great friend, right?"

"Sure," I agreed, wondering if he'd just described me.

"Then what if I told you that I found her attractive?" Charlie paused, and I sure as hell hoped he was describing me.

"All of a sudden we can't be friends anymore," he continued. "Because let me tell you, I like my guy friends. They make me laugh, too. But I don't find them attractive, and that's why I'm not dating a guy named Chuck. Because I don't want to sleep with my friends."

I wasn't sure Charlie answered my question about the movie, but I didn't really care at that point. Charlie wanted to sleep with me. And I had to admit, the idea sounded very appealing.

"So you're telling me that I don't have to be wary of your friends? Because I've never had to compete with a guy named Chuck before."

Charlie laughed. "You've got nothing to worry about."

Then why was I worrying? Why was it becoming even more important that Charlie hold out the possibility of something beyond a string of enjoyable dates? Hadn't Paige, Robin and I always prided ourselves on the fact that we didn't need a wedding band on our finger in order to be happy? Why did I feel like I was letting down generations of feminists as I ate my pizza and let the little twinges of uneasiness overshadow the fact that I was seated between Red Auerbach and a man who was happy just to spend time with me?

"Do you have time to take a walk down by the water?" Charlie asked, after I'd noisily sucked down the last drops of my Sprite with my straw.

I'd told Maria I wouldn't be back until one, and it was barely twelve thirty. I crumpled up my paper plate and stood up. "I have plenty of time."

I refused to let five-tier wedding cakes and sugar-paste flower toppers get the best of me. I'd be damned if I'd let *happily ever after* spoil *right now*.

18

*C*an you meet me for a drink? I want to talk to you about something."

"I think I can swing that." I turned my back to Maria and walked out of the kitchen, making sure the door was shut before I continued talking into the phone. "What were you thinking?"

Neil paused. "I don't know too many places anymore. I haven't been here for a while. Any suggestions?"

I could have gone either of two ways—neutral ground where two old acquaintances would meet or the hallowed ground shared by onetime lovers. I figured I'd give him the choice.

"I could meet you at this cute tapas bar around the corner from the boutique, or we could always just go to the Bell in Hand," I suggested, naming one of our favorite downtown pubs.

He didn't even have to consider the options. "I'll meet you at the Bell in Hand at five."

I didn't have to find a way to be alone with Neil. He'd made the first move and saved me the trouble. It wasn't just idle speculation any longer. It wasn't just me listening to Julie remind me of what I'd given up.

It was a date.

"So, what'll it be, Lauren?" Neil asked when we sat down at a table. "What are you drinking nowadays, assuming you've progressed past light beer and Sex on the Beach." I was sure he meant the drink, not the act itself.

We used to order pints of beer, but I figured an Absolut and tonic would make me look a little more sophisticated. Neil ordered a scotch on the rocks. My, how we've grown up.

"So, what made you call?" I asked after the waitress walked away. "I have to admit—I was surprised."

"I wanted to ask you a favor. This wedding is putting a lot of pressure on Julie, especially since she's here by herself until I move back."

I nodded.

"Julie told me she ran into you at Gamble Mansion and you were a big help. So I was wondering if you knew someone who could assist with all the details, like a wedding planner or something."

"Sure, of course. I have a few I could recommend." A recommendation for a wedding planner? He wanted me to meet him so I could make life easier for his fiancée?

"That'd be a huge help. I've about had it with the daily phone calls about monogrammed cocktail napkins." Neil shook his head at the absurdity. "Who the hell looks at cocktail napkins? What's next? Monogrammed toilet paper?"

"Ever wish you could elope and do away with the big event?"

"What guy doesn't?" Neil laughed. "No, seriously, I know it will be great. It's just that it's taken over our lives. Every free minute we have appointments and decisions to make. Do you really think my friends care if they get candied almonds at their plates as keepsakes?"

"It's tradition. Weddings are a weird thing, aren't they?"

"Weird is one word I'd use. Pain in the ass is another."

The waiter brought our drinks and we both took long sips before I continued. "So, that's why you called? Strictly business?"

Neil grinned. "Maybe not all business," he admitted. "Maybe I was a little curious."

I couldn't help smiling back. "Me, too."

"And what were you curious about?" he asked with raised eyebrows.

There were so many things I was curious about. What

was he like? What was his life like? Did he ever think of me? How did he remember our time together? Did he regret that he left Boston without me?

"Just about what you were up to now, how your life has changed, that sort of thing," I answered.

"Well, I'm moving back to Boston, so I guess not much has changed."

"I guess not, if you don't count getting engaged," I pointed out, and Neil seemed genuinely embarrassed that he'd left out that small life-altering event.

"Well, there's that, too," he acknowledged.

Neil lifted his glass and held it out toward me. "How about a toast? To old friends and old times." He clinked my glass and took a long sip. I took an even longer one.

"So, now you're a super-successful pastry chef and businesswoman. I have to admit—I'm really impressed."

I liked Neil's take on my life. I was like a Virginia Slims ad without the risk of lung cancer.

"I haven't done so bad for myself," I agreed.

Neil sat back and looked at me as if he was taking me in. After taking a breath, I met his eyes and felt up to the challenge.

"If owning the hottest cake boutique in Boston is *not bad,* then you're right."

"What'd you expect me to do? Sit around miserable because you left me?"

Neil pretended to choke on his scotch. "I think that's called revisionist history," he coughed.

"How's that?"

"I left you?"

"Um, you're the one who moved," I pointed out.

"Um, you're the one who didn't come with me," he imitated. "I asked."

"No, asking is when we discuss moving before you decide to do it."

"What do you mean?" He seemed really confused.

"At dinner you told me you got the job and were moving," I explained. "It didn't seem up for discussion."

"What do you call talking about moving to DC, if not us planning to do it together?" I guess I looked confused, because he added, "I mean, you never even said you wanted to stay together after I left. Ever hear of long-distance relationships?"

I don't know why I was playing this game with Neil. He was right. I didn't want to go to DC. And I didn't want to have a long-distance relationship. It wasn't his fault, although I was doing a good job of making him think I thought that.

"It wouldn't have worked. Long-distance relationships never do," I explained away my actions.

"Especially when one of the people doesn't want it to," he replied, seriously. "Regardless, we had fun, didn't we?" Neil smiled at me and cocked his head.

"Yeah, we had fun."

Neil twirled the ice in his glass with his index finger as he spoke. When he finished, he slid the finger between his lips and licked it dry. For some reason it made me uncomfortable. His actions were so blatantly sexual, or maybe I was making more of it than he intended. Looking up from his glass, Neil caught me staring, and I'm sure he could tell that my mind was in the gutter. I looked across the bar, where a table of newcomers were just sitting down.

"I knew the minute I pulled away from the curb that you'd already moved on." Neil waited for me to look at him. "Do you know how I knew?"

I shook my head.

"When I looked in the rearview mirror you were smiling."

"That's not true," I objected. "I was waving."

"Yeah, that too. There you were waving frantically and smiling, like those passengers you see on the deck of a cruise ship. It was like you were leaving; you were going on an adventure instead of me."

"At least I wasn't tossing confetti," I joked before getting serious again. "I don't believe that."

"Believe it. I guess that's why I'm not that surprised that you went on to open Lauren's Luscious Licks and everything."

He was being so honest, I thought it was time to come clean. "That's not exactly true. I was laid off from the ad agency after you left."

Neil shrugged. "But you got the last laugh, didn't you?

You're still so sure of yourself and what you want and how to get it, aren't you?"

Were we still talking about me? Talk about revisionist history. It was as if he were retouching a photo.

"You always had that *I know exactly where I'm going* expression," he continued. "I guess you just weren't going anywhere with me."

"Now you're just making things up."

"I'm not," Neil laughed. "I hate to admit it, but I kind of wish you'd gone downhill since we broke up."

"Downhill?"

"Yeah, maybe lost a few teeth, got a limp, grown a few moles."

"Would you like some errant hairs growing out of those moles?"

"That'd be good. And an eye patch, too. Just so I don't feel like I've missed out on anything. Is that ridiculous?"

"Not so ridiculous."

"So are you seeing anyone?"

That I even hesitated made me feel slightly disloyal toward Charlie. "Sort of."

"He's a lucky guy."

We talked some more about Neil's job and moving back to Boston. Our conversation felt eerily similar to old times but without the issues of a relationship and all the eagerness of a courtship. As he spoke I studied his face, one I'd known so well many years ago, one that now seemed to belong to a stranger. Although he was still easy on the eyes, Neil's hairline was retreating and the jawline that used to make his profile distinguishable to me in any room had become rounder and softer.

"I better get going. We have a meeting with a caterer," Neil finally announced and rolled his eyes. "Before I forget, can I get those planners' names?"

When the waitress brought the check, Neil reached for his wallet. I reached over and took the bill. What was the point of having your ex-boyfriend think you're super-successful if you couldn't buy him a drink? And what was the point of having Neil show up after eight years if not to give me another chance? If I wanted it.

* * *

Neil caught a cab and I walked toward the T station. Outside, the downtown streets were deserted except for the occasional straggler hurrying to catch a bus or make the train home. The interiors of the office buildings were still lit, their empty lobbies under the watchful eyes of security guards who paced across the marble floors killing time before their shifts ended.

I stepped over the cracks in the sidewalk as I walked, trying to decide what to do next. Obviously Neil was wondering what I'd do now that I knew that he was curious about more than just wedding planners. Maybe Neil had even been wondering if he'd made a mistake by leaving without me.

"Lauren?" A male voice startled me and instinctively I pulled my purse close to my side.

"Lauren?" The voice called again, following me. "What are you doing downtown?" I jumped when he grabbed for my arm and almost screamed before I realized this wasn't a random mugging.

"Charlie, are you following me?" I blurted out, guiltily. Deflection was highly underrated when you were buying time.

"Um, no. I work here, remember?" He pointed up at the building.

"Oh, sure. I was just on my way home from Filene's. A little shopping."

"Apparently very little."

What did that mean? Was I that obvious?

"You're not carrying any shopping bags," he explained and then laughed at me. "Are you okay?"

"Sure, I'm fine. Just a little frustrated from shopping, that's all. I couldn't find what I was looking for." It wasn't a total lie. Besides, what did I have to feel guilty about? Charlie and I had gone on only two dates.

"I know what you mean. Sometimes it's harder when you know exactly what you want. You won't settle for anything else." Charlie held up the white paper bag in his hand, a small grease stain bleeding through its side. "I'd offer to go grab a bite to eat with you, but I just ran out to get a little dinner myself. Cheeseburger and fries. It's going to be a long night."

"That's okay. I was just going to catch the T home," I explained but didn't make a move to leave. Being around Charlie made me hungry.

"We're still on for Cambridge with your friends on Thursday, right?"

I nodded. After Paige agreed to go on a non-date date with Hugh, I called Amanda and asked for Hugh's phone number. After promising that Paige was a confirmed heterosexual with little chance of changing her mind, he agreed to meet us all for margaritas in Cambridge.

"Great; I'll see you then." Charlie walked through the revolving door, but instead of stepping out when he reached the lobby he kept traveling in a circle and ended up back outside with me. "And don't be too bummed about the shopping. You'll find what you're looking for as soon as you stop looking. That's the way it always is, right?" He winked at me and spun back into the foyer, where he waved and headed toward the elevators.

19

$\mathcal{R}$obin had asked me to meet her at ten o'clock on Beacon Hill. As I headed down Charles Street, the gas streetlamps lining the narrow cobblestone street reminded me that squeezed between the contemporary shopping haven of Newbury Street and the glass and steel of downtown, historic Beacon Hill lingered as a souvenir of the city's history.

Robin was pacing back and forth in front of our designated meeting spot when I arrived. "It's about time. You were supposed to be here ten minutes ago."

"It was nice out, so I walked."

"Well, this is important and I don't want to be late." Robin looked up and down the street, as if checking to see that I wasn't being followed.

"You haven't sworn off men for good and now want to ask me to be your girlfriend, do you?" I asked, thinking Allison and Amanda seemed pretty damn happy compared to a lot of other couples I'd seen.

Robin crossed her arms. "You should be so lucky."

"Because don't get me wrong—I'd be flattered."

"Are you finished?"

"I guess."

"Okay. Here it is." Robin pointed to the discrete rectangular brass plaque secured to the side of the building. I read the name of the building's tenant, in polished raised letters: The New England Cryobank and Clinic. The brick three-story building looked more like a turn-of-the-century town-house than a high-tech medical office.

"What's a cryobank?"

"It's a fancy name for *sperm bank*. Kinda like *boutique* is a fancy name for *bakery*."

I started to object, but Robin raised her hand and cut me off. "I'm sorry; I didn't mean that. I'm just nervous."

"About what?"

Robin reached for my hand and squeezed it. "I'm thinking about having a baby."

"You and every other thirty-two-year-old woman."

"I mean now. I'm thinking about having a baby now."

"Why?"

"Why not?"

I wanted to point out the anonymous girl holding the rainbow-striped beach ball and the unidentified elderly couple strolling on an unspecified beach—Robin couldn't even replace Mark's pictures with anything more than fillers, and now it sounded like she wanted to replace him with a baby.

"You mean besides the obvious?"

"What's so obvious?" Robin pulled back defensively.

Was I surprised that a week after bumping into her ex-husband, Robin had decided to retaliate by replacing Mark with a child to prove she had no use for him? Unfortunately, not as surprised as I should have been.

"Are you doing this because of Mark?"

"No, I'm not doing this because of Mark," Robin mimicked me. "In fact, I'm doing this to prove that I don't need a man at all."

"And you just happened to decide you want a baby after running into your ex-husband."

Robin walked toward the front steps of the cryobank and sat down, ready to defend her decision and prove that the fact Mark was moving in with another woman had nothing to do with it.

"I want a family and, unlike you, I'm not willing to wait for Mr. Right. I thought I'd found Mr. Right and he turned out to be Mr. Completely Fucking Wrong. I've been looking into it and it's actually quite easy. It's kind of like the turkey-baster method of conception."

I went over and sat next to her on the cool slate steps. "Let me get this straight—you want to have a baby with a stranger?"

"That's the beauty of the whole thing. I wouldn't be having it with anybody. I'd be having it by myself. All I need to do is pick out some sperm. It's like flipping the bird at all those men who think they're indispensable."

"You can't be telling me you're seriously considering this."

"I'm telling you that I don't want to make the mistake of putting off having a baby until I find a man. I've kissed more frogs than I care to recall, and yet the closest I've come to a prince was a bicycle messenger who took me to a midnight showing of *Purple Rain*. So will you come in with me?"

Robin looked so determined, so set on going through with this, that I couldn't turn her down. "I'll go in with you, but if they're offering free samples, I'm running out the door."

"Don't worry. I just need you there to help me pick out my donor, and maybe for a little moral support."

Robin wanted me, a woman trying to figure out whether she should pursue her engaged ex-boyfriend or a guy who eats pineapples Foster for dinner, to provide moral support? "Being a woman of few morals, I think a little support is all I have to offer."

Robin threw her arms around my neck. "This is so great! I knew you'd do it. Thanks."

After the receptionist buzzed us in, she handed Robin a clipboard and asked her to complete a stack of forms. We took a seat in the waiting room, where vintage furnishings were clustered around a marble fireplace.

"I feel like I'm in a bed-and-breakfast," I whispered as Robin started writing.

"Yeah, well, there's nothing quaint about this application. Have you ever seen a semen order form?"

"How'd you even know this place existed?"

"My doctor's registered with the clinic. She's used them before."

"Does she earn frequent insemination points that can be redeemed for magazine subscriptions or free trips?"

"I don't know about free trips, but you'd never think something in such ample supply would be so expensive."

"How much is this costing you?"

"When all is said and done, about twenty-four hundred dollars, assuming it works the first time." Robin stopped writing and looked at me. "Do you realize how many times I've had guys offer to do for free what I'm paying thousands of dollars for?"

I pointed to the glossy brochure I was reading. "Yeah, but did you see how many donors you get to choose from? You'd have to be one busy girl to get this variety on your own. And it says here you can have your order shipped to your door in a liquid nitrogen vapor tank—giving a whole new meaning to the term *male-order delivery*."

After Robin had completed the recipient information form and signed the consent agreement, the receptionist handed her the donor catalog and showed us into a smaller room where we were told to wait for the counselor. I looked over Robin's shoulder as she carefully studied each page in the three-ring binder.

"So, how's this work? They fill up a turkey baster and pretend you're an Oven Stuffer roaster?"

"Actually, yeah. I can even do it myself at home if I want."

"Please—I know you, and if you had a spatula in your kitchen, much less a turkey baster, I'd be shocked."

"I'm not going to do it myself; I just said I could. And it's called an aspirating syringe, but same principle."

"Sounds like something best left to the professionals, if you ask me."

Robin carefully read each donor's credentials, and I couldn't help but wonder whether she really knew what she was about to do.

"Are you sure you're ready to be a mother?"

Robin nodded and stopped turning the catalog pages. "You know, I was reading this book about how families are like little microcosms of the world around us, and we need to create a behavior model of what's acceptable or punishable, just like in society."

"And the catchy title of the seminar I know you're hatching in your brain?" I asked, walking over to the wall to look at the photos of all the happy donor babies the New England Cryobank and Clinic had produced.

"It's a Small World After All: Behavior Models for Better Families. It's just a working title right now."

"Wow. There are a lot of guys in that catalog," I observed over Robin's shoulder in awe of all her choices—from bald and brainy geologists to brawny firemen with varsity letters. "There must be three hundred donors in that book. It's babies à la carte."

"You're enjoying this, aren't you?"

"I'm just saying . . . Look at this." I pointed to the page Robin was reviewing. "You can pick the eye color, the height, even the religion. But where's all the important information?"

"Like what?"

"Like whether or not he puts the toilet seat down when he's finished."

Robin laughed. "You're right. Who cares what color his hair is. They should really ask if he's going bald."

"Or sports a comb-over," I added.

Robin closed the binder and turned to me. "We should come up with a more useful questionnaire they could give their donors."

I reached for a pen on the desk and flipped over one of the handouts I found in a Lucite rack nailed to the wall.

"Question number one: Can he recall every golf shot he's ever taken, including the hole in one he got on the windmill hole playing miniature golf, but can't remember that you don't put aluminum foil in the microwave?"

I scribbled on the paper, thinking that this list would be a hell of a lot more useful than the list I'd found in my storage room. "Number two: Is he capable of replacing the roll of toilet paper, or does he just use the box of Kleenex sitting on the sink until that's gone, too?"

"Three: Can he tell the difference between a boob job and a pair that's au naturel?"

"More importantly, does he prefer the real thing?"

"Right." Robin tapped the page and told me to keep writing. "Five: Does he wait until the last minute to shop for

Christmas gifts and then think you'll love the ninety-four-ounce bottle of Jean Naté body splash he picked up at T.J.Maxx?"

"That's a good one," I complimented.

"Unfortunately, I learned that one from personal experience."

There was a rap on the door and a gray-haired woman poked her head in. "Ms. Cross? Are you ready to begin?"

Robin and I exchanged looks. I gave her a reassuring smile and she waved the woman in. "I'm ready."

"Do you need to get back to the boutique?" Robin asked as the clinic's door closed behind us. We'd emerged with Robin's top five donor choices and a calendar Robin was supposed to use to monitor her ovulation cycle.

It was almost noon, and my next appointment wasn't scheduled to arrive until two o'clock. "I'm fine. Let's get some lunch."

We walked around the corner to the Beacon Hill Hotel & Bistro. The bistro had the warm, old-money feel of a men's club, with raised mahogany paneling, etched glass and a large fireplace. The maitre d' seated us in a banquette, its table top covered in stiff white butcher paper, and I waited to see whether Robin had any second thoughts since she'd put her plan into action.

"That wasn't so bad, now, was it?" Robin asked, her decision obviously unchanged by the counselor's mandatory lecture.

"Actually, it wasn't," I admitted.

"*Cryobank* sounds so much better than *sperm bank,* don't you think?"

I shrugged. "Certainly more high-tech. So you think it's weird that I call Lauren's Luscious Licks a cake boutique instead of a bakery?" I asked, glancing up from my menu.

"Look, I said I was sorry," Robin said.

"I know. But it's not the first time you've said something like that. You said I was a florist."

"Oh my God, Lauren. Most people wouldn't find that insulting."

Most people weren't in the greenhouse killing the flowers

while Maria the gardener was out taking care of a family crisis.

"You don't think calling it a boutique is just a matter of semantics?"

"No, not really. When I was in elementary school my mom would take me to a little local bakery for cupcakes and cookies after school, you know the kind of cookies that were scalloped like shells, dipped in chocolate and covered with sprinkles?"

I nodded, picturing the cookies Robin described. I used to love them, too.

"Well there's no way Lauren's Luscious Licks could be confused with Dinkle's Bakery. I remember they had a tall spool of red and white string they used to tie the white cardboard pastry boxes closed. I loved carrying that box home, hooking my fingers under the string so I could swing the box back and forth as we walked. Of course, the cupcakes always ended up with smudged icing from slamming into the sides of the box, and the cookies cracked, but it never stopped me from doing the exact same thing the next time."

"So, calling it a boutique isn't just some marketing tactic?"

"Not any more than Women in Action calling our seminars *lifecycle management programs* and shedding the whole self-help label, even if that's what everyone else thinks they are. I'd argue that if our clients could help themselves, why the hell would they be sitting in a meeting room at the Park Plaza attending my seminars?" Robin returned her attention to the menu. "So, what are you having?"

"The rare roast beef sandwich with field mushrooms and horseradish mustard."

"Sounds good." Robin closed her menu and placed it on the table next to her bread plate. "What's with the crisis of conscience about what you call your business?"

"The other day Maria had a family emergency and had to go home," I started to explain.

"Maria has a family? The thought never occurred to me. I just assumed she emerged from the belly of a beast, her horns and tail already fully formed."

"Yes, Maria has a family. Quite a big one, from what I understand. Anyway, when Maria was gone I had to fill a few orders—nothing difficult, just a few of our basic cakes. And I blew it. Even Dominique and Georgina were looking at me like I was an imposter."

"You're not an imposter. You're just out of practice."

"But I'm supposed to be a pastry chef, Robin."

"No, you're supposed to make a pretty dessert." Robin sat back in the banquette to give our returning waiter room. After the bread basket was on our table and we'd both ordered a refill on our iced teas, she continued, "And that's what you do, even if you're not the one baking the cakes."

"But my name's on the front of the boutique."

"No, your name is associated with the vision of the boutique. Nobody expects Coco Chanel to be sitting at the sewing machine stitching the seams of a suit."

"That's because she's dead," I pointed out.

"It's obvious nothing I say is getting through to you, so why don't we move on. Did you invite Charlie to join us tomorrow night?"

I nodded. "I saw Neil again yesterday."

"What do you mean you *saw* Neil?" Robin asked suspiciously.

"I mean he called and asked me to meet him."

"What happened?"

"It doesn't matter."

Robin frowned and put her iced-tea glass down on the table. "Then why are you telling me this?"

"Because ever since Neil came in to the boutique I've been thinking about him."

"You are treading in dangerous waters, Lauren. Neil is getting married."

"But is he getting married to the right woman?"

Robin shook her head in disbelief. "I'm going to pretend I didn't just hear that. On second thought, I'm going to suggest that maybe you attend one of my seminars, Time Heals Old Wounds—Ex-Boyfriends Inflict New Ones."

"You want me to take relationship advice from a woman who was just flipping through a catalog of men who deposit bodily fluids in a Dixie cup while watching porn."

Robin paused, pondering the image for a minute. "You think they watch it or read it?"

"They probably put them in a room with a VCR and portable TV and say, 'Today's porn du jour includes *Caddysnatch* and *Auto-Erotica, the Best of Mercedes Bends*.'"

"I'm impressed. You seem pretty current with your porn."

"I just made those up."

"Then I think you've missed your true calling. Either way, they both sound like cinematic tours de force."

"You're telling me it doesn't bother you that your future child may result from a horny stranger watching a woman with silicone boobs and collagen lips take it up the butt."

"Okay, back up a minute. How'd we go from Neil to anal sex? We were talking about you meeting up with your ex-boyfriend, who eight years ago you let move away without you."

"I found my checklist from senior year and Neil matched nearly every requirement."

"I don't even know where my checklist is, but I'm guessing Mark was ten for ten—a perfect asshole. Which just goes to show you—it's not about meeting abstract criteria."

"Then what's it all about?"

The waiter approached, balancing our roast beef sandwiches on a tray above his head.

"That, my dear friend, is the sixty-four-thousand-dollar question."

20

$\mathscr{P}$aige had agreed to go on her non-date date Thursday night, and we decided to meet at the boutique before grabbing a cab over the river to Cambridge. Robin's lawyer had scheduled a last-minute meeting, so Robin was going to try to meet us at the bar when she finished, which was fine with me. I needed tonight to go off without a hitch if I was going to use Paige and Hugh to prove my cake theory for Vivian, and the last thing I needed was to worry about what Robin thought of Charlie.

My last appointment of the day was leaving when Paige arrived.

"She's cute. What'd they pick?" Paige asked, letting the front door close behind the future Mr. and Mrs. Blake Peterson.

I knelt on the floor and hesitated, pretending to rub an invisible scuff mark with my finger while I figured out what to tell Paige. Blake and Claire picked the cake that, in an ideal world, Paige and Steve would have settled on with little debate. "White cake with blackberry filling and white chocolate mousseline," I mumbled.

Paige inhaled a little too deeply, considered this for a moment and then handed me four pages of computer printouts neatly clipped together. The top sheet's photo showed a three-story brownstone with all of its vitals listed below. "Here. I brought these for you."

I stood up but didn't take the pages. "I told you—I'm not ready to buy a place yet."

"Just take a look; you might be tempted." She waved the pages dramatically in front of me, like she was charming a snake.

"The only thing I'm tempted to do is throw them out."

Paige crossed her arms and stood there watching me. "Considering I'm letting you set me up with a strange man mere weeks after I broke off my engagement, shouldn't you be a bit more gracious?"

"Point taken." Paige handed me the listings and I took them into the kitchen, where, true to my word, I didn't throw them in the garbage. I stuffed them in my desk drawer on top of my catalogs.

"What's that?" Maria asked, eyeing me suspiciously.

"Some real estate listings Paige brought over."

Maria perked up. "Paige is here?" She wiped her floury hands on the front of her apron and straightened her bandanna. "I'm going to say hello."

In the few minutes it took me to shut down the computer and grab my coat, Maria had already beelined it into the gallery, where I found her fussing over Paige like a doting mother hen.

"How's that handsome teacher of yours?" Maria asked, inquiring about Steve.

Paige shot me an uncomfortable look but answered Maria. "We're taking a break right now, to think things over."

Maria threw her hands in the air, as if tossing confetti. "What's to think over? You love him, he loves you—you're getting married!"

Paige gave Maria an endearing smile but didn't defend her situation. "We'll see."

Maria shot me a wary look, as if she was trying to piece together what had happened to Paige and Steve and knew I had something to do with it.

"We better get going," I suggested, grabbing Paige's elbow and leading her out of the boutique. "We're going to be late."

* * *

Paige and I weren't late. But Charlie was. Although we easily located Hugh hanging out by the bar with Amanda and Allison, Charlie was nowhere to be found.

"He begged us to come along," Amanda explained when Hugh left us to order our strawberry margaritas. "But now that you're here, we'll be leaving. You be nice to my baby brother, Paige."

Amanda and Allison waved to Hugh and left before he could object to being stranded with two strange women.

"He's cute, isn't he?" I nudged Paige, who was watching for a table to open up.

"Sure," she answered, her voice completely lacking the enthusiasm I was hoping for.

If only Paige knew how much I had riding on tonight. I'd become accustomed to the belief that if I assembled all the right ingredients and carefully followed the directions line by line, I was assured that in the end, everything would work out fine. I wished Paige was a more willing participant in my little recipe for love.

While we waited, I kept an eye on the door and hoped Charlie would show up soon. I wasn't really too worried about Paige and Hugh; after hearing he'd wanted Amanda and Allison to choose a carrot cake, I just knew Paige would like him. Now it was my job to make sure she knew it, too.

"So, Hugh, why carrot cake?" I asked when he returned with our frozen margaritas.

"What?"

"You wanted Amanda and Allison to pick a carrot cake, and I was just wondering why."

"Oh, that. Well, I don't know, I never really thought about it before." Hugh paused to consider my question. "I just like carrot cake. Especially the cream cheese icing."

I elbowed Paige, who seemed more interested in the basket of free tortilla chips than my matchmaking efforts. "Did you hear that? He loves cream cheese icing."

"I heard."

"Ever had carrot cake with spiced buttercream icing, Hugh?"

"No, but it sounds good."

"Did you hear that, Paige?"

"Yes, Lauren. I heard." Paige sipped absentmindedly from her straw, looking bored.

The cake route wasn't working, so it was time for Plan B.

"So what's going on in the world of mortgages these days?" I asked Hugh and finally saw a spark of interest from Paige.

"Do you think rates are going to go down, or will the Fed raise them as the economy improves?" Paige asked, moving closer to Hugh and giving me an opportunity to step back and watch my wizardry at work.

But their eyes didn't lock in passion; there were no fireworks or starry-eyed gazes. I stood by silently listening to Paige and Hugh talk about the real estate market, whether the bubble was going to burst and whether Chairman Greenspan could keep rates low for much longer—not exactly captivating talk from two people I was hoping would discover they were soul mates.

Just when I thought I'd nearly die of boredom listening to Paige and Hugh go street by street comparing home sales data, Charlie pulled the front door open and pushed his way through the crowd, scanning the room for us. I caught his eye and, without even thinking, my hand shot up and waved.

When I met Neil at the Bell in Hand, there was the recognition that goes along with seeing someone familiar, but not the wave of anticipation that surged when Charlie started toward me.

When he reached me, Charlie brushed an unexpected kiss on my lips. It was a kiss that was way more Harry wants to fuck Sally than Harry wants to be Sally's friend.

"Sorry. Work. What can I say?" he apologized.

Charlie looked even more attractive tonight, in a French blue oxford and navy suit, and judging by the appreciative looks he kept getting from passing women, I wasn't the only one who noticed. I wanted to stamp a sign on his forehead: HANDS OFF.

"You're forgiven, but it better have been worth it—did you convince your client to work it out?"

"Not a chance. His wife was having an affair with his best friend."

I introduced everyone and watched as they played the name game, bringing up people they knew at Charlie's law firm or friends who used an agent in Paige's office.

When the small talk died down, Paige scouted a group leaving a table by the front window, and she and Hugh ran to save the spot.

"What were you telling Mel about me the other night at the bar?" I asked Charlie while we waited by the bar for his margarita on the rocks.

"Just how we met. Why?"

"He told me that people in my line of work are a guy's worst nightmare."

Charlie laughed. "That's just Mel. He's a confirmed bachelor."

More like confirmed asshole.

"So what kind of people do you think he was referring to?"

"Probably people who feed the fantasy of the perfect day followed by the perfect honeymoon, where all you do is have sex on the beach as the water crashes at your feet, before you stroll off hand in hand into the sunset."

"Doesn't sound so bad to me."

"Of course it doesn't. Did you know that studies show that married women are more dissatisfied than married men? And why? Expectations."

"So you want women to lower their expectations?"

"Not at all. It would be nice if everyone had realistic expectations. Here, hold this a sec." He handed me his drink and paid the bartender.

Charlie's explanation was no doubt the result of his clients' experiences, which admittedly would probably make anyone look at relationships with a dubious eye. But even though he seemed to believe women and men vowed "till death do us part" with varying expectations, Charlie didn't sound like he was preaching the gospel according to the single man, imparting his wisdom with the irreverent tone of a radio shock jock. This wasn't a guy thumping his chest, ready to divulge all of his hard-earned knowledge of the elusive female of the species. He wasn't making accusations. He was simply sharing observations, as if offering me a hand, an olive branch, hoping I'd accept. He was just my date, trying to find some common ground in a situation that usually put us on opposite sides of the same field.

"So, how do you think they're doing over there?" Charlie tipped his head toward my coupling experiment seated by the window.

Paige was sitting at our table trying to look interested in something Hugh was saying. She must have felt my eyes on her, because she looked over at me. I waved and took my index finger and pointed to the smile on my face. Paige shrugged, *I'm trying*.

"She's still there. That must be a good sign." Or at least I hoped so. If I was going to convince Vivian, I needed Hugh and Paige as living proof that my cake theory was more than just wishful thinking.

"Shall we join them?" Charlie asked, holding out his elbow to escort me across the bar.

I accepted and we made our way toward the table. I noticed that Paige's margarita glass was already empty; only a shallow pool of pale pink slush lay melting in the bottom.

"We're going to get a bite to eat. Want to come along?" Hugh offered.

Charlie didn't give me time to answer. "Thanks, but we were going to stay and grab something here."

Hugh and Paige left, his hand resting on the small of her back as they walked single file out the front door.

"That was pretty brazen of you, sending Paige off into the night alone with Hugh."

"I'm not opposed to playing matchmaker. Besides, it's a nice change, my contribution to creating universal equilibrium. What goes around, comes around."

We ordered a couple of fajitas and hung out until the waitress was giving us the evil eye, impatiently waiting to turn our table over to another group of paying customers.

"What do you say? Want to come over to my place for a bit?" Charlie asked as the waitress practically took my margarita glass out of my hand in midsip.

He didn't have to ask me twice.

* * *

We took a cab over to Charlie's apartment on the border of the Back Bay and the South End.

"It's not exactly a prestigious address, but it's an easy commute," he told me, unlocking the door.

The loftlike apartment was a wide open space with one large room and a kitchen set off to the side, separated from the living area by a black granite breakfast bar in front of shiny stainless steel appliances. The space had obviously been rehabbed, because although the unit wasn't ornate, it was definitely new. The interior wasn't exactly designer-finished, but it wasn't fraternity chapter room either. It was a grown-up man's home. Unless you counted the foosball table in the corner.

"Big TV, total cliché," Charlie pointed out before I could.

"Four remote controls; I'm impressed."

"Are you kidding me? I'm a novice compared to my friends. They think I'm slumming it with my VCR instead of TiVo."

Charlie left me alone to change out of his suit, and I wandered around taking in the scenery. On a console table lined up against the living room wall, *Sports Illustrated*s were stacked next to a *Fortune* and a *People* magazine. I picked up *People* and was thumbing through its pages when Charlie returned wearing jeans and a plain white T-shirt.

"Big fan of Britney Spears?" I asked him, pointing to the cover.

"My mom got me a subscription for Christmas. Beats last year's present." He pointed behind the dining room table, where one of those framed inspirational prints usually hung in corporate cafeterias was leaning against the wall: SOME PEOPLE DREAM OF SUCCESS . . . WHILE OTHERS WAKE UP AND WORK HARD AT IT. "Don't you just love the sunrise over the golf course? I don't even play golf."

"Remember, it's the thought that counts," I reminded him. A guy who cared about his mom enough to keep cheesy Christmas presents definitely got along with his family. Add another check to the list, please!

"Do you play?" Charlie asked, taking a backgammon briefcase off the bookshelf.

"I've been known to."

Charlie set up the board while I grabbed beers out of the refrigerator. "These are the last two," I told him, handing over a Heineken.

"I know. I'm probably a big disappointment, but I haven't been to the store. I think there's some vodka under the sink." Charlie scavenged a half-full bottle of Absolut from the kitchen cabinet. "Let's see. For mixers we're looking pretty bleak. There's water," he said, sounding hopeful, and held up a Brita pitcher. I shook my head. "Okay, we can rule out milk. What's this?" Charlie stood up and kicked the fridge door shut with his foot. "Three cans of cream soda?"

"That works."

Charlie won the first game of backgammon, after which we decided to keep playing and broke open the vodka.

While we played I told him about Vivian and the book.

"I bet that would be great for business, wouldn't it?"

"It should be. Vivian says I could be the next Emeril."

"You won't forget all us little people once you're a big star, will you?"

I scratched my head and stared at him blankly. "I'm sorry. What was your name again?"

Charlie smirked. "Harry."

After the fourth game I was down three to one and the vodka was gone.

"I hate to even suggest this." Charlie got up and came back with a bottle of ouzo. "A housewarming gift from my college roommate."

"I'm not sure I'd consider someone who gave me ouzo a friend."

"When I got into law school, he gave me a six-pack of Old Milwaukee. I actually considered this a step up."

I set the board up for a fifth game and Charlie brought us back two shot glasses. He poured a round of ouzo and we toasted before swallowing the licorice-flavored liquor that reminded me of the thick black cough medicine my mom used to give me.

I winced. "Real smooth."

Charlie laughed and poured another round.

"The ouzo was supposed to remind me of the summer before law school when my roommate and I went to Europe. You know, the whole backpacking thing, staying in youth hostels hoping to meet willing young women."

I felt an irrational twinge of jealousy as I imagined the score of nameless coeds Charlie woke up with but couldn't resist asking the question. "And did you?"

"I plead the fifth. What did you do after graduation?"

"Nothing as exciting as touring Europe on my back. I got a job."

Charlie rolled the dice and moved his white checker three places. I rolled doubles and landed on two of his checkers, sending him back to the beginning to start over.

"So where'd you go in Europe?"

"All over: France, Italy, Greece, the islands."

"Which ones?"

"Why, you've been?"

"No, but I'd like to. I've read a lot about them—Corfu, Mykonos, Hydra, Naxos, Santorini."

"You know a hell of a lot more than I did when I went there. Why don't you go?"

"At first it was the boutique and getting it up and running. And then, I don't know. It never seemed like the right time."

What I didn't tell Charlie was that the idea of visiting a romantic Greek island by myself, with its whitewashed arches and domes set against a sapphire sea, sounded about as much fun as an Outward Bound solo excursion.

"Go, Lauren," Charlie told me, seriously, as if it was his personal duty to make sure I didn't miss out on the experience. "You'll regret it if you keep putting it off. Just go."

That's when I realized what was different about Charlie. It wasn't the way he looked at me, but the way he saw me. Maybe it was something they taught you in law school, or maybe Charlie didn't even realize he was doing it, but he held my gaze with an interest and intensity that made me not want to look away.

In spite of the beer and vodka and shots of ouzo, or maybe thanks to all three, I managed to even up the score at three games apiece. Charlie didn't make a move to reset the board for another game, content to let us tie.

"Why don't you set the board up while I get this mess out of our way?" I stood, ready to take the empty bottles and glasses into the kitchen, when Charlie reached out and pulled me down onto the couch, where he leaned me back on the cushions and looked at me for a minute before brushing his lips against mine. I closed my eyes and let my hands run up his back, feeling his muscles tighten as he pressed against me.

I knew where this was going, and I wanted it to go there, even if I was breaking about eleven canons of prudent dating. Here was my opportunity to prove that I wasn't the least bit concerned about Charlie's lack of marriage potential.

All of a sudden Charlie pulled back. "One more game. Winner takes all."

We played another game, but my concentration was shot.

I became acutely aware of his body, the way his jeans bunched around his thighs when he moved toward the board, the way his T-shirt fell away from his body when he leaned forward to roll the dice, even the three-inch scar above his ankle when he rested his bare feet on the table.

"How'd you get the scar?" I asked, just in case he caught me staring.

"Fell out of a tree when I was a kid. The bone went right through my skin."

I made a face. "Did you learn your lesson about climbing trees?"

"No. But I did learn my lesson about falling."

The game was over quickly, with Charlie defeating me easily. Being the good sport I am, I led Charlie straight to his bedroom, where the winner was going to get justly rewarded.

I can do this, I kept repeating to myself. Not only could I do this, but I was going to enjoy every minute of it.

Game, set, match. Charlie won hands down. Neil who? I couldn't even imagine that sex was ever that good with Neil, that slow and fevered and tender and aggressive.

Afterward we lay on our sides facing each other, Charlie stroking my hair away from my face until it was fanned out on the pillow under us. Up close I could see that his eyes weren't brown; they were golden and soft, like melted brown sugar.

Okay, maybe I can't do this after all.

"What?" I asked, curious for an explanation for the amused look on his face.

"Emeril would be proud of your ability to kick it up a notch, but I'm actually a little disappointed."

I pulled away and propped myself up on my elbows. "Disappointed?"

"Yeah. I kept waiting for you to yell *'Bam!'*" Charlie pulled the covers over our heads and laughed at me. When we started to suffocate under the flannel sheets, we poked our heads out and lay there silently until both of us were on the verge of finally succumbing to an alcohol-induced sleep.

But I had to go to the bathroom. I knew it was either now or later, in the middle of the night in a strange room where I'd probably end up accidentally squatting in a closet. I waited until Charlie's breathing was heavy and then slipped out of bed.

"You're not making a quick getaway, are you?" Charlie asked, watching me in the dark.

"Don't get your hopes up. I'm not that easy."

"If I thought you were easy we would have played Trivial Pursuit."

In the bathroom I looked for some clues to the man in the other room. But there was nothing extraordinary, nothing that would make Charlie stand out in a room of other thirty-something men. When I was younger, situations like this were usually carefully planned. A quiet bathroom, a dainty flush, a quick tiptoe back to the bed, where I'd slide under the covers and lay there with my stomach pulled into my belly button and my back slightly arched—a move every woman on a beach in a bikini has attempted at some point. But there was nothing dainty about a drunk and naked thirty-two-year-old woman trying to find her way back to a strange bed in the dark.

As I crawled back under the covers it occurred to me that movie sex was so unrealistic, so neat and clean. You never see the woman hop out of bed and make a quick retreat to the bathroom before the remnants of her encounter slide down her legs and onto the ceramic tile. The guy never needs to wipe his private parts with a pair of boxers or socks discretely left on the nightstand for exactly that purpose. Where'd they toss the liquid-filled condom so it didn't spill all over the place? And, if these things never take place, then how come we never see one half of the happy couple make a face when he or she inevitably rolls over onto the wet spot?

"Come here." Charlie ran his hand along the curve of my waist and then pulled me closer in to him. "You're so nice and warm," he whispered, wrapping his body around me until I could feel the fine hairs on his chest pressed against my back.

Even though Charlie fell right back to sleep, I couldn't get comfortable. It wasn't that I was physically uncomfortable; as a matter of fact, Charlie made quite a cozy sleeping companion. No, the problem was in my head. There were restless thoughts in there that wouldn't give in to the temptation of Charlie's warm skin and flannel sheets that still smelled like fabric softener.

So if my bravado didn't give me proof that I was a carefree woman who could have sex with a man she was attracted to without wanting more, then what did it give me? Amazing sex and a voice in my head that couldn't figure out for the life of me why I couldn't just enjoy the fact that Charlie wanted me here. In his apartment. In his bed.

As much as I wanted to just close my eyes and let myself drift off to sleep, my mind wouldn't let me. Instead I wiggled away and turned over.

"Is everything okay?" Charlie asked, his eyes still closed.

"Everything's fine," I lied.

I don't know why I was so bothered by his admission. I'd slept with men before who didn't want to marry me. Shit, I'd slept with a couple I didn't even want to know my name.

I attempted to channel the woman that Neil remembered and fell right to sleep.

When I opened my eyes the next morning, Charlie was on his side with an arm resting across my stomach. As he lay there I studied his face. A night's worth of stubble blanketed his cheeks and upper lip, creating a shadow that looked soft despite the prickly whiskers, like suede. The clean-shaven guy from the night before had been replaced by a more rugged version, more Marlboro man than George Michael.

Maybe my middle-of-the-night reservations were a result more of ouzo-induced delirium than of any true misgivings about Charlie. Watching him sleep so comfortably beside me made it easier to overlook the tiny matter of our uncertain future—not *easy*, just *easier*.

I ran my finger lightly along the stubble and Charlie's eyelashes seemed to shiver before his eyes opened and he looked back at me, not saying a word.

"It's almost seven-thirty," I whispered, figuring a lawyer must start his days earlier than the owner of a cake boutique.

"Shit," he moaned, his voice scratchy. "Note to self— throw out ouzo."

"There's none to throw out. We finished the bottle."

"How're you feeling?" he asked, laying his head on my chest and running his hand along the inside of my thighs.

"A wee bit queasy, but other than that, I'm still here."

"I'm glad." Charlie looked up at me, his hair in disarray. "So, I'd say that was a pretty successful third date. What do you think?"

What did I think? Bed head, a full bladder, morning breath and visits from the sandman. I was no Meg Ryan. Then again, she had better hair than I did.

I slid down under Charlie's body until we were face to face, my legs curled around his calves, pulling him closer. "Remember, *Some people dream of success . . . while others wake up and work hard at it.*"

21

$\mathcal{O}$liver was waiting for me when I got home. Luckily he didn't ask me where I'd been or question why I was still wearing last night's pants and shirt, which smelled like I'd rolled around in an ashtray before washing off in a fountain of grain alcohol. He just sat perched against my pillows looking happy to see me, his thin, frayed threaded mouth still managing to curve upward even as the ends were unraveling.

Round two with Charlie had been just as enjoyable as round one, even if we had slowed down a couple of times to keep last night's ouzo from making an unwelcome morning appearance. When he put me in a cab and kissed me good-bye I was even feeling quite good, if you didn't count the dull pounding in my temples and a bad case of dry mouth.

But as the cab got closer to home the same sinking feeling that had crawled into bed with me last night decided to join me in the backseat of the taxi. And by the time I walked through my front door there was no denying that the churning in my stomach wasn't just a mixture of margaritas, beer, vodka and ouzo shots, but an unlikely combination of pleasure and remorse.

I'd taken one on the chin for independent-minded women everywhere and ended up feeling like the *Playboy* centerfold who claims to love the political writings of Socrates and Plato. Without the perky breasts, of course. No matter how many times I told myself it didn't matter, no matter how illogical my feelings toward Charlie were, I'd been fooling myself.

Granted, at the time crawling under the sheets with Charlie seemed extraordinarily easy, even effortless. And there was no denying that when I was bent over the side of his bed I was more concerned with whether the neighbors could hear the headboard smacking against the wall than whether or not Charlie was reconsidering his stance on marriage. Even though sleeping with Charlie seemed to change everything, it really didn't change anything. And it definitely didn't change the fact that Neil had walked into the boutique and practically held up a sign that said I'M YOUR MAN.

"What do you think?" I asked Oliver as I sat on the bed and unbuttoned my shirt.

True to form, Oliver remained quiet. He always was the strong, silent type.

I stood up and continued undressing in front of the mirror, looking for evidence of Charlie. But instead of fingerprints or hickeys, all I could find was a satisfied smile on my lips and a worried look in my eyes.

Even if Oliver wasn't any help, one thing was clear. I needed to take a shower and get to work. And I had to figure out a way to wipe that smile off my face. The last thing I needed was for Maria to make a comment about my postcoital glow.

I noticed the commotion in front of the boutique when I was a block away. Two police cars and at least four white vans were parallel parked, and three policemen were standing on the sidewalk talking into their walkie-talkies. My heart started beating fast and my eyes immediately looked for signs of a raging fire. I ran right past Starbucks toward the ambulances. But when I reached the boutique I saw that it wasn't walkie-talkies the men were lifting to their mouths; it was cups of coffee. And the spheres on top of the vans weren't sirens; they were satellite dishes. And the logos on their side panels weren't from Mass General; they were from TV and radio stations. And that's when I really panicked.

I pushed past the cluster of reporters loitering around the doorway smoking cigarettes, and entered the boutique.

"Lauren!" Vivian cried, rushing over to me. "Where have you been? The press conference starts in fifteen minutes."

Vivian, Bradley Potter and a woman I assumed was from the publicity department were all dressed in dark business suits, which pretty much matched the somber look on Maria's face as she watched me through the window in the kitchen door.

Vivian looked me up and down. "You're going to have to hurry if you plan on changing your outfit."

I hadn't planned on changing. I hadn't planned on standing up in front of twenty reporters in my Levi's and Nike baseball shirt, either. I had to think quickly.

"But this is what I usually wear in the kitchen when I bake."

Vivian waved the publicist over. "Lauren thinks we should show what she looks like when she bakes instead of making her look press-ready."

The publicist nodded. "That's not a bad idea. We make her look accessible, like she just stepped out of the kitchen after measuring the ingredients for a cake."

"Exactly," I agreed, but the publicist just gave me a sidelong glance.

"But that doesn't mean she has to look like she had a rough night drinking. Let's get some makeup on her."

I'd averted the fashion police, but I still had to face Maria.

The reporters were filing into the boutique and taking seats in the rows of chairs Vivian had rented for the occasion. I wended my way through the growing crowd with their pads of paper and mini tape recorders, and met up with Maria in the kitchen.

"What's going on?" Maria demanded.

"It's just a little press conference."

"Little? That Vivian and her crew were here at seven o'clock this morning rearranging the boutique. On a Friday. We have cakes to prepare for tomorrow, or did that small detail escape your mind?"

"They're not coming into the kitchen, and they'll be out of here as soon as it's over."

"Why didn't you tell me about this?"

"I forgot."

"You forgot." Maria shook her head at the tile floor.

"I'm sorry, I should have told you. My bad."

"You need to get your act together, Lauren."

"I said I was sorry. Now where can I find a clean apron?"

"An apron?"

"They want me to look like I was just in the kitchen baking."

Maria went into the back room and returned with a neatly pressed white cotton apron. "You didn't tell me this book was a work of fiction."

I took the apron and shook it out, smoothing the folds. "They'll be out of here in an hour, I promise."

After the publicist quieted the reporters, Bradley made a brief pitch about Pegasus Publishing and its commitment to quality before introducing Vivian.

"Thank you, Bradley. We're here today because Pegasus Publishing is excited to announce that Lauren Gallagher, owner of Lauren's Luscious Licks and pastry chef extraordinaire, will be partnering with us on her first book. Lauren Gallagher revolutionized the way we all look at wedding cakes when she opened her cake boutique right here on Newbury Street. She built Lauren's Luscious Licks one cake at a time and today is recognized for her exquisite cake creations, her craftsmanship and her unwavering dedication to her craft."

Vivian paused, and for a minute I almost expected Maria to burst into the room and put a stop to this entire charade. But while I was seated beside the podium receiving praise for my baking talents, Maria was in the kitchen baking.

"As I'm sure everyone here knows, Lauren Gallagher's clients read like a who's who of Boston society, from political leaders to business titans. In her yet untitled book, Lauren Gallagher will give readers a behind-the-scenes look at a preeminent pastry chef's secrets."

Vivian turned to me and smiled. "It is my pleasure to introduce to you today our very own Lauren Gallagher."

A polite round of applause welled up and then faded as I took my place at the podium for questions. As I stood there calling on the raised hands, the publicist shot me a thumbs up from the back of the room. After a rocky start that included a poor wardrobe choice, bloodshot eyes and the guest of honor dry heaving into the toilet as I attempted to put on my lipstick, it was all going according to plan.

22

$\mathcal{W}$hile I was busy dazzling the press with my extensive knowledge of wedding confections, Robin was being deposed in a law firm's conference room downtown, and Paige was one day into my matchmaking experiment. We decided to meet for breakfast early Saturday morning to rehash the events of the past twenty-four hours.

"We went out for Thai food after we left you and Charlie at Julio's," Paige told us. "It was good."

"The food or the date?" Robin asked, but Paige was too busy finishing her tomato juice to answer.

I decided to assume she meant the date, which put me that much closer to a blockbuster book.

"Hugh sounds great. I wish I got to meet him." Robin added some positive reinforcement before spreading a dollop of cream cheese on her bagel. "Are you going to see him again?"

"We'll see."

"I promise I'll be there next time. Believe me, given the choice I would take margaritas with you guys over a meeting with my lawyer any day. You would not believe all the crap he wanted to go over before the deposition on Friday. My God, it was like I was being prepared for a public stoning."

"So how was the deposition?"

Robin cringed. "Can't you see the rock marks? They made me sound like a bitter, angry control freak."

Robin paused for a minute and waited for one of us to assure her she wasn't any of those things, but our mouths were full so instead we shook our heads reassuringly.

"Afterward Jeremy came running up to me in the hall, saying how sorry he was or some other bullshit before his brother-in-law pulled him away. Man, I was fucked."

Paige smirked. "You're not the only one."

Robin's eyes shot to Paige, who shook her head and pointed to me.

"Oh my God; you slept with Charlie?" Robin practically gasped, leaving me to believe that she and Paige had probably decided I'd given up on sex altogether.

"I had to. He beat me at backgammon."

"You wagered with sex?"

"Not exactly."

"Sounds like you were the real winner. So was it something you'd like to do again?"

I looked up, straightfaced. "The backgammon or the sex?"

Robin laughed. "Wow. I'm impressed. Indiscriminate sex on a Thursday night wasn't exactly what I was expecting to hear about with my morning coffee."

"You also realize, of course, that you'll probably never hear from him again. You should have waited until the fourth date," Paige suggested. I didn't bother pointing out that she'd slept with Steve before they even returned from Key West.

"Come on, what's the big deal? It's not like she's going to marry him, right?" Robin defended me and at the same time managed to hit a nerve that had felt exposed since I left Charlie's apartment Friday morning.

"I'll have you know that he called yesterday, a mere six hours after I left his apartment. But I'm not sure if I'm going to keep seeing him."

Robin threw up her arms. "Wait a minute. You found someone you like, who is intelligent and fun and apparently good in bed, and you want to stop seeing him?" Robin turned to Paige. "Did I miss something here?"

Paige shrugged. "I'm lost. What's up?"

I took a bite of my bagel to avoid answering. What they didn't understand, and what I didn't tell them, was that there was no recipe for a relationship with Charlie, no way to know how it would turn out. And even though I'd left it blank, I was beginning to figure out what line number one on my list should have been. Numbers two through ten didn't mean a thing if the man I described didn't want the same ending I'd been waiting for.

In the silence, Robin's expression turned from confusion to understanding. "I think I get it. Is this because he told you he doesn't want to get married?"

"Or because Neil does?" Paige asked.

"Why are you worried about getting married all of a sudden?"

"I'm not worried."

Robin looked around for our waiter and signaled for the check. "Then keep sleeping with him."

Sure, just continue sleeping with Charlie. Have mind-blowing sex. Keep dating. Become his girlfriend. Fall in love. Spend holidays together and exchange thoughtful gifts. It sounded easy enough.

Paige placed a five-dollar bill on the table. "I've got to get to the office. I made an offer on the house near Cleveland Circle and they're supposed to get back to me today."

My bagel stuck in my throat as I envisioned the ants industriously building their fortress on Paige's kitchen counter. "Please tell me you're not buying that hellhole."

"Oh, yes, I am," Paige replied emphatically and then turned to Robin. "I don't know what she's talking about. The place is great."

"Better you than me." I took one more bite of my bagel and offered to walk with her on my way to the boutique. "Are you coming?" I asked Robin.

"I think I'll finish my juice and then head off to Baby-Gap to do a little pre-insemination browsing. You ladies enjoy yourselves."

Pre-insemination shopping. I doubted BabyGap had a gift card for that.

Paige and I collected our coats and were about to leave the table when Paige ducked back down into her seat.

"Don't look now," she instructed, barely moving her lips in an effort to remain inconspicuous.

"What?" Robin twisted around toward the front door.

"Did you not understand what I meant by *Don't look now*?" Paige hissed, but it was too late.

"Robin, can I talk to you?" Jeremy was standing next to our booth, while Denny and Mitch watched him from their spots at the lunch counter.

"Are you fucking kidding me?" Robin shot back. "After what you did to me yesterday in that room? Go to hell."

Robin stood up, grabbed her jacket and pushed past Jeremy. But he wasn't giving up that easily and followed her outside.

I looked over at Denny and Mitch, who just shrugged and went back to their Western omelets.

I tossed my money on the table and Paige and I went after Robin and Jeremy.

After walking half a block with Jeremy on her heels, Robin stopped and whipped around to face him. "Do I need to get a restraining order to keep you away from me?" she shouted.

"I just wanted to apologize for yesterday. I had no idea my brother-in-law was going to go after you like that."

"What the hell did you think was going to happen? It's a *lawsuit*! Did you think we'd sit down and share a few laughs over tea?"

"I meant I didn't know he'd attack you personally."

"Nice try, but too little, too late."

Robin stormed off, probably the angriest customer ever to walk through the doors of BabyGap in search of pink gingham jumpers and baby blue onesies.

Jeremy turned back toward the diner and saw us standing there observing the scene.

"I swear, I had no idea my brother-in-law was going to put her through that yesterday," he explained again. "Is the entire male population of the species destined to pay for her ex-husband's sins?" he asked me.

"Unless you can find someone else for her to blame, I think so."

Paige nodded. "Your omelet's probably getting cold, Jeremy."

Jeremy passed us on his way back to the diner, shaking

his head at the ground as he walked. But whether Robin's re-action pissed him off or he felt sorry for her, I really couldn't tell.

"Why don't you ever mention Steve?" I asked Paige as we passed storeowners unlocking their front doors in prepara-tion for Saturday's shopping crowd.

"What's the point? It's not going to change anything." Paige stared straight ahead as she answered, and I had to as-sume that she was dealing with this the only way she could—by removing her heart from the equation and letting her head do all the work.

"Has he called you?"

Paige stopped walking and turned to me. "Let's not do this, okay? I did what everyone thought I should do. It's over. Yes, he's called me. Yes, he's stopped by my apart-ment. Is the wedding back on? No." She resumed her stride. "So what are you going to do about Charlie?" she asked, her tone returning to normal.

"What do you think I should do?"

"I think you should keep seeing him."

I felt obliged to take Paige's advice. After all, she'd taken mine.

23

On Sunday morning I lay in bed longer than I should have. The sun streaming through my bedroom window was deceiving, giving the impression that outside the dusty pane of glass a warm summer day awaited. It was one of those brilliant early spring sunshines, the kind that reflects its rays off everything it touches and turns the windshields of cars into traveling mirrors, and the ground, still wet from melted snow and the occasional shower, blinds you even as you turn your face toward the sun, basking in its warmth. All it took was one palm on the glass to determine that even though the sun was ready to shine, it was still April.

My only plan for the day was a trip to the bookstore. Now that we'd announced to the world that Lauren Gallagher was going to impart her cake insight to the masses, I thought I should have some idea what other books were already telling future brides. Besides, I wanted to get my hands on the Vera Wang book Vivian seemed to revere so highly.

After spending Saturday night alone, I thought that Paige might need some company. I rang her up to see if she wanted to meet me at Barnes and Noble for a little browsing.

"Sounds like fun, but I can't." Paige spoke fast and was oddly upbeat for a Sunday morning.

"Are you working? Because I could stop by, and if you're not on an appointment, maybe we could grab some lunch."

"I'm not working. I just have plans."

Paige was being awfully evasive, but she sounded too

happy for a woman with plans to go grocery shopping. "Are you seeing Hugh?"

Paige hesitated. "Yeah."

A second date. My plan was going to work out just as I'd anticipated. Bring on the carrot cake! "Why didn't you just tell me?"

"I didn't want you to make a big deal out of it."

"I wouldn't do that."

"Please." I could practically hear Paige rolling her eyes. "Don't even pretend you weren't just thinking about carrot cake."

The girl just knew me too well.

Since it looked like I was flying solo for the day, I had plenty of time to get down to the bookstore, and enough time to clean my apartment. I collected the supplies from under my kitchen sink and rolled up my pajama sleeves. It wasn't as if I had to clean a double sink and whirlpool tub, so in all of seven minutes I'd managed to mop the floor and organize the clutter under my sink. While I was stooped over the bathtub scrubbing the remains of my volumizing shampoo, I decided that I should partake of the fruits of my labor. I set myself up in the bathtub with a tall glass of orange juice, a bowl of strawberries and a little light reading—my college yearbook.

I propped my elbows up on the side of the bathtub and held the book above the steaming bubbles. I turned the pages slowly, stopping when I came to one of the many pictures of Paige, a proud and smiling leader of several extracurricular activities. I flipped past a portrait of a woman I recognized from my senior ethics class. She'd shown up one day our senior year with the biggest rock I'd ever seen on her finger— at twenty-two! That meant she'd probably been married almost ten years by now, assuming she was still married. Ten years since graduation, and what did I have to show for it? A glass tasting table, a Lalique vase and an appointment book filled with other people's special days.

When I reached my senior picture, I examined the portrait closely, trying to find a clue as to what that young woman was thinking, to see the person that Neil described. I looked into my own black-and-white face, and what I found was a broad smile and wide eyes that seemed to be devoid of any panic about her future. I was fearless. Or maybe just young and stupid.

There were so many unknowns ahead—moving into my own apartment, finding a job, breaking up with Neil, losing a job—and instead of being fazed by it all I remember looking forward to it. All that ambiguity that followed graduation, the uncertainty of a career, and I wasn't fazed one bit.

Even when I was in my studio apartment I experimented with different cakes and ingredients, throwing out about every fourth try because I'd screwed something up. But there wasn't any room for trial and error once we moved into the boutique, and now it seemed I was destined to follow recipes to the letter, every time, so I'd be assured of the outcome of every cake.

Maybe I hadn't been as fearless as I looked in my yearbook picture. After all, I'd come up with my first recipe during senior year, even if I didn't realize it at the time. Although it was written on notebook paper instead of typed on an index card, I'd written down the ingredients for my perfect man.

I removed the list from between the pages of my yearbook. The ten criteria for my perfect companion were still listed in my bubbly handwriting. They hadn't gone anywhere and they hadn't changed. As I held the list, water from my pruned fingertips spread across the page. I was so engrossed in my dissection of the nine sentences and the single empty line that when the phone rang I jumped and my list fell beneath the bubbles.

As I skimmed the bottom of the tub for the piece of paper, I reached for the portable phone I'd left on the bath mat, trying not to get suds on the receiver or drop the slippery handset into the tub and seal my fate with death by electrocution.

"You want to grab some lunch?" Charlie asked.

I was so surprised to hear his voice, I stopped searching for the list. "Sure. What were you thinking?"

"I wasn't really thinking anything in particular. I'm at the office finishing up some work that's due tomorrow. I was pretty useless on Friday, needless to say."

"Why don't you meet me at the Barnes and Noble at the

Prudential Center. I wanted to do a little research for the book."

We agreed to meet at one-thirty, and I resumed my search for the waterlogged paper. I finally found it settled around the drain, the writing smudged and barely discernable.

At Barnes and Noble, I wandered the aisles until I found the wedding section, actually a combined display of wedding and etiquette books. How ironic that the bookseller paired wedding and etiquette but stacked the relationship books four aisles away, by psychology. I guess it was more important to know how to identify the correct fork than it was to know how to identify the right spouse.

Vera Wang's timeless tome stood proudly on the top shelf, a large, elegant volume hermetically sealed in shrink-wrap, as if it contained secrets only a privileged few could share. I had to admit, the cover, with its misty, out-of-focus black-and-white photo of a veiled bride gazing out a window, was beautiful in a timeless way, like pictures of war brides. I turned the book over and learned that Vera's secrets didn't come cheap—a whopping sixty-five dollars.

I set Vera's book back on the shelf and ran my fingers along the spines of the other books, which came in every shape and size and addressed every possible wedding subject.

There were books on weddings—elegant weddings, outdoor weddings, romantic weddings, big weddings, intimate weddings, easy weddings, inexpensive weddings, and my personal favorite, instant weddings—although I was disappointed to learn that an instant wedding in fact takes four months to plan.

There were books for all types of brides—buff brides, second brides, petite brides, modern brides, conscious brides, and frugal brides. There were also books for the men these brides were marrying, the titles of which didn't bode very well for their future wives. The men were mostly of the foolish variety, as if the day a man slipped a diamond on a woman's finger all his common sense went out the window—the *Pocket Idiot's Guide to Being a Groom,* the *Clueless Groom's Guide,* and the *Reluctant Groom*. Grim.

To keep everyone else from feeling left out, several books

addressed the special needs of the mothers, fathers, siblings and friends of the bride, as well as all the special events they'd be planning—bridal showers, bachelorette parties, wedding toasts, speeches and, of course, honeymoons. The shelves were also packed with enough planners, calendars, organizers and guides to make wedding planning seem like a full-time job. Which is why I wasn't surprised to find a book on guerrilla weddings.

And if all this was a little overwhelming for a bride-to-be, there was always *Chicken Soup for the Bride's Soul*.

I flipped through a few of the books that included sections devoted to receptions and took note of the cakes they featured. It seemed that Vivian knew what she was talking about. Although there were books exploring just about every facet of the wedding, from flowers to hairstyles, I couldn't find a single book that helped women design a fitting cake, one that reflected the unique characteristics of the couple and their future together. I had my work cut out for me.

"There's a lot to know, isn't there?" A woman knelt on the floor next to me and reached for a book on vows.

"There sure is," I agreed.

"When's your wedding?" she asked, flipping the pages of her book.

"There's no wedding. I'm just doing some research on wedding cakes. You know, wedding cakes were originally a rite of fertility," I explained and then glanced over at her. She was probably in her late twenties, with curly black hair that she'd tied back with a scarf. From the diamond solitaire on her finger, it was obvious that she wasn't just browsing. "When's your wedding date?"

"We don't know yet. I just got engaged last night." She held up her hand and waved her fingers at me. "It still feels so weird."

"Congratulations."

"Thanks." She smiled at me and then looked back down at her finger. "You know, I never thought it really mattered, but the minute Todd got on his knees and asked me to marry him I realized that this is it. This is what I'd been waiting for. You know what I mean?"

I nodded, but instead of returning her smile I looked down at my own empty hand. "Yes, I think I do."

Charlie was waiting by the entrance at one-thirty, dressed more casually than I'd ever seen him—if you don't count being naked. It was the first time we'd seen each other since I left his apartment Friday morning, and all of a sudden, spotting him standing by the magazine rack flipping through *Time,* I was nervous. What if he expected us to wind up in bed again this afternoon? Worse yet, what if he didn't?

"Did you figure out how to give Vivian a best seller?" Charlie asked as I approached, his warm smile dissolving any fears I'd had.

"I'm working on it," I told him, determined to enjoy our day together without worrying about what came next.

Charlie suggested we take advantage of the sunny afternoon and walk until we found a place for lunch.

"How'd Paige and Hugh do?" he asked, reaching for my hand and lacing his fingers between mine.

Not as good as us, I thought. "So far, so good. She's seeing him again today."

"Speaking of seeing someone again, the marathon goes right by my friend's place in Brookline, and he's having a little party next Monday. A bunch of the guys are going to the Red Sox game that morning, but I thought you could meet me at his place afterward."

"I'm not exactly a big runner, but I think I could cheer on those more ambitious than myself. Especially if all it requires is sitting on someone's porch and clapping occasionally."

"I promise, the only physical exertion required all day is the ability to stir the celery stalk in your Bloody Mary."

We turned down Newbury Street and walked past the familiar stores I saw every day. Upscale boutiques with security men placed near the entrances mixed with the staples of contemporary shopping—Gap, Banana Republic, Ann Taylor. Above street level, chic hair salons and designer showrooms overlooked the strolling patrons below.

A mother-and-daughter team of shoppers passed us carrying their loot in oversized stiff paper shopping bags.

"Look at all these people who think shopping on Newbury Street is a special occasion, and for you it's probably no big deal."

"Somehow I always end up here," I observed, glancing up at the third-story bay windows where designer wedding dresses were displayed on headless mannequins. The billowing skirts and beaded sheaths were close enough to seduce you, but just out of reach.

As we stood on the corner of Dartmouth waiting for the light to change, I recognized the lanky gait coming toward us in thick rubber-soled hiking boots and my stomach jumped. Steve was about half a block away when he cut across Newbury Street and ducked into Starbucks.

Charlie watched my eyes follow Steve into the store.

"Who was that?"

"Paige's ex-fiancé."

"Oh." Even though the light changed, Charlie didn't make a move to enter the crosswalk.

"Do you want to go say hi?" he offered.

I debated what to do. It was totally different from running into Mark. Steve didn't crush Paige. Robin and I did.

"Can we just walk by?" I asked Charlie. "Maybe if he sees us I'll say something."

We crossed over to the other side of the street, and as we passed the plate-glass window I caught sight of Steve sitting at a small round bistro table. I was about to wave when I noticed he was seated across from a woman with a ponytail poking out the back of her baseball cap. I couldn't see her face, but I had a clear view of Steve as he reached across the table for her hand.

I quickly pulled Charlie away from the window.

"Did you see him?" he asked.

"It wasn't Steve."

But it was Steve. Steve and another woman sharing a coffee. I'd been right. We'd been right. I didn't have to feel bad for Steve anymore. Without intending to, Steve had absolved me of my guilt.

Charlie and I kept walking until we reached the public garden. The warming day had lured parents and their children into the park, where they were playing together on the softening grass. Under the gated arch of the Arlington Street entrance, Charlie stopped and turned me toward him.

"It's too bad the swan boats aren't back yet. We could go for a ride." He placed his hands on my hips and pulled me closer. "I think they return next week. We'll have to come back."

Charlie leaned down and kissed me, his lips soft and gentle, lacking the urgency of that first kiss on his couch. "So, what do you say? A date with the swan boats in two weeks?"

"Sure, maybe." More like maybe not. After Neil left for DC I started to slowly rediscover Boston as a single person. I ventured to the banks of the Charles to read a book and to the band shell for the Boston Pops Fourth of July concert. But I never reclaimed the swan boats as my own. They seemed reserved for couples and families, and since Neil had taken me on numerous swan rides around the lagoon, I always thought of it as *our* place. Charlie's suggestion that we revisit the swan boats together may have sounded romantic, but it was just not going to happen.

"I have a great idea." Charlie raised his hand to hail a cab.

"Where are we going?"

"If you won't go to Greece, then I'll make Greece come to you. We're going to a Greek restaurant for lunch."

At that moment, a black Lincoln Town Car pulled up to the Arlington Street stoplight, its darkly tinted windows shielding its occupants from our prying eyes. Even though I couldn't see the people in the backseat, I knew they could see me. And I wondered what they glimpsed when they looked at us standing on the curb, waiting for a ride.

Before the light changed and the car pulled away, I saw two people reflected in the smoky windows, the arch above their heads creating a wrought iron frame for the still life. I saw two people who were possibly on the verge of discovering something special. And I couldn't for the life of me figure out why that didn't seem like enough.

24

The Boston Marathon is run every Patriots' Day, a state holiday that's supposed to commemorate the start of the revolutionary war but really just gives everyone in Boston an excuse to hit an early-morning baseball game and then litter the streets along the course to cheer on the 17,000 runners who trained months for this day.

Most businesses were closed, including the boutique, so I had some time to kill before meeting Charlie in Brookline. Robin was holding an all-day seminar for women desperately in need of an intensive eight-hour workshop, so I decided to drop in on Paige at the new house. Even though the place was a total eyesore and should probably be condemned, Paige was excited to start on the repairs that would bring the place up to code and hopefully transform it into a building that was habitable for more than just six-legged creatures.

The front door was open when I arrived, and I could see Paige crouched in the living room, sanding down the newly exposed wood floors.

"So how'd the inspection go?" I yelled above the gritty sound of the sandpaper, startling Paige.

She hesitated for a minute and then stood up, the knees of her jean overalls powdered with dust. "Not bad. A few things here and there, but nothing I can't work with. Structurally, the place is sound." Paige wiped a rubber-gloved hand across her forehead and dropped a soggy sponge into the bucket beside her.

"This is for you." I handed Paige the potted violets I'd picked up before I hopped on the T. "Sorry about making fun of the house. I hope you have fun with it."

"Thanks." Paige took the plant and placed it on the windowsill where the freshly cleaned glass panes looked transparent in the sunlight. "What are you doing here?"

"Enjoying a break from the boutique. If I spend one more minute talking about basket-weaved buttercream, I'm going to scream."

Paige picked up an empty bucket and came over to me. "What's wrong?" she asked, turning the bucket over and using it as an impromptu seat.

"I don't know. This thing with Charlie isn't going anywhere."

"That depends on your definition of the destination, doesn't it?"

"What's that mean?"

"Just that I think you should see where it takes you before you write him off completely."

But what if it took me down a long, winding path to nowhere? I remembered how adamant Robin was about proving that she was different from those women we felt sorry for, the ones we imagined surrendering themselves to marriage, the ones who conceded to the idea of marriage as an achievement. Even though she took Mark's name, in the two years they were married, Robin hadn't shared much else. But now I wondered if maybe Robin hadn't been so afraid that finding Mark meant losing herself, their marriage would have turned out differently. Even though none of us said anything out loud, there were times when I got the feeling we were all thinking that the traditional roles we fought so hard to avoid sounded awfully appealing—to relinquish some of the control was also to relinquish the responsibility for the outcome.

"You know what I hate even more than the idea that Charlie never wants to get married? That I care so much when all along I thought it didn't matter."

"If you think it doesn't matter, just ask Robin," Paige reminded me.

"Do you think Charlie will change his mind?" I asked.

"I don't think you should ever go into a relationship with the idea that the other person has to change." Paige didn't look at me as she offered her advice, and for a minute I wondered if she was talking about Charlie or Steve. "Look, I don't even really know Charlie, but I do know that in the three years you were with Neil, I didn't see you this worked up."

"Does Hugh have you worked up?" I asked.

Paige cleared her throat and got to her feet, taking the bucket with her. "Sure. Everything's going great."

"You don't sound very convincing."

Paige picked up a mop and started wiping down the floor. "We've gone out only a few times. What do you want me to say, that he's my soul mate?"

"Would that be asking too much?"

"Yeah, it would."

Above our heads the ceiling shook with the weight of heavy footsteps.

"What's that?" I covered my head as little flakes of plaster floated to the ground.

"What?" Paige continued mopping, ignoring the banging that had just started on the second floor.

"Paige," a man shouted from upstairs in a voice I thought I recognized. "I need you."

"Just a minute. *Lauren* just stopped by for a second," she called out, almost intentionally emphasizing my name by stretching it out into two distinct syllables.

Paige gave me a sheepish look, and I immediately understood. "Why didn't you tell me Hugh was up there?"

Paige shrugged and started walking toward the door, which she held open until I followed her. "Thanks for the plant."

I didn't even have a chance to say good-bye before the door closed behind me.

Out on the sidewalk I gazed up at the second-floor window, where paper-thin shades shielded Paige's and Hugh's shadows from prying eyes. The yellow light in the background elongated their hazy figures, and as they embraced they seemed to combine to form a single thin line framed by the peeling exterior of the house.

Watching the scene unfold like a silent movie gave me goose bumps, the fine hairs on my neck perking up at the idea that my theory was now more than just a silly notion. There just might be a carrot cake in Paige's future yet.

But my voyeuristic spying also left me feeling hollow, as if the small bit of hope I'd carried with me since Charlie made his announcement had finally been worn away by watching Paige find what I didn't even know I was waiting for.

I caught the green line down to St. Paul Street and found Charlie's friend's apartment. Marathon spectators were already lining the street, holding the balloons and clappers and noisemakers that were supposed to provide the encouragement needed to carry the runners along the final three miles to the finish line. There was a crowd gathered around the door to the apartment building, but I couldn't find Charlie. I finally asked someone if they'd seen him and was told he was tending bar upstairs.

The apartment was filled with people I didn't know, so I followed the line and waited until I reached the bar.

"What can I get you, ma'am?" Charlie asked, tossing a plastic cup up in the air and catching it behind his back. "If this law thing doesn't work out, I think I've got a second career waiting for me. Just don't ask for anything that requires more than two ingredients."

"A Bloody Mary is fine," I told him.

"A Bloody Mary it is, then." He filled the cup from a pitcher sitting on the counter and stuck a celery stalk among the ice cubes before handing the drink to me. "I'm glad you're here."

Without even thinking, I smiled back. "Me, too."

"Let me get someone to fill in, and I'll meet you over there." He pointed to the couch.

I stepped out of the line and walked over to the window to wait for Charlie.

I'd considered blowing off the party. After I'd seen Paige and Hugh, the last thing I felt like doing was going to a party with Charlie. I wasn't exactly feeling celebratory. It wasn't that I was jealous—I wasn't. I'd never experienced a twinge of jealousy when Robin married Mark. And when Paige showed me the ring Steve presented to her on Christmas morning, there wasn't a second that I wasn't happy for her. It was great. It was wonderful. It was something I wanted for myself someday, but I didn't wish I could trade places with either of them. It was like watching your best friend accept the Oscar—it just reminded me that I hadn't had my moment, but it didn't mean I wanted to take her moment away from her. I wanted the achievement and recognition, but I didn't want the parts Robin and Paige played to get it.

I always hated the stereotypes about women smiling through gritted teeth when their friends got a fabulous promotion, or won an exotic trip to some tropical island, or held out a hand donning a sparkly new diamond. And that's why I hated how I felt watching Paige through that shaded window. I didn't feel envious watching them. I just felt empty.

"How's that drink?" Charlie asked, coming over to me.

"Not bad. Were you expecting a tip?"

"Maybe you can repay me later." Charlie reached for my hand and led me toward the balcony, where there was just enough room for us and the small gas grill that stood in a corner.

I leaned over the railing to look at the crowd, while Charlie waited in the doorway. Without even looking, I knew he was close behind me, and when I finally turned around we stood face-to-face. In one fluid movement Charlie placed his lips on mine and parted them with his tongue, the taste of gin and lime awakening my taste buds. I let my hands run along the waist of his jeans until they settled into his back pockets.

Beneath us, the noise from the crowd of spectators rose up and enclosed us.

"They just hit Coolidge Corner," somebody called out from the kitchen. "The runners will be here any minute."

Charlie pulled away. "Thanks for coming."

The room started emptying out as everyone headed downstairs to watch the race. I turned to leave but Charlie held me back. "We can stay here and watch from the balcony, if you want."

Why couldn't my head and my body get on the same page? I should have been running from Charlie, not making out with him. Nothing good could come of this.

"There they are." Charlie pointed up Beacon Street, and I could see the small figures coming toward us, their feet pounding the pavement in rapid succession.

"Have you ever thought about running the marathon?" I asked, moving back to the railing.

"Sure. Except there's the small matter of running twenty-six miles." Charlie joined me at the edge of the balcony. "I don't think I have it in me."

"You know, I never understood why people run marathons. It seems kind of useless to train for so long, run the race, and then it's over."

The first runners passed us quickly, and we watched as the stream of racers flowed in behind them until the street was completely covered with brightly colored nylon shorts and skin glistening with sweat under the searing rays of the midday sun.

"I think it's more about pushing yourself, proving you can do it. Even the last person to cross the finish line knows that he met the challenge."

Meeting the challenge. Isn't that what I'd set out to do with Charlie? To prove that Charlie would change his mind? To prove I wasn't the type of woman who'd practice writing *Mrs. Charlie Banks* on paper, wondering what baby names sounded best with his last name? But I'd been wrong. Maybe the real challenge was going after what I wanted.

Charlie reached for my hand, but I pulled away. "I've got to go."

"Now? You'll hit tons of traffic."

"There are some things at the boutique I need to take care of," I explained quickly. "Thanks for inviting me. I had a great time."

I rushed past Charlie and ran out of the apartment, biting my lip the whole way, taking one last taste of him.

25

*I*f I was going to be honest, I had to admit that I was like that woman in the bookstore, that I wanted the culmination, or at least the promise of it. I was swallowing my pride. I'd been proud that I didn't need the wedding, confident that I was unlike the women I met at the boutique who seemed so wrapped up in the idea of becoming half of a newly formed whole. And what did that make me? I wasn't so sure anymore. Because if you want it, you're weak. If you need it, you're desperate. But if you go along like none of it matters, you're strong and self-possessed. In control. Given the choice, which would you choose to be?

I couldn't see Charlie anymore. And even if she wasn't the biggest fan of holy matrimony, I knew there was one person I could count on to take the side of a woman in need.

I took the T to the Arlington Street stop and walked the three blocks to the hotel, past lingering marathon watchers and street vendors selling souvenirs, until I reached the doorman busy assisting visitors under bright red awnings. He greeted me with a tip of his hat and held the door open. Inside the elaborate lobby of the Park Plaza, shallow chandeliers hung from the ceiling like crystal flying saucers. A piano player sat at the baby grand in the open-air entryway to the Swan's Court performing a tune I recognized as an old Nat King Cole song, and a few stragglers were still seated at tables in front of the court's mirrored wall, lingering over half-eaten scones with strawberry jam and clotted cream as the formal afternoon tea wound down. I made my way around the obscenely large floral arrangement squatting on a table in the center of the room and went to check the meeting board. I traced my finger down the list until I found Women in Action, and then started up the stairs toward the White Hill room.

There were still another twenty minutes left in the program, so I snuck in the door and waited at the back of the room. I looked around to see who would fork over seven hundred and fifty dollars to spend a day learning how to get over a broken heart. Women of all shapes and sizes sat taking notes in the standard-issue metal and vinyl hotel chairs. The audience seemed to be either twenty-something women, undoubtedly there to try to get over the guy they thought they'd marry, or forty-ish women, undoubtedly there to get over the guy they *did* marry.

Robin didn't usually speak at the seminars—her program managers were responsible for handling the events—but every once in a while she liked to get back up on stage to watch the body language of attendees as they listened to the program. She'd told me that lots of nodding heads was a good sign. People absentmindedly doodling on the free notepad was not.

I listened to the last minutes of the seminar, wondering whether this is where I would have ended up if I kept seeing Charlie—seated between a housewife in stretch jeans and a girl in a belly-baring shirt with a barbell through her tongue, all three of us trying to figure out why we'd wasted months, maybe years, on a man who couldn't give us what we wanted.

At five o'clock I waited by the double doors as the attendees shuffled up the aisle and spilled into the hallway.

When Robin emerged, it was as if a celebrity had walked into the room. A swarm of women descended on her, patting her on the back and trying to shake her hand—even a few sticking pens in her face, hoping to get an autograph on the seminar program guide.

"Robin." I reached out and tapped her on the shoulder. She turned around and a look of surprise crossed her face.

"Hey, what are you doing here?" she asked, before a teary-eyed attendee wrapped her in an embrace.

"I wanted to talk with you about Charlie."

"Okay, but I've got to run and talk with my program manager, and then I have to stop back at the office to drop off some materials. Why don't you meet me in the lobby in fifteen minutes and you can trail along?"

Robin left her adoring crowd to huddle with the program manager and I headed to the lobby to wait.

An hour later I was seated in Robin's office at Women in Action.

Robin's offices were right out of *Architectural Digest*, tastefully appointed by her personal interior designer. Oversized Georgia O'Keefe prints hung in the waiting room, sensuous flowers that suggested both strength and femininity. With its tumbled-travertine floors and oversized cocoa-colored leather sofas and chairs illuminated by small pendant lighting strung from exposed steel wires, it wasn't exactly homey. But it definitely sent the message that Robin and her company of women were all business. The only splash of whimsy hung on Robin's office wall, an abstract print aptly titled *Ordered Chaos*.

"So, what's up with the book? Is Vivian treating you right?" Robin leaned back in her desk chair and kicked her heels up on the desk. She popped open a can of Diet Coke and quickly put her mouth over the top to keep the caramel-colored foam from spilling onto her buff suede pants.

"Everything's great. The staff and Maria are baking like crazy for tomorrow's photo shoot, but that's not why I'm here. I've been thinking about Charlie and Neil and I decided—" But before I could get to the punch line the door to Robin's office swung open and Jeremy marched in, chased by Robin's frantic assistant.

"I tried to stop him," Leesa apologized, practically in tears. "I really did."

"It's not her fault," Jeremy told Robin. "She tried to tell me you weren't here."

Robin swung her feet off her desk and stood up, pointing to the door. "Leesa, call security. Now!"

Jeremy stood in front of the door, blocking Leesa's exit. "I don't want to make a scene, Robin. I just want to talk to you and explain some things."

"Fine." Robin reached for her phone and started dialing. "I'm calling nine-one-one. You can explain this all to the police."

Jeremy walked up to Robin's desk and pressed the lit button on the dial pad, disconnecting the outgoing line. "You know what I find the saddest thing of all in this whole situation? That for someone who likes to act like she's so strong and in control, you seem to relish your role as the victim. You can't even look at yourself honestly and admit that you were responsible, that you made a mistake, because it's more important to you to be the one who's angry. And if your friends aren't willing to tell you, then I'll tell you—it's time to get that chip off your shoulder, Robin, before you forget what it's like to be happy."

Jeremy turned to leave, but before closing the door he faced me. "You're not doing her any favors, you know."

Leesa ran to the door and closed it behind Jeremy, leaning against the frame as if the curves she earned from daily cardio kickboxing classes would be enough to keep Jeremy from bursting in on us again. "Do you want me to call security and have them stop him?"

Robin shook her head but remained silent. Leesa stood there, awkwardly waiting for Robin to say something.

"It's okay, Leesa. You can go now," I told her.

"What the hell was he talking about?" Robin asked me after she'd gone. "What does he want you to tell me?"

A psychology class in college didn't qualify me to play therapist to Robin. "I don't know."

"I think he's unbalanced." Robin finished her Diet Coke and tossed it into the garbage can behind her desk, where it landed with a clank.

"So, everything's going well with the book; good for you," Robin repeated, as if trying to rewind our conversation and get back on track. She gave me an encouraging smile, but it quickly faded.

Jeremy's remarks had gotten to Robin, and even though she'd asked me what he meant by his accusations, the pained look on her face showed me that she knew exactly what he was saying. I watched as she distractedly shuffled a few papers on her desk, as if looking for something she'd misplaced, and for the first time since I'd known her, I felt sorry for Robin. Jeremy may have had a point, but he had no right to dump on her like that.

"I've got to go," I told Robin and gave her a quick hug before running out of the office to find Jeremy and give him a piece of my mind.

When I reached the lobby and the elevator doors slid open I saw the back of Jeremy's blue windbreaker about to enter the revolving doors.

"Jeremy," I called out, my voice echoing in the massive marble tomb. He turned around and paused as I quickly crossed the floor, just a step shy of running.

"Who do you think you are acting like you know what Robin's been through?" I demanded, trying to catch my breath.

"I've had my heart broken, too, Lauren. Everyone has."

I hadn't. And I was taking great care to keep it that way.

"That still doesn't give you the right to attack her like that. And why the hell are you getting on my case? You don't know what we've done to help Robin."

"I know that you let her act like some sort of martyr for women instead of telling her the way it is."

"And how is it, exactly, Jeremy?" I stood there with my hands defiantly on my hips, waiting for Jeremy to impart his wisdom.

"Nobody can make you into a victim unless you let them, Lauren. It's too bad you haven't pointed that out to Robin."

"She needs time to work this out for herself," I countered. "Her husband walked out on her, Jeremy. I think she's justified in feeling a little cheated. He was the one who was wrong."

"Does she want to be right or does she want to be happy?"

"For now she wants to be right."

Jeremy nodded as if agreeing with me. "And I'm sure that will offer cold comfort to her in years to come." Jeremy turned his back on me and raised his hand in a dismissive wave. "Good-bye, Lauren."

26

*W*hat's that?" Maria asked, looking over my shoulder.

I covered the page with my hand and looked up from the desk. "A list."

"Like a grocery list?"

"Sort of." I'd laid the waterlogged paper from my bath next to a blank piece of paper and hoped that I could figure out why yesterday's date with Charlie had left me feeling so unsettled. It wasn't that Charlie had done anything wrong. In fact, what bothered me was that everything seemed so right. And yet, even after I'd rearranged the list's order, I was still left with a blank next to number one, leaving space for something that I couldn't quite put my finger on but that I was sure shouldn't be *A guy who wants to date me for a long time*.

Maria reached for my list and snatched it out from under my hand. "Do you find a nonsmoker in the frozen food aisle or in produce?" she asked, holding up the list for further inspection.

"Forget it." I grabbed the sheet back and turned it over. But it was already too late.

"That list is a bunch of crap," she told me, as if I'd asked for her opinion. "Next thing you know, I'll find you writing out your recipe for a relationship—add a pinch of charm, a dollop of good looks and bake for one hour at three hundred and fifty degrees."

Maria chuckled and then smacked her head as if she'd

suddenly remembered something. "Oh, and don't forget to set the timer so it doesn't burn!"

I sat still and waited for Maria's ominous shadow to walk away, but she hovered over me like a black cloud. Sure, my list seemed crazy to her now, but maybe if she'd taken the time to make a list she wouldn't have had to turn down Mario Spinelli.

"Oh, yeah," Maria added nonchalantly. "A woman named Julie called. She said she was Neil's fiancée and wanted you to call her back." She looked up at me and waited for a reaction.

I shrugged, as if my ex-boyfriends' fiancées called here every day asking for me. There was no way Neil told her about our little date. Maybe Julie just wanted to talk about the cake—the cake! Maybe she changed her mind about the almond cake, which would mean that she and Neil didn't agree. And Neil and I did.

I was expecting my first appointment at one o'clock, which meant I had two hours to screw up my nerve and call Julie. At 12:45, my nerve still wasn't screwed up, but I was. I knew it was now or never, and so I dialed.

"I just wanted to say thanks for all your help," Julie told me graciously. "It's been such a pain coordinating the wedding in Boston with Neil still in DC most of the time, and you made choosing the cake so easy."

"I'm glad I could help." Was Julie calling to show her appreciation, or did she have a feeling, like I did, that there was something between me and Neil that needed further investigation? It just didn't seem possible that she'd called to thank me. Nobody was that nice.

"And we really appreciate it," Julie repeated.

"Are you sure you liked the almond cake as much as Neil?" I asked, prodding Julie for an admission that she really wanted the lemon cake. "I sort of got the feeling that he was more interested than you were, and it's very important that you both agree on the cake."

"Oh, no. I love the cake," Julie assured me. "And now we've got one less thing to worry about. If Neil likes the items I put on our registry when he looks at them, then we can scratch two things off our list."

Neil was back from DC?

"Where are you registered?" I asked, implying that a gift was in order and not the interception of her fiancé.

"Macy's. I asked Neil to go over there after work today to look at the patterns I picked out."

I couldn't have asked for more valuable information if I'd tried. Obviously Julie had fallen prey to my subversive interrogation tactics. Or maybe she really was just too nice.

"I'm sure he'll love what you chose," I assured Julie, all sweetness and light.

But just in case, I planned on being there to help Neil with his registry selections.

27

*H*ey, Lauren. What are you doing here?"

I let my jaw drop open in sheer surprise as if meeting up with Neil in the bridal registry section of Macy's was just about the most amazing coincidence I'd ever experienced and wandering around Macy's aisles looking at Lenox gravy boats was the most natural thing in the world. "What are you doing here?" I asked him right back.

"We're registering at Macy's."

I clutched my hand to my chest in utter surprise. "No way."

"Yeah, Julie picked out some things and she wanted me to come and see what I thought."

I placed the Marquis stemware back in its spot on the shelf, surrounded by matching relatives. After loitering in the china department for almost an hour, I was sure the saleswoman thought I was casing the joint for a sophisticated heist of crystal decanters. I kept waiting for the security guard to show up and ask me to leave.

I offered a logical explanation for our unexpected meeting. "Sometimes I like to see what my clients are registered for, to give me a better feel for their tastes."

Neil grinned. "I have to admit, this registering-for-gifts thing is pretty nice. Have you seen our list?"

Did he mean the dining section, with the Wedgwood Promenade dinnerware, or the cooking section, with the Calphalon tri-ply stainless steel pots? The first thing I'd done when I arrived was check out everything on their registry, right down to the Ralph Lauren washcloths. "No, I haven't."

"Well, then let's take a look together."

I smiled politely at the saleswoman as she printed out the registry, a smile that said *See, it's perfectly normal to browse through china and crystal and silver settings for hours and then act surprised when your ex-boyfriend shows up.*

"This is too weird, isn't it? We don't see each other for years and now we seem to be bumping into each other everywhere we go—almost like it was meant to be." I nudged Neil playfully, which he obviously wasn't expecting because he almost knocked over a display of crystal vases as he fell backward.

Neil caught his balance and righted a teetering bud vase. "Hey, thanks for that list of planners. I think we're going to use Gloria Caldwell, if she can fit us into her schedule."

From *We're meant to be* to *Thanks for the wedding planner*? Was this the same guy who wanted me to get an eye patch? "Sure, no problem."

We found the Wedgwood Promenade dinnerware and Neil shrugged. "They're nice, huh?"

I took the dinner plate from Neil's hand and turned it over, as if inspecting the china for imperfections. It was your basic wedding china, white with bands of platinum trimming the edges. Julie wasn't going out on a limb with that selection.

"I guess, if you want something understated. But what about this one?" I placed the boring plate back onto its stand and reached for a bold blue and green pattern. "Now this Villeroy and Boch is beautiful, and you can mix and match the patterns." I picked up the dessert plate and held it up next to the dinner plate. "See, you have the swirling waves on the rim of the Costa pattern contrasted with the checkerboard trim of the Castell. It has a lot more pizzazz."

"I don't know." Neil shook his head, unconvinced, and picked up the Promenade plate again. "This is nice and simple."

"True. But I love the colors in these; they're very Mediterranean." I swept my hand in front of the impromptu place setting like a model on *The Price Is Right*.

Neil hesitated and then shook his head. "No, the white is fine. That way they'll go with everything."

"Sure, you're right," I halfheartedly agreed, reluctant to put down the plates. They really were beautiful.

"Why don't you get yourself the plates if you like them so much?" Neil asked, searching the shelf for the Tuscany stemware Julie had picked out.

"I don't think so." I guess I could live with plain white if I had to.

Neil held up a tall, bulbous wineglass and shrugged. "This is a wineglass all right."

"What about this one?" I showed him the glass I'd picked up. "See how it has a little wave going through it? That's different."

"What's with this wave thing you have going on? It matches the plates you picked out."

Neil was right. The stemware was practically made to go with the Villeroy & Boch setting I liked. How could Julie pick generic glasses and boring plates when she could pick something with a little flair? Here was the chance I'd been waiting for.

"You know, if you don't like the patterns Julie selected, we could choose new ones," I suggested. I thought I saw the saleswoman glare at me from behind her granny glasses, her squinty eyes letting me know that I might be fooling Neil, but she was on to me.

"No, this one is fine. It's just a wineglass, right? Is that the silverware?" He pointed to the Weston spoon with its slight indent at the tip of the handle, the only hint of interest on the entire sterling silver handle.

"Works for me." He held up a fork for my appraisal.

"Sure." If you wanted to hold the most boring silver fork ever made.

Neil scanned the rest of the page. "Do you really think we need to look at the sheets and towels?"

The idea of looking at items designed for their joint showers and evenings in bed wasn't exactly on my list of things to do tonight. "Probably not."

Neil agreed and we returned the registry to the saleswoman, who seemed pleased that my mission had failed.

Obviously my idea that we'd bond over flatware and table settings wasn't working out.

"Want to go get a drink?" I asked on our way to the escalator.

"Didn't you have client research to finish?"

Oh yeah, that. "I was just finishing up when you got here, so there's time for a drink, if you're game."

Neil contemplated my offer. "Sure. There's a bunch of guys from work meeting a few blocks away."

I hadn't planned on making our date a group affair, but maybe it would be good to meet some of Neil's new friends.

We walked four blocks until we reached the bar that Neil suggested, an after-work haunt favored by the pin-striped-suit crowd looking to escape the mazes of cubicles.

Barnaby's front window was illuminated by fluorescent blinking beer logos. A stool propped open the front door and I could hear the sounds of laughing, music and clinking beer bottles inside the basement bar.

Neil obviously wasn't out to impress me.

I followed him down the cement steps and into a small room with low ceilings. The after-work crowd was in full swing; ties hung slack around necks and shirtsleeves were unbuttoned and rolled up to elbows, so that what were probably accountants and lawyers looked like fraternity guys ready to arm wrestle.

We found a small round table and sat down. While we munched on the basket of popcorn and waited for the waitress to take our order, a group of guys walked into the bar and headed in our direction, slapping backs and cracking jokes on the way. Neil's face lit up when he saw them.

"Those are the guys I told you about," he explained, standing up ready to greet them. "Grab those chairs over there and we'll make some room."

Not only was he not trying to impress me, now he wanted me to lug four chairs across Barnaby's sticky floor. Obviously a conversation about our destiny would have to take place another time. When we were alone. And when I wasn't trying to suck popcorn kernels out of my teeth.

Once Neil's four coworkers sat down, I was relegated to the role of the agreeable nodder, the person who chirped in with an occasional *Uh-huh* and tipped her head to the side as if thoroughly engrossed in the prospects of a new first baseman for the Red Sox. Although Neil slid a cold bottle of beer in front of me every time a new round was ordered, I wasn't exactly an active participant in the table's conversation.

Finally, I tapped Neil on the shoulder in a request for attention. "I'm going to go now."

There was no begging or even feigned disappointment at my departure—just a quick *Okay* before he rejoined the speculation about a price increase for tickets to Fenway Park.

Now, that did not go as I'd planned. When I asked if he'd like to have a drink, I was thinking something more along the lines of a quiet restaurant along the water, not a hole-in-the-wall with Bruce Springsteen on the jukebox lamenting the plight of the working man. Then again, who knew what would have happened if Neil's work cronies hadn't arrived. Maybe we could have had the conversation I was hoping for, the talk where we got beyond just reminiscing about what we were and got around to figuring out what we could be.

28

$\mathcal{P}$lease come out and meet Pietro," I begged, my hands clasped together in prayer as if a superior being could get Maria to change her mind.

"No," Maria insisted.

Only weeks after the contract was signed, Vivian had managed to set up the photo shoot and book Pietro. Bradley Potter wanted to publish the book in October, when all the June brides were in full-planning mode, and with Pietro planning to spend the next six months in Europe, Vivian acted fast. I pored over my index cards with Maria, selecting cakes that reflected Lauren's Luscious Licks' best work, and then the staff got baking. In nine days they were able to complete thirty-six cakes of all shapes and sizes. Because most of the cakes were going to be photographed whole, only the dozen cakes that we'd chosen to include with pictures of actual slices had any filling. And, luckily, because the cakes were being photographed and not eaten, it didn't matter if they were stale when Pietro arrived.

"But he wants to meet you, and I want him to meet you. You did such an amazing job on the cakes."

Maria sniffed and continued scraping the offset icing spatula along the side of a fourteen-inch round cake. She'd moved on to our orders, as if today was just like any other day instead of one of Lauren's Luscious Licks' defining moments.

"Please?"

Maria pointed to Betty Friedan's wise words posted above the butcher-block bench. "I did my part. I created the cakes that no one will ever even eat. Now you do yours."

I gave up and left Maria alone with the cake and her philosophical musings.

"Maria's a little tied up right now," I explained to Pietro and his crew, relishing the fantasy of Maria secured to the oven with bungee cords, her fat little fingers working behind her back as she tried to break free. In my mind I took the bandanna off her head and used it to muffle her screams—if I was going to fantasize, I might as well go all the way. "We have a lot of orders to fill."

Pietro frowned, but his team of stylists and assistants continued to strategically place lights and reflective shields around the set they'd created in the center of the boutique.

When the white backdrop was in place and the lights were up, Hector and Benita removed the first cake from the walk-in cooler and assembled it on the silk-covered platform the stylist had designed.

The cake, four tiers with a faux fondant finish in lavender Italian meringue buttercream icing, was dotted with hand-sculpted violet blossoms in brilliant shades of amethyst. Bands of white fondant swags circled each tier and were "tied back" with the delicate flowers.

Finally, after an assistant went a few more rounds with the light meter, Pietro's camera started clicking.

By the third cake, a champagne-colored fondant-iced design embellished with roses, sweet peas, fall leaves and burgundy grapes cascading down offset oval tiers, I started to understand the bored look that models seem to have perfected. In a way, my cakes were just like those leggy, vacant-looking models in magazines. Sure, they were beautiful and pleasing to look at, but they weren't exactly accessible. The clothing and accessories models wore looked stunning set against exotic locales, but in real life, they'd look ridiculous. Like my cakes at a photo shoot.

It was as if Pietro and his team were trying to make the cakes into something more than they were, like owners who dress up their poodles in evening gowns, feather hats, and fuchsia-polished toenails. I watched as Maria's creations were primped and positioned until Pietro found the ideal angle to *capture their essence*—his words, not mine.

But with each cake, I started to think that maybe they weren't meant to be admired from afar, or from a photograph. Lauren's Luscious Licks was supposed to be about sharing scrumptious cakes, desserts that you couldn't wait to eat and that, once eaten, left you satisfied. Like my first vanilla-bean cheesecake, the fun was supposed to be in watching people eat the cake, not admiring it from afar like some unattainable standard.

I'd asked Julie if I could use the almond cake with raspberry filling and chocolate ganache in the final group of cakes, but I hadn't included it, even though it would have been beautiful with fresh raspberries, slivered almonds and a wreath of variegated ivy for decoration. It felt too personal, especially now that Neil and I shared it.

I'd decided to call Neil and ask him to meet me again once the flurry of activities surrounding the photo shoot died down. Our afternoon at Macy's hadn't turned out as I'd planned, but I couldn't ignore the signs that I'd paid such close attention to in the past.

"Do you need to get that?" Vivian asked, pointing to the phone.

I shook my head and watched Pietro try to coax a mound of hydrangea to sit still without smudging the dotted Swiss icing. "Maria will get it." Eventually. On the fourth ring she finally picked up.

I listened, waiting for Maria to call me into the kitchen. Charlie had called the boutique five times this week, and every time Maria took a message she shoved it at me and shook her head. I knew her patience was wearing thin.

I still thought about Charlie the way you remembered childhood ballet lessons—they sure were fun, and maybe if you'd stuck it out you could have learned some of the more graceful moves, but it wasn't like you had any chance of being a prima ballerina. At least not without some serious sacrifice, boxes of bunion pads and a couple bloodied toes. I was hoping he'd get the hint and stop calling. The last thing I wanted to do was face him and admit that I'd been wrong or confess that I'd overestimated myself on our first date.

The photo shoot lasted almost ten hours, and by the time the crew was packed up and out the door, I was exhausted. Maria stayed late in the kitchen to dispose of the cakes, muttering what a waste it was to make a cake just for show. It was too late to call Neil, but I vowed to pick up where we'd left off at Barnaby's—even if it meant luring him to meet me under false pretenses. I mean, this my future we were talking about, after all.

When I left the boutique, I slipped my key from the keyhole and jiggled the doorknob to make sure it was locked. When I was convinced the bolt was secure, I turned to leave and smacked squarely into a yellow and blue lattice-striped tie.

"Hey, stranger."

"Charlie, what are you doing here?" I bent to pick up the keys I'd dropped, but Charlie got to them first. He held the keys in his hand, in what seemed like a hostage situation intended to make me talk.

"You haven't returned my calls and I wanted to make sure you didn't have some sort of icing emergency," he smiled, trying to make light of my conspicuous avoidance. "I know how treacherous that whipped cream can get."

"Spring is one of our busiest seasons," I stammered. "I really haven't had time to call anyone."

"I know. I left a few messages with a woman named Maria, but she said I should stop by around seven and talk to you myself," Charlie told me and then grinned. "She was really sweet."

Yeah, real sweet.

Charlie's hand still clutched my keys. "And, besides, I'm not just anyone. I thought we were considering a joint venture."

"I know, I'm sorry. I just don't think now is a good time to get involved. You understand, don't you?" I smiled weakly and avoided looking into his eyes.

"No, not really." Charlie wasn't going to make this easy for me. "Is there a better time?"

"It's just that I'm not sure we want—"

"The same thing." He finished my sentence with horrifying accuracy. Charlie gave me a forgiving smile. "Yeah, I think I understand."

He held out my keys, dangling them from his finger, and I took the cool metal edges in my hand and squeezed tightly. "Thanks."

Charlie stepped back from the door and studied me for a minute before walking away. "You know, it's too bad," he called out, turning and walking backward so he could face me. "You were a hell of a backgammon player."

He turned around again and never looked over his shoulder to see if I was still standing in the doorway.

I dropped the keys in my purse and noticed the ridges left in my hand from the keys, deep indents outlined in red. I rubbed my hands together trying to make the impressions go away, but it would take some time before the marks would fade.

I had a choice to make. Charlie or Neil. Uncertainty or a sure thing. There really wasn't any choice at all. It was an obvious decision.

The front windows of the boutique were dark, but back toward the kitchen a faint light shone through the small window in the swinging door, and I thought I saw the shadow of a face watching me.

A taxicab's horn blew at two young girls crossing the street, and the swearing that followed grabbed my attention away from the boutique. The girls ran into Starbucks, leaving the cab driver stuck at a red light. When I looked back toward the kitchen, the shadow was gone.

29

My unexpected run-in with Charlie wasn't exactly what I'd planned; in fact, I was just hoping he'd give up and stop calling. But it was probably the best thing. Rip the Band-Aid off quickly, even if it stung for a little while afterward. Still, the only thing that made me think of was the box of Barney Band-Aids sitting on Charlie's bathroom shelf.

Running into Neil at Macy's was step one. Or maybe my surprise visit to Gamble Mansion was step one, but I definitely thought I'd have some time before I was forced to come up with my next move. When I dialed Neil's cell phone, I had no idea he was in a cab racing out of the Sumner Tunnel—a mere twenty minutes from the boutique's front door. But when I told him I had some concerns about the cake, Neil immediately offered to swing by. He told me he had time to kill before meeting Julie, and two seconds later he was repeating the boutique's address to the cab driver.

"Why don't you meet me at the swan boats instead," I quickly suggested. "I'm looking at the gardens for a client."

Neil agreed and I took a deep breath before hanging up. This was it.

I waited on a bench by the lagoon. When I saw Neil approaching, I quickly ran my tongue over my lips, hoping to make them glossy and luscious. Instead I tasted the mustard from my lunch.

"You have a little on the corner, too," Neil pointed out when he reached me, dabbing at his own lips to guide my hand.

Nothing like a little French's yellow mustard to turn glossy and luscious into just plain gross. Unless Neil fantasized about kissing a ballpark frank, I wasn't starting out on my best foot. I swiped at my mouth with the back of my hand. "Thanks."

Neil gave me a perfunctory hug and the familiar scent of Obsession cologne sent a wave of recognition through my body. It wasn't desire, or even nostalgia, just my senses acknowledging his presence.

I sat back down and Neil joined me, leaning against the arm of the bench so we faced each other. There was a good two feet between us.

"God, I haven't been here since the week before I moved, remember?"

I did. We'd come down to the lagoon for one last ride on the boats. "That's the last time I went for a ride, too."

Neil tipped his head to the side and smirked. "Really? That was eight years ago."

"Really." I nodded. "Does Julie know you're here?"

"Not yet. I called her when my plane landed, but she was still out with her mom dress shopping."

Not yet? So he was planning to tell her, which meant he wasn't planning a grand seduction where he made crazy love to me on a blanket in the public garden.

"So, what did you want to talk about?"

"I have something I want to show you." I took Neil's letter out of my pocket and unfolded the crumpled paper. "I found this the other day."

Neil took the page and read.

"Remember when you used to turn Oliver around when we were in bed?" I asked him, hoping to subtly jog his memory.

Neil's eyes scanned the page and then he let out a laugh before folding the letter back into its envelope. "That bear always creeped me out."

Oliver wasn't creepy. "In a bad way?"

"Um, yeah. That's what *creeped-out* means, Lauren."

Neil shook his head. "So where is good old Oliver these days?"

"My bedroom."

"No way! I thought he'd be reduced to a lint ball by now."

So there'd be no reminiscing about Oliver. Time to change tactics.

"It's weird, isn't it? After all these years you walk into the boutique and it's like it was meant to be." I reached out to take the envelope and instead let my hand fall on Neil's arm.

Neil reacted like my touch was about as welcome as a scorpion's stinger. "What are you talking about?"

"You and me."

Neil stood up and backed away from me. "Maybe coming here was a bad idea."

"Why? Because then we'd both have to admit what we should have known eight years ago—that we made a mistake when you moved to DC?"

"*We* didn't do anything when I moved. *You* stayed in Boston," he pointed out. "What the hell is going on here? I thought you wanted to talk about the cake."

"I do." Right words. Wrong context.

I stood up and moved closer to Neil, who at this point was practically drawing a line in the dirt hoping I wouldn't cross it. No such luck.

"I made a mistake," I admitted.

"What is this, a joke? I'm getting married! Why are you saying this now?"

"Because it's true. Because seeing you again made me think that maybe we should give it another try."

"You're confusing the hell out of me, Lauren. You're the one who didn't want to move to DC. You're the one who barely blinked when I left after three years. Why the sudden revelation?"

I swallowed hard and stepped closer to him. "Because you picked the same cake I wanted for my own wedding."

"So did Julie," he reminded me. "I think you're reading more into this than there is, Lauren."

I reached for Neil's elbow and pulled him back down onto the bench with me. I kept a firm grip on his knee so he couldn't get up. "But we have to be," I said, trying to keep my voice from shaking.

"Why?"

Because if I was wrong then I'd broken up Steve and Paige for no reason at all. Because if I was wrong then everything was left up to chance.

"Because if there's no way to tell whether two people are meant to be together, then it's just a crapshoot."

"Of course it's a crapshoot, Lauren. Nobody offers relationship insurance; the premium would be too high."

"But I really can predict if a couple will work out or not by the cake they pick. I've done it a million times, and I did it with you."

"Funny how you couldn't tell eight years ago."

"So my timing was off."

"I don't think it was your timing, Lauren. You knew exactly what you were doing."

I did know. I was taking a chance. I was risking something that was safe and easy because I knew there was something else out there.

"Look, why don't we just forget this ever happened." Neil patted my knee, but his touch was more reticent than reassuring.

I looked away from Neil and instead watched the mothers and children and couples waiting their turns to step onto a swan boat. They lined up in pairs, the ticket collector playing a modern-day Noah as he handed over their stubs and helped them step down. Even though I'd managed to start a business and take care of myself, when Neil moved away I never returned to ride the boats because I still thought there were some things you saved until you could share them with someone else. It was almost as if having someone else there meant it was more real, more meaningful. But all I'd done was miss out on opportunities to create moments with my own meaning.

My hands went to my face and I covered my eyes, wishing that I could rub away the events that had just transpired. Instead all I managed to do was lose a few eyelashes.

Neil just sat there watching me, keeping a safe distance

between us. I let out a laugh, even though there was nothing funny about making a complete idiot of myself in front of a guy who probably already thought I had a few screws loose.

It wasn't Neil I wanted. It was the person I was when we'd been together. Or, more accurately, the person I was when I watched him drive away.

"Do me a favor; don't tell Julie about this, okay? I feel foolish enough."

Neil's shoulders relaxed and it was as if we'd made it safely to the other side. "Are you kidding me? I couldn't tell Julie. She'd kill me if she thought I'd blown our chance to have you make our cake. I mean, I could care less about the cake, but Julie's got her heart set on it. You'll still make it, right?"

I almost told Neil that I wasn't the one who made the cakes, but I didn't want to ruin the illusion. And maybe I would make his cake; at least then somebody would get to have the raspberry-filled almond cake I'd been saving for myself.

"Sure, I'll still make your cake," I told Neil, even though he could care less.

Neil stood up but instead of hightailing it away from me, as any person would have in the same situation, he waited before leaving. "You know, I thought you were the one—at the time."

In the silence that followed Neil's declaration, I wanted to say the same back to him. But it wouldn't be true. Back when Neil left I didn't see it as an ending. I saw it as a sweet beginning. I did love Neil, but if I'd followed him to DC it would have been more out of fear than anything else. And even though it would have been a neat and tidy ending to our story to have him meet me by the swan boats and declare his never-ending devotion, it wouldn't be the right ending.

I looked up at him and noticed the receding hairline and few strands of gray that were already paving the way for others to follow. Neil was still familiar, but he was a different person. And so was I. After eight years, the fact that he selected the right cake with the right filling and icing didn't change the fact that we still didn't belong together. No matter what the cake said, no matter how much I wanted to be able to predict my future, to stack the odds in my favor, the fact that life was more like a surprise party than a carefully planned wedding reception was becoming all too clear.

"Then why didn't you write me when you got down there? Why didn't I ever get a drunken call from some bar in Georgetown?"

"Is that what you were waiting for?" Neil asked.

"Not really." I shook my head. "But it might have been nice."

"Then what were you waiting for?"

I hesitated, keeping the answer to myself. Nothing and everything.

"Tell Julie that the cake will be exactly what she's always dreamed of on her wedding day," I told him.

Neil waved good-bye and I watched him walk away until he went through the wrought-iron gateway leading to the street. Number one on my list had nothing to do with finding someone else, and everything to do with finding me.

Once I lost sight of Neil I didn't waste any more time. I made my way down to the boathouse and stood in line at the ticket stand.

"How many?" the ticket agent asked.

"Just one." I handed my money over and eagerly received a single red ticket. I was about to begin one hell of a ride.

30

*W*hen I arrived home, I walked straight to the living room window to let in some fresh air. It took me a few tries to shimmy the window's edge away from the paint-caked sill, but once it cracked free the air rushed in and called my apartment to attention, rousing anything that wasn't heavy enough to resist the unexpected breeze. After leaving Neil and taking my first swan-boat ride in years, I wasn't afraid to make a stir, and the first place I was going to start was at home. It was time to pack away my winter clothes and retrieve my summer things from the storage room.

I spent the next hour in my closet removing shirts and pants from hangers and refolding my sweaters neatly like the salespeople at the Gap. While I worked, Oliver sat on my dresser watching the mountain of knitted wool grow until I had a stacked pile that was ready to go downstairs. As a last thought I took Oliver and placed him on top of the mound, like a proud explorer who'd just conquered Mount Everest. The only thing missing was a flag in his paw. He looked triumphant and tired. It was time to retire Oliver to the storage room, too.

I threw some sweaters into a shopping bag and was on my way out the door to get my Rubbermaid containers from the storage room when the phone rang.

On the other end of the receiver Robin seemed to be gulping for air.

"Robin, what's wrong?" I asked, but she couldn't get any words out.

"Robin, you're scaring me. What's going on?"

"He's engaged." Robin's voice was shaking.

"Who?"

"Mark. He's getting married."

"I'll be right over."

Paige was pulling into a parking space in front of Robin's building when my taxi drove up.

"How'd she sound?" Paige asked, pushing the button on the small black rectangle hanging from her key chain. The automatic locks ducked into their holes and the car beeped.

"Horrible."

Paige dropped her keys in her jacket pocket and threw her shoulders back. "I'm glad you called me. This isn't going to be pretty."

Paige and I waved to Robin's doorman and walked straight to the elevator. As the doors slid closed, he returned our friendly gesture with a soldier's salute, as if he sensed we were about to enter a combat zone and attempt to bring our compatriot out alive.

As the elevator carried us in silence to the sixth floor, I noticed that Paige was wearing the charm bracelet from Steve, a single sterling silver heart charm dangling off her thin wrist for the first time since she broke off the engagement. It looked like Mark wasn't the only one who was moving on.

Robin answered the door but didn't even bother saying hello to us. Instead she just turned back toward the living room, where a box of Kleenex sat on the coffee table amidst a heaping mound of soggy, balled up tissues.

Paige and I followed Robin, dropping our coats onto the bench lining the entryway as we passed.

We'd all been here before under similar circumstances. When Robin had called me after Mark left, Paige and I raced over to console her, just as we'd done tonight. But even though Mark's declaration that he wanted a divorce had produced tears and the same pile of tissues, I could already tell that this was different. The night Mark left Robin's tears were quickly replaced by a seething anger so primal Robin had paced around the apartment like a caged animal. After the shock dissipated, Robin wasn't sad—she was pissed.

This time Robin wasn't furiously moving around the room calling Mark names, or punctuating every sentence with *mother fucking prick*. Instead, she sat in silence as the tears slid down her cheeks and landed like raindrops on the *Boston Globe* in her lap.

I waited for Paige to start the ball rolling, to offer some words of consolation that would get Robin talking.

"Can I see?" Paige asked softly, pointing to the newspaper.

Robin handed the wilted *Globe* to Paige. We stood together reading the engagement announcement:

> Mark Manning (of Boston), son of Howard and Elizabeth Manning of Marblehead, to Kate Farridy (of Boston), daughter of Frank and Doris of Hingham.

It was such a simple sentence—it didn't proclaim their undying love or include a tasteful black-and-white photograph of the happy couple sharing an intimate moment. But with just three little lines, the *Boston Globe* had broadcast the announcement's meaning loud and clear: Mark was leaving Robin behind.

"I can't believe it's over." Robin slowly shook her head in disbelief and stared at the dwindling box of tissues. "I feel like I'm suffocating."

Paige folded the paper and placed it on the floor, announcement side down, before taking a seat next to Robin. "It was over two years ago, Robin," Paige reminded her in a voice that was low and patient and filled with meaning without explanation, like a parent explaining to a child why the helium balloon she let go drifted away into the sky without delving into the complexities of gravity and the infinite space of the universe.

"It's like we never happened. He'll have a new wife, she'll take his last name, she'll have the children and the husband and the house with Mark—all the things I thought would be mine."

Robin let out small, lingering moans as she started to rock herself, her eyes closed.

As Robin's sobs grew louder, her tears flowed and she buried her head in her hands. It was all emptying out of her for the first time, all the pain she'd set aside in favor of anger. For the first time, Robin was mourning the death of her marriage, the end of a game she'd managed to keep alive by herself even though Mark had walked off the court a long time ago. Two years of the emotional iceberg Robin had let build up melted and flooded the room, and all I could do was hope Robin didn't go along with it.

There was nothing we could say, no piece of advice or assurance that would make Robin feel better. So, instead, Paige and I sat on either side of her, our arms over Robin's shoulders and our heads bowed against her own, and we were just there with her so she wasn't alone.

We sat huddled together until the room grew dark, our eyes adjusting to the dimming interior of Robin's apartment.

"I just wish I knew what I did wrong," Robin said into her hands, her voice grainy from crying. "I just wish I knew why he couldn't love me. What's wrong with me?"

I reached for Robin's face and turned it toward me. Even in the dark I could see her swollen lids and the exhausted eyes they were cradling. "What was wrong with you was that you fell in love. That's not a fatal flaw, Robin. That's life."

Paige stood up and reached for the light switch. "Okay, I think we need to feed you and get you dried out. All this crying is making you moldy."

Robin smiled weakly. "I am a little hungry."

Paige went into the kitchen to order a pizza, and when she returned she handed Robin the blue gel eye mask she'd taken out of the freezer.

"Here, put this on."

Robin tipped her head back against the cushion and let Paige lay the chilled mask against her lids.

Robin sat like that while Paige and I straightened up the apartment, clearing away the tissues and making the rumpled bed that Robin once shared with Mark. When the pizza arrived Paige opened a bottle of red wine and brought three glasses out to the living room. Robin's tears were gone, but her face was still damp and the skin around her eyes inflated, as if straining from the pressure of the sheer volume of tears underneath.

We didn't talk about Mark while we ate, and instead I told them about the photo shoot and Pietro's ridiculous attempts to coax the cakes to cooperate, as if they were swimsuit models—*You're beautiful! Luscious! Look at you, all white and creamy! You're sweet, you're moist, you're perfect!*

Paige laughed when I imitated Pietro's affirmations, and Robin even seemed vaguely amused. But when the conversation died, Robin cleared her throat and took a deep breath.

"Mark is getting married," she said, listening to herself say the words out loud. "He's getting married."

"I always thought you'd be the one to leave him," I admitted, as if that would make her feel any better.

Robin nodded. "Me, too."

Robin had never said those words aloud before, but I could tell that as the admission escaped from her lips she realized it was true. Even though she loved him, there was a part of her that also knew that maybe she and Mark wouldn't make it, that she wasn't prepared for the sacrifices she'd be required to make.

"We were never really together, were we? We shared the mortgage and the laundry, but when it came right down to it, we weren't sharing a life." Robin was shredding a paper napkin as she talked, the white fibers dropping onto her lap like snowflakes. "I thought if we got married that would change. I was thinking big picture, starting at the top instead of working on all the little things that add up to a marriage."

"The trickle-down theory of happiness?" Paige asked.

"Exactly."

"Nice theory, but it doesn't work in practice."

"You know, we never even had an engagement announcement. We thought it was just a dumb formality. I guess he changed his mind—about a lot of things." Robin looked at Paige. "Before I saw Mark's girlfriend at your office I kept wondering if she was prettier than me or smarter than me. I thought she had to be better than me in some way because Mark wanted to be with her and he didn't want to be with me. But she was just normal, not some extraordinary super-model with a PhD from MIT. And when I saw that announcement, you know what I realized? She wanted an announcement. She was ready to share her life with Mark and let the whole world know. So what it comes down to is that she was ready to *be* married, and I was ready to *get* married."

"I know that hating Mark gave you something to do, some way to keep him around. But maybe it's time to move on," I suggested, realizing how trite I sounded only when the words were out of my mouth.

"That sounds easy enough, doesn't it? But how do you get over the fact that someone can fall out of love with you? How do you forget that someone can love you and then decide one day that he doesn't anymore? I've tried to understand, I really have—I've been like a goddamn postnuptial Quincy practicing the art of marital forensics, and I still can't come up with an answer."

"I don't know if you'll ever find the answer, Robin."

"But he wasted six years of my life, Lauren."

"And you've wasted two years trying to piece together where it all went wrong. He didn't take those years away from you. You gave them to him."

"Let's call him," Paige suggested, finishing her second glass of wine.

"Mark?" Robin held her flopping pizza slice mid-bite. "You want to call Mark?"

"Yep. Let's call him and get you the answers you need, if that's what it will take."

"I'm not calling Mark. I don't even know his phone number," Robin lied. Of course she knew his number. She'd had two dozen anchovy pizzas delivered to his apartment every day for a week when he first moved out—a delivery that required providing his phone number to the pizzeria.

"Fine. I'll call information." Paige stood up and steadied herself against the coffee table. "I'd like to tell him exactly what I've always thought—he never deserved you."

"No." I stood up and joined Paige. If this was what Robin

needed, then Paige and I would give it to her. "We'll all call. And we'll tell him to go fuck himself."

We watched Robin consider Paige's offer. Instead of wondering, Robin could finally get her answer straight from Mark. But even if we did call, and even if Mark didn't hang up on us the minute he realized why we were calling, I doubt it would have made a difference. Because as Robin stared at the phone and contemplated dialing Mark's number, I could tell that she knew the answer, that she'd known all along but kept hoping it could be found in Mark's direction and not her own.

Paige and I watched Robin replay her own words in her head—*Mark's fiancée was ready to* be *married. I was ready to* get *married.* And at that moment, when Robin acknowledged to herself that by blaming Mark she'd been able to keep him in her life, and that he wasn't the only one who contributed to the demise of their marriage, I knew that Robin didn't need to pick up the phone.

"Sit down. We're not calling anyone." Robin finished taking the bite of her pizza and slowly shook her head before laughing at herself. "Oh my God. You must think I've been truly insane."

Paige nodded. "We knew you were off your rocker, but that's what friends are for, to listen to all the insane thoughts that funnel through your brain every day but that you can't say out loud because everyone else would think you were nuts."

"You want insane? Do you know how many times I've imagined that I'm out for drinks or dinner, looking absolutely gorgeous, of course, and I bump into Mark, and he realizes that he made the biggest mistake of his life. We end up going back to my place together, where I rock his world in bed and when it's over he wants to go to sleep. But instead I kick his ass out of bed, out of my apartment, and out of my life for good because from then on I'd be the one who did the dumping and he'd be the one left behind."

Paige let out a long whistle. "Wow. You've spent a lot of time thinking about that one, huh?"

Robin took our paper plates and tossed them into the empty pizza box. "Way too much time."

"What insane thoughts do you have?" Robin asked Paige.

Paige became serious. "I think about spending my life with a man I've known for less time than my dry cleaner."

Paige's confession hung in the air, and Robin shifted uncomfortably in her seat.

"And you?" Robin asked, waiting for my contribution to this purging of insanities.

"That if I'm patient and I wait, one day I'll have everything I want."

Robin was less forgiving of my admission. "Waiting doesn't require patience, Lauren, just the ability to ignore what you need and watch while the rest of the world passes you by."

"How can you say that you don't have what you want? You have a great business and fabulous friends, right?" Paige looked over at Robin, who held her wineglass up in agreement. "What don't you have?"

I remained silent.

"Look at us!" Robin demanded, jumping up. She grabbed our hands and pulled us in front of the fireplace, turning us all toward the mirror above her mantel. Robin, Paige and I stared at our own reflections. "This is so pathetic. Why do we still need a relationship to feel anchored in our lives? What's so bad about swimming by yourself and going where the current takes you?"

"The fear of drowning?" I ventured, watching my lips move as I spoke.

"The sharks?" Paige added.

Robin shrugged. "Haven't we made any progress?"

"I'm so sick of hearing about progress. What's so great about progress? Progress would imply that we always need to be moving toward something. Why can't we just be happy where we are?" Paige asked the three women in the mirror, as if they'd have the answer. "Why are we stronger by following our heads? As if intellectualizing love or trying to reduce it to some mathematical equation or a proof that can be solved is any better—if x then y. But there is no right answer, is there?"

If there was, none of us had it.

The woman who looked just like me spoke first. "Why

must marriage be the goal we all aspire to? Why can't I aspire to create the perfect flourless chocolate cake?"

Robin's reflection answered. "Because diamond companies are telling us we need right-hand rings when what we need is to stop saving our left hand and start decorating any fucking finger we want."

The three women in the mirror laughed, and Robin seemed to enjoy entertaining them.

"Are we all hopeless?" I asked.

"I think we're all hopeful," Paige replied.

Robin turned away from the mirror and we followed. "Okay, so now we know we're all insane."

I held up my glass for a toast. "And doesn't it feel great?"

31

*A*lthough Robin seemed to be in better shape than when we'd arrived, Paige and I decided to spend the night anyway. Just to be sure.

Paige slept in Robin's guest room and I crashed on the couch, which would explain why the next morning Paige and Robin were well rested and chipper and I kept rubbing my neck.

We decided to go out for breakfast to a diner around the corner from Robin's apartment.

After the waitress brought our cheese omelets and Paige's bowl of Special K, Robin told us she'd changed her mind. "I've decided not to go ahead with the insemination."

"But I was looking forward to shopping in BabyGap," Paige teased. "Now I'll never be an aunt."

"Maybe someday, but not right now. I think I need to let all this settle in." She turned to me and paused. "Just please promise me one thing. If they come to you for a cake, please don't do it."

"I think I can handle that."

At least she didn't ask me to lace it with arsenic. I saw that as a promising sign.

The rest of our breakfast was uneventful compared to the past twenty-four hours. I didn't even bother telling them about Neil; it all seemed so silly compared to what Robin had just gone through. Instead we talked about our plans for the day, which seemed a lot safer than trying to plan well into the future.

We'd all been afraid to surrender—our independence, our identity, our idea that by being in control we'd get exactly what we wanted. I wasn't sure we'd exorcised all our demons, but maybe we were just learning to peacefully coexist with them instead.

After breakfast Paige went home to change for work and I took a cab to the boutique. Amanda was waiting for me at the tasting table when I got there.

"I hope you don't mind. Maria let me in. I wanted to stop by and show you the flowers we picked out." She laid Polaroid photos on the tasting table, each one a picture of a different flower. "After much debate, we settled on peonies, poppies, lilacs and sweet peas in white, pinks and purples. What do you think?"

"They're gorgeous. Will you be carrying identical bouquets?"

"Nope. I'll have the pinks and whites, and Allison will have the purples."

I thought for a minute, trying to picture the cake they'd selected. "Then we'll make the topper a combination of both."

"Exactly." Amanda collected the photos and slipped them back in her purse.

I walked her to the front door. "So I guess Hugh and Paige hit it off."

"Really?" Amanda looked surprised. "I knew they went out that one time, but I thought that was it. As far as I know, Hugh really liked her, but she said she wasn't ready for a relationship."

"But he was at her new house the other day helping to fix it up."

Amanda shook her head. "Not Hugh. He hasn't seen Paige since Julio's. It's too bad, because she seemed nice."

Why would Paige lie to us? And who the hell was upstairs kissing Paige?

"I hope Hugh doesn't give up on women altogether."

Amanda grinned. "I didn't; why should he?"

* * *

I was still dressed in last night's clothes, which, judging by the way Maria looked me over when I entered the kitchen, didn't go unnoticed. I was ready for a sarcastic comment about my attire. Instead she surprised me.

"So was Neil the one?" Maria asked, stooping in front of the wall shelves that held all the dry ingredients.

"How'd you know I saw Neil?"

"Who do you think you're fooling? I know you better than you know yourself."

"I met him by the swan boats," I admitted, taking a seat at my desk. "We talked and then he left to meet Julie."

Maria stood up and came over to me.

"So it didn't pan out for you and Neil after all."

I shrugged and didn't bother to point out that it hadn't worked for Paige and Hugh either. I was oh for two.

"Wake up, Lauren. You're saving experiences the way we used to save sex, hesitating to *use up* all the things you want to do before you meet someone to share them with."

"I'm not doing that."

"Oh, please. Life ain't a dress rehearsal, Lauren, and the sooner you figure that out, the better." Maria leaned against the wall and crossed her arms. "Your cake theory crapped out."

And so did my blockbuster book.

What was I going to tell Vivian? She'd coordinated a press conference and announced that I'd reveal my secrets—which had then been repeated in newspaper articles and talk radio and other outlets that only served to increase my pending public humiliation. Now the only secret I'd have to reveal is my total lack of judgment.

I had no valid theory. No relationship guarantee. A book deal hanging by a thread. I couldn't even call Charlie and have him crack a joke that would make my situation seem bearable. And for some reason, that depressed me as much as anything else.

Maria went back to the shelves while I let her words sink in. I sat there watching her organize the ingredient bins, a small round woman in a red bandanna who, after seven years, had decided it was time to set me straight.

"What happened to Paige and Steve?" she asked, never one to miss an opportunity to twist the blade.

I had two choices: lie or tell the truth. Nothing had actually happened between Paige and Steve. They were both stressed out about the wedding, but there was never a huge argument or defining moment where they decided it wasn't worth it. Even after the intervention, Paige never admitted that she really didn't think they'd work it out, or that she didn't love him. The outcome of the intervention really didn't have to do with Paige and Steve as a couple as much as it did with what I thought about their cake.

At this point I didn't have much else to lose by telling the truth. Besides, Maria's well of witticisms and snide remarks had to run dry sooner or later, didn't it?

"I told Paige about my cake theory."

"And she listened to you? I thought Paige had more sense than that."

"But I've always been right."

"Really?" It was a simple word, but Maria's sarcasm was biting. "And that's why you and Neil are living happily ever after now?"

Neil was, but I didn't feel like telling that to Maria. She obviously had an endless supply of unpleasant comments to fling my way.

When the bins were put away and the deck ovens turned off, Maria untied the strings of her apron and turned toward me. "I'm taking a break."

"What do you mean, you're taking a break?"

"Effective immediately, I'm on vacation."

"You can't do that. We have cakes to make—we have six weddings next Saturday."

"Then you better get baking, Chef Gallagher." Maria handed me her apron, grabbed her coat off the hook and walked out the door.

32

*T*hree hours later I realized that Maria really wasn't coming back, and I called a meeting with the staff to tell them about her impromptu vacation. To say they looked scared is an understatement.

"But what about the orders?" Benita wanted to know.

"Who'll manage the baking?" Hector demanded. "We can't fall behind."

"Can't she come in a few hours a day?" Georgina asked, biting her lip.

"Okay, look." I held up my hands and waited for them to calm down. "We're a team and we can do this if we work together," I assured them.

Dominique's eyes welled up. "Can't you just call her?" she practically squeaked.

All four were quiet as they waited for me to give in and call Maria. But I couldn't. I wouldn't. This was Lauren's Luscious Licks, not Maria's.

All the cakes for the day's orders were already completed and ready for delivery. I could handle a few days in the kitchen. After all, with Saturday's orders out of the way, I had a few days before I had to worry about the next weekend's cakes. Maria had trained her staff well, and I could get back into the swing of things. I had to.

"No. We're doing this on our own," I told them firmly. I had everything under control.

By Tuesday, however, I was starting to get nervous.

Three days after she left, I got the feeling that my idea of a little break was different from Maria's. I hadn't heard from her since she'd walked out—not even a phone call checking in on the weekend's orders. Every time the phone rang I was torn between jumping for it in case Maria was on the other end, and letting it go to voice mail so I wouldn't have to talk to Vivian again.

It didn't help that Vivian was calling every day asking if I'd thought about the copy that was going to accompany Pietro's photographs.

"The proofs are amazing," she'd told me breathlessly. "The cakes look like works of art."

I couldn't bring myself to tell her that the whole concept behind the book had gone bust. Even if we left out the theory, Vivian would just suggest we go back to her original idea—a big glossy book with pictures. But the whole point of telling Vivian about my theory was to make it more than a pretty cake book, to make it something that readers could learn from. I needed to come up with a new idea. Fast.

I finally decided to get an answer. I called my afternoon appointments, rescheduled their tastings, and left Benita and Hector in charge of the kitchen. I ran out of the boutique and caught a cab to the North End.

I'd never been to Maria's home before. In fact, the only reason I knew her address was that I had it in the accounting system. It wasn't like she'd ever invited me over for Thanksgiving dinner. She'd never even offered to grab me a bottle of water from the boutique's refrigerator—and they were free.

I hadn't been to the North End in years, since Paige dragged me to the festival for Saint Agrippina di Mineo—one of the many street fairs that took place during the summer. I remember several muscled men hoisting a one-ton statue of the saint on their shoulders, the statue adorned with dollar bills according to some sort of tradition. Paige said it reminded her of a bachelor party, except instead of stuffing money down a woman's G-string they taped the dollar bills to carved stone.

The cab wound through the narrow curving streets of neighborhoods that seemed to be put together piecemeal, compared to the planned organization of the Back Bay. The improvised neighborhoods were a hodgepodge of buildings. Square, squat, nondescript structures that once acted as tenements for European immigrants sat next to brick three flats with bay windows and stained glass. I caught quick glimpses of hidden courtyards as we passed.

When the taxi stopped in front of Maria's address, I was surprised by the old-world charm of her building. I'd expected a building like Maria, something cold and a little forbidding, but the black iron fire escape that zigzagged up the front of the building like a zipper was covered with blooming flowers potted in terra-cotta planters.

Just as I was about to press the buzzer next to Maria's last name, the front door swung open and three little kids practically knocked me down as they ran by screaming something about being chased by a big bear. I grabbed the door and held it open, but before I could step into the black-and-white-tiled foyer, the big bear appeared, yelling for the kids to wait for her to catch up.

Maria would have walked right by me if I hadn't said something first. "Hi, Maria."

She turned around and saw me holding the door open. I'd never seen Maria out of the starched white chef jacket and checked pants she wore to the boutique every day, and so I was surprised to find her in a cardigan sweater and tartan plaid skirt with fleshy tights. A pair of black rubber-soled flats made her seem even shorter than usual.

"What are you doing here?" she asked, not even letting on that she was a little surprised to find me on her doorstep.

"I wanted to talk with you about your vacation."

"Ever hear of a thing called the phone?"

"I thought we could talk in person."

"I'm taking my grandnieces and nephew to the Children's Museum," she told me and then called the kids back from the street. "I don't have time to talk."

"It won't take long. I promise."

"Fine," Maria grunted. "You can come with us, if you want."

A family field trip with Maria. Maybe we were entering a new phase of our relationship. "That'd be great."

Maria took the hand of the curly-haired little girl. "But I'm not paying for you," she added.

Then again, maybe we weren't.

Maria corralled the children, whom in my head I'd been calling Nina, Pinto and Santa Maria, but who introduced themselves as Connie, Mary and Joseph. On the ride to the museum I was a silent observer as Maria pointed out the sights to the kids and explained history. She never even glanced in my direction or explained to the children who I was. They didn't even seem to recognize my name, so at least I knew Maria wasn't saying nasty things about me when she got home at night, though I couldn't for the life of me understand how she could spend more than forty hours a week with me and never once mention my name at home.

Maria sat in the backseat with the kids while I kept our non–English speaking driver company and wondered if I'd smell like a combination of evergreen car freshener and clove cigarettes when I emerged. No one talked to me on the ride, even though I hung over the back of the seat like a puppy starved for attention. When the museum's trademark forty-foot milk bottle came into view, the kids could barely sit still and our driver couldn't wait to get us out of his car.

I paid my own admission fee, and the kids took off toward the exhibits that encouraged touching, pushing, pulling and any other action a child could employ in a place where hands-on was the order of the day.

"My niece will be here soon to meet us. What do you want to talk about?" Maria asked, as we walked slowly behind the children, their little bodies always in our view.

"I was just wondering how long you planned to take a break."

"I haven't decided yet," Maria answered shortly, not taking her eyes off the children.

"Well, we have a lot of orders coming up, what with the spring weddings and all."

"Can't you handle them?" she asked, the tone of her voice implying that the very idea amused her. "According to the press, you're the queen bee of cakes."

I was damned if I said I could handle the spring orders, because I'd look like an idiot for even going to see her. But I was damned if I said I couldn't, because, well, that sounded even worse.

"I probably could, but I just need to know how to plan for the next—" I left my sentence open-ended, hoping Maria would fill in the blank. A couple of days? A week? Months?

Maria found a bench under a suspended sculpture and sat down for a rest. "It's only been three days. I think I've earned a vacation, don't you?"

How could I argue? Maria had barely taken a sick day, much less a real vacation, in the seven years she'd worked for me.

"Whatever you need is fine. I just wanted to be able to schedule the staff appropriately and make sure we can handle the orders on our own."

"The *staff* is fully capable of taking care of things, Lauren. After all, I'm the one who trained them." There was no mistaking Maria's tone now.

"I'm the one who used to bake the cakes, Maria. Remember?"

"I remember, Lauren. Do you?" Maria asked, almost challenging me.

This circular conversation wasn't going anywhere. All I wanted was an answer. "So, when are you coming back?"

Maria stood up to go after the children, who were running toward an airplane exhibit. "I'll let you know."

I'd already wasted almost two hours trying to get an answer from Maria, and all I'd gotten in return were cab receipts and a nine-dollar ticket stub from my brief visit to a museum where Arthur the aardvark was the featured attraction.

On my way through the lobby I passed a woman who looked like a younger Maria with longer hair. She was even wearing the same fleshy tights.

"Excuse me. Are you Maria's niece?" I asked as she hurried by me.

She stopped a few feet away and answered slowly while she looked me up and down. "Yeah. Who are you?"

"I'm Lauren Gallagher." Maria's niece showed no sign of recognition. How was it that for seven years Maria never mentioned me? I mean, I signed her paychecks! "I work with Maria."

"Oh."

She couldn't have been less interested. This woman was definitely related to Maria.

"I was just wondering if you knew why Maria didn't marry Mario Spinelli."

"Sure," she answered but didn't elaborate. It must have been really bad.

"Did he cheat on her or do something horrible?" I ventured, thinking that maybe he tried to hurt her.

"No, nothing like that."

"Then what?"

"She just said that her heart wasn't in it."

"That's it? Her heart wasn't in it?" I've never seen Maria smile, so I hardly doubted it was Mario's fault. "There was nothing wrong with him?"

"Not as far as I know." Maria's niece looked around distractedly. "Where is she? Have you seen my kids?"

I pointed toward the Boats Afloat exhibit and realized that there had to be more to the story than what Maria had told her family. I mean, as far as I could tell, Maria didn't have a heart.

33

$\mathscr{I}$'d forgotten how physically demanding it was to run a kitchen. My fingers ached from working the pastry bag, and the muscles in my back were pulled taut from bending over the rotating cake stand for hours on end. At first I was a little rusty, and as I scraped wilting blue delphinium off a cake and started over, it was like déjà vu. I'd done it all during those first few months in my studio kitchenette when my initial attempts to create something people would enjoy were rarely my last.

A few of the gerbera daisies I attempted to cascade down the side of a three-tiered cake looked like they were dying on the vine, their petals drooping forward and curling into one another in defeat. Eventually I got the hang of it, and spending all day in the kitchen mixing and blending and discovering was like the beginning, when Lauren's Luscious Licks was more about learning than trying to create the illusion of perfection.

And that's when I knew what to tell Vivian. The book shouldn't tell the secrets behind a cake theory, but the secrets of how cups of flour became a white cake layered with fresh strawberries and covered with piped whipped cream. But I didn't have time to think too much about it, because things around the boutique had changed now that Maria wasn't in the kitchen to manage the staff and ensure that the orders were filled.

I rescheduled my morning tastings and pushed them off

till the afternoon. I was at work by five o'clock every morning instead of strolling in after my customary caffe latte, and even though I was exhausted by the time I fell into bed at night, it felt great. When the cakes were lifted into the delivery trucks, I experienced a sense of accomplishment I hadn't felt since I ceremoniously handed Maria her first apron and traded in the kitchen for the gallery floor.

I kept busy and tried not to think of Charlie when I was home alone at night, but it was hard not to. I kept reminding myself that it was better this way, but I always ended up wondering if he'd already found someone else, or if he was also lying in bed at night exhausted but unable to sleep. Was he thinking of me and drowning his woes in ouzo while I waited for him to show up outside my apartment window like a love-obsessed John Cusack, a portable stereo held high above his head as Peter Gabriel blasted from its speakers?

On slower days, usually the beginning of the week, I experimented with new ingredients for fillings and flavors that weren't part of our standard offering and even considered introducing a few of the more original cakes for the summer season—maybe even a couple of everyday offerings like a lavender lemon Bundt cake that would bring customers in more regularly rather than just thinking of Lauren's Luscious Licks as a place only for special occasions.

Although the idea was exciting, in reality I knew the staff was already on the verge of their breaking point with existing orders, and creating a whole take-out business would mean installing display cases and changing the layout of the gallery I'd painstakingly designed to look nothing like a bakery. As it was, I had enough of a challenge handling both the tastings and the baking.

Spending fifteen hours a day at the boutique meant I didn't get to see Robin and Paige. The sun was lingering longer in the evenings, and spring was trying to become more than just a fleeting promise. Homeowners were once again lined up outside Paige's office, ready to put their homes on the market and make the leap to the suburbs once school let out. Robin had been laying low after the news about Mark, and she seemed to be spending more time on the phone with her lawyer than with anyone else.

Although we tried to keep in touch, we kept missing each other, and so neither of them knew Maria was taking a break from the boutique. Whenever I'd tried to call Paige, she was either on a showing or not home. I'd left a few messages for her but I never heard back.

I was elbow-deep in a fondant-wrapped gift-box cake, each layer decorated with different pastel-colored wrapping paper and bow, when Robin called and asked if I could meet her for lunch.

"Why you don't you grab some sandwiches and come by the boutique?" I suggested, hoping I'd be able to finish the orders before meeting Vivian at her house in Cambridge. Even though I didn't really have the time, I thought it might be helpful to fly my new idea by Robin before seeing Vivian, just in case Robin wasn't interested.

"But it's so nice out. How about meeting me in the public garden, by the ducks?"

It was the end of April, but I knew Robin wasn't talking about the feathered variety. "Fine. By the ducks at noon."

I walked down Newbury Street toward the public garden's entrance, where Commonwealth Avenue started at the foot of the imposing gates that let visitors into the park, which was bound by a wrought iron fence. The snow had disappeared and the public garden was awakening from its winter nap. Tourists posed in front of the George Washington statue, snapping photos of the proud equestrian on his steed. I made my way along the winding path, past the bulbous bushes that lined the trail like brilliant green gumdrops and the large, lazy willow trees hugging the shore of the lagoon. The swan boats floated lightly on the water, enjoying their return from winter hibernation in storage.

Past the edge of the park on Beacon Street, Cheers fans lined up outside the Bull & Finch, hoping to share a draught in their favorite TV bar. Little did they know that the inspiration for the friendly neighborhood bar where everybody knows your name was nothing like the television show—in real life, the place didn't even vaguely resemble where Sam and Woody tended bar.

When I spotted the nine bronze waddling figures in the distance, I noticed that Robin had staked out an empty bench opposite the parade of statues—eight tiny ducklings following their mother, inspired by the book *Make Way for Ducklings*.

She was waiting for me with two turkey clubs and a couple of Sprites.

"So, what's up?"

"They dropped the lawsuit."

"That's great."

"Yeah. But my lawyer suggested we tone things down a little moving forward. Just because Jeremy backed out doesn't mean some other attendee won't get the wrong idea and take matters into her own hands." Surprisingly, Robin didn't complain that the attorney wasn't aggressive enough or lament the demise of her right to free speech. "Besides, maybe it's time to come up with some new programming."

"Retire SCALPEL? What are you going to replace it with?"

"I've been doing some more research on my small-world child-rearing idea, and I think it could be good."

"But what about the book?"

"Who knows. Once I tell Vivian we're going to be concluding the program, I doubt she'll still want to go ahead and publish it. You know, it's been almost three years since I first launched SCALPEL, so I think it's in the final phase."

"You mean *Letting go*?"

Robin laughed. "Yeah, maybe that, too."

By the Charles Street entrance, a toddler broke free from her mother's grasp and ran up to the bronze mommy duck. She stood eye to eye with the statue and imitated quacking sounds. Robin watched and smiled as the little girl crouched down, patting a duckling on the head.

The little girl's mother stood aside until it was time to leave, and then folded the child's small hand in her own and led her away.

"Well, I had a brainstorm." I washed down my potato chip with a sip of Sprite and told Robin my idea. "What about cooking programs?"

"In case you've forgotten, I don't cook," Robin reminded me.

"But I do."

"You do? Since when?"

"Well, I've sort of been thrown back into the kitchen. Maria's taking a break."

"What's that mean?"

"I don't know. She needed a little time off and she said she'll return when she's ready."

"And you let her just walk out?"

"What were my choices? She hasn't taken a vacation day in three years."

"So you're making the cakes?"

"Yep."

"Good for you. I always thought you should be back there instead of sucking up to brides who want to believe there's a difference between a cake boutique and a bakery. Besides, now I won't be afraid to ask for free samples." Robin smiled. "Maria scares me."

"You and everyone else." I laughed. "So I was thinking that we could come up with cooking programs and offer them at the boutique."

Robin wrinkled her nose. "How?"

I explained my idea for the classes. "We'd start with a focus on cakes, and if that went well we could expand the classes to include other desserts, like chocolate raspberry tartlets and soufflés, that sort of thing. The boutique's reputation would pull people in, and with your expertise organizing, promoting and managing programs, they'd be completely professional. It's perfect."

"But why do people need to know how to make desserts when they can just buy them?"

"Because it's about learning to enjoy the whole process, not just the finished product. The classes wouldn't so much be about right and wrong, even though we'd teach students the proper techniques, of course. They'd be about trying new things, experimenting with ingredients and understanding why some desserts work out and some don't."

"Our database has thousands of women we could market the programs to." Robin sat forward, and I could tell she was warming up to the idea. "We could even develop programs for different demographics, just like we do now—have mother-daughter afternoons where they bake cookies, or weekend evenings for single women looking for a fun night, or theme programs like An Evening of Chocolate Decadence."

Robin's eyes were sparkling and I could tell there were already a million ideas running through her head. "I love it."

"Me, too. And I thought we could tie it all in to my book launch, make it a joint coming-out party."

"But the book is just pictures of wedding cakes," Robin pointed out.

"We'll see about that. I'm going to talk with Vivian tonight."

"Poor Viv. Here she thought she had two ringers and now we're changing everything on her. Well, let me know if she goes for it. I think it's a great idea." Robin looked at her watch and started packing up. "I better go. I'm meeting Jeremy for coffee."

I nearly choked on my potato chip. "Plaintiff Jeremy?"

"Yeah."

"You're cavorting with the enemy?"

Robin stopped crumpling her napkin. "After my lawyer called to tell me the suit was dropped, Jeremy showed up at my office and wouldn't leave until I talked to him. He wanted to talk to me after the deposition, but his brother-in-law kept telling him he couldn't talk to the person he was suing." Robin smiled. "He's really not a bad guy, but I don't think we'll be going to a barbeque at his brother-in-law's anytime soon."

"So, you're dating Plaintiff Jeremy?"

"No, we're not dating. I'm just getting used to the idea of being divorced. But I haven't ruled out being friends."

"That's mighty understanding for the founder of Women in Action."

"Hey, if you can remember how to cook, I can remember what it's like not to have all the answers. Being a modern woman doesn't mean hating modern man."

"Jesus, you sound like you've had a religious experience."

"Nah, just quoting an article I read in *Marie Claire*."

I'd asked Vivian to meet me after work, and she'd suggested I come to her house in Cambridge. She greeted me in running shorts and tank top and led me through the kitchen and out onto a slate patio. Even though it was after six o'clock, the sky was still a brilliant blue, its clear color set off by the cottony white clouds that sporadically floated over us. Vivian's yard was fragrant from the springtime blooms crawling up the back fence and along the hammock strung up in the far corner, while long, stringy wildflowers dotted color throughout the garden that bordered the patio. Although the long, narrow backyard was typical for a city row house, very small and completely fenced off from its neighbors by brick walls, Vivian had created her own little garden of Eden.

She gestured to a padded garden chair and took a seat on the opposite side of the wrought-iron table. She poured fresh-squeezed lemonade from a chilled glass pitcher on the table and waited for me to talk.

"So, what's up?"

"I'd like to make some changes to the book."

"Weren't you happy with Pietro? I know he can be a bit much sometimes."

"No, he was fine. But I had another idea."

"What's that?" She sat back in her chair and crossed her arms expectantly.

"I don't think it should be about my cake predictions."

Vivian laced her fingers together and sat forward, resting her elbows on the table. "Remember that little event we had at that boutique? The one attended by more than twenty journalists who showed up to hear you tell them you'd be revealing your secrets?"

"I can still do that, only they'd be different secrets I'm revealing." I paused and waited for Vivian to object, but she was still listening. "I was thinking we include recipes, but also a behind-the-scenes look at how the cakes are made, pictures of the kitchen and the process as well as tips on how to select a cake that the bride and groom can both enjoy. It would still be wedding-focused, because that's what we're known for, but maybe it could lead to other dessert books—special-occasion desserts, seasonal desserts, children's desserts, that sort of thing."

Vivian squinted and brought her hand up to her chin, where it stayed while she thought over my idea. I was afraid she'd outright reject my suggestion, but as long as Vivian was seriously considering the change, I decided to continue.

"Let's be honest. Not many brides are actually going to bake their own wedding cakes. But you said I could be like the Emeril of wedding cakes, and Emeril doesn't just show you pictures of the food; he lets you come into his kitchen and watch how it's done."

"I see where you're going with this." Vivian let her hand drop to her hip. "You're thinking it would be a glimpse into what goes on behind the scenes, the nitty-gritty work behind the finished cakes, the inner workings of Lauren Gallagher's sugary sanctuary."

I sat back in my chair and started to relax. Vivian got it. "Exactly."

"Lauren Gallagher's recipes for love," she mused. "We can use Pietro's photos for the cakes, but I want to reshoot the interior of the boutique, get you in the kitchen. We need to show you working. Maybe this time we'll go with someone a little less polished, more raw. It's fantastic."

"I don't know about a recipe for love, but definitely recipes for some amazing cakes."

"I love it."

"Good, because I have another idea. Robin and I talked, and we think there's a ton of opportunity for us to work together."

34

$\mathcal{T}$he general contractor was at the boutique by nine o'clock sharp the following Monday morning. I showed the four men through the gallery and into the kitchen, where the stainless steel workbench had been moved aside to give them room to set up their tools. As they assembled the saw-horses and snaked the extension cords around the floor like orange spaghetti, I stayed out of the way, observing from my desk until the noise of sledgehammers crashing into the wall between the gallery and the kitchen became too great, and I finally gave in and took the architect's blueprints into the gallery to take one more look around the boutique as I knew it.

Once we'd decided to go ahead with the cooking program, I didn't waste any time putting our plan into action. Paige knew just about every architect, developer and building inspector in the city, and she put me in touch with a small firm in Cambridge, which in turn recommended a contractor who had room on his schedule for a small renovation and the contacts to get the permits needed for the work.

The architect had translated my idea exactly as I'd envisioned. The large, empty gallery was going to be split into two sections. The first section, the smaller of the two and the area you stepped into immediately upon entering the boutique, was going to take up the first eight feet and be a miniature version of the existing gallery, with the tasting table and chairs taking up most of the space. A half wall of glass bricks would separate the tasting section of the gallery from the classroom. Although I'd originally thought that we'd have to divide the gallery into two separate rooms, the architect suggested that by using a five-foot wall of glass bricks we'd be able to create distinct areas while allowing the classroom to be viewed through the front windows and from the scaled-down tasting gallery. This way, when I was seated at the tasting table with clients, the kitchen would still be visible through the new picture window the crew was installing in the wall—and that was the whole point of the change, to allow clients to see the cakes being made, the mixing and beating and icing that resulted in the beautiful desserts.

I'd cleared my schedule for the week, and by Thursday the bulk of the construction was expected to be completed. That would still give me time to fulfill the weekend's orders.

As I waited on hold for confirmation that the new butcher-block island and surrounding workstations would be delivered by Friday, I was interrupted by impatient knocking on the front door. The boutique was closed all week, and the sign on the front door explained that, but the knocking continued so I looked up. And there was a short, stocky Italian woman staring at me through the front door.

"Why didn't you just use your key?" I asked Maria, as I shut the door behind her and slid the deadbolt back into place.

"I wasn't sure I'd be welcome." Maria looked around the boutique, her eyebrows furrowing as she took in the paint-splattered drop cloths protecting the hardwood floor and plastic sheeting hanging on the walls to keep the sawdust off of the pictures. "Love what you've done with the place."

"We're doing a little construction." The air-compressor hose and nail gun started pulsating in the background as if I'd asked for audible proof.

"Are we still in business?"

"Yes, we're still in business. In fact, Robin and I are working on something that means we'll be doing much more business, even if it is a little different than what we're used to."

I took Maria over to the blueprints laid out on the tasting

table and explained how I came up with the idea for baking classes.

"So you've been doing all the baking yourself?"

"Yep."

"Good." Maria squeezed my arm and gave me an approving smile. It was the closest she'd ever come to giving me a compliment.

"What did you expect me to do? I wasn't given much of a choice."

"I didn't know. I wanted you to get yourself back into the kitchen, to do what you were doing when you first hired me. I was beginning to think you'd forgotten that most of the pleasure in this business is in the creating, not the end result that gets packed up and shipped out to some hotel's ballroom. I was afraid you'd find someone else to come in here and pick up where I left off." Maria stopped talking, waiting for the high-pitched whine of the saw to stop. "I can tell you that I never imagined I'd come back to this."

Despite myself, Maria's reaction made me feel like I'd made the right choice.

"You know, I've never regretted turning down Mario Spinelli," she said, out of nowhere.

"Really?"

"Not once." Maria shook her head with authority and I knew she meant it.

"So what do you think?"

Maria surveyed the room and nodded appreciatively. "It's about time."

"Better late than never."

The contractors completed the finishing touches on the classroom by Thursday afternoon, and just as I was about to begin the weekend's orders, the UPS driver was at the back door ready to unload the butcher-block workstations. I'd ordered six stations and twelve wooden stools for seating, and once I realized that the driver was simply going to park all the boxes on the kitchen floor, I handed him a twenty-dollar bill and asked if he wouldn't mind putting all the boxes in the classroom instead. As much as I wanted to unpack the boxes, we needed to start making the cakes if we were going to get them finished and delivered on time.

Maria had offered to come in to help, but I told her to enjoy the last few days of her vacation and to come in on Saturday morning as usual. I could have used her assistance, but I was looking forward to the time alone, without contractors or clients or the staff. Just me and the possibility of what was to come.

Once the batters were mixed and the cakes were poured into their pans, I set the timers, grabbed an X-Acto knife and headed into the classroom. It was weird, seeing the towering brown cardboard boxes where once there was nothing but open, empty space. As I started to unpack each workstation, carefully unwinding the bubble-wrap cocoon that had protected the wood as it traveled from the factory, I tried to imagine how different the boutique would be from here on. Even though I'd still have to schedule tastings and meet with clients, I couldn't wait for the classes to start.

"Looks like it's starting to shape up," Robin commented, coming through the front door.

"You're welcome to help me with these." I pointed to the stacks of boxes and Robin rolled up her sleeves.

"Have you heard from Paige?" she asked, taking the X-Acto knife from me.

"She said she'd stop by this week to check out the new space, but she never showed. I just figured she was swamped with showings."

"We were supposed to have lunch yesterday but she canceled. And when I called, her office told me she'd called in sick—sick! Paige doesn't call in sick."

"Maybe she's just tired. She's been working really late the last few weeks."

"No, she hasn't. I ran into Sheila and she said that Paige has been dashing out of the office by five every night, all giddy."

"Giddy? I didn't know a thirty-two-year-old woman could act giddy."

"You don't think she's sleeping with Hugh, do you?"

"She can't be. Amanda stopped by the other day and told me that Hugh hasn't seen Paige since their first date."

"Then why was she telling us they kept going out? Did you ask her?"

"No way. The last thing she needs from us is more meddling. I just figured she wanted us to leave her alone for a bit."

Robin set up the workstation she'd unpacked and stood back to observe. "These are exactly what the classroom needs, but what's the rush? The classes won't start until September."

"I just wanted to get used to the idea. Besides, this way clients will see the classroom and start telling their friends about the classes. Maybe I'll even get some advance reservations."

"Hey, I thought I was the one in charge of bringing in the students. Your job is to teach them how to bake."

"What?" I asked Robin, just so I could hear her say it again.

"Your job is to teach them how to bake," she repeated.

I let the words swim around my head and settle in comfortably. I could practically smell the vanilla beans as their thick skins were slivered, see the melted chocolate squares begin to slowly bubble in the double boiler. And it was going to be my job to share that with our students.

I glanced over Robin's shoulder at the stools lined up against the wall waiting to be put to use. In a few months they could be filled to capacity or sit empty. There was no way to tell whether or not anyone would embrace the new Lauren's Luscious Licks. According to Robin and Vivian we'd have a waiting list, but there was always the possibility that people didn't want to learn what went into making their desserts. It might be like pulling back the curtain and discovering that the wizard is in fact an average little man with funny ears and a megaphone. Maybe the result would be somewhere in between, but either way I was willing to take the chance.

And that's when I knew that, for the first time in years, my heart was in it.

35

$\mathcal{W}$hat are you doing here?" It wasn't like Robin to drop by on a Saturday afternoon. Then again, it wasn't like me to be in the boutique trying out new recipes on a Saturday afternoon.

"I thought I'd come by and say hi. The contractors did a great job."

They did. Even though the gallery had been divided up into two distinct sections and the new window in the back wall gave visitors a view of the inner workings of the kitchen, the effect wasn't as hall-like as I'd feared. Instead of feeling like a long, narrow space, the new design followed a natural progression—first the kitchen, with its large ovens and sinks and industrial-sized mixers, then the learning space, where clients would have hands-on instruction, and then the tasting area, where the final product was presented.

Robin walked over to the large plate-glass window separating the gallery from the kitchen. She knocked on the glass and Maria looked up. "I see Medusa came back."

"Yeah, she's back."

Robin waved to Maria, who blew away a stray hair that had fallen out of her bandanna and went back to work. "What's she think about the cooking school idea?"

"She said it was about time I got my hands dirty again."

"We won't be using your dirty hands as a selling point in the brochures." Robin came back to the large butcher-block island in the center of the classroom area and took a seat on one of the wooden stools.

"She does know that you're the one who'll be teaching the classes, right? We can't have her smacking the knuckles of our paying clients with a rolling pin, no matter how incorrectly they're separating the egg whites."

"Don't worry. Maria has no desire to get involved with the classes. She's content to stay in the kitchen filling orders. But, you know, if we're going to begin offering programs in the fall, we have a lot to do—there's the curriculum and the ingredient lists, not to mention all the new equipment I'm going to need to buy for the classes."

"That's kind of why I'm here."

My heart dropped into my feet. This couldn't be happening. "Don't tell me you're backing out. You can't do that."

"No, I'm not backing out. I just wanted to say thanks for asking me to do this with you."

"Don't thank me. I couldn't do this without you. I still can't believe it."

"Me neither," Robin admitted before a small smile crept across her face. "It's going to be fun, isn't it?"

"It's going to be a blast. Here." I handed Robin one of the Polaroids I'd taken of the new space. "Maybe you can put this in one of those frames you have at home."

"This is awesome. Thanks." Robin smiled at the picture for a few seconds before asking, "Are you scared?"

I looked around the boutique at all the changes. "Scared shitless."

"Well, I'm happy for you; I really am." She stood up and came over to hug me. I was all too happy to hug her back.

"What's this?" a voice called from the front door. "I go away for a few days and you two go all sappy on me?"

"Where have you been?" Robin demanded, pulling away from me.

Paige came toward us, beaming. "Las Vegas." She held up her left hand, where a thin gold band circled her ring finger.

"You got married without us?" I cried, rushing toward her. "What about those Vera Wang dresses you promised we'd be able to wear again?"

Paige shrugged. "Looks like we'll all be doing without the gala at the Four Seasons, but it certainly was memorable, nonetheless. We were married by Elvis."

"I'm assuming that when you say *we* you mean you and Steve, and not you and Hugh."

"Yes, I mean me and Steve."

"Is that why you've been avoiding us? Have you been sneaking around with Steve?"

"Not sneaking around, just trying to figure things out. And in a way, I have you two to thank for that."

"Us? What'd we do besides make you lose your deposit at the Four Seasons?"

"You set me up with someone who was perfect for me in every way, and it made me realize that love wasn't about being perfect."

"You sound like a fortune cookie. Let me get a good look at this thing." Robin reached for Paige's hand and inspected her ring. "So, you were married by the King? Would that be the young, hip-swaying Elvis or the bloated, pill-popping Elvis?"

"We're talking full-on-Vegas Elvis, complete with white rhinestone-studded jumpsuit and big bushy sideburns. It was unbelievable."

"Sounds like you didn't miss the ballroom and the horse-drawn carriage."

"You know, not at all." Paige reached into her bag and pulled out two T-shirts. "They may not be the most appropriate bridesmaids gifts, but I think they're more fitting, given the circumstances."

Paige handed us each a T-shirt and we held them up to read the flamingo pink writing scrawled across the fronts. MY FRIEND GOT MARRIED IN LAS VEGAS AND ALL I GOT WAS THIS STUPID T-SHIRT.

"It's classic," Robin said. "Thanks."

I folded my T-shirt and placed it on the tasting table. "So when did you decide to run off to Vegas?"

Paige stared at the T-shirt and absentmindedly toyed with the heart hanging from her charm bracelet. "It wasn't as sudden as it sounds. Steve and I started talking again, on the phone at first, and then we started going out—not having sex or anything, but just hanging out together again without the cloud of the wedding hanging over us." Paige let go of the charm and turned to me. "Remember that night when you told me that if I was asked where I'd be in ten or twenty years, I'd be able to give you an answer right away? Well, when I thought about it, really thought about it, the only place I wanted to be in twenty years was with Steve."

"Well, then I'm glad you decided not to listen to us. I'm not so sure that cakes should be used to determine the fortitude of a relationship," I admitted. "So, what did your parents say when you told them you were given away by Colonel Parker?" I asked.

"Steve and I decided to have a small reception in the city in a few weeks, mostly so our parents don't think we've completely excluded them. Of course, we'd still love a cake, but something a little simpler this time around."

"Like cupcakes?"

Paige rolled her eyes. "I'll pretend I didn't hear that."

"I'd be honored to make you guys a cake, but maybe there's another gift I can give you as well."

I walked into the kitchen and opened up the desk drawer filled with catalogs. I slipped out the listing Paige had brought to me the night of her non-date date and headed back into the gallery.

"Here." I handed the sheet to Paige. "Since you've forfeited all those fancy wedding gifts, maybe a hefty commission check will come in handy."

"This is the unit on Comm Ave," Paige told Robin, showing her the picture of the brownstone.

"Yep. But if there are others you think I'd like, I'm willing to look at them, too."

Paige started clapping. "Oh, this is so great! I have tons I can show you. Are you still hell-bent on Beacon Street or have you decided to expand your definition of what's perfect?"

"Among other things."

"Super. When I get home I'll see what I've got and we can start on Monday—or even tomorrow, if you want."

"Monday is fine," I assured her, afraid she'd immediately drag me out of the boutique and on a tour of all the available units in the Back Bay.

"Well"—Robin folded her T-shirt and tucked it under her arm—"I'm going to head home and let all this sink in."

"I'll drive you," Paige offered before exclaiming, "This is all so exciting!"

I couldn't stop grinning. It *was* exciting.

After they'd gone, I headed straight for the kitchen.

My gift to Paige was as much a wedding present to her as a gift to myself—permission to stop waiting and to do all the things I'd been saving for someday.

As I sorted through my Rolodex for Charlie's phone number, Maria watched me from the sink. "I sure hope you're calling who I think you're calling."

Neil had been my safety net, and after he moved to DC, I made my way off the platform and ventured out onto the tightrope, oblivious to the fact that I could fall. But his reappearance made me look down, and only then did I realize how precariously I was balanced. But while Neil may have offered me safety from a devastating fall, Charlie had urged me to enjoy the view.

Although I didn't know exactly what I planned to say when I got him on the phone, I was still disappointed when his familiar recorded message answered instead. It had been more than a month since we'd last spoken and for a brief moment I considered hanging up. But I could feel Maria's eyes on me, so I left a message for Charlie to meet me at 75 Chestnut at eight o'clock. I wasn't even sure we'd be able to get a table, but at least we could have a drink at the bar and maybe share a little dessert.

"Now what are you doing?" Maria asked.

I removed the stack of glossy pages from my desk drawer and placed it on my desk. "I think it's time I cleaned out this drawer."

I picked up the Pottery Barn catalog, took my Visa card out of my wallet and flipped open to the first dog-eared page.

The Bordeaux dining table, with its curved cabriole legs that were at once elegant and rustic, had been merely a decision and a dial tone away. I was about to find liberation in a seventy-two-by-thirty-eight-inch piece of mahogany. I wanted that table; I wanted to sit around that table on the slipcovered linen of a Megan chair under the muted lighting of the Brittany chandelier's thirty faceted glass teardrops. I was ready to take the plunge.

It would all arrive within seven business days, which meant I had to find a place soon or else I'd be sharing my eight-hundred-square-foot apartment with two thousand square feet of furniture. But it wasn't just furniture; it was emancipation from everyone's expectations, especially my own. And it had all been available in a catalog, a mail-order life.

While I waited, on hold, I decided to ask Maria what she thought. After all, she hadn't done so bad for herself.

"Hey, Maria, do you think you can have your cake and eat it, too?"

Maria put down the spatula in her hand and paused just long enough to give me her two cents. "Who knows, but I bet you have a hell of a better chance if you're the one doing the baking."

The customer service representative came on the line. "Sorry to keep you waiting. Are you ready to begin?"

I answered with a resounding yes.

Read on for a sneak peek of
Jennifer O'Connell's newest original novel

INSIDER DATING

Available from New American Library
in May 2007

Recently divorced, top financial analyst Abby Dunn has learned the hard way that when it comes to relationships, there's no sure thing. But now Abby's decided to use her knack for risk management to change all that—and give a whole new meaning to mergers and acquisitions. She's creating a members-only club where women share the inside-dating information they need to invest in their greatest assets: themselves. And she's got underperforming men running scared.

$\mathcal{H}$ave you ever loved someone so much you wish him happiness, even if it's not with you?

Good luck. Be happy. I hope you find what you're looking for. Those words sound so bittersweet, so achingly perfect when they're spoken over soft background music right before the final credits begin scrolling up an oversized screen.

That's the way it's supposed to be, right? When it's all over and his name is permanently deleted from your Palm Pilot, after you've divvied up the wok and all of the accessories you were supposed to use to re-create the sesame chicken from Ming Garden, and returned your now-favorite sleeping shirt to its rightful owner, you're supposed to wish him well. Because that's what grown-ups do.

And I thought I was a grown-up. I had all the accoutrements of an adult. A job that I couldn't blow off by pinching my nose shut and pretending to be sick while I left a message on my boss's voice mail. I had a mortgage that required proof of my dependability and ability to pay bills on time. And I had a reverence for my youth, including an ongoing weakness for SweeTARTS and the firmly held belief that pink Jelly sandals were the perfect complement to a pair of Jordache jeans with zippers at the ankle.

Adults forgive and then they forget. They bury the hatchet and let bygones be bygones. They learn that to err is human, but to forgive is divine.

But what I learned was that I'm not that forgiving. I want answers. I want an explanation. I want penance.

And, once I finally admitted that, once I said it out loud, I learned something else.

I wasn't the only one.

They say that *hell hath no fury like a woman scorned*. But we weren't scorned—we were armed with experience. We had information, and information is power. In fact, there were enough of us around to form the biggest support group in history—if we wanted to sit around and do nothing but cry into our cold mocha lattes. But I'm not a crier. And I don't drink coffee. So I had a better idea. Instead, we could create a network that helped women look out for one another. A secret sisterhood. An underground information superhighway where women could find the dependable data they needed to avoid mistakes and shitty boyfriends who didn't stand a chance.

And I was just the person to make it happen.

Score one for the girls.

We're expected to remember our *first*. A first kiss. Our first day of school. The first time we considered the idea that maybe the presents under the Christmas tree had more to do with the locked closet in the basement than a bearded man in a red suit. Firsts are supposed to open up a whole new world to us, to offer a sort of introduction to what lies ahead. In a way, they're the start of one thing and the beginning of the end for others. A first kiss eventually leads to sex. Kindergarten leads to college. And the realization that Santa Claus is more wishful thinking than Toys "R" Us gravy train sets us up for a lifetime of last-minute shopping and the Christmas Eve rationalization that a pair of one-size-fits-all gloves from the revolving rack beside the Stop 'n' Shop checkout line is exactly the right gift, no matter who the recipient.

I do remember a lot of firsts, although I'm not sure they're the monumental occasions everyone expects. There was the first time I realized you should never jump on a trampoline if you have to pee. And the night I first discovered that the only thing worse than bed spins is experiencing the horizontal whirls at two a.m. In someone else's bed. On the top bunk, in a fraternity house where the bathroom doesn't seem nearly as convenient as simply leaning over the edge of the mattress. The poor guy on the bottom bunk also experienced a first that night. And I'm sure from then on he made it a point to never sleep below another freshman drunk off keg beer and peach Riunite.

But with all the firsts that have filled my life, the one first I never thought I'd be experiencing was the first anniversary of the end of my marriage.

Now, three hundred and sixty five days after I signed my name with the new Montblanc pen Maggie and Claudia bought me especially for the occasion, I was seated at Kingfish Hall for a celebratory lunch. Only the occasion I was celebrating had nothing to do with rejoicing in my ability to successfully navigate the legalities of marital dissolution, and everything to do with the fact that I couldn't get out of celebrating my coworker's birthday.

Not that Verity Financial was some touchy-feely financial services firm, as if such a thing existed. There was no employee fitness facility, and we weren't encouraged to have a life outside the floor-to-ceiling glass windows of our Exchange Place headquarters. Birthday lunches were not the norm, nor were they as celebrated as beating the S&P 500 or landing an interview on CNBC. But when the birthday boy's portfolio is returning twenty percent three years running, Verity ponies up. A seafood lunch isn't nearly as expensive as losing a top fund manager.

"How's the salad, Abby?" Jason asked me from across the table. Seven pairs of eyes waited for my answer, waited for me to admit I should have tried the chowder like they'd all insisted.

"Great," I told them, and went back to picking the anchovies off my Greek salad. The dingy, limp strings now lying across my bread plate were my attempt to placate an entire table that couldn't understand how a woman who lived in Boston didn't eat seafood. To them I was the culinary version of Benedict Arnold, a Midwestern transplant who swore off gifts from the sea after an early childhood being force-fed Gorton's fish sticks dipped in ketchup.

My coworkers smiled at me and went back to their lobster rolls and scallops, but not before giving one another knowing looks that said they didn't believe me for a minute.

I took a bite of the salad, still salty from the discarded anchovies, and reminded myself to order a burger next year.

The lunch crowd continued to grow around us, the tables turning over faster than the shrimp rotating on the dancing fish rotisserie, their crescent-shaped bodies speared through the center by spikes that made the cooking apparatus look less like an open pit grill, and more like an S-and-M carnival ride.

"Here, sign this," Sarah whispered in my ear, before discreetly passing a card under the table until it rested on my lap. There was no writing instrument included with her covert instructions. I reached into my purse, just as I had almost one year ago to the hour, and pulled out a stainless-steel Montblanc pen.

"The salesperson wanted us to get a classic black one, but we thought this was better suited to the task," Maggie had explained to me when I opened their gift the night before Alex and I were meeting at our lawyer's office to sign the papers. We couldn't share a home, a life together, or a future, but Alex had suggested we share an attorney. Despite Claudia's insistence that I needed my own representation, in the end working with one lawyer just seemed easier, seemed more civil than getting an attorney to oppose his own. Maggie couldn't believe I was being so nice, but that was really the point, wasn't it? To prove I wasn't the bitch he wanted to move out on, to demonstrate I was still the woman he'd wanted to marry. To show, once and for all, that I was still the girl he fell in love with. Besides, not going along with Alex's suggestion would have been like admitting I wanted to drag it out, that I wanted to prolong what was quickly becoming the inevitable. And I didn't want Alex to know I wasn't ready to give up, that I wasn't ready to give *him* up. So I said yes, and the attorney's retainer fee came out of our joint checking account.

I'd taken the gift box from Maggie and slipped the heavy metal pen from the blue velvet. "It's gorgeous," I told them, noticing my reflection in the polished stainless-steel barrel.

"It's the Montblanc version of steel balls," Claudia added. "Not that you need any help, but it can't hurt."

And it didn't. The next day when the attorney handed me a black Bic pen, its logo worn away from all the couples who came before us, I took out my stainless-steel Montblanc and held it up to the light. I was packing my own heat. I had my very own silver bullet. If this was the last time Alex and I would face off, if we weren't going to share anything from this day forward, not sharing a pen seemed like a good place to start. I placed the eighteen-carat gold nib on the page and signed on the thin black line.

Now I used the pen to sign a card featuring Snoopy and all his pals declaring *Happy Birthday from the Gang!* It was chosen from the hundreds of cards marking today's event, and it wasn't lost on me that there wasn't a single card commemorating my own un-anniversary, my own anti-celebration. Divorce wasn't exactly a Hallmark holiday.

In the past few years I'd added a few unexpected items to my list of *firsts*, although in hindsight I should have seen them coming a mile away. I was the first of my friends to get married, but only because Claudia didn't accept a proposal from an overeager mime who pledged his undying love by falling to both knees on the cobblestones of Faneuil Hall.

I'd experienced my first engagement, my first wedding, and my first marriage. And after that disintegrated, I earned a new title: Alex's first wife. And here I thought I'd be his last.

When I called Claudia and Maggie that now infamous Friday night, they'd sprung into action, almost as if they anticipated something like this might happen, like they were the relationship equivalent of an emergency rescue team just waiting to slide down the pole and rush out to the scene of the crime. They were at my door, a door that until that day I'd considered *our door*, before I could even begin to comprehend the profound rippling effect two little words—*I'm leaving*—could have.

I'm leaving. I'd heard Alex say it before, so it wasn't the words themselves that sent a shock through my body like my synapses firing bullets instead of electrical currents. He'd say it every Saturday morning before heading out the door for the dry cleaner, his arms overwhelmed by wrinkled dress shirts, folded pants, and worn suit jackets turned inside out so only the shiny satiny lining was visible. He'd say it in the mornings before walking out the door for work, and in the evenings after he'd changed into his running shorts and a faded Princeton T-shirt that by now was more rusty-marigold than Tiger orange.

No, it wasn't the words themselves that made me take notice. It was the way he managed to turn two little words, three little syllables, a contraction and a word that dropped its *e* before adding *ing*, into a declaration. An announcement. It was his emancipation proclamation. He wasn't just leaving. He was leaving me.

My two best friends didn't waste any time circling the wagons, didn't hesitate to close ranks. The enemy had been identified. He was tagged and labeled for future reference. The enemy was my soon-to-be ex-husband. The enemy was Alex.

Zax Auto Wash - Livonia
29067 Plymouth Road

C a r # 2 8 2

02/07/2021, 01:19 PM, Shift 1
XPT2,   Sale # 31521848882

Express   5.99
Penny Power   0.01

               Total   6.00

MasterCard x8353   6.00
(Sale Appr # 308495)

By pre-determined agreement with
the Sales and Use tax authority,
the above sale total includes
applicable sales tax.

INSIDER DATING

by JENNIFER O'CONNELL

Abby Dunn, barely thirty and recently divorced, has taken herself off the dating market. Instead she's using her experience to turn the tables on the opposite sex by building a dating database to rank underperforming men and set women straight when investing in their greatest asset: themselves.

Now, what started out as a pet project is becoming a full-time enterprise. But while Abby is busy, someone is skewing her data and threatening to ruin her model. Even worse, he's about to teach Abby that, while it may be perfectly legal, nothing good can come from insider dating.

Available wherever books are sold or at penguin.com

A whole new spin on reality from

Jennifer
O'Connell

Bachelorette #1

Sarah Holmes is one of the glamorous young
hopefuls on America's hottest reality TV show. But
she isn't just another bachelorette—she's a married
undercover reporter. And she's about to discover
an alternate reality far more seductive than she
could have ever imagined.

OFF THE RECORD

by JENNIFER O'CONNELL

Jane Marlow is a true-blue good girl: plain, predictable, and perfectly responsible. But when her brother catches an episode of Music One's "Off the Record," he discovers that former pop sensation Teddy Rock is actually their childhood neighbor Theodore Brockford, and that his one-hit wonder twelve years earlier wasn't just a catchy tune that took the charts by storm—it was a song about Jane Marlow! Now Jane has a chance to live life off the record, but is she ready for the changes it brings? And even if she's willing to take the risk, is she willing to face the music?

Available wherever books are sold or at penguin.com